In Times of War
A Tale of Ardalencor

Andrew Zimba

Library of Congress Control Number: 2021916667
ISBN: 978-1-7377031-0-5 (paperback)
ISBN: 978-1-7377031-1-2 (eBook / EPUB format)
ISBN: 978-1-7377031-2-9 (eBook / Kindle format)

ardalencor.com

Andrew Zimba Publishing, LLC
Spring, TX

To my mom, who taught us when boredom looms,
use your imagination.

ACKNOWLEDGMENTS

Thank you to Sue, Tony, Elena, Richard, and Sam for reading
initial portions of the story and for your comments.
A special thanks to Tina, my lovely wife, for her ongoing
support, inspiration, and input as this tale of Ardalencor took
shape.

AUTHOR'S NOTE

Ardalencor, at first, may seem an unfamiliar and uncharted land. To better understand the movements of people, armies, and the importance of certain places, an overview map of Ardalencor is provided. The map depicts the large towns, major rivers and forests, as well as other notable features and landmarks.

A glossary of selected characters also is included at the back of the book.

More information about the country of Ardalencor and its people can be found at ardalencor.com

— Andy

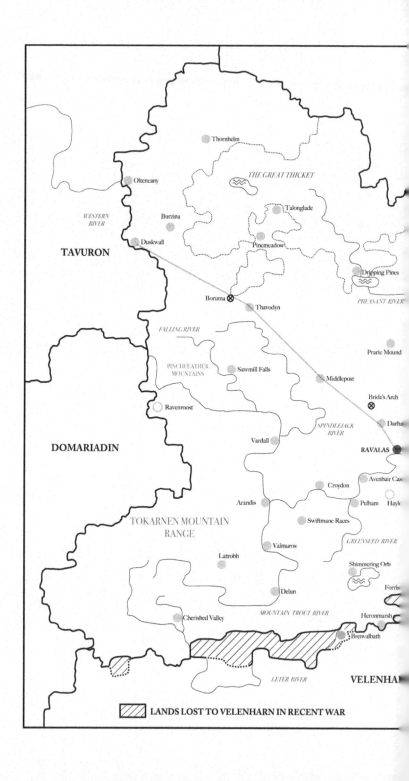

LANDS LOST TO VELENHARN IN RECENT WAR

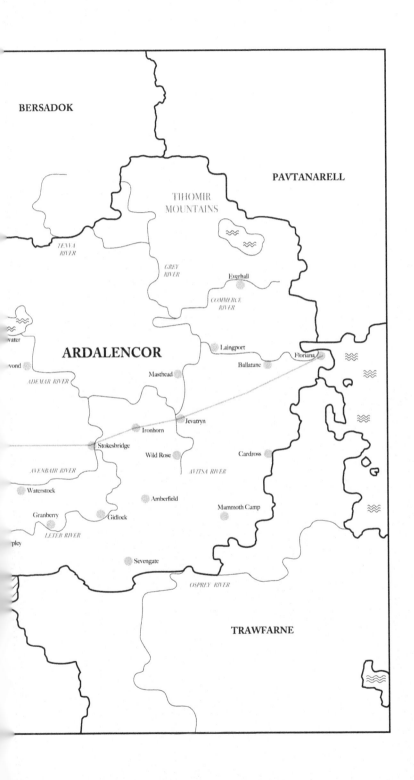

PROLOGUE

Eight grim faces looked at one another, perhaps for the last time. A day passed since the stone walls of the Burzina Monastery, an outpost of the Faith of Indalos, had been breached. This group of steadfast defenders, recently much larger in number, retreated to one of the few buildings which initially escaped the bombardment of siege engines. An incessant chipping of chisels and hammers continued throughout the night but took on a renewed frenzy at daybreak. Concussive sounds rippled through the building's exterior walls.

The country of Ardalencor was at war and again the victim of foreign invasion. Less than a month before, the invading armies of Tavuron crossed the border and encountered only paltry resistance before besieging the monastery. The crown army of Ardalencor had yet to arrive, and hope of temporal deliverance amongst the Burzina defenders rapidly faded.

This group of survivors fortified themselves in a pair of rooms at the end of a scorched and rubble-strewn corridor. Piled stone, splintered furniture, and tangled webs of flesh and steel: bodies twisted together with wide stares marking the delivery of death blows, formed the last line of defense. After midnight probing attacks were foiled, the defenders gained a brief reprieve, but the air swelled with rank stench, and a red-black slime spread and congealed on the mosaic floors.

Above the din of quickened chisel work, the hallways reverberated anew with the torturous screams of captured defenders and then gentle offers of safe passage if the remaining defenders surrendered.

"Why do they keep coming?" screamed a young woman as she covered her ears to block out the mad swirl of sounds.

"They are searching for the relics and sacred tomes. The Tavuros want to consume their power," replied a thin, elderly voice.

"And they're butchers. Their blood is up. Hundreds of their dead lie across our holy grounds. They'll chop us up and strew the pieces around the fields," said a male voice with jaunty despondence.

With that morose remark, roof beams shifted, and another ray of light stretched into the bleak room to reveal slate fragments splashing to the floor.

"Shut your mouth!"

The sudden crash of heavy slate set teeth chattering to signal another shift between resolute tranquility and despair. Means of momentary escape found several forms: whispering prayers, scratching limbs raw, or ripping hair.

"Forgive me," beseeched the elder monk. All eyes searched for him in the shadows of the corner. He was old but looked to have aged another ten years since the retreat to this final hold-out. He struggled, moment upon moment, to maintain a protective field which kept several crossbeams in place and prevented the entire roof from collapsing.

"I can help you," offered another voice from across the room.

"No, it's all right. Save your strength. I have maintained and protected these walls nearly all my life. In full view of my ancestors, I will honor my vows to Indalos."

A familiar voice pleaded for the remaining defenders to surrender.

The elder monk exhaled deeply. "That is not the voice of our blessed sister. Her soul is already free and on its way to the Starry Fields."

The outside wall shook as stone flecks and dust pulsed from multiple points. The strides of armored men and shields scraping along the walls were heard approaching down the corridor. The defenders nearest the barricade threw stones as the footfalls quickened, and a war cry was raised.

A portion of the once three-foot-thick exterior wall was punched through with an iron chisel. Hurriedly two glass phials were pushed into the room followed by a spear shaft. A defender lunged but was unable to catch the phials, and they shattered on impact.

"Sulfur!"

Another defender quickly conjured a gust of wind, and the suffocating vapor was deftly directed out through the crevice from which it came. Coughing and sputtering was heard on the other side, and the spear retreated.

The elder monk tenderly put his hand on a nearby cheek to still a quivering lip. He addressed the group. "Let fear pass from your heart. Give the Tavuros no satisfaction. You have the blessing of life. Do not let it pass cheaply from you. Duty is yet before us."

CHAPTER 1

"It never felt natural to me. Never quite right. Predation with a bow, I mean. I never got the touch for it. I do most of my gathering with neck snares and dead falls. Maybe a basket trap. Catch them alive, if I got the time and mind to, but make quick work of it when the time comes. Don't let the animal suffer in an iron trap all twitching and frightful, you know?"

The big half-orc glanced up from sharpening his double-headed axe more to see if the man was done talking than to agree.

The man continued, "Having the poor creature sitting there struggling and waiting for the end or trying to chew its own leg off to get away." He shook his head. "We are blessed to have the animals. They permit us to survive, give their lives for us. They don't need to suffer."

Clad in a gray homespun shirt, jerkin fringed with elk fur, scuffed leather pants and boots, and a tattered deep green cloak, the wiry, middle-aged man set down his carving knife and added another log to the campfire. He gave the two skewered hares a quarter turn on the spit. "The others will be back soon."

Amongst the silence and receding light of the forest, the half-orc scanned the narrow hallows between pine and pale birch. He sniffed twice and looked at the man.

The man smiled wryly. "Even with your orc eyes and smell, you can't locate them? Maybe they are coming in from upwind? Maybe you just smell yourself?" He smiled genuinely to soften his earlier words and through eroded teeth spit a glob of chewed brown leaf. "Listen for them, Dronor."

Dronor, a towering, green-gray boulder, man and orc, gave an incredulous look and turned his fevered head. "There's no one here. How close are they?" he challenged. "Did they find anyone else?"

"I didn't say they were here. I said they would be back soon." The man put his finger to his lip to quiet Dronor and remind him of their three companions sleeping by the fire. "How is that poultice working on your leg?"

"Smells like shit."

"Cow dung from the pasture we walked through. And hot ash. Heal you up good. It'll keep the rot away. I'm cap and carriage impressed you were able to walk all this way with such a nasty gash. That would drop any man."

Feeling the attention on his splinted left leg, Dronor shifted uneasily, grimaced, and slumped back against a stout birch tree. "What did you say your name was?"

"Bambenek. Some call me Bam. Others Ben. Your pick." Bambenek gave a look at the firewood pile. "This white birch is tough to burn. Got to strip the bark. Get rid of some of the moisture, especially during this time of year, but it'll be alright. Tell me again. How did you get that gash?"

"Cavalry lance. I tried to sweep with my shield but still got gouged pretty good. Ripped the muscle open." Dronor simulated the movement with his hand and looked off blankly into the thicket of birch and pine spindles. "The first line did not stand against the charge, and the mess was on. Battle lost as soon as it began."

"I was in the second line and tried to rally men to stand. Don't have a spear; I needed a few to stay with me to slow down the horses so I could take some good whacks and clear saddles." The half-orc wiped his slick brow. "I'd grab some by the arm or shoulder and get them to reform. Run, and you're dead. Stand and live. I stopped a sergeant and a flagbearer, too; that helped rally more of the boys. How did you come to join this bunch?"

"I deployed in the skirmish line. Slinger. As any man, I've been tossing rocks since I was knee high to a goose, but I stuck with it. We traded a few volleys and then withdrew behind the infantry when the enemy cavalry advanced. First line in their chain mail and shiny helmets got spooked like deer and started to force their way back into us and the second line moving up."

"Now the second rank got eyes wide like holiday wafers with a tangle of panicked boys plowing their way. I was between both lines. With the trample of men and mounts, we're all starting to get the feeling of the ground giving way and starting to walk that old, thin line towards the horizon."

"Where was our cavalry?" Anger washed across Dronor's broad, angular face.

"Some boys were saying the left wing deserted. Duke Padazar went over to the Tavuros. That son of a bitch called the coiling snakes right to the nest and left us for dead." Bambenek slammed one hand against the ground. "And our right wing wilted like an autumn leaf."

As the two hares roasted and a soup of leafy greens threatened to froth over the walls of a hollowed log, Bambenek stood and nudged the three convalescents crumpled and caked in bandaged blood. "Lads, time to get up. Get some food. Our friends will be back soon."

Dronor flared his nostrils slightly and tilted his head as if to give more credence to Bambenek's assertion.

"Friends returning," called an approaching voice, familiar but still obscured within the forest dusk and falling shadows.

"Welcome, friends," Bambenek called back.

Within a few moments, a wounded and winding column of about forty armed men closed in around the makeshift camp. Bambenek anxiously studied the arrivals, a swirl of drained and dirty faces, some known and some strange. His search met the eyes of Humphrey Cotterill, a major of the Chartered Cities militia. Within the country of Ardalencor, the Chartered Cities were a confederation of eight primary cities and dozens of villages and hamlets which had been able to secure and maintain a degree of representative and guild self-government outside of noble control. The Cities were answerable only to the High Lord of Ardalencor.

Cotterill was Major of the Everhall militia column, the largest of the Chartered Cities, and second in overall command of over a thousand men at the start of the day. His command nearly evaporated as sun and stirrups surmounted the battlefield. Cotterill, a virile orator and respected merchant, in his early sixties but still gifted of hue and health, a man proud and protective of his station and city, lowered a face heavy with despair.

Cotterill's dented breastplate, a patchwork of muck, elegant ornamentation, and faded parade ground luster gave off a disconcerting reflection in the campfire light. Rage and sorrow wetted his eyes. The gauging stare of Dronor's slate-colored eyes brought Cotterill back to his duty.

"This is what remains." Cotterill forced an air of control and detachment. "No sign of Commander Jerris. Maybe he was captured?" He paused. "Knowing Jerris, he may already be negotiating his own release," he said with the shallow trace of a smile.

Bambenek nodded in acknowledgement but offered, "Others got away. Have to be more units who escaped. We're a way out here in the woods, and you found some more of ours. There must be many more scattered or already reforming at Thavodyn. Did the High Lord survive the battle?"

Major Cotterill just shrugged his shoulders. "If fate and fortune oblige him."

Turning to the group, Bambenek called out, "You all must be hungry. There is enough soup to go around. Were the village folk forthcoming?" As he finished, a few of the soldiers lifted some small sacks, a bushel of turnips here, a wheel of cheese there, and four strangled ducks.

The men with Cotterill started to make room for themselves near the campfire. Those farther back began to prepare new cooking fires and scratch out a place to bed down for the night. All the men looked at Dronor in a blend of reverent fear and then quickly turned their heads as soon as they felt Dronor's gaze.

When standing, Dronor would be nearly two heads taller than many of the encamped men, but even when seated cast a towering presence. Whispers of the half-orc and the day's battle went about the men. Most were truly boys and of an age that the horrors of the so-called Orc Wars were only tales and the actual existence of orcs a spinster's yarn.

All of the arriving men allowed for a wide space away from Dronor, at least battle axe length and then some, just to be sure. One soldier, after seeing to his men, approached Dronor without trepidation. "You saved my life and that of others here. You gave many more a fighting chance. I would be honored to drink with you." The soldier shook his head. "It has been a great while since I have seen fearlessness and guts like that."

Dronor accepted the pale blue bottle and took a long swig of some unknown sour village brew.

"Sergeant Kellin Farrior. Line infantry. Eighth Broad-shield, Armstead's Roamers. Twelfth Banner Company," he said with the formality of countless repetition but accented with the dignity of career service.

Now better recognizing Farrior without his helmet, Dronor asked, "Your flagbearer make it?"

The man with short sandy hair and bushy mustache let out a sigh. "He died of his wounds on the way here. We left his body with some villagers to give him a proper burial. He was a good kid. He protected that banner. Valor," Farrior said defiantly and then gave Dronor a departing nod.

Between the campfires, the men more or less freely shared their provisions, although most had some square of hard biscuit or bite of greasy sausage squirreled away in a belt pouch or inner pocket as precaution against future hungers.

"Friends," said Farrior, "we will all be fed with what little there is to go around, but," the veteran sergeant pointed to Dronor, "this..." He paused. "This warrior," Farrior recovered, "deserves a hero's portion of tonight's food, not only to help him recover from that brutal wound, but in recognition of his bravery and indomitable will to fight."

The spattering of claps and cheers for the half-orc faded into silent remembrance of the fallen and the shared disaster.

"Thank you, Sergeant," said Cotterill, his eyes dismissing Farrior, as he now stepped closer to the center of the men and firelight. With the help of his aides, Cotterill had removed his breastplate and chain mail to reveal a grimy doublet of refined orange and vermillion brocade and a simple pewter talisman of Indalos about his neck. "Sons of this land." He suppressed a wheeze and puffed out his chest now free of the protective weight.

Cotterill raised his hands and swept them in an arc across the men as if to gather their attention. "As night descends upon us on this dark day: a day of betrayal, a breach of sacred oath, and a breach of honor." The merchant-soldier statesman, whether for effect or to calm himself, ran his hands through his silver-blond locks. "We are still here. And while we grieve for those fallen, we must fortify ourselves to carry on to defend our lands and drive out this menace. Tomorrow we must go and form up with forces still bound by honor and duty to High Lord Eadolan."

Voices leapt forth from around the flames.

"Find the High Lord? Where?"

"How do you know he is still alive? Probably dead."

"Captured."

"We need to defend our homes and families."

"He lost his throne. We don't need to find him another one!"

"Watch your loose words. If the High Lord is dead, there will be greater tragedy, and what of your families then? I don't intend to spend the rest of my life lurking in the forest. What kind of disgrace and cowardice is this from you?" Cotterill exclaimed, eyes ablaze. "The High Lord may still be alive and fighting on. I know he is! His family assuredly is. Loyal units must rally to him. You are still soldiers and sworn men under his standard."

"How do you know you won't get a better deal from Tavuron and Padazar as the High Lord?" called an inquisitive voice.

"What!" Cotterill shouted back, his face starting to match the color of his doublet.

Men started to reach for their weapons as a nobleman stood.

"There'll be no need for that." The nobleman stuck out his palms to show he only wanted to talk. "Calm yourself, old man. We are merely discussing today's events and, more importantly, what to do next. I have no intention to stay in this waste any longer than necessary, but let's be clear. We all fought for the High Lord and under flags raised in loyalty to him. So, while you are a distinguished merchant, I must say, I am a bit surprised by your reaction to even the mere mention of striking a deal, because isn't that how you've made your way?"

The square-jawed man in his twenties gave Cotterill an inquiring and penetrating look but again raised his palms to restate his intentions. "Indeed, you are a successful coin counter, but you are not in command of line infantry, like our dear sergeant here, nor of me and my knightly companions. You have charge of your venerable militia, so when we discuss obligations and duties, let's all abide by the existing terms."

The nobleman turned his attention. "To all friends gathered, you must forgive me, for although the Major and I became acquainted on our leisurely wooded trek, I don't believe I've had the pleasure to meet all of you. To those in our present brotherhood of the campfire," he said mockingly and then changed his tone, "my name is Sir Dallen Portnay, guardian of and heir to the fertile estates and stronghold at Amberfield. The knightly Evret Hufyn and seven squires are here with me."

The knight and squires nodded to the group. The foot soldiers did not return the courtesy and looked more interested in a fresh meal and famishedly eyed the troopers' horses tethered to nearby trees. Portnay continued, "I am a cavalry bannerman serving with the honorable Esselrig Gidlock in pledge to Duke Urric who commanded the right wing and stood loyal to the High Lord."

A flurry of denouncements struck the air.

"You caused this!"

"Where was Urric? Where was your attack?"

"You abandoned us! You left us for dead!"

One of the line infantrymen slowly got to his feet. "We're all busted and bleeding, and you look like you don't have a scratch on you. Where in the righteous name of Indalos were all of you? Watching the ass end of the horse in front of you as you ran away!"

Portnay rolled up his honey-colored silken sleeves to reveal bruises and minor cuts on his forearms. "We did not exactly run away, you short-sighted fools. Many fell who were under my command, so mind your disrespectful tongues!" The infantryman quieted instinctively at the sound of a nobleman's reprimand.

Portnay assumed a more measured, rhetorical tone with his next words. "What has come to rest in my mind is that the Tavuros did not equally divide their cavalry. While plainly I was not on the left wing, it is evident to me that Padazar's move was pre-arranged. We were outnumbered on the right wing and, you are correct, could not stand the weight of the charge. The Tavuros must have placed only a token force to create a veneer on our left and overloaded on our right side."

Mumbles rippled through the men as they considered this option.

"Padazar is a traitor and deserves to kneel at the block," remarked Portnay. "My point is whom do you trust? We are a fraction of a proper army. When we emerge as a sliver from this forest, if we encounter a group of any number, have we found a friend or foe? Cotterill, your Chartered Cities collect scales and curled parchment, but the nobility control land, and that is the real power in this realm." Portnay further fixed his attention on Cotterill. "You want to rally men? Who will they follow? You?"

"I led you and your men to the safety of these woods, and I will lead you back to your duty and the defense of the country. You've spent far too much of your life with your balls cradled in a soft saddle! You left us in the cauldron, but we pious crafters and keepers fought our way out of that roiling blaze which your noble eminence did little to prevent from happening in the first instance! You created this catastrophe but now graciously offer your service to no doubt make worse the misfortune that has befallen us." Cotterill gasped and wheezed deeply. He started to bend forward and several men, including Portnay, rushed to steady him. The men helped Cotterill sit and handed him a cup which seemed to calm the old man.

"Enough of this bickering," said Bambenek as the lone figure still standing around the central fire. "Pointless barking in the dark. Look to your wounds. Look to your brothers. Get some rest. There will be enough to do tomorrow." He agitatedly threw two more logs on the main fire. Seeing no one else exercising command, Bambenek asked, "Sergeant Farrior, may I trouble you to set the watch for this evening?"

Farrior rumbled an affirmation through a mouth swollen with bread and cheese. Cotterill nodded a ceremonial approval to Bambenek's proposal as one of Cotterill's aides helped steady a piece of food in the Major's hand. Portnay's light blue eyes glanced scornfully at Bambenek's impromptu sorting of affairs as he wheeled around and walked back to his companions.

Dronor's lips moved, but no one seemed to notice as he slurped the last of his soup and then sat almost imperceptibly still. Few of the men had cloaks or blankets. None had tents. All of the heavier gear and packs were left in the camp before the battle, now likely in the possession of the victorious army or sifted and strewn about the field by local foragers. Some men, within the safe confines of a campfire's aura, tried to cut and gather a bed of boughs to carpet the half-dry ground. In a haze of smoke, dull moans, rote and improvised prayers, others just huddled in the damp as close to a fire as they could manage.

Dronor closed his eyes to the sight of Sergeant Farrior instructing line infantrymen to keep watch and to tend each campfire through the night.

CHAPTER 2

As a bleak and growing darkness covered the battlefield, the Duke of Delun, Horace Padazar, was comfortably back in his war pavilion: an opulent tent of red and blue silk ribbed with pine and skinned with a sturdy, featureless canvas. The massive pavilion dominated the concentric circles of smaller tents and wagon parks which formed the rest of his camp. A shallow entrenchment had been hastily dug around the camp the evening before.

Padazar, much to the displeasure of High Lord Eadolan, was slow to join the army on the eve of battle and established a separate camp a long mile west of the main camp. Padazar had explained to Eadolan and the other members of the war council that he had done so as the main camp was improperly laid out to accommodate his soldiers, and he needed proper grazing space for his horses.

Duke Urric of Vryvond, Padazar's counterpart as the commander of the Ardalen army's right wing, had to acknowledge that Padazar's banners accounted for over twice the number of knights and retainers that Urric would have under his command. Duke Urric's demand that Padazar, as one of the most prominent nobles and leader of the left wing, stay in the encampment came to naught as Eadolan demurred on the issue.

"Duke Padazar is here for the council. Battle will be before us tomorrow. This is not the time to be moving tents and wagons," High Lord Eadolan had said to close the discussion. "What matters is that we defeat the invaders and drive them back across the frontier."

Padazar smiled deeply as he recalled the preceding night. As he had departed the war council, he bowed slightly to Eadolan and said, "Orders are clear. We need not wait for Silverface. Victory tomorrow is assured."

The victory today, for Padazar and the Tavuros, was a crushing rout. Padazar looked up from the map positioned on a wide table, motioned for the cups to be topped off, and looked at the men before him who had abandoned one oath for a deeper fealty.

"A toast, to a new era and the revitalization of our country. For too long have we tolerated the decline and erosion of our lands. We ascend to take our rightful places in Ardalencor. With the good fortune and favor of Indalos, you, distinguished and victorious Brothers, have done great service for our families. We hold these lands dear as any man, and while some in other provinces may question the alliance with Tavuron, know that these interlopers are merely tools at our disposal. They can never hold these lands without our assistance and therefore are dependent on us. The other lords, even Urric and the like, will soon see the wisdom of deserting Eadolan, returning peacefully to their homes, and acknowledging me as High Lord."

Horace Padazar, foremost nobleman in Ardalencor's Southwest, was a man consumed by the wrenching humiliation of his family and the injustices done to the people of Ardalencor's southwestern provinces. He, and many others, had laid responsibility and the rotting corpse of betrayal at Eadolan's feet four years ago. Now Padazar had the long-sought moment to settle accounts fully and permanently.

Despite having recently seen his forty-second summer, Padazar's mid-length hair, moustache, and goatee were still a deep black. He wore a yellow robe with iron gray embroidery and had about his waist a sash sewn in his family's heraldic red and light blue. The sash was adorned with peregrine falcons in heavy black thread. His feet were studded with polished crimson boots. He enjoyed another sip of golden mead and tapped the map twice at Ravalas, capital of Ardalencor. "We take Ravalas, and the whole affair is resolved."

Three of Padazar's sons accompanied him to this battlefield. He marveled at them with paternal joy. The three teenagers looked back in the youthful meld of pride and uncertainty.

"Today was a thundering testament to the justice of Indalos," Padazar said gravely, intertwining thoughts of mortality and posterity.

"Indalos, protect us. Guard soul and soil," intoned a man in clerical vestments.

Padazar turned to his friend of many decades. "Ray, you Sharp Spur, I've seen your earlier dispatches, but recount for me and for those now gathered the course of our victory. Tell us a valiant tale."

"May it please Your High Lordship, I trust you did receive the thick stands of captured banners."

"Indeed! Yesterday was your birthday, and today you have given me quite the present."

"Before I recount bright deeds of enshrined triumph and bravery, let us all raise our glass to the true High Lord of Ardalencor, Horace Padazar."

"To High Lord Horace Padazar!"

Balian Latrobh and Drevell Swan grinned flatly as their peer began the performance.

Corneleo Ray flashed an impish grin and savored a long drink. His rings clinked on the goblet as he set it down and wiped the glistening twists of his moustache. "It was a delightful chase. It took Eadolan, that old goat, a while to realize what was happening. We crashed into his slow-footed Hearthguards, but his mounted crossbowmen put up a good rate of fire to cover the flight. Those damn elves, pale lynx, got to give them their due; they have ice in their veins and a steady eye. Lyjos is the best commander in their whole army."

The stocky Ray, fresh into his forty-first year, grew more animated in the telling of the tale. "The air seemed to buzz with hornets, stinging and slowing our advance which allowed the Hearthguards to extricate themselves from a tight spot. Our rear echelons did rightly capture more than a few Hearth-guards, it would be right to note. They aren't much when it comes to real fighting, but the horses they ride are fine breeds. I'll have far better use of these steeds; maybe hitch up some new stallions at Swiftmane." Swiftmane Races, hereditary possession of the Ray family, was the most famous racetrack and horse breeding farm in Ardalencor. Every year in early summer, Swiftmane Races hosted a great festival replete with races, tournaments, and jousts.

"The boys and I gallantly leaned into the swarm and braved our way forward to keep the fright on. We spied the outskirts of the camp and could see panicked carters and bull-whackers," Ray laughed recalling the sight, "trying to get the oxen hooked up and mules loaded to get away with Eadolan's wardrobes."

"The camp was guarded by some archers and militia forma-tions, but we netted most and a number of convalescents in the camp. These wounded men said they were involved in the initial skirmishes when the Tavurite armies crossed the frontier. They are mostly border guards who were pushed out of the custom house at Duskwall and secondary points down the main road. Anyway," Ray dismissed the thought with the wave of a fleshy, ring-studded hand. "I left some men to secure the camp as well as sent word back to our camp infantry to march over in strength lest any stragglers from the main line try to reclaim their packs. Back to the scramble, I spurred on the boys and surged around the edge to try to block Eadolan and his fleeing rabbits spilling onto the road."

Ray paused for effect. "The spellbinders. Remember, Horace, when you said just a few were in camp last night? Well, they were coming up the road late and lethargic as ever. A whole train of carriages and wagons and schools of apprentices at the ready with fine parchment to copy down spells or wipe their ass or whatmayhaps. Now there is a jam on the road. I think we can nab the whole lot. Just then the wizards start to lay down a barrage of bolts and blasts which charred man and beast alike. A ghastly sight. It would have been reckless for me to advance my men any farther, even in the numbers we had, but we made true that they kept up the retreat and hazarded no attempt to retake the camp or join the central fray. My boys did a fine job. Did their fathers proud." He scratched at his razor-short hair and looked pensively, hoping Padazar approved of his martial achievements.

The clergyman looked at Padazar, but Padazar pretended not to notice.

"Well done, Sharp Spur! I would not expect us to bag all the foxes in one go." Padazar patted Ray on the shoulder. "We'll follow them as they run back to the den and that will be the end." Padazar threw some half-eaten beef bones to his two faithful black and tan bloodhounds who were lounging close to a brazier.

"A stirring description, Ray, of your exploits on the periphery of the battle. There is no need to chase after a tiger when its neck has been sliced. My Lord, Brethren, let me now relay to you the decisive moment, the jugular strike, to Eadolan's army," said Latrobh as he pushed back a strand of flat, lanky hair. A single, hazel eye peered out from a glowering face. His left eye had yielded to an arrow bequeathing a shallow socket now concealed by a taut eye patch.

"Better an eye than a life," the long-limbed Latrobh would often say when recounting the flight of the arrow from an orc's bow that pierced his helmet's visor and lodged just beyond. He was fourteen at the time. Nearly four decades later, Latrobh, called the One-Eyed Buzzard for his sweeping, deliberate way of surveying a swirling battlefield, was one of the most methodical killers on the continent.

The master tactician's family seat of Latrobh was a modest settlement on the banks of the Antler River. The people along its watershed were impoverished, subsisting on trapping and fishing or scratching a crop from rocky soil. While the stream-creased land was barely fertile, the region's women were the opposite. The reality of a thin and overstretched resource base and bleak prospects for surviving second sons created the Antler River basin's greatest export crop. Hungry and hardened young men found ready employ and their surest path to social advancement as line infantrymen in the royal army, in retinues of Southwestern nobles, or as soldiers of fortune under a foreign banner.

At times, Latrobh himself had served as an officer and military advisor in far-flung lands. His outward appearance reflected the unique blend of hardscrabble rustic, ambition, and opulence. He wore a sapphire blue tunic, a luxury item imported through Ardalencor's lone seaport of Floriana. Along with the tunic, he wore simple, loose fitting brown pants and the plain boots of a freeholder. Doeskin gloves were tucked into his belt next to a jeweled saber worth the equivalent of several farmsteads.

The curved saber scabbard was inlaid with emeralds and pearls. The hilt of the elven-forged blade found shape as an elk's head which began at the pommel. The elk's neck constituted the grip. From the pommel, faint antlers twisted around and contoured the grip and then fully extended to form an intricate hand guard. Latrobh adjusted the sword belt; the hilt and the scabbard shimmered preternaturally among the pavilion's multitude of candles and braziers.

"The Tavuros did their part in forcing the movement of the skirmish line and shield wall. I led my steel-fisted knights to link up with our infantry in the center." Latrobh motioned at two men around the table. "Barrett and Gerdeon did their part in detaining the fleeing skirmishers and convincing others not to resist." Barrett Drummond and Gerdeon Bune, Southwestern nobles, commanded line infantry broadshields largely drawn from their home provinces.

"The coordination of infantry and cavalry is paramount," instructed Latrobh. "It has an unnerving effect on even the sturdy man and showed others with the approaching glint of Tavurite cataphracts that immediate safety lay under our protection. Any reluctant sergeants or flagbearers were quickly dissuaded. Our men in the line infantry started collecting tiger standards like kindling sticks. With the Southwestern liners now flying the black falcon banners and moving in precision with my men, the nearest mercenary companies switched sides on the spot."

"We secured the bulk of the center and permitted units still loyal to Eadolan to stagger into deeper contact with the

Tavuros. The real fighting was on the right side of the line against Tavurite units. Our forces remain at battle readiness. Most of the killing can be attributed to the invader."

"The men are being sorted, nobles and officers separated out. Our boys are guarding the nobles and officers. The mercenaries are guarding the rank and file," Latrobh said. "We are trying to get units overtaken by the Tavuros transferred to our control. It's promising that they'll take the offer. They'll be able to throw more men forward without the burden of watching prisoners." Latrobh peered at Ray and then shifted his gaze to Drevell Swan. "Drev, perhaps you have news about this?"

"This has been arranged," Swan said with detachment. More envoy in dress and manner than soldier, Drevell Swan commanded the portion of the left wing that made contact with the Tavuros at the start of the battle and rode to meet with Nabrensus, the Tavurite King. Swan was no stranger among the Tavuros. He had led the clandestine discussions over the past several months.

Swan was a thin man in his sixties, clean shaven, with a white-brown trim of hair round back and to his temples. An unflappable man of cool words, many believed Swan to have the cold heart of a lizard. He frowned at Padazar. "As I have only recently returned, forgive me, High Lord, but I must interpose the valiant tale with troubling news."

"Lord Ray pranced around this topic as he extolled his courageous trotters." Swan scowled as flames licked over a nearby brazier. "As our present allies overran the custom stations at Duskwall crossing, some border guards and local gentry with their families, who did not retreat down the main road, sought refuge in the Burzina Monastery. As Your Eminence may well know, this is not a simple building but a well-maintained, walled complex. A respectable stone fortress in wars gone by." Swan's words became more inflected. "You may recall the living tales of the scarred and lamed elders who, in their dearly-traded youth, defended their sanctuary and drenched the solemn grounds in successive tides of orc blood."

"Oh, get on with it, Swan," hurried Ray. "This is one of a hundred sites of defiance to those eradicated monsters. We all know the stories. Stop distracting us with some obscure history lesson."

Swan had lost an uncle and a cousin at the Burzina Monastery. No one else gathered likely remembered this detail, but for him the memory was a constant companion. His relatives, knights, along with other warriors, sworn monks of Indalos' holy order, local ploughmen, and shepherds had defended the hallowed grounds against countless, frenzied orc assaults. Family stories had it that the sworn fallen, his kin, were interned in a common grave beneath a victory pillar outside the walls. Swan paused to consider the probable fate of that heroic rest since the Tavurite intrusion.

Hoping he appeared outwardly placid, but recognizing he would be seen as belaboring the point, Swan transitioned calmly. "The elder monks refused to surrender and determined to hold out once again. Rather than surround and contain the petulant node, the Tavuros stopped. Their infantry spent days investing and reducing the place to near rubble with siege weapons. After spending some time amongst the Tavuros, my men heard many wild whispers that the Tavurite force took heavy casualties as they went stone room by stone room, with chisel and torch, if need be, slaughtering all within. Our men placed in the Tavurite camp confirm this disquieting news."

"Some of the invalids captured by Ray's troopers are certainly aware of people seeking haven in the monastery but could not know of its fate. This has all barely begun, and the understanding to respect the faith has come to naught." Swan was not a genuine believer but well understood its power and utility. "News of this will gallop faster than a fleet mare," he said morosely.

"Burzina," said a voice that let the name linger in the air. "Burzina was a brood of schismatics. The walls kept out the orcs and the wicked but not the untamed impiety of the wilderness," said Donald Woolfolk derisively. Dressed simply in white cassock and green cape, the Conservator of Delun's largest Starfield paced with a limp and cradled his lame right arm. In spite of the physical frailties, an inquisitive zeal animated his being and illuminated his piercing ice-blue eyes. Woolfolk's wavy, full head of hair was a hoary white in challenge and reflection of his age. His wide face, otherwise shaven, was framed with bushy side whiskers to the jaw line.

He pointed an accusing finger at no one in particular. "That monastery was founded three hundred years ago to secure the name of Indalos in those lands. Without constant vigilance, rodents will defile any garden. While there are many weeds in this field, they can be removed, and the soil restored to proper bounty. The consecrated field endures."

Woolfolk's right arm started to twitch, and he strove to steady his arm and emotions. "The Tavuros have desecrated a holy site and must atone for this transgression. Despite all their peculiarities, the Burzina monks did proclaim Indalos as protector and defended their vows to the last! Warriors of Indalos deserve remembrance, but we must remember them in mournful silence for the time being."

Woolfolk touched a pewter talisman about his neck and said a quiet prayer.

Padazar observed Woolfolk with a cautious unease. "Thank you, Conservator. Enough. Your words sorrow us all. This will be righted in time. We have spent many a contemplative night in preparation for today. Reevers brought calamity to our homes twice in a lifetime. We have persevered. Your piety continues to be an example to us all."

Padazar swept his hand over the map and looked at his companions. "We all know this is no light undertaking. We have tremored the earth and must tread a mindful path. We are branded as traitors by many, but, in time, these very same will proclaim us the restorers of the land. Conservator, Lord Swan, I will address Burzina with Nabrensus at an opportune moment."

A sudden noise stirred the bloodhounds as one of Padazar's couriers walked in. Uninterested in the courier, the bloodhounds snorted lazily and drifted to sleep.

"Yes?"

"Apologies, Your Eminence. Nabrensus has requested your presence tomorrow morning at first light to plan the next moves of the campaign."

Padazar nodded to acknowledge the message and dismissed the courier.

"Nabrensus intends to besiege Thavodyn and no doubt wants Barrett's and Gerdeon's infantry as dirt mules and breach fodder," said Swan.

The two men blurted a worried "No!" in unison.

"Thavodyn is an unnatural place. It bears the witching mark of Silverface and his blasphemy," said Woolfolk turning to Padazar's sons. "Remember your lessons on natural deduction. The order put forth by Indalos has been interrupted there. The rocks remain a pristine black, unweathered and unchanged to a red or brown as most basalt in open air. This is the meddling of Silverface and his vulgar attempts to warp the creation of Indalos."

Amos could not restrain himself any further and offered his own thoughts. In a voice between squeak and growl, he said, "Let the Tavuros try to force the gates of Thavodyn. They can spend the winter freezing before its walls. We'll have captured Ravalas and pried the country from Eadolan's hand before the walls come down."

"A fine strategy and wishful thinking, Young Master, but we must see it through," said Latrobh. "Thavodyn is a fine chicken coop but an empty one. Why would the Tavuros just not bypass Thavodyn when Eadolan is bone thin on cavalry? He can do little to check their movements. Nabrensus is a man of the saddle not the mud of a siege line. Do you think he would besiege the fortress and give us the free hand to claim the country for your father? Ally and enemy are one in the same with the Tavuros. They will not abide our agreement if given the chance."

Latrobh added, "Save for the belt of plains west of the Thicket, all the good pasture lands are farther east. If the Tavuros are east of Thavodyn for more than a pipe and a piss, we'll also have to fight them, or they'll ravage the central provinces."

"The Tavuros despoiling the lands of Duke Urric and demonstrating for all our countrymen that he is little more than an impotent sot would not be a bad course of events." Padazar relished the thought.

"If Burzina is any indication, they mean to subdue and conquer, not just gallop through. They'll besiege Thavodyn," said Swan.

"Drev, are the Tavuros moving on Thornhelm as well?" asked Gerdeon.

"While I was in their camp, I heard no mention of that rotten tangle of log and sod."

"Ethan, have the homing birds been dispatched back to your mother and brothers?" said Padazar.

"Yes, Father, quite some time ago," answered Ethan.

"Good." Padazar nodded. "Your brothers will be in the

saddle shortly." Padazar turned his attention back to the larger group. "We'll stay together a few days to sort through the nobles and see who may be of the mind to reconsider their opinion of Eadolan. In support of our allies, Lords Ray and Swan and a portion of the cavalry and infantry will remain with Nabrensus."

Padazar returned his focus to his sons. "Ethan, Amos, you will also stay with Lords Ray and Swan. Asmund, you will remain with me."

"What!" gasped Padazar's three teenage sons.

Padazar cut them off. "You will serve your family and country. Ethan, Amos, your presence demonstrates to Nabrensus our commitment to the alliance. Lords Ray and Swan will watch over you. The rest of our forces will return south with me to secure the towns and crossings along the line of supply. We will all be together again in due time."

"We'll keep the Tavuros here. When they're nearly bled dry, we'll capture Thavodyn," offered Swan.

"How?" asked Latrobh skeptically.

Corneleo Ray just twisted the ends of his moustache and smiled widely at Latrobh.

CHAPTER 3

"Help! Help!" came the echoing cries of Cotterill's two young aides. Men groggily peered around, but Bambenek was first to his feet and steps ahead of the rest. Bambenek saw panic in the eyes of the scribe and courier and motioned for them to move back. The sun had not quite risen, but, in the rose-gray dawn, Bambenek could see the clammy pallor of Cotterill's face.

Bambenek lightly slapped Cotterill twice on the cheek and shook his shoulder. Cotterill's muscles were unresponsive; his eyes greeted Bambenek with a vacant stare. Bambenek checked for a pulse on the neck and found none. Quickly glancing at the still motionless chest, Bambenek discreetly checked Cotterill's mouth for obstruction. With the gathering crowd and no visible blockage, Bambenek did not want to linger but thought he noticed a slight discoloration in the back of Cotterill's throat as he started to stand.

To be able to stand, Bambenek had to push back some of the Chartered Cities militiamen crowding in to see their leader.

"He is too far gone," said Bambenek. "Myron. Quinby. What happened during the night?"

All eyes turned to the two aides, both teenagers of well-appointed families in the Chartered Cities. "I don't know. We just found him," Myron bleated. "I woke up and checked on him. I slept through the night."

Sergeant Farrior roused the men who were on watch during the night. "Report!"

"Nothing unusual, Sarge. Some boys more or less stayed awake than face the specters in their sleep. A few went to piddle now and then, but perimeter was secure. Quiet night really," said one of the watchmen.

"You saw the Major's condition yesterday. He was in distress," Portnay offered. "I fear the weight of the day tipped the mortal scales. May he find peace in the tranquil fields of Indalos and have toll ready for the gates. Boys, if you will kindly step aside."

Portnay swept his hand to request a pathway to Cotterill. He knelt down, recited a short prayer, and placed two gold crowned tigers on Cotterill's eyelids. The nobleman then cut a silken strip from the hem of his tunic and tied the strip around Cotterill's head and eyes to keep the coins in place.

Portnay stood and stepped away from the crowd gathering to pay their respects. As he passed through the crowd, he wiggled his fingers to send the trace of death scurrying away.

The men of the Chartered Cities led the singing of the prayer of passage.

The time has come to bid farewell
Tranquility in sweet repose
Gently travel to gracious fold
Rolling fields and blooming rose
Look kindly on fam'ly who remain
As we hold you dear in memory's refrain

Hoping to prevent listening to another solemnity, Portnay returned to the crowd. "As the departed aptly reminded us yesterday, we must look to our duty." To Myron and Quinby, he said with an air of piety, "Gather some men and bury Cotterill's body."

"No!" stammered Quinby. "We should take him with us." He paused to summon words and courage. "He deserves better than to be buried here. He should be interned in his family's crypt."

The other militiamen backed the pensive Quinby. He stood a little taller at the sign of support.

"We'll not disgrace Major Cotterill with some trench in the forest deep," said Hodger Hill. "We are free men. As far as we are concerned, you tell us nothing!" Hill signaled to some of his fellow militiamen to find a cloak to cover Cotterill and to cut wood to fashion a litter for the body.

"I did not catch your name, but in any case, my position and privilege are manifest to tell you precisely. But, if you want to haul his fine threads and bones back home, you can carry him, but tell me this: when we encounter the enemy again, will you spend your time guarding a corpse or protecting the living?" Portnay wasted no time for an answer to his question. "Have your morning meal and make ready to break camp. We will be leaving this place before the day is too far along."

Other than Hufyn and the squires, everyone ignored the order.

At the sight of Portnay's sneer, the grizzled sergeant gave reply. "There you have it. The extent of your command. I can't imagine you have seen much actual combat before today or are aware of soldierly protocol beyond the pomp that your tutor made you memorize. So, permit me, Sir Portnay, to give you a lesson from the soldier's book. With the present absence of unified command and the current size of our group, what we have is an independent company. An independent company chooses its captain." Farrior paused and cleared his throat. "Fellow soldiers, I declare for Bambenek Morley. He is the man best fit to lead us."

"How is a scout the best qualified to lead any group?" Portnay gasped in rebuke.

"I thought he was a skirmisher?" wondered a line infantryman to those nearby.

Bambenek heard the remark. "Yes, that too. With the Tavurite army immediately in front of us, the need for my scouting acumen was much reduced," he replied flatly.

"He's a man from the regular army and born in the Chartered Cities," said Farrior.

"He is of a lower rank than you, Sergeant. How irregular for a sergeant to listen to a subordinate?" Portnay challenged.

"Rank or not, I think he is the best man to lead us. We can sort out ranks another day."

The infantry and militiamen, having seen Bambenek's coolness in the battle fray and reassuring presence over the past day, shouted their approval.

With the noise subsided, one of the Chartered Cities militiamen, Simon Audley, a thin, peevish, erstwhile bookkeeper, could not resist returning a verbal thrust at the knight. "The gallant Dallen Portnay and his eight bent-legged saddle squatters. Here to save the realm. You would strike a chivalric image leading such a miniature host. Or," he smiled, "you would be picked up so quickly by some cavalry patrol that your fretting father would be pressed to deliver up a huge sum for your safe return. Would he trifle to spare even a copper for your squires?"

Audley swept his eyes to each of the squires and nodded knowingly. "Well, seeing as how Padazar has already upset the natural order, he may not be in the mood for keeping the heads of current nobles attached to their shoulders for much longer. As you said yourself, Amberfield does have fertile soil. That would make a tantalizing reward for one of Padazar's stable boys, don't you think?"

Portnay glared at the grinning Audley but made no reply.

Bambenek waited a moment and motioned for the group to quiet. Possessing the moment, he hesitated and then shook his head. "Brothers, I don't know that I am equal to the task and honor you are bestowing on me. I think someone else is better qualified."

The soldiers shouted their adulation.

"You always looked out for us."

"You led our poor hides to safety and will lead us out."

A solitary, phantom gust seemed to slam into Bambenek. He rocked weightlessly, cautiously, on his heels. Returning to the still and present air, Bambenek recovered, gnawed his lip, and spat near his toes. He looked back up and hesitantly said, "I humbly accept the duty to be this company's captain until such time that my service is no longer requested, or the company has disbanded."

The soldiers cheered and patted Bambenek on the back and shook his hand. Over the congratulatory offerings, Bambenek said, "I nominate Sergeant Farrior and Hodger Hill as selected men to lead the line infantry and militiamen." The men only nodded their heads at the formality as Farrior and Hill were already of rank and liked by their men.

"Sir Portnay, when we return to the army, proper standards

and banners will reform. In the meantime, I ask you for your partnership and counsel as leader of the mounted wing. The men have not selected you to lead this company, but we understand who you are and what you represent outside these woods. It is a rare thing for a man to be training with a sword since he learned to walk. We understand the talents you possess."

Bambenek's words seemed to placate Portnay.

Bambenek now turned to the half-orc. "What say you, friend Dronor? Will you help us?"

"Mighty Dronor," Portnay interjected. "Will you serve under my command? You have no ties to these lands, but I will pay you well. You shall not want for pay or whatever you desire. You would have the place as champion in my personal guard."

Dronor grumbled and mindful of his wrapped and splinted leg, slowly, and with aid, rose to his feet. He scratched his jutting lower jaw edged with stumpy tusks and appeared to sort the choices for several moments.

"What say you, Orc?" said Hufyn, eyes bloodshot from lack of sleep.

Portnay immediately shot Hufyn an admonishing look.

Dronor just stared at Hufyn.

"Never mind his hasty words. He lost two brothers on the field," Portnay said with a trace of an apology. Portnay's face contorted, and he seemed to reconsider his offer as he saw Dronor's quilted and crusted leg in plainer view.

Dronor cleared his throat to ward off any further parlay. "Well, I know that some scavenger has my pack, your High Lord has my money, and some horse boy has a drinking tale about how he dropped an orc. I'm owed a few things. I intend to collect what I can. I've taken payment from many purses, but I serve no one." Dronor looked at Hufyn and Portnay. "I agree

34

with the boys. Bambenek. With his help and some luck, I will keep my leg."

"Old village cure. No luck to it. Keeps the blood from getting tainted. It will heal good," Bambenek said confidently.

"I owe you a debt. You have my blade at the ready," Dronor said to Bambenek and raised his axe, firelight flickering in his feral black eyes.

"He's worth ten men," said one soldier.

"Twenty," said another.

Bambenek nodded and smiled. "Boys, I want a full roll call after breakfast. Need to sort the status of things including general vitality, provisions, and condition of weapons. And lastly, anyone know any spells? Any campfire magic? Any disciplined study of mystical forces? I know the wizards don't like to hear of unregulated and sorceress ways, but with our present condition, we need any edge we can get."

Everyone listened apprehensively, shrugged their shoulders, and looked at each other.

"Well, seeing as no one is offering up, hear me kindly. If we get into a pinch and you know how to fix a hex, launch a fireball, or even scatter a few cinders, do it."

After a slim and motley breakfast, the men formed up in ranks, and one by one came forward to report. All men were wounded or damaged in their own way with Dronor being the worst off in terms of visible injury. The more severely wounded had been left on the field or succumbed to their wounds before entering the forested refuge.

All the line infantry stood abreast in their hauberks over gray gambesons with thick blue and orange cuffs. They wore shallow nasal guard helms and had swords whether from their original assignment or appropriated from the fallen. A few men had the spiked maces of dispatched enemy cavalry. Some had retained their shields despite the weight while fleeing pursuit. Most had abandoned their spears, whether splintered on the field or dropped in flight. Sergeant Farrior stood at the head of his men defiantly holding the ragged, blue and orange banner of the Twelfth Company.

The Chartered Cities militiamen were in a leaner condition. Their standard weapon was the thirteen-foot pike, but these were more cumbersome to handle at a quickened pace than the line infantry's eight-foot spear, and even more so at a sustained run. All pikes were discarded. Most still had their iron kettle helmets, but a few tossed the iron brims to gain a step. These same men would have dropped their breastplates and tassets had a calm-fingered neighbor been willing to undue the buckles.

Among the militia, swords were not standard issue in the ranks, but a myriad of daggers, knives, hatchets, and even one sharpened entrenching shovel were counted. Both Myron and Quinby yet carried their ornate, vestigial dueling swords which were gifts of their respective fathers when commissioned as aides to Cotterill. No flag or ensign lofted above the militiamen.

The archers were nearly out of arrows, but to a man, had held firmly to their yew bows. Bambenek recalled that they disposed of their missiles with defiant, unhurried movement, rather than in a panicked scatter. The bowmen, in leathers or padded cloth, were all from the militia and had spare bowstrings in plenty and skinning knives, most being hunters and trappers in gentler days. As Bambenek passed them, he remarked, "Good, boys. No sense in marveling at quivered arrows after a battle. Better to give those screamers a ride."

Bambenek craned his head up and gave Dronor a nod. Dronor stood, weary, but at attention in his full panoply. He wore a soiled, dark blue, long sleeve and thigh-length padded jack with a separate tightly-woven woolen collar and hood of roughly the same color seated atop. A double-thick, leather pauldron further protected his right shoulder and was buckled with straps across his chest. On a broad belt hung a wide knife and a dagger to the right and a giant arming sword to the left; this belt, lacquered in residue, had been cinched timely to Dronor's leg to prevent him from bleeding out on the battlefield.

His drab linen pants were tucked into sturdy, massive mid-calf boots. The right pant leg was greased and flecked with blood and earth; the left leg above the knee was nearly concealed behind a crusted, weeping slag of poultice, moss, and snug cloth and leather wrappings. Despite the wound, he easily projected a dominating air amongst the men. In his near kettle-sized hands, he gripped a great double-headed axe and metal-studded, oaken shield.

After a few moments of esteem for the big half-orc, Bambenek gave an accounting of his own armaments. "Boys, I am flat out of lead shot, but I scrounged a few forest stones that will fly just fine from these slings." He flipped the slings over his shoulder and pointed to his waistline.

A woven belt patterned yellow and green secured a horizontal leather sheath. The sheath sheltered a foot-long knife when measured tip to pommel. Bambenek touched the pommel with a knowing smile. "An efficient tool for several occasions."

Underneath the woven belt, Bambenek had a second, plainer belt which supported a short sword scabbard. Bambenek removed the weapon: a curved, single-edge blade, narrowing towards the hilt and widening at the opposite end before concentrating at the point. The handle was formed in the shape of a falcon and leafed in a weathered gold. All of the militiamen and most of the other soldiers had not seen such a blade before.

"It was not forged in these lands. A relic I picked up on a distant field," Bambenek said when he saw their expressions.

The earlier phantom gust seemed to return and then as quickly recede. Bambenek blinked and renewed his focus. "The shape distributes the blade's weight to allow for a long slicing edge and also for similar impact to an axe blow; however," he smiled and pointed to Dronor, "not with the viciousness that our friend can deliver."

Bambenek did not mention his carving knife, now concealed in a sheath inside his right boot, and stood aside as Portnay presented his retinue. A black flag with a yellow fess and bundled wheat in the hoist presided over the review. The black field represented the fertile earth; the yellow stripe and symbol, the bountiful harvest of the Portnay family's Amberfield estates.

As a member of the nobility, a self-isolating minority obsessed with dominating the broader society, even within his present diminished grandeur, Sir Dallen Portnay had been taught to manipulate every occasion; to use ostentatious displays as symbols of unbreachable wealth and power to the desperate, barefoot serf. "Men of Ardalencor, I present to you the chivalric knights and squires here assembled."

Portnay and Hufyn cut a gallant image in freshly shined armor. Idleness, a fear for home, and a longing for routine in an unfamiliar place prodded the squires to scrub and polish the chain and plate. Most of the dried blood and carnage had been meticulously pried loose of ringlet, dent, and crevice. In his left arm Portnay cradled a sallet helmet finely etched with wheat sheaves and flourishes and theatrically raised a gilded, basket-hilted broadsword with his right. His lead squire, Talvert, held his lord's alternating black and yellow eight-part gyronny shield. Talvert, like the other squires, was clad in chain mail under a yellow and black surcoat.

Hufyn, his armor lacking some of the detailed magnificence of his benefactor's, was nonetheless expensively equipped. To signify the allegiance to the Portnay family, his shield bore the Portnay colors: halved into upper yellow and lower black portions but with the silhouette of a rearing stallion in the upper left corner to denote his own distinct noble standing. His shield was smashed, gouged, and draped in a bloody veneer but still maintained its sturdiness. As the squires cleaned the arms and armor, Hufyn held back his shield as legacy of his failed attempts to protect his two brothers who were unhorsed, hacked and trodden into an all too embracing ground. "In the name of Indalos, my brothers will be avenged," Hufyn whispered and gripped the shield tighter.

After Portnay introduced each of the squires, the horses were paraded through the encampment. The dapple gray and sorrel brown war steeds were pristinely brushed with improvised birch combs. Most were remounts, simply saddled, but one was covered with a black caparison, densely patterned with wheat bundles sown in golden thread. In all, Portnay had eight men under his command and four horses. With two mounts between the seven squires, he begrudgingly had an orphaned infantry command of his own.

Moving his eyes across the congregation, Bambenek muttered, "Forty enduring souls."

"Captain. Hey Captain! We got one more," called one of the soldiers.

A few trees back of the sequenced men slumped a man plastered with fever and clutching his right arm. Between the shakes and whimpers, it took a few moments to figure out that the man could communicate with them only in an abridged military tongue utilized by mercenary companies drawn from multiple compass points.

"Why did no one bring this man to my attention?" asked Bambenek.

"He's a mercenary. We didn't understand what he was saying. Just a slap of words every now and then. He just kept to himself and only asked for something to drink," one of the men said.

The mercenary had a scarred, olive complexion and deep-set, dark almond eyes. His studded leather shirt with reinforcing metal staves was mangled and rank. Bambenek motioned for the man to pull back the shreds of the upper sleeve. The man winced as did some of the other men when presented with the sight.

"That arm is all pus and fester," said Bambenek. "Why did no one help this man?"

"He stayed back. Kept to himself. We didn't know his arm was bad," someone replied.

"He probably got the beginnings of that wound a few days back," Bambenek stated. "That arm has curdled."

"It will need to go, nearly to the shoulder," Portnay said.

Bambenek nodded. "Anyone take off an arm before? I mean in a meticulous fashion. We first got to cut away the dead flesh, then saw the arm bone, and sear shut the mess of it. Get some of that village water and a proper stick for this poor traveler to bite on."

Bambenek pulled his crooked knife and began to strop the blade. One of the infantrymen handed a bottle of sour mash to the man which he sniffed and roughly pushed back into the giving hand. The man now started to push himself away from the others. Farrior motioned for three of the line infantry and two of the larger farm boys from the militia to hold the struggling man down.

The outlander was strong and muscled. It took much effort to keep his arm straightened and elevated on a crosswise log they had placed underneath. The mercenary tried to wriggle free from the press of men as much as from the necrotic throb of his arm. One of the men poured some of the spirits down the man's throat, most of which he spit back up. Another of the line infantrymen was looking around for some piece of metal large enough to heat in the fire to cauterize the wound. When the infantryman turned, Dronor stood next to the main fire, a side of his axe blade already deep in the flames.

"I'll take the arm. One swing and seal the wound. Keep him calm for a little longer, and we'll get this done."

"It's got to be precise, Dronor. This is not felling a tree," Bambenek warned.

Dronor grunted. With one side of the axe warmed, the half-orc approached the panicked man who began to struggle again. Dronor grimly lifted the stout haft and great blade in one deliberate motion. The man's shriek, even with the clenched wooden bit, seemed to rattle the leaves and curl the roots of the trees. Dronor pressed the fallen blade firmly against the stump.

One of the militiamen moved forward to remove the bit and offer a cup of cooled herbal tea. Another soldier covered the distressed vestige with moss and tied some cloth tight to keep it in place. The man was lifted up. He sat with his legs pulled close and moaned to the rhythm of a steady rocking.

Dronor patted the man on the head, picked up the rancid arm by its lifeless fingers, and disinterestedly tossed it in a nearby fire. The shocked man looked into the flames, entranced, as his livelihood, his sword arm, crackled and faded.

"Any more surprise amputations needed?" said Bambenek confoundedly. He spat. "Boys, explore these woods, but don't go too far now. We need to find some materials for arrow shafts, javelins, and spears. Kindly ease out a bit and see what you find. Make what you can. We are leaving as the sun falls."

Only Bambenek, Dronor, Farrior, Hill, Portnay, Hufyn, and the convalescent remained in camp as Portnay had instructed his retainers to try to locate forage for the horses.

Portnay looked at Bambenek. "What? Why the delay?"

While he would not have suggested the idea, Hodger Hill quickly grasped its sagacity. "We can't be walking out of here with the sun dancing off your armor."

"We'll leave around dusk and hug the tree line as long as we can. Get a sense of things and who has what," said Bambenek.

"Can't get caught with our trunks out taking a piss on open ground," chided Farrior.

"We can stay concealed for a while, but we'll eventually have to cross open ground to get to Thavodyn's walls much less figure out who will answer the gate when we knock." Bambenek added, "Sir Portnay, we'll need your men to do some scouting work in the dark and report back. Even with traveling at night, it may be after daybreak for the boys on foot to reach the fortress. Do your men know the ground?"

"Yes."

Farrior detected the lie. "On the last breath of my ancestors, I am tired of this! I don't care who you are!" The angry sergeant struggled to control his voice. "You'll not get me and my men killed. You had your chance at that already. If you are planning anything other than to rejoin the army and stand with the rightful ruler, leave now. If you try to string us along, at any time try to double cross us, I will stick this spear so far in one end and out the other that I'll roast you on the spit and eat your fucking heart!"

In an instant a wide-eyed Portnay had brandished his sword.

"Let's have it out," Farrior growled. "Let's see what you got."

Portnay flicked a lunging strike, but Dronor was there to interpose the face of his axe and swat away Portnay's thrust. Bambenek steadied his calloused hand on the sergeant's shoulder. Dronor gave the approaching Hufyn a tusk-filled snarl that seemed to stop his heart for a moment. Hufyn slowed his step.

"If you both are still so inclined, you can paint this pine cone when the Tavuros are driven out and Padazar is a head shorter. Until then, blades towards the enemy; but since we briefly speculate on the topic, if I had to wager," Bambenek mused, "I'd say you, Portnay, likely have more nimble and alacritous swordplay than the Sergeant, but Kellin Farrior is a survivor. I reckon he would just as soon bite off your nose if spear and sword were not enough and smash his own face in just to smash yours. How would you present yourself to the courtly ladies then?"

Bambenek gave Portnay a moment to digest the thought and then continued sternly. "Sir Dallen Portnay, on your honor as a titled and esteemed noble, I need to hear you say that you will remain with the company at all times. At all times," he stressed, "some of your men may venture to search and survey, but you will always remain with the main body."

"I agree," Portnay said slowly.

"On your word and honor."

"On my word and honor."

Dronor, Farrior, and Hill all gave Bambenek an unsettled look. Bambenek said nothing and walked into the surrounding wood.

CHAPTER 4

"You were very late." High Lord Eadolan's eyes bored holes into Rallis Stadrys, the Archmage of Ardalencor.

"Eternal apologies, Your Grace. We arrived as soon as practical. Without the careful provision of supply and spell book, we wouldn't have been much better than infantrymen. I dare say, although delayed, we arrived at a prescient moment."

The High Lord was a glittering beacon on the walls, dressed in his golden, full armor and a silken cape of a richly intricate design in purple and silver. A sleek golden diadem rested on his forehead and ruddy blond hair spilled down to his shoulders.

Squinting at the sun-splashed armor, the Archmage gave the High Lord an assessing look. "I am sure you had a good reason to give battle prior to my arrival."

"The Tavurite army and Padazar will be before the walls tomorrow," replied Eadolan pretending not to have heard the Archmage. For Eadolan, looking out from the massive black basalt ramparts, each blink and breath was an anxious moment in which the outline of the horde could appear in the approaching distance.

"Thavodyn is a proper treasure." The Archmage, known amongst the common folk as Silverface, smiled knowingly and stroked his long, snow and silver-streaked beard. "I was here with your grandfather when the cornerstone was placed. I selected this precious location. Yes, to the perceptive mind, this is fine placement astride the Ravalas road and a worthy gateway to the heartland, but so more importantly, it is atop a font of resonant energy. I infused the cornerstone with an ethereal warding. There is great protective magic imbued in the stone and mortar. My dear High Lord, I know this place very well."

The Archmage's age was a matter of some debate. He once had remarked that he was a youth when Behan IV, Eadolan's great grandfather, was High Lord. No doubt he was old, but he had an ageless quality. Beneath the distinguishing beard, his face was slightly gaunt with cheerful brown eyes and a slim aquiline nose. His head was shaved except for a long, gray-white stretch of hair from the crown of his head which formed a single lock draped across his forehead.

The Archmage dressed in his finest garments, an ankle-length powder blue robe of exquisite lightweight wool but still befit a martial character. The sleeves and bottom hem were a lattice of orange and silver-threaded patterns. The upturned collar had a similar pattern with the inside trimmed in red fox fur.

He wore a stole of durable fabric with a bright orange satin finish which rested broadly across the back and shoulders, angled at the chest, and merged at the navel and then on to extend, underneath a belt, to just below the knee. Metallic warding eyes, two on each side of the chest and a larger one on the back, punctuated the stole. Each of the amulets was firmly secured and linked to one another by shimmering, fine silver wire. The entire stole was trimmed subtly with white mink and filled with orange hummingbirds of varying sizes stitched with silken thread.

Over the robe and stole, a wide belt made of supple, brown leather contained a multitude of pockets and pouches for potions and vials. Two small brass bells on the left added a decorative flare. Low-cut, weld-yellow leather boots and jeweled, inscribed rings on both his middle fingers completed the attire. While a shade or two off, the Archmage had clad himself in the colors of Ardalencor. He hoped that even the densest yokel would make the connection and take heart seeing in old Silverface a living banner of the country.

In close proximity on the walls and engaged in separate conversation were Alwyn Lyjos, Commander of Eadolan's personal guard, Grammel Erstchester, Castellan of Thavodyn, Jakob Rukez, the army's Quartermaster, and Duke Urric Boscawent, owner and liege of sprawling lands on both sides of the Avenbair river and yesterday's commander of the unfortunate right wing. Members of the garrison stood in pairs at regular intervals along the walls, and three elven bodyguards of Lyjos' command stood at a respectful but vigilant distance from the High Lord.

The High Lord stepped back from the parapets and motioned to Duke Urric and the others to join him and the Archmage.

"Including the garrison, how many men do we have inside these walls?" asked the High Lord.

Erstchester was first to speak. "The garrison is at its full, peacetime complement of five hundred and twenty. All well-drilled. They know these rocks," he said with a mild air of deserved boasting. "Four hundred and seventy-three currently available for duty. Gracious Lord, when you brought us news of this disloyalty, I immediately had all the garrison men from the Southwestern provinces seized and locked in the jail. The conditions are cramped, but they are receiving normal rations."

Erstchester shook his head in disgust. "Forty-three in total, including two officers of the cavalry squads. They all protested that they had no knowledge of this and would not give aid to the invader. I do believe them, but I will not take that chance. This betrayal of brothers and shadows of suspicion, these are the poison roots now curling through our lands."

The barrel-chested, balding, fifty-year old Erstchester was a career soldier: a deliberate man, stubborn, tenacious and not one easily to be pried loose from his bastions. "Handfuls of our boys from the battle appeared at the gates during the night. The guards would not open the gates until daylight but dropped some bread and water to ease their wait."

Duke Urric continued, "About a hundred men in total. Some are in bad shape but are committed to fighting on. Surely more will arrive before the siege lines form. In the fighting back to Thavodyn," Urric chose not to say retreat or flight, "we have a count of almost two thousand from my cavalry command, over two hundred from the camp guard, and as Quartermaster Rukez was just mentioning, more than sixteen hundred camp laborers, servants, and followers. As you know, Your Grace, several wives of our noble brothers, including Bernard Tarpley and Clayd Vraim, accompanied the army. They shriek for their husbands and ask about them incessantly." Duke Urric looked down his snub nose and added disdainfully, "They are asking to meet with you and, forgive me, are demanding to know what you are doing to secure their release." Urric hesitated and thought to himself, if they are not yet in the fields of Indalos.

"Everyone has the same question, I am sure," said Eadolan irritably.

Lyjos shielded the High Lord from the pressing expectation for him to say more. Lyjos was fluent in Ardalen but never put aside his elven accent when speaking in another tongue. "For the Hearthguards and Lifeguards, of the six hundred, ninety-one were killed, captured, or missing. All from the Hearthguards. Some of my men are wounded, but all accounted for."

Always neatly trimmed with just a fresh, flaxen budding on his head, Lyjos steadied his pale green eyes and slowed his tone to mask his contempt. "Sir Ellard sends his regrets about not being present. He is in the infirmary under the care of Wizard Telfair and is expected to recover." Lyjos bowed ever so slightly to signal he was finished talking. Most of the officers in the army thought Lyjos was between seventy and ninety, but with pureblood elves living two or three times as long as a typical human, it was difficult to say for certain.

It was left unsaid but known to all that the Hearthguards were more of a noble social circle, a patronage of hunting parties and drinking bouts, than a cohesive fighting force. Ellard Ajhax, a cousin of the High Lord, was not held to a particular standard of martial readiness. Lyjos and the elves of the Lifeguards were just the opposite. With rare exception, all were born outside of Ardalencor, forbidden to own land or engage in enterprise, and were invited to the country for a singular purpose. Under the peerless direction of Lyjos, these warriors in glistening scale armor and conical helmets were drilled, disciplined protectors of the High Lord and his family.

Eadolan drew in a deep breath and held it for a moment. The situation further seeped into his being that nearly nine in ten men from his army had vanished through one method or another: killed, captured, missing, or abandoning him. How did this happen? How would his father and all his ancestors judge him? Yesterday was still a fresh nightmare, an immovable fact, but he still drew breath and still was High Lord.

He exhaled and returned to the inescapable present. "Immediately send all the noble ladies, wives, wardrobe attendants, whores, and whoever else not directly attached to the army back to Middlepost under a strong escort of three hundred cavalry. From there they can find their way on to Darhax and Ravalas. They must leave now. With Padazar's betrayal, that damned, treacherous snake, the road back to Ravalas is now in danger of being cut."

Middlepost was more or less the halfway point between Thavodyn and Ravalas. Thavodyn to Middlepost was sixty-five miles on the main road and about another sixty miles farther to Ravalas.

"Once the escort reaches Middlepost, keep an honor guard assigned to the column and keep them moving. Strengthen the garrison at Middlepost with the bulk of the cavalry to control the road and reconnoiter the surrounding country. We must quickly ascertain whether Padazar has men north of the Falling River at Sawmill Falls and over the north bank of the Avenbair."

Duke Urric, who was Eadolan's father's most trusted general, had smoke white hair cut short and capstoned by a receding widow's peak. A two-day stubble accented a full and contoured moustache. His eyes fidgeted about the horizon as he hurriedly dictated instructions to a page.

Rukez handed the page a second, more extensive note to ensure that the column was provisioned during the march. "You must move quickly. The column must depart before midday." The page nodded and hurried off.

"Before the battle, Your Grace, you saw the refugees fleeing the Tavurite advance assembling at the Park. The road south is already clogged with carts and livestock," the logistically-minded Rukez said referring to Thavodyn Park.

While many forts situated along commercial routes eventually ceded their circumferences to trading posts and towns, Thavodyn observed a strict two-mile radius in which no structures, however temporary, were allowed. No buildings and no trees were permitted in this zone. Nothing that would provide cover or resource to an invader. Merchants and travelers were not even allowed to stop for the night in this radius, but just beyond the basalt boulder marking the two-mile limit on the main road south of Thavodyn, a caravan waypoint and trading station developed in its own right.

Eadolan gave Rukez a half-crazed look, seemingly strangling him with his eyes, as to why Rukez was bothering him with such matters.

In yesterday's tumult and confusion, with Eadolan and his entourage sheltered in Thavodyn's citadel, the exhausted Rukez had done the necessary, and unacknowledged, work following the battle and through the night in making reasonable order of the jumble of panicked and injured men, wailing women, blood-spooked horses, lathered beasts and mazes of wagons, carts, and carriages. The fort's mustering grounds were repurposed as sleeping areas and lines of carts used to create temporary pens immediately outside the walls.

Jakob Rukez, the only son of a Jevatryn surveyor, was insular and aged beyond his thirty-odd years. While still possessing soft, kind eyes, his frame had soured and withered over time after the twin misfortunes of losing his wife to fever and then losing his newly betrothed to a resurgence of the fever a season later. Rukez had a rare talent for order and method, rising quickly, as few with comparable talents desired the quartermaster post, preferring commercial pursuits or a field command.

"I'll personally see to the expeditious departure of the womenfolk," Rukez said awkwardly as he withdrew.

Eadolan's eyes followed Rukez as he disappeared out of

sight down the staircase. "Once the womenfolk are headed towards safety and we have some room to move about this place, we'll do as we discussed last night. I'll lead the knights and cavalry back to Ravalas and gather new armies to crush the rebellion in the provinces and drive out the Tavuros. I hope to return in time while Padazar and the invaders are slowed before mighty Thavodyn. The camp guards and other returning men I place under your command, Castellan."

"Thank you, High Lord," said Erstchester. "That will give us about eight hundred men to hold Thavodyn until your return. Our larders hold more than a year's worth of twice-baked crackers and smoked meat for a thousand mouths. Your Grace, may I ask you to reconsider leaving cavalry detachments. Many of the men currently in the jail, including the two officers I spoke of, are some of my best horsemen. I have only about seventy active mounted fighters, and we are lean on remounts. The walls will be well held, but, if we are to be more than a black tortoise, if we are to disrupt and harass enemy lines of communication, I simply need more troopers. We will be no more than a bump in the road. Forgive me this blunt talk, but even to scout and forage, to cut hay and gather wood will be an issue."

"Castellan. I understand your point. I have already provided you the services of three hundred men. I will leave a few supply wagons as well. Requisition all you need from the Park." Eadolan paused. "I left Ravalas over a week ago with an army. When I return, I want to show that I have not lost it completely!" He fumed with exasperation. "I have already dedicated mounted units to Middlepost. You can coordinate your efforts with them. I need to keep a strong core on which a new army can be rallied lest this whole land give into despair. The whole Southwest of the country may now be in open rebellion. Most of the prominent nobles and best units of line infantry may be dead or held prisoner by the Tavuros and their puppet."

Erstchester nodded in understanding but also disappointment. He added flatly, "Birds and riders were dispatched yesterday to your brother with news of the battle and to hurry the gathering of a second army."

"Many of the noble formations were slow in gathering. Damn laggards. Many more formations will be on the march soon," mentioned Duke Urric. This was an innocuous way of saying that the harvest was poor in several provinces and many nobles, including Duke Urric himself, kept additional armed men back to ensure their granaries and barns were filled first as bread would likely be in short supply by next summer.

"Your Grace, declare Padazar a traitor and outlaw. Hold all his hereditary lands and titles forfeit!" said Urric covetously. "Be it the same fate for all who forsake their allegiance to the High Lord."

The Archmage let Urric's comment linger briefly and then stated apologetically, "Your Grace, I must make a slight modification to your plan from last evening. I will stay here with some of the wizards and apprentices. Our baggage train is cumbersome, heavy on the axles, and will slow you down. Castellan Erstchester and I will hold this keep."

The Archmage repeated his earlier comment. "Thavodyn is a proper treasure. This energy font must not pass from our hands. Let the people know that we hold strong." He stroked his beard. "Let them know that Erstchester and old Silverface will defend this gate."

Anticipating Eadolan's reply, he added, "My High Lord, I have stood loyal and provided counsel to many in your family. Today my place is here. Despite my personal adjustment to the plan, please do not worry. Mage Albright oversees the

Academy in my absence. All are steadfast in pledged service to Ardalencor."

The Archmage paused and then continued when Eadolan remained silent. "We continue to pass through a long day, but one question you have not answered fully and one we have not squarely asked remains a burdensome companion." He took measure of the young High Lord and stared at him gravely. "Will you countenance some arrangement or understanding in return for our men? If you instruct us to refuse any parlay or terms, are you prepared to accept that the Tavuros may slaughter thousands of soldiers and distinguished noblemen?"

CHAPTER 5

Around midday the men of the independent company started to filter back into camp with slim trunks and branches and set to work. A reverberation of cutting and carving began to show results; a few pikes, crude spears, javelins, and anti-cavalry stakes began to take shape. The arrows required more precise work.

While all in camp could shoot a bow, the five militia archers were wary about anyone fashioning the arrows other than themselves. Two of Portnay's retainers with short bows received such a cold reception when they approached the archers that they quickly turned back. In truth, both of their covered saddle-mounted quivers were nearly full, a fact that they did not share.

The archers returned to the urgent task at hand. The arrows' stiffness had to be assessed and sorted in addition to attaching the fletching. For fletching, the men preferred turkey feathers, but in lieu of feathers, pine sap was used to fix pine needles or birch wood. Once a few arrows were completed,

Mardin Tanner, a father of four from the village of Broadford, grabbed the initial batch and set to test the pitch and yaw.

Not long after Mardin's departure, Bambenek returned, carrying the limp body of an ensnared marten robed in a fur of gray and golden straw. "Not much of a catch, but there is always another day and another snare. Martens are kin to weasels. They have a wily and elusive disposition, but sooner or later they'll come across a bounded path, and the neck will find the noose." He gave a glance towards Portnay and let it rest a moment longer. Bambenek deftly skinned the animal to preserve the pelt, removed the guts, and set the remainder to roast over the fire.

"Good progress on our new arsenal." Bambenek moved to the center of camp and lowered his hands to signal them to stop work. "Now, Boys, please stand and hear me clearly. When we move out of here, what are we going to do? If we should happen upon the enemy cavalry, or they upon us, we must stick together at all times. Line infantry, militia, archer, knight and retainer, must remain as one, or we are licked. We are but a small formation seeking to rejoin the main army."

"You must obey my commands at all times. If we encounter enemy cavalry, we will form a square. Archers in the middle, squires hobble the horses and shelter them within, and men with the spears and pikes up front. Don't spread yourselves too thin. We need a dense thicket. Drive the charge-repelling stakes you've been fashioning at twice your arm's length in front of your feet. I want line infantrymen spread on all sides. Sergeant, if the time comes, please kindly see to that. Militia form up closely near or behind the line infantry. If practical, put the shield and spear in the front with the pike's reach to support and bristle our enclosure. We must hold at all times. There are not enough of us to try to mend a leaky bucket. If you run, well, that is not an option. We all ran yesterday, but we will not run again. We are moving in the right direction."

He paused and looked each man in the eye. "Our homes are under attack, and we must quickly rally, but we must do it smartly. We must do it wisely. We are making a lot of ruckus with all the chopping and cutting, but we are swaddled in the birch and pines and are safe for the time being. When we emerge, travel softly, discreetly; we must conceal our banners for the moment. We do not know who we will find. We are but a drop in the rough sea, but we know these waters and will weather this storm together."

Some men looked worried; others nodded in agreement.

"Gather what forage you can because we will leave this forest as the day starts to slumber. We'll travel through the wood and then peer around in the dark. A good while before dawn we'll march straight on Thavodyn's black walls as we'll have just the darkness to cloak us. I know hunger can be a pesky thing. It will rumble your tummy and pick at your bones, but as we march through, you surely remember these are our people. Most of us here are common folk or sons of peddlers from small hamlets and holds. These are our people. You must not injure them. You must not steal from them. There isn't too many a farm or stead between here and Thavodyn, but we'll ask them for charitable provisions and pay what we can. If we encounter any difficulty, you come to me. We will not thieve from our own. This only aids the enemy if we sow discord by taking our cousin's harvest. Crops came in not too long ago, so barns should be full and shareable."

Portnay and Hufyn had looked on blankly as Bambenek addressed the men, but, hearing that last statement, both gave each other a disquieted look.

"It is my sole intention as the elected captain of this company, to, as rapidly as possible, rejoin the army and let us all be supplied, let us all be fed, by the proper storehouses and accumulations. In your conduct, you must remember that you are soldiers and duty-bound militia. You are not a degenerate and despoiling rabble. You will spare the good people of this land. I will deal harshly with any derelictions. Is this clear?"

"Yes, Captain," the men answered.

"Now." Bambenek started to walk back and forth through the men. "Mardin Tanner, I know your wife and kids are proud of you. When the enemy approaches, can they count on you and your fellow archers to fire steady shots to keep roaming horsemen at bay?"

"Yes, Captain."

Bambenek took a few more steps. "Tryk Bearward. Fryll's Broadshield, Second Banner Company. Your father served in the line, and I knew him well. He is looking on favorably this day. Can he count on you to repulse the enemy?"

"Yes, Captain."

Bambenek moved down the lines. "I don't know your name, Son. How old are you?"

Through depleted eyes, the young man said, "Cirnu. Cirnu Millend. I'm almost seventeen."

"Well, Cirnu. I am Bambenek Morley. Pleasure to meet you. Take heart. That is a mighty weapon." Bambenek pointed to the birch pike. "It will hold strong as long as you hold strong. A horse will never willingly impale himself." Bambenek looked at the other men as well. "That only is plain sense, right? A horse can be guided even if you are not riding it. Use your prickly reach to influence its mentality."

"We lost a battle yesterday, but we fight on today. Extinguish the fires. Make ready and prepare to break camp," ordered Bambenek. "Sergeant Farrior, set the line of march. We'll head east through these woods for a mile or so yet."

Mardin and another archer, Abo Fletchbinder, approached

Bambenek. Mardin spoke first, "Bam, the wood we found was not the best. We only have a handful of crude arrows for the five of us."

"I understand. But I also know you understand that we cannot stay here until the quivers are full. Do what you can and make each one count." He touched both men on the shoulder.

Bambenek returned to the main fire, lifted the skewered marten and took a bite. As one of the infantrymen moved to smother the fire, Bambenek picked up the marten pelt and walked over to the litter with Cotterill's body. "Leave that skewer. I'll be back for it," he playfully admonished.

The litter had been built up with side walls and extended cross beams to allow four men to carry it. Moss and leaves were placed to cushion and immobilize the body inside. A few wooden runners were wedged inside the walls to keep the body and armor in place during transport.

Bambenek crouched and said a few words as he placed the pelt on Cotterill's chest. Like Portnay chose to voice earlier, Bambenek thought it better to bury the dead and tend to the living. He did not think it prudent to tie up four men with carrying a corpse. Via the most direct route, the men were over two hundred miles from Everhall, the largest of the Chartered Cites, but a discussion of distances was not one that he wanted to have now with militiamen composing about a third of his command.

Bambenek grabbed the remainder of the roasted marten and walked over to the one-armed outlander. "Sabkano."

The man looked up and turned to let Bambenek see the bandaging. Bambenek nodded and handed him the skewered marten for a few bites. "Time to march. Grab a javelin. Fall in with Farrior's men."

"You see those birds, those cardinals, sitting in the tree?" Bambenek said to a group of men as they took their place in the column. "The couple over there. You see them up in the tree? That's a good sign." Bambenek grinned and nodded in agreement with his own assessment. The welcome diversion pushed a smile to the men's faces.

Bambenek then caught Farrior's eye and motioned towards the east.

Sergeant Farrior squared his shoulders and bellowed a resolute, "Company. Men of Ardalencor. March!" The column moved towards the wood's edge, Thavodyn, and the main road beyond.

CHAPTER 6

"Ah, Commander Jerris. Thank you for coming. I do hope that you are well. Do you need to see a physician? Would you like something to eat?" Padazar motioned for a servant to bring in some food.

Maneol Jerris, Commander of the Chartered Cities militia, his armor and sword confiscated seemingly long ago, looked back at Padazar with an expressionless dignity.

"Please sit down." Padazar poured Jerris a drink. "Golden mead. A favorite of yours, if I recall?" He set the drink down in front of Jerris. Jerris did not move and glanced suspiciously, cravingly at the glass.

"I have a proposition for you." Padazar took a sip from his own cup. "It's really quite good." Padazar paused briefly as if to coax Jerris to try his own cup. "I want to send you home. I want an alliance with the Chartered Cities. I know you are a wise and shrewd man who cares greatly for his home. I will make my best offer plain to you now. I think you will find it very reasonable. Look at the present situation. The field is ours; thousands have been taken prisoner, and Eadolan ran away barely with the hair on his own head. He has no army."

"You say this with such detachment," Jerris started coolly, "when you brought the Tavurite swarm down upon these lands!"

"Hardly. They will be gone soon enough. They need never come within sight of the Grey River if we can strike an accord. Eadolan is spent and near naked of support. Acknowledge me as High Lord and the Chartered Cities keep all their rights, privileges, and obligations. We have not been able to locate Duke Urric. He is presumed to have fled with Eadolan. I know the disputes that you and your Cities have with Urric. He is encroaching on your yeoman farmers around Raymondton and Fairfield. I hear troubling reports that his troops are regularly burning homes and barns to drive out the small tillers and that he is claiming the plots and orchards for himself."

Jerris grimaced, and Padazar instinctively paused. The brooding Jerris seemed to be listening more intently now.

Padazar continued, "Eadolan did not put an end to this. Some High Lord he was, unable to adjudicate a dispute in his own lands? Or did he just turn a blind eye?" Padazar looked at Jerris with wide, demonstrative eyes, took a lengthy swig, and crunched down on an apple slice from a nearby platter. "I will acknowledge and maintain all your boundaries and titles. By Indalos, I may even consider expanding them."

"What of my men you hold captive? Where are Cotterill and the other officers?"

"Cotterill?" Padazar raised his voice and looked at an aide standing some feet distant. Padazar agitatedly gestured at the aide as if the man had made some mistake. "Please go check on the whereabouts of Major Cotterill and bring him here." The flustered aide acknowledged and briskly departed.

Padazar turned back to Jerris. "You must excuse me. We are still sorting the men and officers. I am sure Cotterill is in good health. Your men and yourself will all be permitted to return home in due time. For this to occur, I only need you to agree to my terms."

"I don't have authority to agree to anything. It would need to be submitted to Gann Goodwinds, the Cities, and the Guild Assembly."

"I know. But you will convince them. You are far too modest about your own role in the Assembly. One does not become Commander without a certain level of support and influence. You will maintain all your rights and privileges. All I ask in return is your word and a visible guarantee. Garrisons in Laingport, Everhall, and small detachments in your other cities. Eadolan kept a clutch of customs agents and tax collectors in Laingport. I don't ask for much more. When this situation is sorted out, when the Tavuros return home and when Eadolan is deposed, I will begin to remove detachments and release militiamen, the sons of your lands, to return home. It is in everyone's interest that this whole matter be resolved quickly. Your men will be well cared for until that time."

Jerris looked at him and shook his head in disbelief. "We won't accept the imposition of garrisons in our cities. You are no better than the blasphemous Tavuros!"

Jerris pulsed with anger. "In fact, you are far worse. Betrayer of your own people! You invited or welcomed the enemy in. I know you despise Eadolan and the treaty he made with Velenharn four years ago, but this, of all things, Horace, you..." Jerris trailed off and finally took a drink from his cup and stopped to consider the contents. Jerris realized that the mead was from a keg that he himself had brought in his personal supply wagon.

"I know you had quite a go of it yesterday, but I think you will find that what I am offering you is very generous."

Padazar's affable tone turned sterner. "Several weeks ago I heard rumors that a vein of copper was found in the hills southeast of Everhall. I hear it is a massive strike. Very lucrative for your guilds. You have gone to great lengths to block outside merchants from your Cities. Very determined, and I must say, very effective on your part. But your lands are now open. Your militia is here. I can march my army where I please." Lightning seemed to cross the whites of Padazar's eyes. "If I had a mind to do so, I could turn the copper over to the dwarves. They will burrow so deep into the mountains that you and your grandsons and their grandsons will never get them out. Guild control, guild rule, and the integrity of your lands will be broken."

Fear swept over Jerris' eyes, but Padazar altered his tone before Jerris could speak. "But let's not think of that for a moment further. I respect your decision to ban dwarves and foreign merchants from venturing beyond Laingport. As for me, I don't mind the dwarves. They are an industrious lot. There are a number of them living in my town of Delun with their shops, forges, and small works."

Padazar leaned in a little closer to Jerris. "But I do keep my eye on them. Can't let them get too comfortable. If a bunch of brawny and newly rich dwarves appeared in your lands, some of your local girls may take a liking to their bushy beards and choose them over your own shit-covered swineherds." He gave Jerris a knowing wink.

"We'll keep the dwarves out of the Cities. You control the mines and honor your obligations to me as High Lord. I want to be friends with the Chartered Cities. I have no quarrel with you as Urric has. I offer you the opportunity for glory and honor to secure the position of your Cities and to see the safe return home of many fine men. Think of the joy of the families when they return. Think of the sorrow and your burden of guilt if they never were to return. I don't think that your own people would judge you well. What would they say of you then?"

Padazar gave Jerris a benevolent look, patted his shoulder, and sat down. "Please be calm. I have no time for threats. I only ask that you consider my offer, very just and fair conditions. I will be speaking with some of our more famous noblemen later today and make them all various offers. I don't need all of them to agree to my proposals, so if some agree more readily, I will have less need of those who take more time to ponder. As I said, give it some thought and let me know by morning, but I am more apt to listen now if you have questions."

CHAPTER 7

The distance was not all that far, but the pace was slower than Bambenek would have liked. He was the captain, not a scout, at least for the time being, and progress was made not at his own stride, but by the collective movement of forty others. For the squires, finding a path for the horses proved a challenge through encroaching birch and guiding them across the steep banks of cuts and streams. The militiamen fared about the same and nearly dropped Cotterill's litter into an unnamed creek as they tried to climb the opposite bank.

Kellin Farrior raised his hand and signaled the column to stop. Seeing the break in the tree line, Bambenek came forward and took a broad view of scrub grass rolling out beyond the forest.

"Open road," said Farrior extending his hand.

Thavodyn was still miles off beyond the horizon, but neither friend nor foe appeared to be awaiting them at the wood's edge.

"About damn time," said Portnay as he and Hufyn strode up.

"Sir Portnay," said Bambenek, "I would like to borrow one of your horses and ride out to scout ahead with one of your squires."

Portnay and Hufyn had to restrain their laughter. Portnay chided, "Your captaincy is a far cry from being the High Lord. Your new-found title gives you no claim to confiscate the property of a nobleman. I've kept to the terms of our arrangement while you appear to have not. I will be the one to instruct any squire to ride out and scout around."

Bambenek said nothing and turned his head to study the open tract ahead. When two squires, Talvert and Aaron, were mounted and started out at a trot, Bambenek called, "Be careful. See what you can, but watch for those watching you. If you see our flag still flying, ride to Thavodyn and let them know we are coming during the night."

The squires never once turned around as they moved the horses to a gallop.

Hufyn placed a gauntleted hand on Bambenek's shoulder. "Don't worry, Captain. We've already provided the squires with proper instructions. Kindly leave matters of horsemanship to the knights." He smirked. "I saw a few nice rocks, real smooth, back there that you may want to add to your little pouch. Run along and track them down."

Bambenek Morley had lived a hard forty-five years but was still as agile as men half his age. He spun rapidly, swept Hufyn's hand from his shoulder, grabbed Hufyn's other wrist, and smashed him with a headbutt to the bridge of the nose. Hufyn stumbled back and clutched his nose. The remaining squires and Portnay rushed towards Bambenek while his back was turned.

66

"Hold!" Mardin screamed as he and the four other archers nocked arrows.

Portnay and the squires hesitated. Hufyn, seeing spears and pikes also leveled, attempted to atone for the situation. "No need for the theatrics. Lower your spears. The fault is mine and mine alone. A poor joke. Captain Morley, please accept my apology for this misunderstanding."

"Mammoth shit. Don't let him off so easily!" called an infantryman.

"Morley. Morley, listen to me," said Portnay in a steady voice. "Honor is satisfied. Let this pass."

"You have no honor!" rebuked Fletchbinder, but he nonetheless relaxed the tension on his bowstring.

A few moments passed before Bambenek spoke.

"Even when things are bad, you nobles sure find a way to make a plum shit mess of it. Tormentation must be in your blood." Bambenek paused and looked around at the men of his command who just a moment before were ready to fall upon one another. He sighed. "Thavodyn. The army." Bambenek's words faltered as he looked at Hufyn. "I accept your apology." Bambenek thought he would say more but could not bring himself to do it.

The air jumbled with the retainers' gasps of relief and the bitter groans of all the others as rightful justice seemed to elude a nobleman once again. An acidic cloud of contempt hung heavy in the air. The men passed the next long, anxious moments as silent years awaiting the return of the squires.

The tension finally eased as both squires came back at a good clip, wide smiles on their faces. "The way is open!" exclaimed Talvert as he slowed his horse just before the tree line.

"No enemies in sight!" said Aaron, lest his contributions to this mission be overshadowed.

Talvert, as scouting party leader, continued, "The tiger flies above the walls. Our boys still hold Thavodyn." The squire was referring to the flag of Ardalencor, the snarling face of a great white sabertooth tiger upon a horizontal bicolor of blue and orange.

A heartened cheer went up amongst the men.

"Sir." Talvert was only addressing Portnay. "The way is clear. If we leave now, we can be at Thavodyn in time for supper."

"Brilliant and befitting work, Squires. Well done," Portnay lavished. "It seems the choice is an easy one, Morley."

Bambenek eyed the squires. "While you observed the flag, how close did you get? Did you signal the garrison? Did anyone ride out to meet you? Will they send a guard to cover our movements?"

"Why?" Talvert said incredulously. "We could see straight to the castle. No Tavuros or Padazar's men in sight. We came back as soon as we could to share the good news. No sense wasting time when the sun is still up."

"Why all these questions? Why do we cower in these woods a moment longer?" Portnay said with a rising ire.

"I concur," said Hodger amazed at himself for finding common ground with Portnay.

"Let's get a move on, Captain," offered Tryk. Others were quick to add their acclamation.

Seeing his nocturnal plan rejected, Bambenek grimaced. "Alright, Boys. I hear you true." His shoulders drooped with resignation. "There is a more vigilant course to follow than what you all seem to favor, but I will lead you all just the same. Remember what I said before. If we should encounter trouble, we'll form a spear fort and fight them off. Don't forget those stakes either."

"Sergeant, please form the men into column. We'll move at the double step," said Bambenek.

"Men, form up!" Farrior called.

The men began to assemble outside the tree canopy and under a bare, cloudless sky. Bambenek remained in the forest for the moment and surveyed the marching column taking shape.

"Bam." Dronor loomed near and leaned in to whisper. "That recent patch was a lot harder than the path we took to enter the forest. Anything more than walking across flat ground and these rags will rip." Dronor tried to appear calm but left unsaid, *"Don't leave me here to die."*

Bambenek did his best to hide his concern. "Ask Myron and Quinby for help. Use their sword belts to hold the dressing in place. We'll make it through." He patted Dronor on the forearm and gave him a reassuring nod.

The men readily shook off their trepidation as they soon realized they were alone on the edge of the forest. The radiance of the autumn day was a welcome relief to the shards of light found in the forest. Loose chatter and song verse buoyed the men.

Bambenek lifted his gaze upward. Not a bird or anything larger appeared in the sky, and while after highpoint, the sun still stood bright as it glided westwards.

Portnay, Hufyn, Talvert and Aaron rode while the five other squires fell in with the rest of the foot soldiers. The militiamen were an august and comedic sight as they struggled to carry Cotterill's litter and match the speed of the line infantry veterans. When the column found its footing and rhythm, Portnay ordered his cavalry to spread out as a vanguard. As the group marched, the riders would occasionally recede into yet unseen undulations in the terrain but benignly re-emerge a moment later.

After a time, the pace of the men imperceptibly started to slow as the desire to keep the formation intact regressed to the speed of the slower moving members.

A few moments later, Hufyn stood up in the stirrups and spun his mount back to the column. "Tavuros!" Talvert and Aaron swiftly followed the knight.

"How many?" shouted Portnay.

Sergeant Farrior was already barking orders which drowned out Hufyn's reply. "Square! Fix the toe ticklers. Front rank kneel. Archers to the middle." A porcupine, quills patchy in some areas, began to take shape.

Portnay just shook his head when Bambenek asked that the horses be hobbled in the square. The nobleman instead commanded his dismounted squires, "Find your place within the square."

As the dismounted squires grabbed javelins and plugged an open spot alongside an infantry or militiaman, Portnay commanded, "Sir Evret, Squires Talvert and Aaron, stay on my flanks. We'll counterattack when the square is engaged." The three riders took positions surrounding Portnay who was just to the left of the phalanx.

"Enemy cavalry!" called Bambenek. A line of twenty horsemen neared to about one hundred paces. These were Tavuros, the crowned silver steed on dark blue battle standard fluttering above. These men, unlike the cataphracts, which had shattered the army of Ardalencor the previous day, were of a lighter sort, scouts and raiders.

"Enemy cavalry!" shouted militiaman Simon Audley as another knot of horsemen fanned out beyond arrow range on the right side of the company's position.

Profanity and prayers reverberated amongst the men.

"Steady, Boys," called Farrior.

Bambenek looked at Farrior and said, "We make our stand here, but we'll need to draw them in."

Bambenek raised his voice to be heard by the men. "We cannot move back to the forest, and we cannot stay idle. These marauders gorged on victory and want a belly more. They are arrogant and think we will wilt in the sun. Brave sons of Ardalencor! Your ancestors look upon you."

Bambenek unsheathed his sword and made his way around the interior of the square. "The enemy is before us. They beat us yesterday and think they can beat us again. Can they whip us?"

"No!"

The men cheered and began to knock their weapons together to raise the din. Standing in the second rank, Dronor roared and smashed the battle axe head into the ground to fix his spot and grabbed two javelins.

The Tavurite cavalry squads seemed unfazed by the commotion, but Bambenek spied one of the horsemen motioning instructions to the other men.

"Archers! Squires! Target their leader. Fire a welcoming shot."

The arrows found range but plunked harmlessly around the horsemen.

Seeing the fresh quivers of arrows used by the mounted squires, Mardin extended entreating hands. "Let me ask you but once. Give me a handful of those arrows." The bowman promptly received arrows from Talvert and Aaron. Mardin smiled at the expertly-made bodkin arrows with wicked barbs at the base of the iron heads.

"Archers! Squires! Volley two. Loose!"

Two arrows found targets. One Tavurite horseman, attempting to avoid the barrage, leaned down on the side of his horse, and the horse took an arrow in the haunch. The horse reared in spasm while the rider struggled to maintain control. At the same moment another arrow hit the shoulder of a nearby horse. The two horses thrashed about as the Tavurite leader ordered both squads to unleash a return volley.

"Incoming!" A shower of arrows arced towards the Ardalens. Most of the arrows fell just short. The only hit was to a militiaman who took an arrow to the thigh. He grimaced as he braced himself against his pike. Myron and Quinby grinned as they emerged from cover and inspected Dronor's shield. Dronor let out a chuckle as two archers were quick to extract arrows from the great oaken shield and prepare them for a return journey.

"Kneel," said Farrior and several line infantrymen dropped down in feigned injury. A few of the militiamen, pikes wobbling, followed their veteran counterparts. Seeing the apparent effect of the return volley, the Tavurite cavalry leader raised his sword, and men and beasts started forward on both sides.

"Indalos, protect us. Guard soul and soil."

"Boys, I'll make it plain," said Farrior grinning. "How you handle these next few breaths will determine if you ever get to make love to a woman again. Do yourself and your cock a service and hold the line."

Several men forced a nervous laugh as once again they felt the horizon tighten.

"At ten paces out, spears and pikes up," Farrior said coolly. "Arrows and javelins, release once you get a clear shot. Forget the riders and stick the horses."

The Tavuros were now fifty paces out and moving to a full gallop.

"Hold the line, Boys. Don't get lured out. Use the spikes to your gain," Bambenek said reassuringly. "Use the long reach."

At thirty paces the beasts were a wide-eyed froth. The Tavuros bellowed a battle cry.

Farrior calmed the men to preserve the trap and not trade volleys of martial yells. "Stand firm at your brother's shoulder, and he will do the same. Mark your target."

The cavalry charges were well-coordinated and appeared on course to crash simultaneously into two sides of the square. Sunlight refracted off the swords as the composite creatures of radiant sound and butchery approached the bleeding edge. With contact imminent, the cavalrymen more clearly saw the spikes before them and began to adjust their line, spread and bunch, and disrupt the impact of their charge.

"Up, Boys! Fire!" called Bambenek.

At this range, most of the arrows and javelins found a target.

Two of the lead horses were both hit in the neck and chest. They reared in choking screams and lurched amongst the spikes and staves. Mardin dropped the first horse with an arrow to the eye. Its rider's leg was crushed below, and the Tavuro took a rib-splitting spike to the side as they thudded to the ground. Both forms gave a few fleeting shivers and ceased to move.

The second horse, blood pumping and draping from wounds to chest and throat, dropped a skittering hoof flush on a stave and then frantically lunged forward to free itself. Its rider tumbled from the saddle and was met with a leaf-shaped iron spearpoint in the shoulder and then a second strike to the nose.

The horse, free of its rider, propelled forward. Hodger Hill, preoccupied with the brandished swords of other horsemen, could not avoid the equine boulder. Hodger was kicked in the chest and then trampled as the horse bucked. In the press, Quinby was dropped to the ground and had two fingers smashed by an iron horseshoe.

This breach was soon exploited, and some Tavuros dismounted and rushed in to wedge apart the formation. Tryk Bearward and Simon Audley fought against long odds to hold the corner strong. Supporting arrows whizzed dangerously by as Tryk and Simon contended with a multitude of swirling blows.

Stuck between this hammer and anvil, Quinby swore and slashed to free his pulverized fingers. Once freed, Farrior dragged Quinby aside. "Son, up and to your duty," he said as they both moved to counter the Tavuros' onrush.

"Now! Help us!" Bambenek yelled at Portnay. With the attack on multiple sides, Portnay looked unsure where to direct his men.

A few paces down the line that was fractured after Hodger's demise, young Cirnu reached and missed with his pike. A Tavuro safely passed the sharp end and rushed forward. Cirnu dropped his pike and could only cover. His forearms and then face were hacked open. Bambenek moved up to cut down the Tavuro but not in time to save the young militiaman who slumped disfigured in a broadening pool of his own blood.

Portnay, Hufyn, and the two squires now spurred their horses around the far edge of the square and caught the Tavuros in the flank. Portnay made short work of the two nearest Tavuros catching them in the back as they fought against the line infantry and militiamen.

Portnay's attack brought relief to this portion of the line, but still under attack from two sides, Simon Audley succumbed to an accumulation of cuts and stabs. Tryk, Farrior, and Quinby struggled to hold the hot corner intact. To the right of the angle, the square was also under intense pressure.

"Take your place, Boys!" Bambenek motioned for three of

Portnay's squires on an unengaged side of the square to move to confront the continued threat.

The Wellheard brothers, Osset and Bofred, two big farm boys from near Bathon's Ferry, anchored the right side and fought in tandem, shields and spears, frustrating all attempts to break this portion of the line. Dronor, with his limited movement, fought in support of these infantrymen and had quickly used all available javelins during the initial moments of collision. Still the Tavuros came on.

Not all the Tavurite horsemen had charged. A handful stayed back from the initial melee. This Tavurite reserve may have contributed to Portnay's initial hesitancy to commit his own troops. These Tavuros began to shoot arrows aimed at the sides not initially hit by the two charges. Sabkano was hit in the pelvis with an arrow and then again in the collar when he stumbled. One of the squires not ordered by Bambenek to another sector of the square, Arvid, remained next to Sabkano and was also hit.

Arvid called to other squires as he fell to the ground. "Help me!"

A few archers shifted their focus to the new threat and fired barbed retorts which sailed harmlessly towards the mobile horsemen.

Another arrow screamed in and hit Bofred's shoulder. His spear dipped, and the younger Wellheard brother received a sword hack to the elbow. Bofred called for his brother. "Osset!" The older brother paid for turning his attention and was cracked in the head. The helmet contour deflected most of the impact, but he dropped to one knee.

Several arrows struck more men of Ardalencor.

"Portnay! Horse archers!" came the cries. Portnay and his troopers, having driven off the Tavuros on one side, saw the new threat across the square and wielded around the way they had come. More arrows swarmed into the ever collapsing square.

The Ardalen archers turned to fire back at the horse archers but did little to suppress or even delay a fresh shower of arrows.

A string of Tavurite arrows sailed towards Portnay and his troopers, but all missed.

Portnay abruptly signaled his men to stop next to the square. "Squires!" Portnay screamed to his retainers amidst the chaos. "This is lost. Get on!"

"What about Arvid? He can't move!" called one of the dismounted squires. "And Bayard? He is on the other side."

"There is no time. Get on now, or we'll leave you all here!" yelled Hufyn.

"Sorry" was all the three dismounted squires could muster as they started to move past Arvid.

Arvid reached for his friends. "Don't leave me!" he cried, but his hands were kicked away. The three squires ran on and doubled up with Hufyn, Talvert, and Aaron, and the Amberfield knights rode away.

The men who observed the noble departure felt the forlorn crash of their stomachs.

The other side of the square was still heavily engaged. The Wellheard brothers and other line infantrymen had thinned the Tavurite assault, but still the enemy came on. With the sibling shield wall down, Dronor careened forward and slammed a Tavuro to the ground with his oaken shield. He swung his battle axe above him to keep approaching horsemen away. Dronor released his shield and stood as an intense pain rippled through his leg.

Dronor kept advancing and gripped his battle axe in both hands. With wild cleaves he sliced the nose of a horse which hissed blood and recoiled. As the heavy blade swung around, the big half-orc chopped the wrist and knee of another rider. A Tavuro on foot rammed his sword into Dronor's side, but Dronor turned and the blade tore into his padded jack and did not find flesh. With the sword twisted in the jack, Dronor grabbed his attacker by the forearm. Dronor pulled the wide-eyed Tavuro towards him and sunk the battle axe deep into the man's face.

Dronor wrenched the great two-headed axe clear and let out a bestial howl. The remaining Tavuros all along the line started to disengage at the frightful sound and shifting tide of battle.

Tavurite riders in the last rank threw lassos at the towering warrior. Presented with such a clear target, these expert horsemen easily snared their quarry. Both lassos caught Dronor around the neck as the Tavuros started to gallop and draw the ropes tight. Dronor sought to brace himself and raise his axe, but his wounded leg gave way. He thudded to the ground, shoulder smacking first, and the axe jarred free from his hands. He tried to reach for the axe, but it was beyond his grasp. The ropes stretched, and he clutched at his constricted neck.

Fletchbinder thumped an arrow into the back of one of the riders. In the slackened reprieve, Dronor searched for his dagger, but another Tavuro grabbed the fallen lasso and started off. With effort the horses started to drag the half-orc who desperately flailed at his neck, the lassos, and the ground. Serpentine coils bit, injecting pain and pulsating swarms of asphyxiating color.

"Dronor!" came the cries from the men as they tried to chase off or cut their way through the remaining Tavuros. The horses picked up speed, and a third rider joined to help drag Dronor farther away.

Suddenly the three galloping horses jerked to a stop. The spooked horses reared and snorted frantically at an unseen force. The riders were shaken in their saddles, and one lasso snapped loose. The riders tried to steady their horses and turn their mounts. Dumbfounded, they saw their big catch and a length of the ropes entwined with the ground itself. In the shift of fortune and with the heavy casualties already sustained, the Tavurite leader signaled the attack to end. The Tavuros unleashed a few parting slurs and arrows but withdrew.

Several men ran to Dronor as the scrub grass and vegetation receded.

Bambenek instructed the men still in the square to look to the wounded. Bambenek did not move. He hoped for an unobserved moment as his legs buckled and he fell to one knee. Bambenek released some crushed leaf and root fragments from his hand and exhaled so deeply and wearily that the men stared for a moment.

"Captain?"

"I'll be fine," he managed eventually. "Look to the others."

"What from the black abyss was that!" called Myron as he approached the half-orc.

"Don't just stand there. Cut the damn ropes off him!" ordered Farrior.

Tryk and other infantrymen cleared the lassos and removed Dronor's hooded collar.

"This saved your life," said Tryk holding the thick collar. Dronor could only cough spittle between his teeth and tusks.

The men of Ardalencor held the field. After the resounding defeat yesterday on the plains near the village of Boruma, the seizure of trophies from the Tavuros took on heightened importance. The crawling wounded were finished off, at times in gruesome fashion. The men went among the Tavurite corpses plucking earrings, smashing out gold teeth, lopping off ringed fingers, and taking whatever they could find in pockets and pouches, no matter how insignificant the prize.

"Everything will be collected and divided in kind," said Farrior. "Each man gets his fair share of the spoils."

As the remaining men of the company considered their next move, Tryk Bearward looked at the fallen men and the stark contrast of Cotterill's unscathed litter still in the middle of the square. "How many more bones do you boys intend to carry back home?"

CHAPTER 8

Innumerable craggy rivulets traced the mountain sides and sloshed out a wide basin. The conjoining watershed, cold and clear, moved with the rhythmic vigor of awakening snowmelt. The river gained shape, narrowing and deepening as it descended. The watery sinews formed a writhing host which inspired distant wanderings and tales of hypnotic sprites still remembered alongside the doctrines of Indalos.

The torrential course plowed the stone valley with a frothing rush and then hurled itself down a thousand-foot drop to inspire the cartographer's inking of Falling River to the map. Within far sight of the skyward mists, the town of Sawmill Falls sat on the north bank above a pocket bend in the river.

The town of about two thousand inhabitants was a frenetic sprawl of muddy and partially planked streets. Hydraulics drove the industry of the town with sawmills, gristmills, and trip hammer forges spread out along the bank. Simple but finely-hewn wood buildings of one and two stories dotted the rows and ways. Pens for chickens and goats, vegetable gardens, and flower beds leaned out between the houses. A thin wooden palisade ringed the landward side, constructed with a mind to keep domesticated animals in and wild creatures out. Canals, coves, and fish ponds had been dug alongside the riverbank to provide a measure of tranquility from the swift current.

Not long before sunset, ten riders bounded into town under a blue and orange banner. The market stalls on the town's only notable square were beginning to close, but a sizeable crowd remained.

"Townsmen! Brothers and sisters of Ardalencor! Hear me! I am Captain Ocklef. Royal courier. I bring urgent news of the war. A great battle has been fought. The Tavuros have won, and Eadolan is in flight. Pray tell me, where is the mayor?"

The crowd looked on with surprise and a creeping fear.

A woman approached the courier. "Can you tell me what happened to my son?"

"Please, Dear Mother, I do not know your son."

"Owen. My son is Owen." She moved closer and tried to grab the courier by the hand but pulled away when the cloak sleeve flattened to a nub.

The courier spun his horse and said, "The mayor. Where can I find the mayor?"

"His shop is on Woodwheel Street," called a voice. Dozens pointed the way.

"Green sign out front," called another.

The horsemen bounded down the plank road and reined up in front of a long shop with "Pelt & Sons" carved and painted white into a green sign. The front of the metalworking shop was open to the street and covered with a broad awning. A teenage boy behind the counter jolted to attention at the clomp of hooves.

"I am Captain Ocklef, royal courier. Where is the mayor?"

The boy gave no response but immediately sprinted through a door. A moment later a man of middle height and middle age with strong hands and a fleshy chin emerged through the doorway.

"Mayor Pelt."

"Yes."

Most of the riders turned their attention back up the street as the crowd from the square had been joined by other curious townspeople and were converging on the forge and foundry of Dobbins Pelt.

"I bring urgent news and must speak with you alone," implored Ocklef.

The mayor gave an uncertain look and then stepped out on the street to wave the crowd away. "My friends. Please. I beg your leave to speak with these men." On the second appeal the crowd began to withdraw.

Ocklef and two other riders dismounted and followed the mayor deeper into the workshop and closed the door to his office. The din of the waterwheels and trip hammers permeated the walls.

"I have urgent orders from General Stokes to secure this town."

"Against what?" Pelt scratched his soot-spattered brow and asked with a hint of trepidation. "Are the Tavuros coming this way?"

"Is this city loyal? Are you, Mayor, personally loyal to the High Lord?" said the courier with a rising inflection.

"What? You insult me with the very question!"

"Permit me to finish, Mayor Pelt," Ocklef said as he handed him a sealed role of parchment.

"A broadshield of infantry is marching here as we speak. As you see in the letter, the command of the gates is to be turned over to me. I need your help, Mayor. Ardalencor needs your full cooperation in this uncertain time."

"Yes, of course," said Pelt. "What happened to our valley boys?"

"I wish I could bring less bitter tidings. Tavurite cavalry is roaming the countryside and falsely riding under captured standards. Eadolan fled the field. I am not sure of his current whereabouts. This is why I bring to you this written order from General Stokes."

"What can I do? I am at your service."

"Assemble the local rangers. Bring in the livestock and crops from the countryside. Implement a curfew starting at dusk and close the palisade." Ocklef leaned in a little closer. "Are there those in town you suspect of disloyalty?"

Pelt fidgeted. "I don't know of anyone disloyal to Eadolan. We mind our own business up here."

"Well, call the mountaineers to assemble here and ensure all unmilled grain and crops are quickly brought in. Can't have that falling into enemy hands."

"Quite right," said Pelt with an air of relief.

"There is one more thing that you can do, Mayor."

"Please call me Dobbins," Pelt said as he grabbed a cloth to strip the layer of grime from his hands.

"I will state this plain. The Tavuros are perhaps within a day's ride of here. We have lost many towns across the border-lands. We may have to take each one back the hard way. Once we drive the Tavuros from our lands, we'll take the offensive and will need stone throwers ever still. Sawmill Falls must provide twenty. All the parts, properly assembled, then disas-sembled and ready for transport. Massive throwers with cow baskets."

The mayor gave Ocklef a startled look.

"Never heard of a cow basket? A soldier's term. The cow basket is the large counterweight. One of my men will provide the specifications. The wood from the uplands and your town's mills are just what is needed. Work must begin at sunup."

With a deep sigh, Pelt's troubled gaze pulled away from Ocklef and found narrow escape in the floor boards.

"Is there a problem?"

"No, no, not at all. It's just, we have a number of obligations, and the mills are already behind. I can't fully call a town council. Two of the members went to Vardall and won't be back for a few days. Is the river still open? We have a good town here, but we are not like the fancy folk downriver. We are loyal to Ardalencor, but, well, you are asking for a mighty big rhubarb. It will impoverish many a sawyer and farmer. What will remain for us through the winter with these requisitions you are making?"

"You are a fine steward. Worry not. Eadolan will pay for it all. Your support will not go unacknowledged." Ocklef motioned to one of his men, and a small pouch was produced. "That's for you, Dobbins," and after a pause, "for the fine people of this town."

The mayor felt a gentle pressure inside his temples. He squirmed momentarily but relaxed to greet the sensation.

"Well, I suppose. Gold, silver, or copper?" Pelt sputtered, while hefting the pouch and glancing around the windowless room.

"All gold."

"Very generous." He coughed back a smile. "I'll see what can be arranged."

"I trust you will. Say, Dobbins, you got a man up at Dog's Rock?"

"Little Dog's Rock," Pelt corrected. "Yes, the fire watch is always manned. Probably hard to see now with the sun dropping behind the mountains, but when the beacon is lit, you'll see it hot and bright."

"How far can the signal be seen?"

"Miles, especially when the moons aren't out. We got a few birds up there, but the birds only know one way. Just like the logs we send downriver. Otherwise, to get a message up there would take more than a day to make that trek."

"Last man up there claimed he saw a griffon moving between the peaks. Every now and then someone will have a griffon sighting or swear some pixies are frolicking near the tower. Hearing all that falling water, one's mind tends to splash around a bit. Too much idle time for a man spent watching for some fire to break out in the timbers. If the mountains could talk, I am sure they would tell the stories. The trees out here sing though." Pelt smiled. "Oh yes, they sing just fine as they glide through the mills."

Pelt laughed and slapped Ocklef on the shoulder. "It's good to recollect an old joke in these troubled times."

The mayor headed towards a large iron safe in the corner of the room. "If you fine soldiers could excuse me for a moment, I will join you outside. My wife was not expecting guests at the table, and she isn't really that fit of a cook to be feeding men on royal business. May I interest you all in a good meal all the same?"

"Very kind of you," agreed Ocklef.

"Let's go get a shank and a tank at the Grizzly Goat. The best fermented milk you'll ever have. You ever been round this way before?"

"No," replied Ocklef.

"Well, then you are in for a treat. A real prize on the grill tonight!"

"Dobbins." Ocklef raised his voice gently to stop the mayor. "I think you should say a few words. Let your people know that you are a dependable leader and that they will be shielded. Tell them we are here to protect the town, and they in turn must help save the land."

"Yes," affirmed Pelt as he considered his ascending place in the unfolding events. "I think I shall."

The trip to the Grizzly Goat led them back towards the main square and then down Calver Street. The Goat was the center of town life after sundown. Along the route, Ocklef dispatched most of his men to close and guard the town's two gates.

The mayor led his three guests into the roiling serenade of sounds, smoke, and smells. The high ceiling beams sheltered two levels. Supported by thick posts, the second level sprang up on portions of three sides and mushroomed with small tables and chairs. A stout railing prevented sloppy revelers from tumbling on the patrons below. A large roasting pit dominated the center of the main floor.

"Damned souls. What from the depths is that?" said one of Ocklef's companions abruptly.

Four cooks worked the multiple skewers and spits – seasoning, turning, slicing. A few iron grates were set over smaller fires for gravies and roasted tubers. A small brick oven regularly birthed bubbling disks of hot bread. Tonight, the main edible spectacle was a stonewater alligator or known to the locals as a galaswack. This creature was a mysterious, isolated relic from a bygone era. Found nowhere in Ardalencor save for the Falling River valley, it was suited uniquely to cold temperatures and known to skulk along the banks and even venture into the forests in search of food.

At the time of its demise, this galaswack was dust gray in color but with its chromomorphic skin, had the ability to blend in with the forest floor, fleck its skin white in the snowy season or mimic the rocky banks at the base of the falls. The gator was a smaller catch, head to tail just slightly beyond seven feet. It had been gutted and placed in an iron grilling cage stationed on sturdy supports. A jib and pulley system secured to the Goat's ridge line helped to raise and lower even the largest of catches.

"Oh," smiled Pelt. "You are in for a real treat. Galaswack! Only place you can find it is in these waters. Nasty, nasty beast, but very tasty. Lots of fat and lots of flavor. They caught this one trying to sneak into a fish pond. Too easy of a kill, really. Braver men have lost their lives hunting these monstrosities. The jaws will fetch large coin downriver."

A long bar anchored one side of the Goat's wooden ribs. Friendly and ever-moving barkeeps kept the patrons in good spirits. At irregular intervals waiters and wenches would emerge from the back kitchen with more complex dishes than those prepared at the central pit. An elevated platform diagonal to the main entry provided a stage for minstrels, theatrical productions and civic orations. No performances were scheduled for tonight so additional benches were placed to accommodate the large crowd. The startling news proclaimed by Ocklef at the town's square had pulled ever more to the Grizzly Goat for gossip and comradery.

All activity slowed as the prominent group wound its way through the labyrinth of long and round tables. Mayor Pelt stopped to shake several hands, but eventually the group made their way to the stage. Pelt gave a few tugs on his stretched chin as he considered his words.

"Kin and kindred of our fair valley. Many of you had heard the news that these men have come to warn us of danger. Let me also tell you that there is infantry rushing here to secure the town. Now as for our own boys who went off to fight, I am sorry that I don't have any more news. We hope for their safety and ask the protection of Indalos. The Tavuros are lurking about and may be riding under our banners, so as a precaution, I am going to put a curfew in place and keep the gates closed throughout the night."

Groans and grumbles swirled from above and below.

"This is just something for the time being. I don't want people sneaking into town and using the movements of our good people as cover. I am sure you all agree with me." He nodded his head and got several in the crowd to repeat the gesture. "Stay vigilant and keep an eye out for new travelers or passersby in town. Enjoy yourselves tonight. I'll come calling on some of you tomorrow about what we can do to help in this time of need."

"What happened at the battle?"

"Where is the High Lord?"

"Where are our sons and fathers?"

With the deluge of questions, Pelt readily acceded to Ocklef stepping forward. "Good people, I was sent by General Stokes to bring succor and relief to this valley. The High Lord," Ocklef shook his head in disgust, "forgive me the blunt words of a soldier, fled the field like a skittish hare. Other units held themselves to a better account. Duke Padazar, the Defender of Delun, as should be no surprise, acquitted himself valiantly."

Ocklef paused for effect. "We'll see your boys home safe. I am sorry to trouble you with the curfew. I asked Mayor Pelt for this. I hope you can understand. But let me not intrude upon your evening more than I already have. The next round is on me. I entreat you all to raise a toast to the brave men of the valley and the defenders of Ardalencor!"

A hundred cheers came in resounding reply.

As the cheers subsided, Pelt said to Ocklef, "I want you to speak with Jon Heward. He is one of our finest foresters, and he served our country well during the recent war. He is back by the door. I'll introduce you."

The way back was a circuitous rite of handshakes and

raised glasses. The man they sought was surrounded by a small crowd discussing the latest events. The crowd greeted the mayor, Ocklef, and the other couriers and then took their leave.

"Hey, Jon! Well, the river just got a lot deeper. Quite the day," said Pelt.

A man in his early thirties with tousled dark brown hair and horseshoe mustache motioned for the men to sit down. He wore a gray tunic with sky blue piping, deep green trousers with leather patches on the knees and seat, and buckskin shoes. A black cloak with faint red patterning was clasped around his shoulders.

"Jon, I want you to meet Captain Ocklef. We need your beavers to get to work tomorrow. Big job. High Lord needs our help. He is looking for our mills to supply twenty stone throwers, cow baskets and all."

"Dobbins! Hey, Dobbins! Mayor!" called an inebriated man. The man bumped and threaded his way through the crowd to get closer. "Dobbins, how long are you going to put this off?" He lurched forward but steadied himself on a nearby chair. "When are you going to get Brumfus to fix that damn berm along the canal? A part wider than my house eroded. Whole thing is slipping to a muddy mess!"

"Alright, Melvin, you slosh pot! Step backways, and I'll come talk to you." Pelt turned to Ocklef. "Excuse me for a moment. Jon, please talk to the Captain."

Ocklef was first to speak. "I'm told you were in the army?"

"I was in the line infantry, for a time." Heward took a long drink of fermented milk and winced. "This is not their best batch."

"Where were you posted?"

"I squandered two years of my life on garrison duty at Sevengate," Heward said with a chuckle. "Months on end staring towards the border. This was before the war with Velenharn ever started. We'd go on these long, forsaken patrols into the marshlands. Battled more flies than we did find smugglers or some scheming kaldoon. Those swamps and marshes, such a wasteland. I could tell you some stories."

Heward paused for a moment as serving girls placed galaswack platters and beer before the couriers.

"Everyone we'd find there was half-crazed, or the pumpkin had totally rotted through, you know? Living in little soggy shit hovels. We'd build skiffs and dugout canoes and paddle around when the land dropped off. Never know what you would find. Maybe a poisoned arrow in the back or, well, one time," he said shaking off the melancholy just as easily as it had come on, "we saw a huge herd of mammoth." He recalled with a growing smile, "Must have been a hundred of them. Just off in the distance. Unbelievable. Now that was a sight to see."

"You weren't in the line for the full twelve?"

"No," he slapped his leg. "We were approaching a smuggler's hideout, and I stepped on a sharpened stake just below the waterline. The fort surgeon barely saved my foot when we finally got back. He credited this ring that I was able to hold on." Heward ostentatiously removed a milky green ring from his hand.

One of the men with Ocklef gave a dismissive look when the ring initially was presented but quickly switched to a nodding smile when Heward turned his way. "Very impressive. Toadstone?" he said as a smile widened on a leathery and life-etched face.

Heward tipped his cup in affirmation. "Whatever was on that stake left me a little touched so I was discharged. Came back to the valley after that. I've recovered since then. Mostly," he winked.

"I thought Dobbins said you were in the war against Velenharn?"

"I was. I raised a volunteer group of rangers and log dogs."

"Well, so you actually fought?"

"Many fought, and I did my part. I was at Pelham. Part of the ambush," Heward said proudly.

"Pelham," said the other courier with a smile.

"Did the Tigerclaw really slay ten men in single combat before the battle?" asked Ocklef with raised brows.

"I recall it closer to four before the Velens decided to stop sending out champions, but he slew or maimed them one by one while they were agreeable. He would gallop around between the armies and goad them to send out another. Bought us the time we needed to lay the trap."

"The boys were saying that just before he rode out, he said, 'Boys, don't worry. I will fight the whole army one by one if I have to. I figure we are five times outnumbered, so if I kill more than five of them, then I did my part.' He trotted off with his seconds and then shouted, 'If I don't make it back, listen to Crosstimbers. He will see these bastards back across the border!'"

All the men laughed and clinked their tankards.

"He's got a pair that rival some of the big stones near the falls! You know that his family are valley folk from way back?" said Heward. "Ever heard of a general willing to stand for single combat?"

Heward grabbed a bit of bread, smeared it with lard, and offered the small platter to the rest to the soldiers. They declined, more content with the generous portion of galaswack before them.

"Let me pick up a fresh egg," said Heward as the smile receded from his face. "How did Stokes get separated from Eadolan? Something awful must have happened. Where is our army now? How many standards were lost that the Tavuros are secretly loose in the countryside?"

Ocklef gave him a troubled look and contemplated the smoke wafting in the rafters. "Eadolan is prone to impulse. He may have locked himself in Thavodyn or run back to Ravalas. Men like Padazar and Stokes hold the realm together."

"Why is a broadshield marching here? Seems like the men would be better served staying with the army then spread out in little towns. What is in such vital need of protection here?"

"Why all the doubt, Brother?"

"I don't know. Unless Eadolan has some grand army already at his call, something just doesn't sit right. Just seems like a leaning tree. Not sure I can quite see where it may land."

Ocklef's companions sat with impatience and rapidly narrowing eyes, but Heward was too baffled and focused on teasing out his own thoughts to notice.

"Twenty gigantic stone throwers. I've been out of the proper army for a while, but I don't recall hearing about any large fortifications between Thavodyn and the frontier forts."

Heward suddenly grew more concerned. He gripped the table edge, leaned in, and said in a whisper, "Are you asking because Thavodyn has already fallen?"

Ocklef grew wide-eyed, glanced around, and considered his response. "As a fellow soldier, I am sure you understand that military matters necessitate a measure of discretion, but know that Thavodyn is safe." Ocklef gave a pitying shake of his head. "I ask you, Jon, humbly, forget your speculations and not send others to fright with rumor. What the country and," he stressed, "the valley need most is for you to do your part."

"That's just a huge amount of lumber," Heward said running his hands through his hair and imagining all the stacked wood. "All that hewing and hauling, you'll need scores of men to assemble, and I don't know how many carts and mules to carry it off."

"And now you know why a broadshield is headed this way."

Heward seemed to relax, forced a long sip, and nodded in affirmation. Ocklef's companion who had earlier dismissed the toadstone ring perceived that beneath Heward's display, doubts lingered.

"Well, I sure appreciate you being patient and talking to an old liner. If you'll excuse me, I live outside of town and best be on my way."

"Fair enough," said Ocklef. "We'll see you after sunup at the mayor's shop. We'll check the mills tomorrow and then let you know what additional felling may be required."

"Well, I will leave it to you to tell the mill owners that they'll miss filling a few orders, but I understand." With that Heward bade the couriers farewell and soon welcomed the cooler air of Calver Street.

A short while later, the more perceptive of Ocklef's confidants, the man with the weathered face, crossed from the shadowed threshold of the Grizzly Goat. Out in the dusky street the man saw more people than he anticipated. He looked at each of the small knots of people and waved when they called to him, but he carefully avoided approaching. He milled around for a moment but saw no sign of Heward.

Considering his options, the man did his best to recall the brief tonal fragments. "Seen Jon?" he called to no one in particular.

"Wow, Grady, that milk really twisted your tongue, huh?" a townsman said to a round of laughter. "Jon headed down towards Abran's."

The man stood heavy-footed and started swaying in place.

The people laughed again. "That milk must have turned in the teat! Run along, you blind puppy." The townsman pointed the way to a small inn a few streets down.

The street angled to the right. Soon the crowds outside of the Grizzly Goat were out of sight. The man slowed and made out the dim glow of light leaking through shuttered windows. As he approached the inn, a shallow voice struck him.

"Grady?"

The man looked around.

"Grady."

"Yeah, Jon," the man whispered, recognizing Heward's voice.

Heward stepped out of an alley between two buildings and motioned for his friend to come closer. Something in the recesses of Heward's mind awoke, but he was too disquieted to pay it much attention.

"I knew you would have the same feeling I did. Did anyone follow you?"

The man shook his head.

"I don't know, Grady. All this don't sit flush. It doesn't line up. I don't know. My old wound has been acting up."

With no one else around, the man motioned for Heward to come back to the street and nodded his head in the direction of the river. The man quietly had been in Sawmill Falls at various times throughout the spring and summer, and while he did not know every landmark in the small town, he knew how to find the river.

"Maybe we should go to Finn's house? I got to catch my breath."

The man gave Heward a reassuring pat on the shoulder and led him towards the river.

Heward kept looking behind him but saw no one emerge from the growing darkness.

The gurgle of the river soon met the ears of both men.

As they approached the river, the man kept his head forward, but Heward strained to look at his friend's face as if it was the sole object in the world. The face wavered in a momentary haze. Instinctively Heward took a step back.

"Grady," Heward said laughing, "what was the name of that girl you were telling me about?"

The man hesitated.

"Oh, you know, the one with the harelip and big tits you were with last night? Did you find out she was married or something?" said Heward as he silently drew his knife and circled behind.

Heward moved with the weapon raised but staggered as an unseen force gripped his temples. He groaned and doubled over as he struggled against it, still clutching the knife.

Heward felt a cold then warming blade enter his shoulder, but he pushed away the second strike aimed at his throat. Heward slashed wildly and thought he caught the man, but the man who no longer appeared as Grady moved around to block the path towards the town center.

The vice-like pressure receded when he cut the man, but it returned with greater intensity. All Heward could do was stumble back; his call for help dribbled out in a faint whimper. His knife thudded to the planked street below. The water seemed right behind Heward as his assailant lunged towards him. Consumed in the mental grip, Heward discerned two new cuts to his forearm and flank. Heward tried to move to the right but received a blade scything into his hair. He frantically pulled away and splashed into the water.

Warm trails of blood flowed into the cold river as Heward slipped below the surface.

CHAPTER 9

The fortress of Thavodyn was laid out in a square with the corners oriented to the cardinal points of the compass. The curtain wall, which enclosed an area of more than six acres, stood eighteen feet to the top of the crenellations and twelve feet in width at the narrowest point. The two gatehouses were placed in ordinal directions, the Ravalas Gate to the southeast, and the Duskwall Gate to the northwest, through which the Duskwall-Floriana road traced its most direct path. In truth, travelers on this cross-country road not in state or noble service often were denied entrance and diverted around the fortress.

The two gatehouses stretched thirty feet long and shielded fourteen-foot-wide entrances with machicolations looming over the approach. An iron portcullis protected the gaps in the massive basalt, the outside tracks of which were cut into the walls and into a groove in the stone floor to further secure the portcullis in place. Two segments formed the portcullis, and one could be raised while the other remained lowered. Ten feet beyond were a pair of iron-reinforced wooden doors and the pattern of tandem portcullis and doors repeated at the same intervals. The whole length of each gatehouse ceiling was cut with murder holes and channels for boiling oil or whatever the garrison wizards concocted.

Anchoring the fortress corners were elevated and protruding bastions with steeply-sloped exterior walls of over twenty feet thick. With the closure of reinforced doors, the bastions could be isolated from the courtyard and curtain walls to function as self-contained strongholds. The lower level was deepened with a partial dugout containing a larder, sundry supplies, and a large water catchment cistern. The second level contained a barracks and an arsenal with natural illumination through arrow slits in the courtyard and exterior walls. Atop the bastion's upper fighting platform were movable catapults and torsion crossbows. Guard towers at the midpoint strengthened the curtain walls between the gatehouses and the bastions. On the two sides of the fort without gatehouses, bastions reinforced the walls and were similarly flanked by guard towers at symmetrical intervals.

To support the fortifications and impede the approach of siege towers and battering rams, a ten-foot-wide shallow trench ringed the entire circumference. A movable plank road could be placed over the trench to link the stone-paved main road and the gatehouse entrances.

Nearly to the western horizon stood Fort Traskon, an observation point constructed on the sheer side of a basalt esker and secondary quarry used for the building of Thavodyn. The small garrison within the structure, more signal station than fort, had been rotated and deeply replenished with supplies in the preceding days. Other than approach by a steep and narrow switchback trail, Fort Traskon was considered unassailable up the carved rock faces that had been left in the wake of the stonemasons' work.

ANDREW ZIMBA

Inside Thavodyn's black walls were two stables, carpentry and forging shops, granaries, an infirmary, barracks, warehouses, laydown yards, small fruit and vegetable gardens, mustering areas, and arsenals. Water was drawn from two wells near the southwest bastion in addition to cisterns found at each bastion and tower. Silver rods inserted in the catchments and the talents of the garrison wizards preserved the water's potability.

Offset towards the south corner stood the citadel. Built atop a low outcropping of basalt, the citadel towered over eighty feet and enclosed eight levels, six of which were above ground. The only entrance to the citadel was up a set of stairs cut into the basalt outcropping and then through a gatehouse cut within the sloped fifteen-foot-thick walls at the base.

Machicolations overlooked the rocky outcropping. Torsion crossbows were positioned on multiple levels. Access to the deepest level of the citadel was restricted to the Castellan and the small contingent of garrison wizards and apprentices. The level above stored provisions and food stuffs. The main level contained kitchens and a sizeable gathering hall for ceremonial occasions and feasts. On the highest level stood a signal beacon and a pole holding aloft the flag of Ardalencor. Living quarters and offices for the high-ranking officers occupied the remaining levels.

A heavy knock lifted Grammel Erstchester from his pre-dawn review of the updated duty rosters. "Castellan! You are wanted at the Duskwall Gate," boomed a muffled voice through the thick birch door.

"What is it?" said Erstchester, candleholder in hand, as he hefted open the door.

The face of Constable Harrik Dunbar beamed an irrepressibly wide smile. "The Tigerclaw is here."

"Crowiler?" Erstchester snorted a laugh of disbelieving hope.

"Yes, and others," said the Constable as he briskly motioned for the Castellan to follow him. They both hurried down the citadel's stairs and towards the northwest gate.

Erstchester climbed up to the gatehouse's second level. Soldiers on both sides of the gatehouse already had mirrored lanterns pointed down at the men.

"Sir Crowiler Herring is outside, Castellan. And Lord Tarpley. They say they escaped the Tavuros," a sentry said excitedly.

"Open the damn gate, Erstchester," called a voice from below.

A few moments later a lithe, swarthy man with the faintest nubs of a once stringy black moustache led two dozen or so men into Thavodyn. While in captivity, most of the arrivals had been stripped of any notable armor. Although few carried weapons, Ardalencor's fastest blade, the Tigerclaw, still walked with his predatory charisma. Those present gave a long cheer as the men entered, all searching for familiar faces.

"Raymond!" said a man with a wild mane of gray-white hair, rushing forward.

"Arnost!" came the call back as the man moved to meet his friend. The two men slapped each other on the shoulders and embraced.

"You slippery bastard. Good to see you made it," said Arnost Wolfwind, Thavodyn's Master of Horse, as he started to release the hug and look at his friend's bruised face.

Raymond Fryll grabbed his friend by the forearms. Fryll held the rank of broadshield in the line infantry denoting command of a unit which could range from several hundred to a few thousand men. The term broadshield harkened to the long shield wall formed by the line infantry. Fryll whispered bitterly in Wolfwind's ear. "I left them. So many men back there. General Stokes. The whole of the infantry. Killed or bound."

"Where is my wife?" demanded Bernard Tarpley ending the cheers and impromptu festivities.

"Lord Tarpley, she is safe. On her way back to Ravalas," said Erstchester. "By Indalos, fate and fortune oblige you. What of our men? How many in the Tavurite army? How did you come to be here?"

"Lord Tarpley and I were captured by the Tavuros, but we concealed ourselves with the common soldiers. Had to cut off my damn moustache and hide our faces behind bloody cloth." Crowiler rubbed his face. "Padazar's men were separating out the nobles and officers. Some of our former mercenaries were guarding us through the night."

Crowiler flashed a roguish smile. "They started drinking and later found out they had not confiscated all our weapons. We stole away with as many as we could without raising an alarm. Hid the next day and found our way back after sunfall."

"Where is the High Lord? How many remain in our army?" asked Lord Tarpley with surprise, expecting signs of a larger force still at Thavodyn.

"The High Lord and Duke Urric have returned to the capital with the cavalry. They mean to gather a new army." Annoyed, the Castellan pressed his earlier question. "How many Tavuros are before us?"

"Then Lord Tarpley and I must leave for Ravalas immediately," said Crowiler ignoring Erstchester's question. "Any sign of Silverface and the wizards? That dust pincher was not in camp the morning of the battle."

"Archmage Stadrys is here," said the Castellan without inflection.

Crowiler squinted in response, all words seemingly out of reach.

"Lords, I suggest you leave before the sun is up," said Wolfwind as he walked over to stand next to his Castellan. "I presume Sir Ellard and the remaining Hearthguards will want to accompany you. Forgive the inconvenience, but we are desperately short of remounts. I can only offer you mules. A more fitting mount may be found in Middlepost."

Lord Tarpley did not look pleased, but, when he glanced in appeal to Erstchester, the Castellan only shook his head in reply.

Addressing the other men, the Castellan said, "It is a welcome sight to see you safe. Any other nobleman will be permitted passage to Ravalas. All other officers and soldiers, known and loyal, are hereby added to the garrison."

A young man, not yet acknowledged by anyone in the garrison, stepped forward. "Noblemen and Soldiers," he said with a weighty confidence that defied his years. "I am Jarvis Jernivan."

The Jernivan family name, if at all remembered, was twisted in lore and scandal. For the men to hear someone in their midst claim that tarnished name brought little more than guffaws and chuckles.

The Jernivan family was an ancient and once powerful house, but the intrigues of Jarvis' great-great-uncles against the High Lord led to the loss of hereditary lands and titles for the entire family. The principal Jernivan conspirators were quartered and their hacked bodies hung as ornamentations atop the gates of Ravalas. The remaining family members were offered banishment or to scrape a new existence in the remoteness of the Northwestern Wilds.

The dirty and hollow-eyed young man continued, "Lord Tarpley. I am relieved to know your Althea is safe. Castellan Erstchester, is there news from Burzina?"

"Do not dare to speak with such familiarity, Boy!" said Tarpley with enmity and suspicion. "I'll whip the skin off your back for such impudence."

"Is there news from Burzina?" The young man was more pleading in his tone.

"No news of the monastery nor from Duskwall or Oltencany since the invasion began," said Constable Dunbar.

Panic stabbed across the young man's face. "I left my wife and her ailing parents in the protection of the monks. May they be safe in the sanctuary of Indalos." He trembled, reliving his decision from over a fortnight ago. He tried to straighten himself.

The young man repositioned his cloak and loosened buckles which released a shield from his back. The shield face was stretched with worn and beaten leather. He gently removed the covering to reveal the golden lion of the Jernivan family.

"Not all Jernivans were disloyal, but all paid the price. My father and his forefathers stood loyal. I took the rightful and honor-bound place beneath my High Lord's standard. The High Lord must return to liberate our lands. Please tell His Grace that the Jernivan lion stands watch at Thavodyn."

"The pauper's boy," Erstchester said to Dunbar with the slight curl of a smile. "The emaciated lion still roars."

The approach of faint bells and familiar footfalls lifted Thiepval Bracelaw from his thoughts. The door to his quarters stood partially open, and the Archmage let himself in. Thiepval tried to tidy up an oversized table strewn about with yellowed tomes, phials of assorted minerals and powders, scraps of parchments, astronomical gauges, packets of dried herbs, weights and scales, charts, pieces of basalt, ink and quills, eight nested bowls of alternating silver and brass, ledgers, mortars and pestles, rough and cut crystals, the corroded iron head of a torsion crossbow bolt, a set of rosewood drawers and vial racks, and a jar containing two silkworms suspended in an oily tincture.

The Archmage gave a reassuring smile to the middle-aged man and waved off his housekeeping efforts. This was the first time the Archmage had come to speak with Thiepval without the Castellan or a string of attendants in tow. While much to his displeasure that the title of mage eluded him, Thiepval was a wizard of considerable proficiency and standing in the Zaravandian Order and also second in command at Thavodyn.

"Archmage, you do us an unexpected and, I must say, disquieting honor," he said in a quandary. "I'm still confused by your decision to be here of all places in this time of great emergency." Thavodyn's principal wizard paused as the Archmage noted multiple cups atop a heavy travel trunk. Through weary eyes Thiepval also peered at the remainders of tea and spirits which accompanied him through a sleepless night.

"Falanika and Brenio stay here, but you sent the others back with Eadolan. Why? If you are fastened to this place when the siege lines close, why reduce our capabilities in the face of the enemy?"

"Don't ask questions to which you already know the answer," said the Archmage with an intense look.

Thiepval rubbed his face with both hands. His right hand traced the scars and fissures on his cheek and neck, self-inflicted brands from a careless moment during his distant apprenticeship at the Academy of Alchemy and Arcane Phenomena. "With great hesitation I accepted this posting to Thavodyn. I obeyed my Archmage's request eight years ago and have served without prestige of title. This is a desolate place."

"Are the Park's bawdyhouses not to your taste? Your position here at Thavodyn and within the Order must count for something."

Thiepval ignored the derision. "In all my time confined within these black walls, I fail to see the monumental importance of this place. I detect—"

The Archmage raised his hand to stop him. "Yes, I have your extensive correspondence on the matter," he said with rising irritation.

"In this moment, with you here, tell me, what is the true secret of this place? There are mere wisps of arcane threads woven about this fortress. What else is there? It cannot just be the ethereal warding. What is deep below the surface?"

The Archmage paced the floor, shut the door, and observed his student of many years. "In the hills not far from here there was once the lair of a long-slumbering dragon. Did you know this?"

"No," Thiepval said with annoyance.

"And if you had known this and were alive at the time, this was several hundred years ago, mind you, what would you have done with this knowledge?"

The Archmage was in no mood to wait for an answer. "Restless as you are, would you have gone to count the scales? Would you have let everyone know of this great discovery? Quite a remarkable and toasted fellow you would have become in telling such a tale. Supposing you were more prudent and decided not to risk the journey, rather in your treasured vanity, sparked the curiosity and expeditions of others? How many would need to die as a result of your knowledge before you would realize you should have kept your mouth shut!"

"I will not squat on this black egg for well but eternity like some silly hen. Forever waiting and waiting." Thiepval swept his hands across the chest, sending tea cups and etched glasses shattering to the ground.

104

"Not a hen. A guardian," said the Archmage as he watched the various liquids pool and seep into the slender joints of the stone floor. "An opened box is never fully closed again."

Thiepval then said a string of words, and the multitude of shards coalesced into their original forms and glided to rest in the former places.

The Archmage softened his tone and pointed to Thiepval's armor stand in the corner of the room. The fine smithing of the gleaming hauberk brought a smile. An embossed steel disk riveted to the chest punctuated the armor, a warding eye prominent in the center.

"I selected you above all others," the Archmage asserted. "I know this has not been easy for you, but there is the utmost need precisely for you to be in this place."

A shielding invisibility melted away. An ornate box now appeared hovering between the two men. Numerous miniature rubies and sapphires bejeweled a rectangular box in gold leaf. "Tovenward. This title and position have remained vacant since the mourned loss of our dear Zelfira," the Archmage said with an inflection of time-faded sorrow and then took a more ceremonial tone. "The distinction and duties of Tovenward are availed only to one member of the Order and conferred to a wizard or mage who has exemplified the warrior spirit and excellence in combative arts and battle casting."

The Archmage's eyes locked onto those of his student of the past thirty years. "As Archmage of the Zaravandian Order, and in concurrence with Mage Albright and Mage Farcloud, I present to you, Thiepval Bracelaw, the merited honor of being selected Tovenward of Ardalencor." The Archmage lifted an arcane mace from the box and let it rest in his palms.

"As you know, the original mace which had passed in orderly succession for over two centuries was not retrieved when Zelfira was slain. Despite efforts we are still unsure of its whereabouts. Votark has gone to great labor to recreate and improve upon the initial design."

"I accept, Archmage," said Thiepval as he bit back a smile and garnered the mace. The mace was about the length of a hand and forearm and heavier than Thiepval would have suspected. Constructed in a three-toned silver with intricate geometric patterns, the head of the mace was not a solid mass but formed of five beveled flanges. As Thiepval rotated the mace, traces of old gold would emerge and submerge depending on the light.

"You are the Tovenward and confirmed in all befitting privileges and obligations. A feast will be coordinated this evening in your honor. Mage Albright and Mage Farcloud send their acclamations and regrets for missing this occasion."

The Archmage moved forward and embraced the new Tovenward. "There is no need to suppress your smile. This is a great occasion!"

The hovering box now settled on the table. "Let us not forget a few more items," the Archmage said as he removed a large seal, a signet ring, and the Tovenward standard which had been neatly folded back and forth at the bottom of the box. The war banner was of a dark red silk with four wide horizontal chevrons of alternating white and silver placed just left of center and then the dark red run ended with a swallow tail. Punctuating the hoist edge was the emblem of the Zaravandian Order, the geometric white star composed on a diamond and four triangles arrayed on the facets.

"Thank you, Archmage."

"Discipline, patience, and hope are all of a kind. Hold tight to them."

The new Tovenward changed the topic to cover his embarrassment. He moved to the window and envisioned the gathering wave. The main enemy force was still unseen and distant beyond the two-mile marker, but small clutches of horsemen probed more closely.

Thiepval shook his head and looked back at the Archmage. "A perversion. This twisted fate. These rabid boys who battled to the end. They would not yield a clod of dirt without a fight. They never capitulated. You can't say that about some who still give whispered counsel to the High Lord."

Losing interest in the horizon, Thiepval poured a clear liquid into two cups.

"Now these men stand apart and against us. My mind was a waterwheel last night. Ever moving but fixed in place, forcibly revolving under the weight of memory."

Thiepval took a sip and exhaled heavily. "I remember being there so clearly. My first trip properly south of the Avenbair. Beautiful country. I can recall the rolling hills and orchards in vivid detail. When I arrived, they had been pushed out of Forris and most of the Leteb basin. They swore they would be pushed no further. Valmuros had been ringed with earthen forts, and Padazar already had the population digging in up and down the banks of the Mountain Trout around Delun."

"The Velen army swarmed, blanketing and devouring the opposite bank. Both sides watched each other across the river for about a week; all the while Padazar extended and reinforced his lines. It seemed like everyone in the Southwest was there. All connected by a desperate strength, digging trenches, loading wicker baskets, making arrows, cutting bandages, whatever was needed."

"Latrobh broke the standstill with a raid on the blackest night. His mountain boys sliced through a good many Velens and burned supplies before re-crossing the river. That fire burned long into the next morning. Two days later, the Velens launched the first of eight river crossings. The water was so thick with skiffs and rafts that you could walk back and forth on stems and sterns and not wet a heel. We saw them readying for this one. It was beaten back easily, but then we were fresh. The odds and our own casualties began to take a toll over the weeks. Between the big attacks, they'd keep probing or sending boats with strawmen. We're constantly on guard. Can't get sleep."

"On the fifth attempt, the line broke, and the Velens started to flank positions around Delun. Do you know who was there to still shaken nerves and restore the line?"

The Archmage listened intently to Thiepval but offered no reply.

"Woolfolk. Up and down the lines, sustaining morale and giving comfort and kind word; then just as quickly on the battle line with sword in hand. He was the breakwater. He steadied the line before Latrobh could force march his boys from another sector and Ray could bring up cavalry from north of town. I remember that old man, sword and self, drenched in blood. As more of our soldiers poured in and the fighting bent towards our favor, he climbed the earthworks and began invoking the name of Indalos. Some on both sides stopped fighting and just watched that old man," marveled Thiepval. "He seemed so possessed by force of prayer that it would push the invaders back to their boats. He stood beseeching and admonishing, a bright silhouette. Not a blade or arrow touched him."

"The Velens never gained even as much as a toehold on that side of the river ever again. The blood-soaked course then carried a new name, Indalos the Protector."

The Archmage raised an eyebrow.

"At least in the Southwest, anyway," Thiepval amended. "There was a shimmer about him. He is a channeler of some kind. He was always suspicious of the Order and sought to avoid us if we got too close. I don't think he was there during Ray's attack; we were fortunate in that."

"No doubt he is a fervent preacher. I'm sure you know he made a name for himself as a warrior during the Disorders."

"Yes, I was born in Valmuros, if you remember."

The Archmage nodded and ran his hand over a glint on the astronomical gauges. He glanced at the window pierced with morning's first full light. "Woolfolk may claim divine inspiration, but his supposed thaumaturgy is little more than a kaldoon's mischief. He would find scarce place at the Academy beyond fetching water or keeping the hedges of uniform height."

The Archmage moved closer to the window and with a deft hand felt the rhythmic pulse of the ethereal warding about the stone. "They were brave men. Some of the bravest men in the country, but," he turned again to face Thiepval, "they have betrayed Ardalencor. They welcomed devouring vermin to rape and ravage. For treason, there is no redemption."

The Archmage turned back to the window and studied the horizon. "Tovenward, prepare a raptor force. Those rats will find not an easy road to Thavodyn."

CHAPTER 10

Like wounded dogs the men of the company had limped back into the woods after the encounter with the Tavurite patrols. Despite gorging on roasted horse, a miserable, sleepless night attended the company's second stay in the forest. Bambenek saw to the men throughout the night, but despite his efforts, two men succumbed to their wounds before the sun rose. The company was a sorry lot with total strength reduced to less than thirty. All those who died in field or forest were interned in a common grave.

Bambenek had little to say during the night, and few dared to catch his eye in the morning. At last, he broke the silence. "Soldiers, when I accepted the captaincy, I asked only for what is due any officer. I asked that you obey my commands at all times."

Bambenek spat and swore. "Instead you were persuaded by someone who couldn't be bothered to be with us now. Yesterday the moons were concealed. Tonight will not be so obliging. I figure crossing tonight would be a fat risk even if all of us were not so busted and bleeding because of your precious haste. For those who fell and will not rise today, you can answer to them eternally for your decision. I am so very sad and disgusted, but I will go on. You all must as well. You have no other choice." He paused and looked at the men.

The shadowy force again returned and vanished just as quickly when Bambenek said, "I relinquish the captaincy."

The men shouted their dismay.

"No!" pleaded one soldier. "We should have listened to you. It's our fault!"

Bambenek waved his hands to quiet the men. "Boys, you'll find your own path. I gave my word to Dronor. I'll make good on my promise to save his leg. After this most recent tussle, I cannot truly treat his wounds. I will take him to the healers."

"Bambenek," Farrior said gravely. "Don't match haste with more of the same. Healers? Those woodland mystics are a strange lot, but you know much more than you care to let on. Did they teach you that reaching vine magic? Why did you not use that little trick when the battle started?"

Disgust crept further across Farrior's face as Bambenek gave no reply. "Remember your duty. I know your concern for Dronor. I share it. He is an able blade and warrior. You cannot desert the army."

"I am not deserting. I don't know where my officer is. I know not where the High Lord is. They may be at Pinemeadow or Dripping Pines. If they are not, I'll look elsewhere. I still fight for my country."

Through a fit of gasps and sobs, Myron muttered, "You can't leave us like this. We've lost too many already."

"I can only do so much. I wish you all the favor and protection of Indalos."

Bambenek started to help Dronor to his feet and put a tree trunk crutch under his arm.

"You are going to walk all the way to Dripping Pines?" Quinby asked incredulously.

"I'm not going to sit here and wait for a Tavurite escort. I don't know if you all will find another favorable night before the siege lines are drawn tight. Take a wide step east and try to regain the main road."

Bambenek stood or knelt to shake the hand of each man and bade them farewell.

"Selfish fool," Farrior said to himself as the scout and the half-orc disappeared amongst the trees.

―――――

A sharp sound broke the silent trudge of the companions. Bambenek spun around and smirked as a figure in a black and yellow surcoat sprinted through the deadfall. Bambenek gave the young man an inquiring look.

"You were right. You kept us alive. After they left me and the others," said Bayard, the lone remaining Amberfield squire, struggling to catch his breath. "Fuck those high and mighty knights. If they expect me to chase after them." Bayard's face reddened in clenched rage. He started to hack at the deadfall. "Arvid was still alive. I carried him back. I..." The young man's voice trailed off as the tears started.

"Easy, Son." Bambenek took the sword from his hands and wrapped him up in a deep hug. After a moment, Bambenek stepped back and gave Bayard a knowing look. "Did you run after us just to tell us that Portnay is a son of bitch?"

"Well, no," said Bayard through a snot-filled laugh. "I wanted to know if I could come with you. I got no place in the line infantry. I'm not from the Chartered Cities, and my own noble lord and best friends just left me for dead."

Bambenek gave the renegade squire a steady look. "We're

not going home anytime soon; in fact, we are headed in the opposite direction. What we need now is a healer. Are you a healer, Bayard?"

"No," said Bayard surprised by the question.

"Everyone can be a healer if the proper mind is put to it," said Bambenek lost for a moment in self-reflection. Chasing away the thought, the scout said, "Do your share, and you are welcome to join us."

"Really? Thank you, Captain. I mean, thank you, Bambenek," said Bayard. "I've never been this far west before. Where are we going exactly?"

CHAPTER 11

"I've been giving it a great measure of thought," declared Fiona Padazar, the Duchess of Delun. She looked back at her first born, Jannon, as he led his horse along the water's edge. Her eyes drifted higher. Delun Castle stood forever defiant, overlooking the riverbank, crowned upon the peak of a string of rocky hills. Hopewell Heights.

The water lapped gently against Fiona's riding boots. Her red silk blouse with a green and white vine and floral pattern contrasted with trousers in the style of a common soldier. Belted to her hip, she wore a mountaineer's sword, a short chopping sword with a sawtooth spine, the ubiquitous highland tool. Her hair was dyed tawny to hide worry-fed graying of the once deep brown. A seashell clasp secured her hair, woven and bundled, in a pearl-adorned braid.

Fiona walked farther into the river shallows, reeds bending as she made her way. This side of the riverbank mostly had returned to its pre-war state: wood from the fortifications was repurposed and the diggings and pilings of soil washed away by the annual river floods, yet it was impossible to erase the memory from the landscape.

Preserved structures stood as living testaments to tenacious endurance. Jannon looked at his mother, awaiting what words may come. Beyond his mother, an elevated stone redoubt and supporting nodes of earth and timber bespoke the seeds of future defensive lines. After the armies of Velenharn had overrun the border forces and pushed deeper into Ardalencor, the Duchess oversaw the rapid construction of these works and lifted earth alongside commoner and fellow noblewoman alike. Fortress Fiona, as it was colloquially known, protected the road winding up through the hills: one fork leading to the Padazar family residence and the other to the city of Delun proper built on higher ground along the banks of an eponymous creek and partially concealed from the river by Hopewell Heights.

Peace treaty or not, the Southwesterners had feared another attack from Velenharn. Almost immediately after the armies of Velenharn withdrew, Duke Padazar ordered construction of a new defensive point on the eastern bank of the river to encourage resettlement. Occupying a stony patch and originally envisioned as a fortified observation point, the Peregrine Tower grew in measure.

The Peregrine Tower became, in fact, a stout, if small, fortress built right to, and beyond, the water's edge to shelter small riverboats shuttling soldiers and supplies across the broad river. At the front of the thick-walled fortress, a solitary eight-sided observation tower anchored the eastern flank. Across a river-fed moat connected by drawbridge rose a stone and brick barbican. A hundred paces beyond the barbican began the climb of an earthen rampart which radiated in a semi-circle back to the riverbank. This was the lock, the clasped talons, that reunited the lands east and west of the river renamed by the Southwesterners in gratitude as Indalos the Protector.

At first, the Peregrine Tower rose gloomily over the east bank, the Burnt Acres, the charred desolation marking the aftermath of foreign occupation. In the intervening years, villages cautiously were rebuilt and toiling farmers struggled to reclaim the soil's bounty, such was the devastation wrought by the armies of Velenharn.

Fiona, the graceful and indomitable mother of six, one of the instigators of the civil war now ravaging Ardalencor, determined that war never again despoil her home. She moved her hand across the full sweep of the river. "May we never need use of these walls. Let us take war far from here."

Harvesting the river's bounty, fishermen checked nets for bream, leaping thinlips, mountain trout, and deep-dwelling, wide-body whisker fish. Nets would still get entangled on the myriad of boats and rafts piled at the river's bottom. Fish still hid in the sunken remains long after drowned flesh had been picked clean.

"What troubles you, Mother? All is prepared," Jannon reassured her.

Fiona motioned for her son to come closer. Jannon handed the reins of his horse to a squire and strode through the reeds. The eldest Padazar offspring and now young man in his early twenties had striking features and a kind face. His long dark brown hair fell past the dark blue checkered shoulders on his otherwise powder blue arming doublet.

"Yes, I know. Eadolan is blind to our movements." Fiona's knowing smile compressed her freckles. "Mathis will make a good pace and panic the Midriver nobles. Let them think a hard blow is about to befall their homes when they are off protecting Eadolan. No, I want to share my thoughts on far greater matters. Your brother will fulfill his task splendidly."

Fiona looked deeply into her son's amber eyes, instinctively recalling the first day she saw them. "The title of High Lord has outlived its purpose. Let Eadolan be forgotten as the last. Jannon, you will reunite this land. This will be a more powerful Ardalencor and far greater in its reach. You will be crowned Emperor in a rededicated and reconsecrated Acclamation Starfield in Valmuros. Ravalas is a hive of corruption." Her amber eyes twinkled. "A new capital must be built."

Absorbing the possibilities, Jannon stared at his mother.

"Boldness will place you on the throne, but as future Emperor, be mindful of decisions and what may come." She hesitated for a moment, anticipating her son's response, but pressed on. "Your Polina is lovely but does not have the connections that we need now. Arley Rostenhan is a fine bannerman of your father's but not fitting to be so close to the throne."

Jannon started to protest, but Fiona stopped him before the first word could form. "Eadolan's father's egregious meddling blocked your marriage to a Domarese princess. Are you hearing this story for the first time?" Good, she thought. Her counselors long held their tongues. "You were barely ten when we began arranging a suitable marriage for you. We tried to raise the matter with Eadolan, but he again, or his advisors, refused, and then the war with Velenharn did much to complicate matters." With a slight sigh of disappointment, she added, "After the devastation of the war and the lack of support from Eadolan in all things, your father did not stand in your way when you chose to marry Polina."

Jannon suppressed a burning shout lest curious fishermen begin to take more than casual notice of their conversation.

"Please. If you are only considering this now," Fiona shook her head and reverted to maternal tenderness. "Oh, Jannon, how much I enjoy her. Polina is a woman of great qualities and an excellent wife in other circumstances for another man, and perhaps for you, if you had a different name." Trying to belay some of her son's worry, or perhaps more to comfort herself,

Fiona said, "We will not marry you to a heretic Tavuro. You may thank Swan when you see him for getting Nabrensus to drop that point. The daughter that Nabrensus had in mind is rather plain, I hear."

"What of Polina?" Jannon's eyes and heart lowered and then rose sharply. "You will not harm her!" he barked, scanning the water lest he was heard.

"She will be well taken care of. Do not worry." Fiona shifted her weight in the soft mud. "Do you think I married your father for love? I did not have much say in the matter, but I grew to love him. He is an exceptional man. Look what we have created together."

"Polina is with child. My child!" Anguish crashed across Jannon's face. "I will not submit to this!"

"I know your deep love for her. That does not need to change. You can visit her from time to time. Be discreet, and there will be no judgment."

"Have you no words about my child?" demanded Jannon.

The Duchess had to restrain herself from slapping her son. "It is a great joy," Fiona said with a genuine smile, and then she grew stern. "The child will want for nothing, if we are successful. If we are not, the child will have nothing. There is no option but victory. Have you understood anything? The fate of your entire family is at stake, and all this land!"

Fiona's voice was now thick with sorrow. "I said goodbye to Ethan and Amos, although they do not know it. They are fated to Tavurite captivity, even if a gilded cage, as surety of the alliance. And I will bear your father more children if need be. Indalos, grant me another fertile moon."

Fiona reached up to grasp her eldest son on both shoulders, trying to imbue him with her elation. "A marriage alliance with Domariadin, and perhaps even to the king's daughter or niece, think of it." She reconsidered her words. "But that would be a delicate matter as not to anger the Tavuros, at least not too soon. Or, perhaps better still, a break with the Arkwen tradition." A spark dazzled her eyes. "Barbora Billengrath is unmarried. A marriage to Barbora would do much to unite the country. I am here to guide you. I have dispatched a most trusted courier to Lady Katya to inquire as to which side she is inclined to favor. A marriage between you and Barbora would give Katya far more gain, and quickly, rather than her slithering charms."

"You what?"

"I've done nothing sharply, but she will understand the question posed. We must understand her perspective. No doubt the thought has already crossed her mind. Loans to Eadolan will only take her so far. She will want to back the victor, and we can offer more." Fiona again contemplated her sometimes rival and potential ally. "Glamour and guile. Katya is far too cunning. Barbora has her mother's admirable qualities. Think of the children you would have."

Fiona moved to embrace her son. "Link up with your father and march on Ravalas. Trap those little rabbits in the pot. There are enough friends in Ravalas who share our concern about the fate of the country. Use a light touch with the nobles but grip tightly. Mind the dogs and watch them well. Braithwaite's gold can help win supporters, but gifted gold breeds expectant greed. What Braithwaite managed to carry off is not without limit. Don't let our troops go unpaid. This is foremost lest they be given to pillaging beyond what is customary of an obedient soldier."

Jannon embraced his mother more out of duty than affection. He felt the eyes of everyone near and far on the river and ancestors looking on from well above Hopewell Heights. "It will all be over soon," he said absently beneath the weight of thought.

"I beseech Indalos for your triumphant return. For now, I am all but alone." The Duchess' voice wavered only slightly. "I hope my letter to your uncle will reach him in time."

"One more thing," Fiona mentioned, feigning that she had almost forgotten. "I am sure you are wondering why we are standing in the river."

Jannon smirked irritably, still struggling beneath the torrent of his mother's counsel.

Fiona reached to the small of her back and opened a small leather satchel looped to her belt. "This was consecrated by Conservator Woolfolk." She cradled a brilliantly white pouch bordered in green and blue thread cinched tight with coarse golden ribbon. She gently opened the pouch and pulled forth a small turtle shell bordered in thin bands of driftwood.

Fiona dipped it in the living water and then used her other hand to pour more water four times over the amulet. "Put it on under your doublet."

"Is it fragile?"

Fiona motioned for Jannon to take the amulet, and then she poured water another four times over his hands.

He received it delicately, but the amulet seemed to have a weight and strength beyond. "What does it do?"

CHAPTER 12

"I think Nabrensus is assured of our loyalty, more than even he thought possible," answered Padazar. "At least Drevell said as much when we rode back to camp; he was very cautious translating while meeting with the Tavuros."

After leaving a portion of his forces under Corneleo Ray to stay with the main Tavurite army, Horace Padazar led his army on a wide march to avoid observation from Thavodyn and its watchtower, Fort Traskon. Padazar's troops then crossed the Spindlejack River and traveled south to join forces with his son, Jannon. The army from the Peregrine Lands moved swiftly with the Spindlejack and the spiny lowlands of the Pinchfeather Mountains to shield their flanks.

"The Tavurite King had much cause for joy. We did him a great favor," remarked Woolfolk without cheer as the sun slid behind another bank of clouds.

"Drevell was right. Other than the cavalry, their army is in a weakened state. Their infantry is smashed up from assaulting Burzina, not that it was good for much anyway. Even their Skytamers needed time to recover. They didn't seem to play much part at Boruma, even in the opening skirmishes. If Silver-face and the Order had been present, it all would have been different," said Padazar recognizing his own luck.

"Do you think the monks destroyed all their works?" fretted Woolfolk. "I am sure Nabrensus will remember our assistance when his army has recovered its strength." The Conservator scowled.

"The Tavuros are superstitious and loose-tongued. Nabrensus stooped to listen to that crippled soothsayer he carts around with him. Swan's agents said that soothsayer claimed to see lightning snaking through the splayed entrails of a young mare. He told Nabrensus that the whole army must stop and take Burzina. Nabrensus refused. Then it started to rain, and lightning split a tree in sight of the monastery. The soothsayer demanded that the siege must begin while the tree still smoldered and continue without respite. They are in no condition to assault Thavodyn or Ravalas. They need time to rest and wait for reinforcements."

"I have heard Swan say that the King sees the story of Thezgos in everything he does," offered Woolfolk. "Maybe Nabrensus will be less inclined to listen next time; his army can ill afford another premonition."

"Thezgos. The boy who became king. Out hunting and lost track of a deer." Padazar smirked as he recalled the creation story of the Tavuros. "He picked up a clump of dirt which was struck by lightning, and a horse arose on the spot. Forever fixing the Tavurite ass to the horse," chuckled Padazar.

"A man ruled by myth," ridiculed Woolfolk. "Can he be trusted?"

"Trust? My need to manipulate him is more important than my need to trust him." Padazar glared at Woolfolk, before looking back towards the fateful battlefield hidden well beyond the horizon. "I hoped Silverface had learned of our plan and intentionally slowed the Order's arrival. How else to explain their absence?"

"If that were the case, Eadolan would be your prisoner now. Eadolan showed himself a fool to have fought the battle without the Order fully present."

"He was a fool to listen to me," said Padazar with a wide grin. "He's too frightened to be seen as a shivering coward, especially when a warrior is in his presence and demanding battle."

"The Order would never aid invaders." Woolfolk dismissed Padazar's wish with a flip of his hand. "Silverface is too cautious, too frightened now. The disaster at Balanshan still haunts him. Many of their real fighters were killed half a world away." Woolfolk paused as if rekindling Padazar's hope. "Still, whether Silverface protects the black rock or follows Eadolan like an obedient hound, it'll show what is most important to him. The Archmage may make a deal to protect what he values most. He is a committed son of this land and a warrior in his own way. I am sure he would approve of a martial spirit on the throne, but his support would not be assured easily. We must be rid of the Tavuros and ready to assuage the Archmage's pride and ensure his preeminent position."

Latrobh laughed at the thought, signaling this return to the conversation after intently watching the passing columns of troops. "Easier to chew through a mountain. We'll have to fight the Order."

"Fight, perhaps, but its destruction may not be required." Woolfolk assumed a tutor's cadence. "A single wizard is a test. Many wizards are a tall challenge. The trick is to isolate them and press the attack. To subdue a true wizard, it may take twenty men, fifty, a hundred or more. Once committed, the attack must be pressed. Never relent," stressed Woolfolk.

Latrobh gave Woolfolk a knowing nod and patted the hilt of his elven-forged sword.

"Why do you repeat what you have said so many times?" chided Padazar. The Duke then shouted to the marching soldiers, "That's it. That's it, Boys. Quick on to victory."

The soldiers cheered their Duke in return.

"Because who else will remind you if I am not constantly by your side?" Woolfolk continued once the cheers subsided. "The Order will always show their hand and cling to their most prized places: Thavodyn, Ravalas, and whatever other rat holes."

Latrobh added, "Flip the countryside and the small towns against Eadolan. They'll not resist in the absence of the royal army. The golden boy has just a thin slice of the line infantry left. Isolate any strongholds. Thavodyn is a hollow prize when the cities and then entire provinces capitulate. Holley's boys already are beating feet to Sawmill. He's a hard marcher. They'll sleep in their shoes if need be."

"How many broadshields does Eadolan still have at full strength?" asked Woolfolk.

"Three," said Padazar. "Just three."

"From fourteen to three since the Tavuros crossed the frontier." Latrobh shook his head. "Eadolan can't replace the experience. The backbone is gone, and the body will collapse. He has to raise new troops or lean on the nobles for even more support. He may have withered from fright." Latrobh grinned like a stalking tiger. "If we offer him a fast ship and exile with his wife, he may take it. Maybe she'd quit Eadolan and want to share a hay bed with a real mountain man."

"What news from Ray's courier?" demanded Padazar uninterested in prolonging Latrobh's fantasy.

"At last count a few hundred line infantry are willing to serve with us," replied Latrobh. "Most are from Waterman's

Broadshield. Poor bastards got assigned the spot in the line next to our boys. I think they're tired of being prisoners. Whether they're willing to kill another Ardalen, or just want to avoid winter captivity, whatever their motivation, it should be rewarded. More will follow."

Latrobh chewed his lip, thinking of his previous brothers-in-arms. What were they to him now? "The Lanterns and Paunchy's Broadshield fought to nearly the last man. Overwhelmed by the Tavuros. They deserved better than that. Paunchy's dead, and Cyp is our guest for the time being. Crowiler's and Fryll's men surrendered. Hard to check every corpse, but, as near as we can tell, Crowiler and Fryll made it out. They may have deserted their men and fled. Some of the infantry tried not to say what broadshield they're with or identify their officers. The Eighth, we're not quite sure what happened. Units may have been able get away." Latrobh grimaced. "This broadshield or that broadshield, watching all these prisoners is going to tie up our troops. Leaving them with Ray is right, but if more don't join us, food and shelter will become an issue. I don't see any point in marching them south; half would run away before we got there."

"We could parole some number as a sign of good faith. Perhaps those who distinguished themselves in the war with Velenharn? Let it be our gesture to release them and not Eadolan's doing," offered Woolfolk. "Our quarrel is with Eadolan and not the country."

Padazar considered the option but said nothing.

"What nobles have joined our cause?" asked Latrobh.

"You can ask them for their loyalty now, and it will mean nothing," seethed Padazar, his anger thinly veiled. "If the tides turn and the nobles are freed, they will claim it was given under duress. We need actual signs of support: refusing to send men and supplies to the royal army."

"Jerris agreed but still must play both sides," added Padazar hoping to counter the disappointment on Woolfolk's face. "When a man is covetous of things, honor is just a word. He is a man of trade and thinks, if there is an agreement now, he can avoid future demands."

"Paper is no shield and neither his half measure," spat Latrobh.

"We will abide by all agreements, especially with those who are first to stand with us. You may never get a second," snapped Woolfolk. "I will not see this land drown in blood." Woolfolk sighed. "I don't think Jerris will be able to influence the Cities from afar."

"How about the lesser nobles?" wondered Woolfolk. "Latrobh, you have a touch with those who drink from wooden cups."

"If you consider Hookbill, Roke, and Whitefield to be nobles. There are freeholders that till more acres than them."

"How many fighting men?" pressed Padazar.

"Not enough worth mentioning, but they are from the southern stretches of the Avenbair. They're concerned that Eadolan won't field an army in the south. The little nobles think the larger lords won't protect them. All the more reason for Mathis to press his advance. More may follow the example of these Midriver nobles and swear allegiance."

"Good. More will join." Padazar returned to pondering the Order's disposition. "What of Silverface? Ray said there were multiple wizards with the Archmage. After overrunning the camp, Ray couldn't force his way to Eadolan. The Order still has great power."

"Battle at a distance is one thing." Woolfolk considered his words. "I mean we must place the wizards in a situation where there is no way out. If we fight them in concentration, it must be on our initiative and in circumstances of our choosing.

Silverface won't risk it all for some patch of cow pasture, which is also to our benefit."

"Then our plan remains unchanged. Our army is the only intact and well-led force in Ardalencor," affirmed Padazar. "Thavodyn will be pinned down. The Tavuros need the fort more than we do. Ray and Swan will play for time until stone throwers are hauled up. Mathis will secure the Midrivers and all the south. Jannon will arrive with the flotilla and fresh troops, and we'll march on Ravalas. Nabrensus, however, may ride in pursuit of Eadolan. If Eadolan obliges an open battle and is defeated, we must reach Ravalas before Nabrensus enters."

"Unless they had eyes on the camp, our wide march should have given them the slip. We need to use this time and reappear directly before the capital. They are running scared. All bridges are intact; creek fords unguarded in our path. If Eadolan rides out to meet Nabrensus, we may even find Ravalas unguarded." Latrobh pushed back a lank of hair from his good eye. "I don't like these little errands to and fro. Once the northern crossing at Croydon is captured, it's little more than fifty miles march to the capital. Push all our men towards Ravalas. All of these scheming threads are tied once Ravalas is captured."

The three men smiled at the thought of the capital's imminent fall.

"No Tavuros, not even Nabrensus, can enter Ravalas until it is under our firm control," remarked Padazar, but more as counsel to himself.

"Or the Academy. They must never be permitted entry. The Skytamers should have no access under any circumstance," added Woolfolk. "Give the Northwestern lands due by the arrangement and send them away. They have soiled our lands already."

"What if Eadolan sues for peace, offering a large payment and control of the Northwest? Then we'll be on our own," mulled Latrobh. "We need to end this before winter."

"I have considered this as well, and think it unlikely," replied Padazar. "Eadolan would lose his last shred of authority if he signed a peace treaty so quickly. What would every other nation think? If the Tavuros took the provinces and then left us alone to deal with Eadolan, I think that would strengthen our hand. What does Silverface do then?"

"The Archmage plays the long game far beyond his own years," said Woolfolk. "They need a generation or two truly to recover if they are not exhausted before then. The Order will defend Ardalencor against invasion, but, in a war of common blood, they will secure their position first."

Woolfolk paused for a long while, and his eyes sparkled in sorrow. "Horace, remember how quickly they arrived in Forris at the start of the war with Velenharn? Even when the Velens had captured the lower town, Silverface still ordered more men to sneak into the upper town and the keep. Ketevan Ironbow and the Ronning brothers, all but one died in the end, led a company of the Order's men-at-arms. Silverface was telling us 'keep fighting'; he was trying to show us, our people, that the Order will defend the nation, every inch of it even if Eadolan would not do the same."

Padazar nodded. He knew the story well but added, "Not the command of a cautious man, though. A different man than the one late to Boruma."

Woolfolk seemed not to hear him. "A lot of wizards, true wizards, are attuned to the world. They feel pain. A man will give out and go numb. Wizards feel everything. When the castle was finally stormed, they took Ironbow alive. Barely, but alive."

Woolfolk grabbed his own arm as if overcome with a

sudden chill. "He was sawed in half by the Velens, conscious to the very end. There was no escape. I heard his cries for a long time."

Padazar's eyes grew wide, disturbed at the revelation as Woolfolk had not been anywhere near Forris at the time of its fall.

"The Order must not be destroyed." Woolfolk regained his composure. "We must come to some understanding. They despise the treaty with Velenharn as much as we do. If the Order is destroyed, any kaldoon with an army becomes a threat to the country."

"How can you say this?" pressured Latrobh. "After what they did to your family! You don't want any revenge? Even a little?"

Woolfolk cut him off. "I am old. He is older. They know things I can never learn. The Order needs rest. He and Farcloud are the last, and he knows the nation cannot survive without us; and even with us, with Eadolan on the throne, it will be a slow decline. We have his attention now. No one outside the Order would give their life for it. They don't enjoy the support of the people. They have to work within the structure built by the very people they look down upon. If the people were roused to defend Ardalencor, many would take up arms. If the people were asked to defend their faith, even more would give their life."

"Enough talk. Iron is weightier than any word." Latrobh urged his horse forward to quicken the march.

CHAPTER 13

"Vengeance crawls from these hands," said Brenio, his jittery fingers moving across a head shaved and patterned with dull white scars where his skull had fused together. Hard edges sculpted his appearance and demeanor, a thick graying moustache covering sealed scissures around his jaw.

His voice would rise and fall, a whistled ditty scattered throughout. "Be on our way. Quit poking around in a coward's cauldron."

Lines of soldiers with torches stood to each side of Castellan Erstchester and Tovenward Thiepval as they addressed the raiding force. The Archmage stood beyond the torchlight but still cast a looming presence over the convocation.

"Well done, Lads. Over the past nights we've located and killed two observers within the stones," said the Castellan referring to the two-mile no-build zone around Thavodyn. "These are just probes, testing our response. More will come. When you step outside the walls, keep a wide eye."

"Indalos, guard soul and soil. Do some harm and come back with empty quivers," finished Erstchester as he took a step back to let Thiepval address the assembled troops.

"Raptor Force, we'll observe the Tavurite and traitor camps and wreck what we can. I'll provide more instruction when we're on the way. Master Wolfwind and Wizard Telfair will lead a cavalry troop beyond the outer marker to cover our return. They won't depart until we're well on our way and won't be in a position to support us if we encounter trouble at the start. With eyes on the fort, we need the Tavuros to think this is a standard cavalry patrol and nothing more."

In addition to Thiepval, the following members of the Zaravandian Order were selected for the raptor force: Brenio Pazdan and Falanika Hood, the two wizards who did not make the return trip to Ravalas with High Lord Eadolan, and five apprentices picked for their subtlety and precision in spell casting.

Toasted throughout the country as the Spearhead or Plow for his assault-leading zeal, Brenio Pazdan, an estranged son of a minor noble house, had found great fame since leaving home as a near-starving squire. He had repelled the call of the grave twice through fortuitous restorations by members of the Order. On the second awakening, the wizard performing the revivification had not separated Brenio's body from the other corpses or, imprecisely focused, had unwittingly permitted the intertwining of Brenio's soul with other unmoored spirits. When Brenio's eyes reopened on the blood-soaked field, his left eye shaded green. Once stoic, his personality thrashed about, recalling far-flung events and places: long reflections with intimate familiarity about sheep prices at Woolmarket, a traveling minstrel and her troupe of pickpockets, sailing grain barges down the Avenbair, and assorted foreign venereal diseases.

Brenio tugged at the fasteners of his copper brown jack

stitched in a pattern of alternating bricks. Black and brown scorch marks discolored the knee-length padded coat, but the integrity of the quilted armor appeared uncompromised.

"Move. Come on." Brenio obsessively shook his fingers at a servant.

The servant helped secure steel gauntlets which ran the length of Brenio's forearms and then flared to cover the outside of the elbow. Warding eyes peered out from the darkened steel covering the back of the hands. A spine and ribs pattern of black basalt was inlaid on each gauntlet over the forearm. Once the gauntlets were secured, another servant handed Brenio his black iron pot helmet with a lobster tail neck guard, large perforated plates to cover the ears and an elongated, ghoulish face shield.

"Good," said Brenio as he smashed the gauntlets against one another.

"Save your strength, Wizard," said Falanika Hood relaxed and bemused by Brenio's impatience. Her pretty, but hard-bit face, was mostly covered by the billowing hood of her dark violet robe. Hood was not her family name, that was unknown, but a sobriquet. Once an orphan girl, a street girl, she was discovered malnourished by members of the Order nearly twenty years ago wrapped in a cloak of bright purple fringed in pink. How a street girl came to possess, and possess little more than that richly dyed cloak, few knew the tale. As an acknowledgement of her enigmatic past, she dyed a long braid of her white-blonde hair the purple-pink of foxglove.

"Thiepval, you'd best keep a restraint on Brenio. I think he's ready to assault the whole camp himself." A smile peeked out as Falanika rested her right hand on her cheek with contemplative fascination. Balanced in the crook of her elbow rested her staff of sleek goldenwood. The staff which Falanika had constructed herself boasted a notched, spherical disk with a large, milk white crystal offset from center. On her left hand, concealed by the unfolded cuff of her robe, was a unique piece of jewelry which had been fashioned by Votark and presented to her two years ago when she received the title of wizard.

The exquisite piece was fashioned primarily of silver and rose gold. A thick rose gold bracelet with oval and kite-shaped pink spinels and purple topazes secured with a clasp at the bottom encased the wrist. Fine chains of silver dangled beneath the palm and connected to three rings also of rose gold for thumb, middle, and third fingers. An ornate twelve-sided plate with a prominent warding eye covered the back of the hand and was joined with silver links to the bracelet and to middle and third fingers.

Just beneath Falanika's elbow stood Malu Littlecheek. As a halfling and more closely acquainted with the ground than the others, she knelt down, pushed back her floppy, wide-brimmed hat, and rubbed a pinch of dirt across her brow.

"Sun-splashed earth rest upon me. Vex the press of cold loam," she said quietly to herself in homage to the pre-battle ritual amongst her smallfolk.

In addition to members of the Order, a small number of garrison soldiers were selected for the raptor force. Wizard Tomas Telfair, the fort's physician, walked amongst the soldiers, eight dead-shot archers and a three-man portable torsion crossbow crew, and handed each man a long phial filled with viscous red liquid.

"Boys, drink these tinctures. Don't mind the taste; it's more bitter than last time, but your eyes should be far sharper, real hawk-like." Telfair grinned with accomplishment.

The chosen soldiers, in addition to their accuracy with yew and string, were well acquainted with the physical effects of potions and elixirs on the bones. All forced down the syrupy contents and slipped on dark green hoods with arcane symbols sewn into the forehead. The symbols permitted covert identification while draped in the black of night.

Unencumbered by armor, the marksmen wore wool trousers and lightly-padded shirts also dyed a dark green. Each man carried a short bow and a covered, padded quiver slung over his back. The padded quiver was crammed with arrows to muffle any noise. A small hand crossbow and bolts were attached with a snug crossbelt to their chests.

The crossbow crew dressed in the same manner and carried the components of the disassembled weapon in stout, specially-designed haversacks.

Seeing the archers don their hoods, Malu removed her hat which helped add some measure to her height. She looked a bit embarrassed for not having remembered to remove the bright teal hat before the assembly, but it was her favorite piece of clothing. The warm felt gave her a cozy courage as she made her way among everyday giants.

Her black hair was braided up and soon to be covered by the hood of her black robe. By the glow of torchlight, her face projected a fierce and mighty conviction, but still her cheerful demeanor sprang forth and gave smile and reprieve to those gathered.

"Allow me, Lady Littlecheek." Castellan Erstchester kindly extended his hand.

"Apprentice," the halfling proudly corrected.

"Indeed, Apprentice Littlecheek, please allow me to take your hat. I shall place it above the Duskwall Gate to await your return."

"Thank you, Castellan," Malu said with ceremonial flourish and a slight bow. She gave an abashed grin to her fellow apprentices and pumped her little fist to regain a martial bearing.

"May the small guide by little steps," said Thiepval

repeating a rustic adage. "Apprentice Littlecheek reminds us well. Take only what you need and secure it well." After a moment he turned to Falanika and said, "Jump!"

Falanika, and then one by one each of the silent feathers of the raptor force, jumped to identify any loose or noisy equipment. Falanika jumped softly and deftly with barely a sound.

As the remaining arcanists and soldiers took their turn, calls of "Quiver," "Drinking Skin," and "Scabbard" led the warriors to tighten and secure their kit. Once the alterations had been made, all jumped together with the faintest of sound.

A cheer went up amongst the gathered crowd.

"Tovenward, we'll have Stomper saddled and waiting for you," said Wolfwind as he and Wizard Telfair approached to discuss the final details of where the raptor force would meet its escort for the last few miles of return to Thavodyn.

Satisfied with Thiepval's preparations, the Archmage turned to meet three of his attendants approaching slowly with kettle pots in each hand. The Archmage nodded and led the attendants away from the soldiers who were bade good hunting by other members of the garrison.

Falanika's eyes closely observed the departure of the Archmage, and she soon followed. Approaching, she said in a low voice, "Here, Archmage. Here would be a good spot. The energy is quite strong. You mean to transport us well beyond the outer marker?"

"Is this your first time at Thavodyn?" questioned the Archmage although he already knew the answer.

"Other than just passing through, yes," Falanika said with exhilaration.

"What do you make of this place?" he asked barely above a conspiratorial whisper.

"I have never been in such a place. My senses are sharp, intensified. I dare say this place, the very ground, is alive, for miles in every direction. I wish to know more of this place. A deep spring must flow beneath the rock."

The Archmage glanced at Thiepval who was still talking to Wolfwind, and then the Archmage studied Falanika for a longer moment. "Where did you say the gate should be placed?"

"Just beyond where you stand now," she said with a self-evident point of her finger.

"Prepare the apparition gate," said the Archmage raising his voice so all could hear. "Mark the center." He noted the spot chosen by Falanika with the press of his boot. "Ensure the measurements are precise, and the space can accommodate the nineteen travelers."

One of the attendants, a dutiful man with wispy white hair, conjured a small bead of light which he sent hovering just above the work area. The three attendants then bent towards the ground and with meticulous hands positioned about a foot off the ground created shallow traces in the dirt and gravel of the fort's mustering ground.

With the apprentices beginning their work, the Archmage again turned to Falanika. "Apprentice Littlecheek may receive the title of wizard should she prove herself during this mission. She will not become a wizard without your approval."

"Archmage?" said Falanika unsure if Thiepval had been given the same charge, or if this was another test from their instructor probing deference and initiative. Where Thiepval was ever anxious to find the correct response, Falanika was nonchalant. She figured whatever answer she gave, if not to the Archmage's liking, it would be corrected. She reasoned, why chase what you will never catch. "You already have my opinion. She is deserving, but Thiepval, as Tovenward, should speak for her conduct during the mission."

"Take care of yourself, Falanika. Give counsel to Thiepval.

Presage time and space. This is a raid. Your safe return matters above all else. Above all else. Do you understand?" stressed the Archmage.

Falanika looked astounded, suddenly feeling a far greater weight placed upon her. She struggled to fix a reply to the cryptic scatter of instructions. "Yes, Archmage," she finally said. "I shall work to accomplish the mission and return all safely."

The Archmage turned away and scrutinized the formation of the apparition gate as the maze-like pattern of partial concentric circles and overlapping arcs expanded outward. "Worthily done. The distances must be precise."

"Archmage, at your command." Thiepval approached with the raptor force.

"Victory and vengeance," said the Archmage to Thiepval and then gave a praising wink.

"Quickly. Quickly into the gate. Do not disturb the configuration." The Archmage pulled a heavy chain studded with silver medallions from one of his belt pouches and wrapped it about his left forearm.

As the group entered the circular portal, the three attendants moved with rapid, yet careful, steps to pour from the pots an opaque, gelatinous liquid which gave off steam in the night's coolness. The mixture took to the grooves cleared by the attendants. To the amazement of the soldiers, rather than slowly oozing into the leveled channel, the thick gray liquid seemed to move with its own propulsion, neatly filling the arcing contours.

"Serpent," barked Brenio as he clapped his gauntlets together. One of the attendants tossed him a heavy bearded axe which he snatched out of the air and jerked close to him.

Thiepval stepped into the circle last, dressed in his chain mail over a red-black felt tunic. As he strode confidently, quietly, the jostling chain mail made nary a sound; neither the hovering point of light nor the roiling flicker of torches reflected about the mail or warding eye.

The Archmage lifted his head skyward and chanted as he exhaled. As he intoned, the liquid in the portal arcs began to vibrate, becoming more viscous, but all the while remaining with the sculpted frame.

"The Archmage needs to fix on a point where we will reappear," said Thiepval to one of the wide-eyed archers.

"Reappear?"

The Archmage's head jerked suddenly, and his attention returned to the gate. He raised his arms, the medallions clinking and spinning. His rhythmic chanting grew louder and more forceful. The liquid began to steam and beneath the rising vapor turned a color resembling the orange cherries of summer.

Erstchester stared transfixed at the ritual and only slowly ascertained the hurried smash of footfalls behind him. Jarvis Jernivan weaved between the mesmerized soldiers and twisted loose of grasping hands. "Wait! I'm going. I must go."

Telfair reached out his hand to impede Jarvis' progress with restraining magic.

In a muffled rush of air, the raptor force disappeared from the circle. Telfair watched in horror as the commotion seemed to stir the Archmage momentarily from his concentration.

A frantic tear of panic started to split the Archmage's thoughts. Even with his knowledge of the surrounding terrain and energy fields, he could not divide his attention long or he would risk the lives of those traveling through the portal. Whatever the intrusion, the Archmage expelled it from his thoughts.

Before Telfair's spell could take effect, streaking shards of light and vapor sprung up from nearby arcs and absorbed into Jarvis' shield. In the bright flash, Jarvis was gone.

A gasp went up amongst the gathered crowd. While all were in an uproar, the Archmage intensely held his concentration.

———————

"That'll stop your heart," wheezed one archer collapsing to his knees.

"Your stomach goes out your ass and snaps back in," gulped another archer.

With a sharp burst of light another individual appeared, alert and grasping in the darkness. "Tovenward," said Jarvis doggedly. "I could not sit in that castle. My wife, she..." He pleaded, "I asked. You should have picked me."

Thiepval, faring better than the archers, but still groggy after the rough emergence, spotted the interloper and clubbed him in the back of the head. Jarvis thudded to the ground; his shield knocked loose. Before Jarvis could attempt to lift himself, Thiepval had pinned him face down with the Tovenward mace pressed harshly across the back of his neck.

Panic and pain radiated from Jarvis' head. Blood streamed through his short blond hair and down his right ear and cheek. Jarvis' voice was a scratchy gurgle as he stole slices of air from between scrub grass and dirt. He managed to turn his head and grabbed a breath. "Wait! Please!"

Jarvis flailed and feebly reached for his shield barely a dagger's length away. The Jernivan Shield was not large, little more than an oversized buckler, which had allowed Jarvis to conceal it during his brief Tavurite captivity. The maned head of a proud lion with a span of a submissive moon beneath, both in old gold, covered most of the shield. A blue field completed the design.

In an instant, the shield traveled the short distance to regain contact with Jarvis. The shield pulsed with a golden moonlight; a spectral lion growled and emerged from the shield, smacking Thiepval and knocking him hard to the ground. Thiepval tumbled but regained his feet, more startled than hurt as he watched the spectral lion re-enter the shield. Thiepval looked slackjawed at Jarvis and halfheartedly leveled his mace unsure if he meant to deal another strike or laugh in astonishment.

Regaining her faculties after the bumpy reappearance from the apparition gate, Falanika quickly threw an arcane cloak of silent darkness about her companions. She had been too disoriented to cast the spell prior to the ripple of light signaling Jarvis' arrival, but she thought her magic covered the group before the shield illuminated.

The archers were still slow to react, writhing from the effects of teleportation, several lifting their masks and retching.

Brenio, like the other members of the Order, was in awe at the awakening of the Jernivan Shield. The wizards and apprentices all remembered their own early days at the Academy, poring over the painted pages chronicling the ancient guardian of generations of dragon-slaying Jernivans. "Thought that was some slapdash buckler, but drag me through the abyss, that's the true."

Knowing that the group was magically concealed, Brenio did not linger on nostalgia. "You little shit! That knot on your head is the first smack. We were sneaking out for a late-night garden romp, and you left us cock limp and naked out here. You'll think your butchered forebearers got off easy!"

"This is where I should be. You should have picked me," said Jarvis while trying to stand.

"As a disgraced member of the Jernivan family, you are in possession of an arcane implement without sanction of the Zaravandian Order. By right, and in the name of the High

Lord, you are ordered to give us the shield," demanded Thiepval, yet wary of a repeat of the lion's pounce.

"No. I didn't know it possessed this power. My father only said that the power left long ago," Jarvis said earnestly, woozy on his feet from the loss of blood. He clumsily dropped to one knee to retrieve the shield in its golden gleam.

"Thavodyn restored the shield," Falanika whispered to Malu.

The apprentices glanced anxiously at Thiepval. Thiepval ignored them, still unsure whether he would help Jarvis or let him bleed out. Falanika looked with pity and bitterness at the frightened young man casting about in his lonely desperation.

"I can understand wanting to hold on to what is yours," said Thiepval lessening the air of formality and grasping his Tovenward mace tighter, "but you're not a lion. There are no lions in Ardalencor. The Archmage will want your shield. You claim it's yours, but you know nothing about it."

"I know the stories. If the shield is reborn, then I know what it can do."

"If you surrender it freely, the Archmage may spare you the thief's noose. You almost killed us all. You're not the only one who has ever sacrificed!" shouted Thiepval.

"Do you speak Tavurite?" said Jarvis scrambling to find his place in the group.

"What? Yes," laughed Thiepval with a wry smirk.

"No, I mean, real Tavurite. Have you spent any time there? I can speak it." Jarvis' voice trailed as he collapsed to the ground. "Please help me," he said with wide, panicked eyes. "Please. I need to come with you."

Thiepval considered the entreaty. After an approving flick of his wrist, two apprentices extended their hands; their incantations quickly reduced and sealed the wound.

"Easy, Jarvis. Drink this." Thiepval smiled as he walked forward.

Jarvis sniffed and gulped down the phial of sweet-smelling liquid.

"Blacken that shield, Boy. Can't have you jumping about with that furry candle. Get back on your feet," commanded Brenio. "The call of life is the strongest force. You stand squared shoulder next to me, do you understand? I know a few Tavurite drinking songs, but can't say much else."

Unable to dampen the shield's radiance, Jarvis carefully stretched the leather covering over top.

"Be worthy of the shield and be worthy of the name," said Brenio as he poked Jarvis in the chest with a heavy gauntlet and then reverentially touched the rim of the shield before Jarvis could fully cover it. Brenio thought he heard a faint growl as he touched the shield. "Strange that things you think have passed well beyond reach are so close."

"Now you know how we feel about you, Brenio," chided Falanika.

"Tovenward. If I may suggest, we best be on our way," offered the lead archer.

Thiepval hesitated for a long moment. "Jernivan. You stay here." Pointing, Thiepval said, "It's still giving off light through the leather covering. You don't know how to control its power. You wait here, keep that shield quiet, and we'll come get you on the way back."

"What? I..." said Jarvis as he drowsily fainted. Brenio was quick to catch him.

"I was wondering what was taking so long. I'll have to speak with Tomas. Not the best batch. That mad fool can sleep here until we return. Who'd have thought that the lion shield would return? I can't wait to present this to the Archmage."

"If the Tavuros saw that flash of light, they may check it out," said Falanika.

"You're right. I think you should stay here. Move off a distance and maintain that cloak until we return."

"Me?" Falanika sorted through whether staying with Jarvis was a punishment or a privilege to steward such a fabled item.

"Yes, I'm sure you will be fine. You can see it, but do you detect any magic radiating from the shield?" asked Thiepval. "How about you, Apprentices?"

All shook their heads.

"Well, at least that part of the legends proves right. Explains how they were able to approach a dragon's lair without the dragon getting a whiff of the magic. I wonder if it can resist flame and venom," pondered Thiepval.

"And channel the power of other sources," added Falanika. "I don't think some kaldoon will be able to detect it. The Tavuros don't have our level of knowledge, even their supposed Skytamers."

"Let's hope that's still the case. If none of you can extinguish the light, then it's a wild lion, and we can't afford to take it with us. We'll come back for you, Falanika. The Archmage then can study the shield."

"Very kind of you, Tovenward," said Falanika with a trace of mockery.

"Lad, stay put," said Brenio to the snoring Jarvis.

"I'll blink the cloak," said Falanika. "Fast feet and good hunting."

Having freed themselves from the last tendrils of nausea, the archers grabbed arrows from their quivers and formed a perimeter as the group took in their new surroundings several miles distant from Thavodyn.

"It's a bit chilly," Malu said, now regretting parting with her hat but quickly got to work with the other apprentices in probing the air and ether in ever-widening circles for the presence of foreign magic. "See you soon, Falanika. Stay warm."

When Thiepval and the others were gone from view, Falanika squeezed the hands of the dozing Jarvis. She had no intention of missing a battle and just sitting in silence. She quickly resolved to tease the true secrets from between the tales and tapestries and learn the nature of the shield which still shone brightly within the arcane darkness. She turned the shield's face to the ground to dampen the light.

Jarvis stirred, bewildered, the elixir still coursing through his veins; precisely what Falanika wanted, figuring Jarvis to be more pliant and forthcoming with information.

"Tell me about your wife," she began softly.

After gaining some distance from Falanika's hiding spot, Thiepval signaled the group to stop. "We are the only force of any consequence between here and the capital. We must convince the Tavuros that they can't avoid Thavodyn. Latrobh and Padazar will want to ride straight for Ravalas. We need to slow them until the heavy snows."

Thiepval turned back towards where the apparition gate had appeared. "Apprentices, do you detect the silhouettes of the cloak?"

"No, Tovenward," called one of the apprentices. "Wizard Falanika has formed a completely sealed illusion."

"You're right, but I'm not sure for how long," grunted Brenio. "The light of that shield was growing ever brighter. Some stories called it the Light of Indalos. We'll come to find out how tightly secured is Falanika's cloak. The lion may burst it open. Hurry on."

"Let's get a close look for a king shot," said one of the archers. "End this."

"We have a few miles yet and will need to cross the creek. We'll set fire to part of the camp and linger long enough to get the ant hill to stir. Hit the Tavuros. The Tavuros are the target. We'll pick them off as they come out or snipe the fire watch. Strike fire on our craven people, if you must; but if you see Padazar, be sure to shoot the traitor. We'll rush back, grab Falanika, and link up with Telfair and Wolfwind to escort us back," instructed Thiepval. "If we can spot the location of our captured people, try to figure out how many are there. They may be used as trenchers and shields as the Tavuros approach Thavodyn. If we can find the horse herds, that's a fine target. Poke at the edges. A fly can command the attention of a mammoth."

"There's many a fine lass at the Waterstock Fair, but hard to dance with them all at the same time. They tend not to like that in fact," jested Brenio.

Thiepval nodded. "I know not what we will encounter up ahead. Just the same we should be ready for any possibility." Turning to Malu, Thiepval added, "The place of honor is yours."

Malu smiled brightly in the darkness and sprinted quickly to the front as the raptor force marched forward in a loose formation.

The group traveled swiftly with the main road as a guide to their right. Malu abruptly knelt down and signaled the group to stop.

"You got to be razor keen to notice the change in elevation," chuckled Brenio as he and Thiepval crawled up towards Malu.

Up ahead the orange glow of campfires marked the bridge crossing of Lost Bugle Creek. The creek was more a muddy trough most of the year and ran a jagged course deeper than a man towards the Spindlejack River and then on to the Avenbair.

"The temporary bridges are probably still intact," said Malu referring to the planked spans that were constructed by army pioneers to widen the crossing in advance of Eadolan's march to the fateful battle of Boruma.

"Likely held in force," said Brenio.

"I'm detecting traces ahead. Faint magic. It's either a weak casting or a poor attempt at concealment," Malu explained.

"Where is the source?" asked Thiepval. "How far does the field extend? Does it link to a larger net?"

"It runs out before us and then back to the road near the pickets. I think it's dirty magic. A kaldoon, or two at most, up ahead."

"You think it is a trip for something larger?"

"Maybe for the bridge guard, but not for the main camp. Too far out. Those fires are just flecks on a cat's coat," said Malu as she craned her head. "This is just a lazy screen. Could be some Skytamers at the bridge, too."

"Tavuros aren't known for tight concealment. They're a smoky fire; spot them right away," said Thiepval describing the sight of warping or odd refractions of light when an attempt at invisibility or any concealing deception is rendered poorly. Even to an untrained eye, a crude illusion in daylight would be spotted by distortions approximating vapor emitting from the source. Clean or pure magic, as it was known in the Academy, was undetectable, or at least extremely hard to ascertain. True mastery of the arcane arts produced a double feat: to alter the natural order and to conceal the evidence.

Thiepval shifted his attention to the swarm of campfires hovering in the far distance. "I wonder if Woolfolk is there," mumbled Thiepval more or less to himself, but Brenio heard him.

"Woolfolk is with Padazar. Where Padazar is, there is Woolfolk. You know Woolfolk's?" started Brenio, and then his thoughts shifted. "Little one, go exam the threads. Locate the source."

Not yet moving, Malu continued to study the patterns of the arcane threads. Recalling her years of training, she knew that the thread patterns hinted to their origin and purpose. A flash of mysteries raced through her mind. Is the magic like a string attached to a bell; will it make noise? Or if disturbed, will it release a flash of light? Is the alarm discreet and only the spell's maker will know, or will the whole camp be alerted?

That the origin of the spell could be well outside the camp worried her, puzzled her. She felt the heavy gaze of Thiepval and Brenio and felt that she could not continue to plow through every option like a farmer diligently tilling his acres. Whether this was an attempt at deception or the superstitious camp guards wary of magic users and wanting them at a distance, she at least had a working idea.

It would not be hard for soldiers to intimidate rudimentary casters. Most people, Ardalens, Tavuros, any people, held a well-founded suspicion or fear of arcanists. The soldiers may have sent the casters from camp for their own comfort but still kept them close enough to provide protection. Like the stench of a tanner's shop announced the demand for leather, those unacquainted with magic enjoyed its benefits but disdained its presence. This was especially common among the Tavuros as very crude castings often spooked the horses and other animals.

"You are going to have to get close. You can't make a peep or a cluck. Coiling shadows. Remember what I taught you." Brenio gently touched Malu on the shoulder. "You ever kill anybody? Close up, I mean."

Malu shook her head at Brenio.

"Well, it is a necessity in a place like this. It is alright to look away when the time comes. They may not enter your dreams that way, but make sure you do your part."

Malu bit her lip and gave Brenio and Thiepval a serious bow.

As she slinked forward, Brenio mused, "If they see her, they'll probably think it's a groundhog scrounging around."

Approaching the arcane threads, Malu quickly mastered their construction, deftly plying the threads into more subtle and elongated connections to allow her to pass through, without, she hoped, attracting the notice of the original crafter. The sinews clear before her trained eyes, she spotted more filaments stringing through the ether and concluding about a hundred paces distant.

As she crawled closer, Malu heard faint snoring. Two figures, wrapped in thin blankets, huddled next to one another. On knees and elbows she worked her way within a few feet of them. She assured herself there was no arcane link between this group and the force guarding the bridge.

Her little heart started to race as one of the figures stirred and sat up to rest upon an elbow, shaking himself back awake.

Malu steadied her nerves, clutched the two crystals in her left hand even tighter, and gulped down the pit in her throat. Her fingers rotated, and coilings of thin shadow found their way around the necks of the two figures. She closed her fists. One of the figures, a young boy, who had been struggling to keep watch, gasped and turned to look in her direction with wide, terrified eyes. She locked on the eyes of the boy and spied his frightened soul flailing within. Blanch-stricken and remorseful, Malu released the shadows. Time slowed as she observed the figures, both young boys, barely teenagers, tear free from their blankets. Their mouths started to move, and the closest one tore wildly in the darkness and nearly grabbed a piece of Malu's robe.

Malu struggled to suppress a scream and to reform the coiling shadows on her attacker. The other boy, knife drawn, approached by sound and feel in the night.

A black shade cut across her view. A new figure emerged with gauntleted hands to plunge daggers into the throats of the two Tavuros. The figure then covered their mouths and stared intently at the camp guarding the bridge crossing. There were no signs of alarm from the camp.

Malu found a thimble of air. "Brenio, I didn't hear you coming."

"I know. You were too focused and yet not focused enough. This isn't throwing fire at a distance. It's one thing to have courage when those braver than you are nearby. You don't have the luxury to be nervous or scared; otherwise, we got to pull you back."

Malu lowered her head.

"Why did you look him in the eye?"

"I thought I could do it. I wanted to show you that I was ready."

"Too much is at stake to hang on your experimentation." He wiped the daggers clean. "You are a member of the Order. There are few of us, and even fewer who rightfully earn the title of wizard."

Brenio observed the stillness at the bridge for a long while and then turned back to Malu. "After Waydun fucked up, got my soul tangled all guts and hooks, I remember more songs I've never heard than I do spells it took me years to master." He sighed. "You weren't at the front in the last war, but you're here now. We count on you."

Brenio and Malu returned to meet the rest of the raptor force which had moved closer to their position.

Thiepval raised his eyebrows when Brenio returned. Brenio just shook his head. Master Sergeant Emerik Dudley, the leader of the archers, was signaled to join Thiepval and Brenio for a council of war.

Thiepval ran his hand over his face to suppress his worry. He felt that the war could hinge on his actions during this blind mission. After a long moment, Thiepval finally said, "Options? If we wipe out this picket, it gets us nothing. The Tavuros will reoccupy the bridge tomorrow in greater force. The creek can be planked over anywhere."

"We can bypass it, hit the main camp, and spend the next days or so tacking a wide path back," offered Brenio.

"We'd risk being cut off from Thavodyn if Tavurite horsemen are sent out after us," said Dudley.

"What about Falanika? What if the shield is discovered and taken? We need to go back for her," worried Thiepval wishing that Falanika was with them now. Being down one wizard and Malu being of suspect benefit for this kind of mission concerned him greatly.

"Falanika can take care of herself," said Brenio but acknowledged the point. "Even if that shield is just a lantern, if Padazar had possession, it would seem like the ancients and old magic are rallying to his standard. She could kill Jarvis or knock him out and drag his scrawny neck back to Thavodyn. She'll know what to do if we are not back by breakfast."

"If we attack the bridge, they'll alert the camp and cause a tough road back," said Dudley, "if they have mind to follow us."

"It would take time, and I don't think they'd bother sending a large force in the night," replied Thiepval.

"The defenses will get tighter as we approach the camp. Sun will be up if we stay cautious and check every tuft of grass before we ever reach the camp," Brenio carped. With a gleam in his eye, he added, "What if we take out this picket, grab some horses and make a dash for the camp. Toss around some fire and then ride back? Buzz, even scorch, that mammoth, like you said."

"There are probably close to five hundred soldiers at this camp, but they all think we are tucked up and hiding in the black rock." Thiepval evaluated the options. "We are going to encircle this group, just not a full circle. Let's make sure to preserve a few at the end for questioning and spare the horses. Brenio, do what you can about those makeshift spans. Block the other side of the bridge, but don't stay too long."

"Dudley, put three of your men to screen Brenio. Don't let anyone get near him."

Before Thiepval could continue, a man carrying a torch began to walk and call for the two teenagers recently silenced by Brenio. Hearing no reply, another man from the camp, also with torch and sword, began to follow.

Malu was already on the move, racing back to where the bodies lay.

Through hand signals down the formation, the raptor force started to move toward one side of the camp. "Brenio," cautioned Thiepval, "if you can't get to the far side of the bridge, at least keep the pressure on and make them think twice about crossing."

Thiepval said to Master Sergeant Dudley, "Tell Rufus and Dahey to keep the line curled on this side of the road. That's the end of the line. We don't need to fight a twenty-to-one encirclement. Panic the Tavuros, but we'll give them a way out, just not a sprint over the bridge."

Thiepval turned back to try to locate Malu and watch the approach of the two Tavuros.

Malu slunk in between the two bodies, the folds of her robe sopping up the pooling blood. She made a guttural snoring noise which drew the men closer with a slew of curse words. Malu started to shake the nearest body, and the Tavuros' excoriations grew louder. She glanced back and saw the raptor force fanning out in the dark. Malu wanted to garner every moment that she could for her companions.

As the Tavuros approached, swords gleaming in the torchlight, Malu sat up and formed two energy pockets which exploded in a dull pop just before the throats of both men. The expert casting shattered the larynx and shredded the throat muscles but did not rupture the skin. Malu saw the tiny waves pulse within each man. As their eyes grew larger, she ignored their faces and cast another spell which fixed them in place. She strained against their strength to keep them upright and the swords and torches still.

Ready signaled Rufus and Dahey, two apprentices who had honed their battle casting while stationed at Thavodyn. Thiepval raised and then leveled his mace to commence the attack. Arrows hit soldiers on watch, easily marked by the campfire glow.

"Under attack!" came the call in Tavurite, and then the camp rose in a growing mix of shouts, officers calling their men to assemble.

The crew had assembled the torsion crossbow, and the first heavy bolt went thumping high into the camp, ripping through the tops of closely packed tents.

Shouts rippled through the camp as the Tavuros crashed to the ground, scrambling to find what meager cover was available. Men stumbled from the tents in a din and clang to don armor or ready weapons. A man with his helmet and one boot was struck with an arrow in the chest as he emerged from a tent.

The Tavuros yelled to one another, vainly straining into the darkness to find the source of the attack. A few arrows were fired blindly into the blackness. None marked an Ardalen.

With range and accuracy found, the torsion crossbow was sighted lower. A special iron-headed bolt with a hollow lead shaft containing a glass tube filled with a swirling blue vapor was carefully readied. The soft lead would bend on impact and crack the glass casing allowing the heavy vapor to creep along the ground.

As soon as the bolt went ripping into the camp, Dahey and Rufus conjured more than a dozen fiery orbs about the size of apples above where they judged the bolt had struck. An instant later, and just as quickly as the fiery orbs appeared, all but three blinked out. The two apprentices gave each other a worried look, and then the three orbs that remained quickly careened into the area carpeted with the blue vapor, igniting it and sending men hurtling and fleeing in all directions.

Brenio ran along the bank of the creek and saw two troopers stationed back from the far side of the bridge mount and spur their horses to the main camp. He swore and increased his pace, but they were too far out for him to stop them.

Malu dispatched the two sentries as they writhed on the ground and clutched their throats. She deftly removed a red conical cap worn by one of the men. The hat was ill-fitting with its top bent forward.

Brenio snorted from his ghoulish helmet and motioned for Malu to come with him. "Target the wooden spans. Find a safe spot on this side of the creek."

"Brenio!" called Malu as she saw a large group of soldiers moving to defend the spans and signaling their comrades to withdraw over the bridge.

"Roast the chickens!" yelled Brenio.

A sunburst started to rise above the Tavurite camp, but Thiepval suppressed its effect, and the dark was again only illuminated by the spreading fires. The Tavuros had no clear view as to how many attackers were assaulting the perimeter.

The sunburst attempt was repeated, and again Thiepval

displayed his mastery and negated the effect. "They have a caster and no simple kaldoon," said Thiepval as he contemplated whether to send his forces in to finish off an overmatched and isolated caster.

Rufus and Dahey continued to crash fire orbs into the camp. While the number and intensity of the fire orbs they could conjure in the same area waned, the orbs were no longer extinguished by an opposing force.

With the Tavuros making no attempt to counterattack beyond the perimeter of their camp, the other apprentices who had prepared defensive measures switched to summon a deafening trample of horse hooves. The growing cacophony of seeming Ardalen reinforcements drove the last defenders from the camp.

Brenio leapt across the creek and ran towards the bridge. He swung his axe to maintain a distance with any would-be attacker. An eerie shriek emanated from his helmet's ghoulish face which drove the enemy nearest the bridge back in panic.

A crack and crash behind Brenio signaled that Malu had collapsed a wooden span. There were three spans each about the width of a cart on either side of the stone bridge. Brenio extended his left hand, speaking an incantation to target the three spans farthest from Malu. He stood astride the bridge as Malu dropped the final spans closest to her position.

Two arrows stretched out towards Brenio's back, but they harmlessly plinked off his brick-patterned gambeson. The Tavurite archers screamed to their compatriots to avoid Brenio and retreat over the remaining spans. Brenio seemed oblivious as another arrow splashed off his gambeson.

Small groups of fleeing Tavuros ran towards the three remaining spans with weapons leveled to keep Brenio at bay. Ardalen arrows whistled towards the Tavuros, more hitting than missing the clumps of men seeking safety.

Brenio took a defensive stance, feigning concern about the nearby Tavuros. As the first Tavurite soldier stepped on a wooden span, he let out a howl as splintered staves plunged into the soft leather of his shoe. He tried to stop, but his next foot also crashed into transformed wood. Not seeing through the illusion across the spans, other Tavuros running heedlessly trampled onto the rough spikes or collapsed onto the men in front of them, puncturing any soft clothing or tissue from head to toe. With the mass of the wood transformed into a bed of spikes, the remaining span was thinned and snapped, crashing men and mangled wood into the creek. Shrieks to wake the dead rose and just as quickly sank below the muddy water.

An oily acid splashed across Brenio's helmet, obscuring his vision and dropping him to one knee. He coughed and clawed at the oil with his gauntlets but only succeeded in spreading the slick mess.

A Tavurite soldier, crazed by the cries of his countrymen, called for a frenzied rush at Brenio to re-open the escape route. Brenio braced himself for the charge and swung his bearded axe, Serpent. The onrushing Tavuro had anticipated the heavy blow and parried with his sword, but the shuddering impact of Brenio's attack still rattled the Tavuro's bones. A spearpoint rushed forward to skewer Brenio, but the spear and attacker recoiled as Brenio arced the long reach of his axe in blind violence.

Brenio was too disoriented and the press too close to concentrate on magical relief. Any recollection of spells was but a dim star in a storm-strewn night. Seasonal depths in the great bends of the Avenbair south of Ravalas sloshed about his mind. He raged, terrified at the loss of his true memories. Brenio also worried greatly that the acid was corroding his helmet and padded coat the way it was eating through the leather palms of his gauntlets.

Malu ran forward, desperately trying to locate the source of the acid spell afflicting Brenio. Not finding the source, in her rising panic, she decided upon another course of action. She dared not replicate the placement of the energy pockets with the press of Tavuros so close to Brenio. Anger and determination welled within the little apprentice, the energy pooling in her hand. She felt and smelled the searing of her own flesh as the crystals surged with the focused energy, and she only squeezed tighter.

Swords and spears prodded at Brenio. While his gambeson protected him from piercing and slashing attacks, the sheer momentum of the attacks drove him back. Malu saw Brenio falter, unable to find room to maneuver Serpent. Malu found her target at the back of the Tavuros' knees and she increased the force to shred flesh and bone alike.

Gaining a reprieve in the swirl of screams and exploding flesh, Brenio, with both hands, instinctively swung the heavy axe like a scythe. He nearly cleaved the nearest man in two, Serpent biting deep, crushing ribs and bursting organs. Brenio gave a war cry as he wrenched out the massive blade.

Brenio suddenly heard the whoosh of warming air rising behind him. He hacked wildly with Serpent to silence those writhing on the bridge after Malu's crippling attacks. The rising flames comforted him, feeling the familiar arcane warmth of the fiery cordon cast by Thiepval to shield him from attack and persuade any lingering Tavuros on the far side of the bridge to flee to their main camp.

After the initial onslaught of fire and iron, most Tavuros hurriedly fled, finding an easier course of retreat upstream into the darkness. A signal of distinct whistles among the raptor force confirmed the danger had subsided. Two Tavuros, who avoided Brenio's and Malu's attacks, pleaded for mercy at the edge of the creek. Malu discovered that the two crystals had

IN TIMES OF WAR: A TALE OF ARDALENCOR

fused and carried off layers of skin as she gingerly pulled the heated blob from her hand. She bit back the pain and calmly approached to accept the surrender of the enemy.

"Get me rid of this muck!" implored Brenio.

As Thiepval went to tend to Brenio, he ordered the raptor force to inspect the camp.

"That kaldoon may still be lurking in the shadows," warned Master Sergeant Dudley, although he thought it unlikely that anyone would be crazy enough to continue the fight. "Move in groups of two and three. Apprentices, detection and counter-measures, if you please."

The fires had largely burned out, but the smoke and stench still blanketed the area. The apprentices and archers moved by short bursts to clear areas of potential ambush. No resistance remained.

"Estimate eighty dead within the perimeter. Maybe more based on the amount of cinders. Not all are Tavuros," called Rufus grimly, pushing back a dark red lock of long hair beneath his headband. "We found three badly burned but still alive. Not sure they'll survive a trip back. More smoke than sense in them."

"How about the kaldoon?"

"Unknown."

"We'll see him again. I've got an arrow for him," said one of the archers.

"They were careless, weren't expecting us. They think the whole country is running scared," said Dudley.

CHAPTER 14

Master of Horse Arnost Wolfwind and Wizard Tomas Telfair departed Thavodyn with the cavalry patrol not long after the Archmage closed the apparition gate. Emerging from the depths of intense concentration, the Archmage remarked with relief, "Certain they made it through the gate." Adding before he stormed off, his rising anger barely contained, "Go see them back!"

Wolfwind selected sixty troopers for the mission, nearly all those available in the garrison. The troopers were divided into squads of eight to ten men and fanned out in a wide formation. The cavalry, including Wolfwind, was armored in a fashion resembling the field army's line infantry, hauberk with shallow nasal guard helm. To denote their distinguished status as a defender of Thavodyn, troopers had a decorative brass emblem riveted to the front of their helmets, a snarling sabertooth tiger head inside of an upturned horseshoe with a stylized tower in the background.

Depending on the trooper's role, he carried a torch or lantern, small crossbow or short lance. All wore swords on their belts and small shields on their saddles which gently bounced to the horses' trotting. In the wake of the screening troopers, four drivers led mule-pulled carts, the only sign that this was more than a routine patrol.

"Vary your sweeps and spacing," called Wolfwind to the squad leaders.

As Wolfwind's troopers searched for enemy observers, he pondered why Telfair's spell had not stopped the heedless Jarvis Jernivan from approaching the apparition gate. Wolfwind had to catch his tongue, knowing the time was not right, and may never be right, to pose such a question to the wizard. Despite their long friendship, all wizards were known to loathe revealing their failings to the uninitiated.

Telfair was the second wizard of Thavodyn, after Thiepval. Unlike the troopers, he carried no weapon. His saddle, front and back, was covered in bulky saddle bags. He wore a long sleeveless gray wool coat with chevron designs in dark red, yellow, and white on the shoulders and lower hem. Prominent on the right breast of the coat was a warding eye. Large pockets, embellished with silver buttons, adorned each side of the coat. Silver clasps down to the waist were undone, and interior pockets bounced with the weight of small vials.

The Order's geometric white star, composed of a diamond and four triangles arrayed on the facets, patterned the hood and was positioned such that when the hood was up, the star rested on the forehead. The hood was down as Telfair welcomed the chill of the evening on his shaved head to cool his nerves and enflamed thoughts.

Beneath the long jacket, he wore an off-white doublet with a multitude of pockets closed by small copper buttons and red hose tucked into calf-high boots of a rich periwinkle blue.

Wolfwind glanced at his brightly-clad friend and began to imagine what fate awaited Jernivan if he foolishly returned to

Thavodyn without first driving the Tavuros out of the country singlehandedly. He snorted a laugh at the absurdity of the thought but figured Jernivan did not have much hope for leniency from the Order as he had already stretched his rope taut.

At the same time, Wolfwind pitied the young man. Wolfwind's wife and eight of their children were warm and tucked safely inside the family's home near Brightwater. The two-story basalt and timber manor house punctuated the tree-sparse prairie on the southern banks of the Pheasant River.

Wolfwind was not of noble stock but a man who fought and found his own way. He was a charmer and one who intuitively understood the folds and rhythm of the land. He was a man of the saddle, though not a warrior, rather a courier and long rider. With daring, ingenuity, and the care and cultivation of horses, he steadily rose as a man of ever-increasing means, owner of several mills, orchards, flocks, and his treasured horse stables. His notice in royal circles came when as a teenager he crossed flood-swollen water courses and half-dead with chill arrived to bring life-saving elixirs to members of the extended royal family who were trapped by a sudden outbreak of plague while leisuring at a country estate. He created and parlayed his own luck ever since.

Wolfwind married late in life but diligently established a wolfpack of his own. He and his wife, twenty years his junior, had seven girls and three boys surviving long enough to receive a name. The eldest, a daughter, Visandra, was married to a landowner just upriver from the Wolfwind manor. She was a renowned artist, a painter of gentry and peasant life on the rolling prairies and wildlife scenes in one of the few areas of the country where the iconic sabertooth tigers still roamed.

The tigers had learned to fear men over the centuries but occasionally would venture close for an opportune meal. It was punishable to kill the national symbol which placed shepherds and yeoman farmers in a precarious spot in defense of their flocks and families. To help combat poaching and trophy taking, any slain tiger was to be reported immediately to local officials. Despoiling the corpse for the coat, eponymic teeth, or meat was forbidden.

Some daring souls would hunt the great beasts but best did so without sharing the tale. Occasionally a man in the swoon of libacious merriment would show close friends or neighbors the trophies of the hunt. An inquiring knock on the door from royal officials often followed.

While still a bachelor, Wolfwind, a man of certain talents and ambition, spied and soon coveted the hand of a local nobleman's new bride. To achieve his ends, Wolfwind set off alone, tracked the animals, and killed two baby tigers. He then planted the pelts, paws, and wide-eyed heads in the barn of the nobleman. Not long after, an anonymous letter was found tacked to the reeve's door in Brightwater.

The nobleman was arrested, and his property confiscated. Charitably, a large portion of the property was bestowed upon his destitute wife, and she promptly divorced the disgraced man in wake of the scandal. The dashing Wolfwind was not long in taking the young beauty into his bed and incorporating her lands and fruited groves into his own growing holdings.

Wolfwind relished the posting at Thavodyn. It was a recognition of prior acclaims and a bountiful route to even greater accomplishment. Even with the disruption of Ardalencor's economy and loss of tax revenue after the destructive war with Velenharn, Wolfwind was amazed that every request from Thavodyn's Castellan and wizards seemed to be fulfilled. More deeply, Wolfwind was fascinated by the Order's abiding interest in the place although they never spoke to him about it directly. He vividly wondered what the wizards had locked beneath the heavy basalt of the citadel.

Wolfwind was not a practitioner of magic but had a bubbling curiosity over the years of observation and snatching fragments of knowledge. He would try to experiment and quickly lost count of the multitude of efforts. Once through a chance mix of potent materials, rhythmic chanting, and ethereal connection, far wide from his objective, his hands erupted in lesions which radiated excruciating pain on a long ride back to Thavodyn. He was circumspect in explaining the cause to Telfair, but the wizard just gave a knowing smile and admonished, "That will be enough of that."

If any of Thavodyn's soldiers fell out of favor with the wizards, they were promptly removed, but Wolfwind felt little worry. For the five-hundred-strong garrison, it was not a fearful atmosphere that pervaded but one of demonstrating the highest standards. Garrison soldiers earned more than a line infantryman or regular army trooper, and the officers enjoyed other benefits. Wolfwind established a veracious standard.

While most buildings in the midland prairies were of wattle and daub, Wolfwind's home of High Rock was built of basalt, and more black stone festooned the archways of his main stables. The two-hundred-mile transportation of the black stones to construct High Rock, which the locals called Blackwolf Castle, dismayed envious nearby landowners. Castellan Erstchester eventually stepped in to curtail Wolfwind's extravagances.

While personal enrichment came with the privilege of appointment, royal connections or noble titles accounted for little in maintaining one's post. Good character and martial skill, regardless of social station, were the most prized qualities. Garrison life had a grueling side. All but the most hardy withered under the constant drills: spotting forward observers, detecting ambushes, countering infiltrations and night climbers, protecting the walls against ladders and siege engines, containing breaches, building secondary defenses in the fort's interior, disassembling the barricades and then hauling them to cordon another section of the fort, holding isolated bastions and towers from attack on all sides, withstanding deprivation of food, water, and sleep, defending against magical attacks, and undergoing tests of fortitude when threatened with poison, acid, or noxious gases.

For those more inclined and even more disciplined, rudimentary arcane methods to detect and counter infiltrations were selectively taught. A handful of the garrison members, outside of the Order's wizards and apprentices, knew some village magic which was encouraged and strengthened despite the Order's standing prohibition to teach outsiders or permit the practice of magic in other circumstances.

"Well, Tomas, so what do you think?" said Wolfwind to Telfair to break a long silence after they completed several concentric sweeps around the fort's perimeter. Wolfwind rode his favorite horse, Blue Allen, a dapple blue gray with an ash white mane and tail.

"No sign of the enemy. All quiet" came the calls back to the Master of Horse.

"Do I think they made it?" said Telfair peevishly. "Yes, the Archmage said they did."

"No, I mean, how long do you think we'll need to hold out before Eadolan returns with an army?"

"Much depends on the Tavuros and winter," said Telfair looking off into the darkness towards the distant field of Boruma. "It was nice to see your son again, a befitting squire for the Hearthguards."

"Yes, Quinton shall be a fine knight. He may earn his spurs before Greenhallow's Eve. What a feast it will be."

"If fate and fortune oblige him," echoed Telfair.

"I always taught him that fortunes are won," said Wolfwind with a sly glimmer in his eye.

Telfair again did not appear to be listening. Jarvis' bold rush to the apparition gate troubled him greatly. What if Jarvis had wanted to attack the Archmage in his moment of concentration and vulnerability? Who would have stopped him? Telfair cast a spell, but it did not work.

Would Telfair explain to the Archmage that Jarvis had vanished too quickly for the spell to take hold or that the spell could not lock on in the swirl of surrounding magic? Neither answer brought any solace. Telfair was unsure what had happened other than his failure to protect his leader and mentor, and inside Thavodyn's walls at that. He dreaded what censure may await; the guilt weighed heavily already.

"That boy is much trouble," muttered Telfair distractedly.

"It's alright," Wolfwind said to comfort his friend. "Erstchester will bear the brunt of it, and the blame will flow down the ranks." He shook a gloved hand to add to his point. "I'm sure Silverface's attendants got their ears torn ragged. What were they doing? It's a good lesson to the boys gawking at all that wild magic. Don't think any of us have seen such a sight before. Need to stay on guard always."

Telfair nodded with a slight smile to his friend and urged his horse forward a few paces. The mare's coat shimmered black in the torchlight with small splotches of white inflecting the lower legs. "Thank you. I shall scout ahead," he said, raising his hand to deter Wolfwind from following or sending an escort.

Telfair had another sense of foreboding, one deeply hidden from Wolfwind. Tomas Telfair had a son. A son he had seen once. Despite efforts to the contrary, the pressure of memory would flood through the cracks of time and regret and when he would see any young boy attended by a doting father. He remembered the softness of his own son's face, fingers, and breath.

Thavodyn had been constructed when Telfair was an apprentice at the Academy. Years later he welcomed the assignment to the black fortress, isolated from the rest of the country, and was able to lose himself in the open expanses, rocky crags, perfecting of potions and healing salves, intensive horticulture, and running the infirmary. He meticulously took to expanding water storage and preserving its lasting potability. Occasionally he would make rounds to Thavodyn Park and the surrounding homesteads to treat common ailments, set bones, sell low-dose potions, or teach farming techniques to those scratching the rocky soil near Sutler's Creek.

Telfair had made the fateful decision to abandon his own blood. To aid his forgetting and penance, he enjoyed missions like this where his senses heightened in the present and where he undertook responsibility for the care of others.

As then a young apprentice of the Order, his illicit romance and child were discovered by internal agents. The woman and the newborn had been bundled off by members of the Order and sent where, he had no idea. In years of reflection, he figured that this dalliance had been known of for months and, whether out of kindness or spite, the night of the child's birth, his son was taken away. It was Ardalen custom not to name a baby until a twice passing of the two moons. He sometimes wondered, wished, and then hoped that the child was not named Tomas.

He assumed the Order threatened the woman never to reveal the identity of the father or both mother and child would be dispatched as an unsightly blemish to the Order. Tomas only protested meekly when the woman and his child were ushered away. He never sought out the woman or his son. He was never really sure if he regretted the experience or just the inconvenience of the whole affair. He denounced the woman and child and confirmed his loyalty to the Order. The Archmage, in a magnanimous mood, offered forgiveness. Telfair's training continued.

Each time he contemplated the decision, he came to his original conclusion. He marveled at the magical wonders that were revealed to him and the working of the world. That he would never freely give up. This bond endured through all else, but in melancholic moments, part of him mused at the impossible trade of a prior lifetime to spend time with his family now. Having spent decades climbing a steep and snow-deep mountain, he found the summit to be more and more lonely.

But that was the proposition; to achieve a semblance of ethereal mastery demanded total focus, total commitment. Having knowledge of magic and having a family were not mutually exclusive in the absolute, but when offered the chance to unlock the mystery and knowledge of the world, all else had to drop out of focus, or one was not serious about the endeavor.

The Order did not tolerate split loyalties; there was no room for defiant ideas or dissension. Rogue members had nearly split the Order at several points in its history. Severity and restriction created the bulwark against corrupted power, devouring narcissism, and the destruction of the world. Initiation and standing in the Order rested upon humility, obedience, sacrifice. Loyalty and devotion to the Order, total focus on arcane matters, and defense of the nation were the steadfast virtues. Within these principles, members studied from a common body of knowledge painstakingly assembled over the centuries but were allowed great measure to explore, experiment, and retain their individuality.

Over its centuries of existence, the Order forbid relationships or intimate contact between members. Walled off from amorous relations with those in closest proximity, uncurtailed temptations led to sneaking out in a still moment or at night. This led to attempts at blackmailing or smearing the reputation of the Order. Swift, and sometimes messy, correction to such matters followed. Celibacy was tacitly encouraged. Rare, discreet, disguised visits to the whorehouse did not bother the Archmage. This type of jaunt had its own utility to test the subterfuge of the members.

Offspring among those in the Order were forbidden and would carry banishment or worse. The Order did not like to see the initiated just walk out the door under any circumstances, even if it was to have a family of one's own. There were those in the extended ranks of the Order, such as servants and the men-at-arms, who could have children and families, but not those in the inner circles.

Telfair often wondered where his son may be. Telfair may even be a grandfather now. A disturbing thought flashed that his son and grandson may be up the road now. With all of his knowledge, if he were to encounter his son, or an unknown descendent, would he recognize them? For all his superb command of arcane elements, would Telfair be able to detect his own blood?

There were faint whispers that the Archmage had a daughter, but this was a question that was never asked. If the Archmage did, then he did his duty with exemplary commitment and put the Order first. Telfair could find no fault in his leader asking others to hold themselves to the same standard of restraint and obedience. Among those brazen enough to whisper on the streets of Ravalas, some said this rumored daughter of the Archmage was confined in a Starfield. Telfair knew that could never be the case. If the Archmage did have a daughter, he would not turn her keeping over to the clergy and permit them power or blackmail over him. Given the Arch-mage's advanced age, any offspring could already have passed.

Far ahead but always within view of the troopers' firelights, Telfair rode by himself until he reached the marker stones and then waited patiently for Wolfwind and the squads to close up. The trundling of the carts could be heard as they stuck to the stone-paved road.

Periodically setting aside his own brooding, the wizard did not detect the presence of any observing eyes. Even so, he thought, let them watch, better still, let them try their luck and see how long they survive or maybe just writhe on the ground and scream for mother.

"I'm here." Telfair raised his arms, but no reply came.

Blue Allen snorted in the chill and instinctively stepped close so his rider could lean towards the wizard. Wolfwind said, "Quiet night now. Let's not make it more work than it needs to be. Don't go drifting out like a log on the tide." Wolfwind grabbed his friend by the wrist, and Telfair looked up and nodded.

Telfair led his horse in front of the forming line of horse-men. He stopped at intervals and touched the bridle's bit on several horses. A dull red light slowly started to emanate from the bits to push away the darkness. The horses were well trained and not startled by the lights.

"Alright, Boys. Snuff the torches and mind the lanterns," called Wolfwind with growing excitement. "Let's ride out and meet our friends." Two of the squads did not attempt to keep pace and instead stayed close to the carts as well as leading Stomper, the Tovenward's light bay warhorse.

Wolfwind gave Blue Allen a gentle brush on his mane, and the prized stallion nudged out from the line at a quick trot. The horses moved in formation, but then Wolfwind grinned and spurred Blue Allen to push the pace. The two moons peeked out through the clouds, and the Master of Horse let out a playful howl.

"Wolf! You'll spook the horses," called Shaver, a burly squad leader, as he urged his horse to match the strides of Wolfwind's fleet dapple blue gray. "How long you want to keep up this pace?"

"They're still miles ahead. We won't spoil their hunting. If there's a siege, there'll be few chances to stretch our legs like this," Wolfwind said with a wild-eyed glint.

Shaver spurred his horse and propelled it a nose ahead of Blue Allen. Blue Allen bit playfully at Shaver's horse and bolted ahead. The horses and riders knew the ground well; these night races were a favorite pastime for the troopers. The red light, which was difficult to see at a distance, illuminated enough ground ahead to give the horses comfort. The troop had covered more than two miles, and still they raced with the wind. The ride was a reprieve, a chance to feel the exhilaration of the night air.

War, betrayal, and the looming siege vanished for the moment, yet pieces, important pieces, were missing from the ride; thoughts of Vardy, Hagedorn, and the other Southwestern men from Wolfwind's command locked in the jail recalled him to the present. Erstchester restricted the number of people who could visit the jail, and Wolfwind was ordered to stay away.

"Whoa! Halt! Halt!" called Wolfwind. "What is that?"

The troopers pulled the reins to slow their mounts.

A beam of light on the horizon shown straight up in the sky.

"Someone knock over a lighthouse?" joked Shaver uneasily and looked to Telfair for assurance.

"Is that the Tovenward's signal?" wondered Wolfwind.

"No," said Telfair. "He would not be so undisciplined. Something else is at hand."

"What do you suggest?" inquired Wolfwind.

Telfair fixated on the origin of the light. "That's probably where the apparition gate opened. Someone may be mapping the pathway," he said with apprehension. "Have your men ready their weapons, load crossbows. I must get closer, but we should move with caution."

"Weapons ready. Loose crescent formation," said Wolfwind as the message was passed down the line.

The group approached to within a mile of the light source. Telfair had dropped the reins to his black mare, his eyes rolled back into his head, and he chanted softly.

The beam beckoned to the riders and seemed to cut through the clouds, reaching high into the sky. The men gripped their lances or cradled their crossbows, fingers close to the trigger.

A faint arcane wave lapped against Telfair's mind.

"Tomas" came the pleading call from an ethereal voice. "Tomas."

Telfair's eyes fluttered and snapped ahead. "Falanika!" he called and kicked his horse into a full gallop. In what seemed little more than an instant, Telfair was fast approaching the source of the light. He saw Falanika crouched down over another person.

"Tomas! You must help him," screamed Falanika.

Telfair jumped from his horse and came running forward. Jarvis was ghostly pale, vomit streaking and congealing in his shirt. His head bounced erratically, and, when it rolled towards Telfair, the wizard saw a faint gold light radiating from behind Jarvis' eyes.

Telfair hesitated and squinted for a moment at the sight of the illuminated eyes. He was not sure if it was Jarvis' state or Falanika's response which unnerved him more. Telfair had never seen her in such visible distress.

"Be careful," she exclaimed. "The shield attacked Thiepval."

"What?"

"Oh Tomas, you must do something!"

"What is that burning smell?" said Telfair as he cautiously approached to within a few feet. He started to look for burns, but Jarvis was slick with sweat and vomit.

"The leather covering of the shield seared away. Energy from the gate awakened the shield and then went into him."

"Are you sure?"

"What else could it be!" she snapped back.

"Are you able to touch him?" Telfair said in the matter-of-fact tone of a physician.

"Yes. He is shaking tremendously. I've been unable to stop it." Falanika spoke helplessly and pointed to a leather satchel that she had placed to cushion Jarvis' head.

Telfair nodded and knelt down to inspect Jarvis. "For how long has this been happening?"

"It started when I touched the shield. It would have started a grass fire."

Beyond his work as a military physician, Telfair had years of experience treating crazed and afflicted kaldoons, battling with and studying many arcane abominations created by depraved elves, or saving the common lot from the corruption of black sorcery. Yet more bizarre occurrences, he thought, astounded at the night's unfolding events.

"Been a long while since I've been a witness to such a concentrated force," mulled Telfair. Since the end of the Disorders three decades ago, he had not felt such a powerful force conjured by anyone other than by Mage Farcloud or Archmage Stadrys.

Telfair billowed his long coat but carefully avoided touching

Jarvis. He pulled a lime-sized bottle with a broad, corked neck from a sturdy pocket. He gripped the bottle filled with a pale purple and white mixture and considered his next move.

Falanika tried to steady Jarvis' head.

"Keep those eyes pointed away, would you?" advised Telfair. "This batch is six months of labor and refinement. It's a heavy sedative, but no telling if it will work on him. I know it will save some of our troops. Consideration for Thiepval and the others must come first."

Telfair looked towards the approaching troopers. "The carts are still a way back. There's so much magic coursing in him, this sedative may just vanish like paper in a fire."

"I think it's best to wait," added Telfair as apathetically as he could, although contentedly if the young man did not return to Thavodyn. "All this convulsing may break his back anyhow. I don't know if we have any choice. He may not even survive the trip back."

"So, the great potency of your healing magic has met its match? You don't have a slight bit of interest in understanding what is going on around you?"

"Can we do something about the shield?" fussed Telfair.

"Sure, go ahead and move it. Extinguish the light," said Falanika heatedly.

"We don't need him. We're better off without him," Telfair finally said. "The shield wasn't made for him."

"And what do you think happens to the shield if he does not make it?" pressed Falanika.

"The stories never spoke of that." Telfair started to place the bottle in a pocket.

"Give him the sedative," demanded Falanika as she grabbed Jarvis' head tightly to control the seizures. "Do it!"

Telfair glared at her but did as he was told. He forcibly pulled down Jarvis' jaw and gradually poured the liquid.

Jarvis seemed to calm slightly, but his eyes remained illuminated.

"Do you have another?"

Telfair fished out another bottle. "How are we going to transport him back? Maybe we can place the shield on top of his chest. Why don't you go get it?"

Falanika stared daggers at Telfair and then looked at the shield with deep suspicion.

A trample of hooves drummed in the night. The troopers curiously peered at the scene, not ready to fling themselves into an unknown danger until summoned by Telfair. Wolfwind formed a perimeter guard and signaled three squads to press ahead to find the raptor force.

"Gold cat shining brightly," blurted Shaver in disbelief.

"Well, a lion is most active at night," said Wolfwind bemusedly. "Get a damn cart up here!"

CHAPTER 15

"Get a good look," chuckled the captain raising his hand to signal the troopers to stop. "Ever see a turtle move like that, Piper?"

An old woman, heavily stooped, feverishly hobbled across the field, arms frantically waving.

"Why stop for an old biddy?" jabbed Piper.

"I'm hungry. All this riding uphill," griped one of the troopers. "Let's see if she has a pot on."

The captain led his long-range patrol towards the woman, her crackling voice not yet forming words.

"Sirs! Knights!" she exclaimed breathlessly as the horses loped across the clearing.

"No one else around," called a wary trooper.

"Fine soldiers." The elderly woman straightened up to meet her mounted and mailed guests. "I saw you coming up the road while I was tending to my chickens." She put down the pail of feed and bowed slightly in her homespun frock and apron. In an excited and conspiratorial tone, she declared, "I

174

have a man here, a true hero, half-dead, mumbling in his shadows that the Tavuros are in Sawmill!"

"What did you say? How many?"

Pleased that her revelation had the desired effect, she touched her brow and looked to the sky. "I found him shivering, still wet with the river, pale and whispering to Indalos. Lucky the fish did not eat his toes. I saved him, I did. I had sweet Burris drag him back home. Only a woman can save a hero," she warbled.

Her mood fluttered abruptly. "My daughter and grandchildren are in town. I hope they are safe. Have you been to town? I think someone would have sent word." She strained her eyes to the horizon, but the town sat beyond and farther up the mountain slope. "My grandson, Owen, is in the army. Do any of you know him?"

"Grandmother, be still a moment. How many of the enemy are in the town?" snapped Piper.

The old woman ignored Piper, more interested in examining the faces of the troopers to see if any knew her grandson.

"Who is this man you saved?" asked the captain in a tone which regained her attention.

"Jon Heward." The woman seemed surprised that the name did not illicit an immediate reaction. "You should know him. Big hero in these parts. I never met him before, I thought he would be taller. He is in a bloody fog but coming through. I think he knocked his head on some river rocks. I did not want to leave him and with my bent leg, it's hard for me to go over the ridge. Sweet Burris is blind in both eyes and don't fare the rocks and roots well neither."

"Have you seen any soldiers?"

"You are the first."

"How many other people are here?"

"It's just me since Ambros passed. He was the best tooth

puller in the whole valley. Folk would come from as far as Echo Gorge and Farmingwood to have him pluck their sore teeth. Gerta, my daughter, comes to check on me every now and then. Don't get much visitors like we used to," she said with a frown.

"Charitable Mother, take us to this man you saved."

She looked back uneasily, surprised at the great distance she had traveled.

"We'll ride ahead. Two of my men shall escort you back home," offered the captain.

The cavalry patrol trotted forward across the thin upland pasture and surveyed small stands of pine and aspen surviving both fire and saw, low walls of stones pried loose from the soil which marked now empty and lichen-spotted enclosures, modest garden rows, gnarled apple trees, a steep-pitched house swaddled in flower beds of oranges, old gold, and purple, a chicken coop, and other graying outbuildings. An old nag list-lessly raised its head at their approach.

The soldiers, many of who were recently assigned from remnants of the royal army to bolster the garrison at Middle-post, fanned out in martial readiness, still holding a nerve-fraying level of alertness from the past several days. As they approached the log and plank house, they encountered only hens which readily gave way as their rooster quickly aban-doned his show of bravado and retreated to the safety of the coop.

The house door yielded easily. The scent of smoke and herbs lilted in the darkened room. A great stone hearth nestled a few crackling logs deep within. The captain spied a man lying on the floor in the fold of a threadbare quilt. His bandaged head resting on a straw-stuffed pillow only turned slightly as several pairs of heavy riding boots thudded over the threshold.

"Jon Heward," called the captain.

"I am."

"Captain Aubrey Trefsayer, His Grace's garrison at Middlepost."

Heward let out a long, deep sigh of relief, and his thoughts poured forth. "I am an old liner. I was at Pelham, too. I led men in the clouds, did my part. A Tavuro, a skin changer, attacked me in town. He took Grady's face," he said with rippling anguish as he jerked to sit up but collapsed back.

"Is there anything you require? Are you well cared for?" asked Trefsayer as his men inspected the iron pot by the fire and helped themselves to a heel of bread on the table.

"Well enough."

"Why do you think the skin changer was a Tavuro?" asked Trefsayer tearing a dried corner of the acorn bread.

"War." Heward slowly exhaled. "If you are here to finish the job, make it quick," he said with suspicion.

"Padazar turned traitor and threw in with the Tavuros. The Southwest is in rebellion," explained Trefsayer. "You are with friends. The men here are loyal to Ardalencor and Eadolan."

Heward grimaced.

"Do you understand, Heward? We could use your help," said Trefsayer pointedly. "How many soldiers entered the city? How many Blackbirds?"

"Birds?" Heward murmured.

"Men from the Southwest. How many entered?"

"Don't know about any birds. I only saw a few, three maybe. Some officer, one of ours. My mind is all shaky."

"Three in total?"

Heward nodded slowly.

"The skin changer could be an Ardalen, some Blackbird," pondered Trefsayer.

Piper, the troop's second-in-command, gave Trefsayer a considering nod. "Or a Tavuro." He scraped a broad wooden spoon through the iron pot. "Mushroom, carrot, leeks, and some other kind of onion, I think," Piper said after a long, reflective slurp.

"Thank you, Boys," said a voice from outside. "That would have been a great hardship." The elderly woman returned home with two troopers steadying her through the door.

"How long has he been here?" asked Trefsayer.

"Two days. I found him towards the chicken coop. I thought he had been lying there a while," said the elderly woman. The intensity of the recent days now showed distinctly on her face as the two soldiers helped her to a chair. "Too much adventure at my age."

"The town could be crawling with Padazar's men and Tavuros by now," worried Piper.

"We came all this way just to roll down the hill? Worth taking a look and mustering some local forces if we can. I'm just not going to hand the country over," vowed Trefsayer.

"Take me with you," Heward appealed.

"Sorry, Brother, hate to disappoint an old liner, but you'd slow us down. You're not fit to ride."

"Take me with you. I can gather the boys from the hollows."

Scratching his short auburn beard, Trefsayer demurred.

"I can spot the skin changer. I'll know if people in town are being true," cajoled Heward. "I'm a tough old stump. Give me some help to sit up. Just mind my left side." Heward for the countless time felt for his missing ring, but he again figured it was lost somewhere in the rush of the river. "Hand me my clothes," he said, wildly searching the room.

"How can you spot a skin changer?" asked one of the troopers who tossed him his tunic. Heward pushed his fingers through where the skin changer's knife had pierced and sliced.

Looking directly at Trefsayer, Heward said, "I saw his real face, and I've been around kaldoons enough to sense them.

Stealing faces takes its toll. Skin gets a leathery look; most just think it's from sun, too much pipe."

"If you are planning to stay for a meal," the woman said nervously as she saw a trooper sniffing around some clay pots on the shelf, "I won't be able to feed you all. Please don't kill my chickens, and Burris deserves better than that."

"Captain, I think if we spend another moment here, we'll miss the whole war," muttered one of soldiers.

The troopers laughed and discreetly pilfered a few small pots of apple and currant jelly which were passed out the door when the woman bent to remove her shoes.

Two of the soldiers helped Heward to his feet to finish dressing.

"Saddle up!" called Piper, and the troopers stomped out of the home.

Heward lingered a moment, knelt, and touched the hand of the elderly woman. "I owe you my life. Indalos works through the virtuous. You are an exemplar. I will never forget your kindness and I will repay it. I'll find your daughter and keep your family safe."

"A twinkle in the eye, divine stars in the sky," she said with a grin. "It was my pleasure to rescue a hero."

"Do you have some place you can go?" He recognized the absurdity of his question. "When I get to town, I'll send someone for you. Stay well away from the road. You've done your part." He gave the old woman a kiss on the forehead and invoked the abiding protection of Indalos.

Heward squinted as he immersed himself in the daylight. He raised a steadying hand to the doorframe.

"He's on wobbly legs, Tref," said Piper watching Heward emerge from the house. Piper casually moved his hand to get Trefsayer to turn around. "You believe him? Maybe Heward is the skin changer. You said yourself that maybe the skin changer could be Ardalen, and he didn't disagree with you."

"You ever been up this way before?" asked Trefsayer examining the unfamiliar terrain.

"No. You?" Piper leaned in closer. "Hey, maybe the old lady is the skin changer. You believe she dragged a man from the river?"

"Wring the shit from your brain," said Trefsayer. "We got to make straight of all this. If the Tavuros are in the town, there would be signs of a fight. Eadolan runs, and the Tavuros trudge up these mountains. Why here? Makes no sense."

"I don't see these mountainfolk climbing in the nest with the Blackbirds. They just want to be left alone and eat sawdust or whatever they do."

"We've got thirty armed men and a local hero to guide the way. If there are only three in town, then what a great service to the High Lord." Trefsayer slapped Piper on the chest. "We'd save the town. We could be knights," said the newly-promoted captain; there being a severe lack of officers following the disintegration of Eadolan's army.

"Yes," said Piper, eyes alight, grasping the reality of the prospect. "Jola's father would have to give his permission. He'd have to, right?"

"How could he refuse a glorious knight? In the meantime," winked Trefsayer, "there'll be plenty of mountain girls who'll enjoy spending some time with a knight."

"Heward," said Trefsayer. "Can you ride?"

"Yeah," Heward said, expecting a horse of his own.

"Jump on with Lisk. He's skinny. There should be room for you both. Lisk, stick close to me and Piper."

Heward frowned at having to share a horse with the pimpled whelp.

"We'll do the talking," said Trefsayer picking up on

Heward's displeasure. "You just tell us what you see. Don't want the skin changer having an easy way of spotting you. Lisk, give Heward your cloak. And Heward, keep the bandage on. It hides your face a bit."

"How far to the town?" asked Piper.

"Not far. Up this rise and a short stretch to the town; ground will level out as we get closer. Pilot Notch is off the main road towards the river. If the logs get bunched up, it's a spot to get things right. There's rare folk who live here and there in the backwood."

Captain Trefsayer and his men rode with glorious ambition to confirm Ardalencor's flag fluttering over Sawmill Falls and also with grave caution. Marching into unknown territory, Trefsayer wondered if they would encounter a welcoming populace or half the Tavurite army. The young man's mind swirled, and he forced an air of confidence with his men. Short of the gates opening and virgins rushing out with bouquets of wild flowers for the vanquishing heroes, he knew not what to do, but the road thus far was quiet, and it gave him comfort.

The emptiness of the road shattered as a man cradling a heavy crossbow emerged from the woods. The riders at the front of the column jerked their reins and started shouting. The man with the crossbow froze for an instant, his mole eyes straining wide, and then leveled the weapon.

"Tavuros!" the beady-eye man yelled and unleashed a bolt which glanced off the kite shield of one of the riders. The horses with spurs raking their sides thundered up the rise in pursuit. The crossbow spilled out of the man's hands. Perceiving a never-ending file of cavalry erupting over the lip of the ridge, he sprinted back into the woods.

"Orders, Captain? Shall we pursue?" questioned a trooper.

Trefsayer looked unsure whether he should command his men to dismount and give chase into the looming wood.

"Not worth the fuss. You hear the snapping branches? No ambush here. They scattered like squirrels," Heward remarked impatiently.

"We carry forth the justice of the High Lord. Show yourself!" called Trefsayer.

"Damn all. That was a heavy crossbow bolt," complained Lisk as he ran a finger through a groove in the shield.

"Precaution against galaswack. They were probably fishing," said Heward trying to suppress his irritation.

After several moments of waiting, four troopers dismounted and warily entered the woods. They returned soon after with two fishing poles and a chain with a multitude of hooks and gill-stretched fishes.

"A couple mudhuggers and a rock fish," observed Heward dispassionately.

Trefsayer and Piper exchanged glances. The other cavalrymen began to mutter.

"The road is open, Captain," discerned Piper.

"Right." Trefsayer reddened. "We ride with all haste to Sawmill Falls." He stood tall in the stirrups. "No stops until we reach the town square. Weapons ready, and make sure the flag is not all twisted."

The horses pounded in a lather through the thin mountain air. "Town ahead!" expectantly shouted Piper at the first sight of the myriad wooden buildings with their angled roofs poking above the log palisade.

"Seems quiet on the river." Heward gripped his head addled by the hard ride.

The scant buildings outside the town's wall were shuttered.

As the troopers approached the gate, "Identify yourself!" called a man in a fur hat on a raised platform behind the stockade. He was about chest-high above the log trunks which formed the wall. Two others quickly scrambled up to the platform and knelt down, crossbow stirrups and bolts poking out between spaces chopped in the wood.

"Open the gate in the name of High Lord Eadolan!" demanded Trefsayer.

"Cousin, we're glad to see you," said the man in the fur hat with a wide smile. "We got this gate blocked off. Lumber stacked high on this side. Would take a good while to move it all. Would you ride round to the other gate?"

"Any crown troops in the town?"

"We've had messengers warning of the dangers, but, no, we don't get many dignified guests," said the man with a slight bow and tip of his hat.

"Any sign of Tavuros or Padazar?"

"No, we've been keeping watch. Ask for Dobbins Pelt. He's the mayor. We're a small town. The other gate ain't too far. Begging the pardon of you knights for the trouble."

"Form column," called Piper.

Trefsayer waved to the man and signaled his troopers to ride around. "Not to worry, Heward. Your skin changer will be rooted out, if he is even still here. Pull that hood up and do give us a signal if you see him."

"Shouldn't we leave a few of our boys outside, just in case?" asked Piper.

"Why? The war hero thinks the skin changer is in town. The sapling at the gate said there is no one here. Why wouldn't we ride in with everyone? Leaving a detachment outside shows fear, like we can't handle this," snapped Trefsayer. "Numbers count to impress the yokels."

The troopers of Middlepost made their entrance to Sawmill Falls. Two men, crossbows held low, smiled and beckoned their arrival through the open gate. Inside the palisade, the street spread wide, broad enough for four carts to travel. Immediately inside the gate the grounds were relatively open: a small guardhouse, customs station, and a patchwork of mud and defiant grass. A string of small workshops, wheelwrights, carters, farriers, and some stables, marked the start of the town proper.

After all the cavalry entered, the gate was slowly closed. "Just a precaution," said a guard with a reassuring smile.

Trefsayer nodded. "Where is the mayor?"

"You'll want to keep to this road; it'll veer to the right and then," the guard stopped at the approach of another man who raised his voice above the rest. The other man in commoner's clothes stood in the middle of the road.

"Soldiers," the new arrival said, extending his arms. "Grateful for your presence. With whom do we have the pleasure?"

"Captain Aubrey Trefsayer, His Grace's royal army."

"That's not the mayor," whispered Heward. He was about to say more, but Trefsayer was not listening.

"Who are you?" inquired Trefsayer amiably.

"People call me Chat. I'm in charge of the defenses here. We got word of what's been going on. We want to make sure nothing happens to our town. Glad to see you boys here." He gave a scrutinizing look at all the troopers. "Any more coming up the road? We're obliged to any soldier sent to protect our home."

Receiving no reply from Trefsayer, Chat continued, "As you can see, we're still pulling our preparations together, but we like to know who is entering the town, as I'm sure you can understand. I have two short questions, and then I'll give you a tour of our defenses and let you meet the boys we've been mustering. If you have instructions for the mayor, we'll make sure you get to meet him as well. He should be along soon."

"Are you from these parts, Chat? How long have you lived in the valley?" asked Trefsayer.

"I thought you might ask me that. I blame my wife. Her mother and sister are sickly. They've been living with us for a while. I try to get out when I can, but I guess some of their southern speech has rubbed off on me. Hard to keep women quiet."

Trefsayer laughed.

"But you raise a serious question, Captain. You have any Blackbirds in your troop? I mean, still loyal to Eadolan."

"Yes, four. Good men. They love their country. This rotten soul, Padazar," said Trefsayer contemptuously. "They want no part."

"True bonds of loyalty," affirmed Chat. "Boys, let me get a good look at you. Want to make sure nothing bad happens as you get settled in here. Don't want you to get mistaken for someone you're not."

"Will you all be requiring lodging? We'll see to that." Chat quickly moved on without waiting for a reply. "Last question, you got any here with magical trickery? Anything special if the Tavuros show up?"

"I'm sure you can understand the urgency of our visit," forced Trefsayer with thin politeness. "Please lead us to the mayor."

"Of course. Please follow me. Mind your horses. The streets are a bit churned up in places."

Piper caught Heward's eye and gave him a probing look with raised eyebrows. Heward gave a shake of the head. "Not him," he said softly. "I don't know him."

The street remained wide, but the buildings started to pack in closer. Signs identified inns and boarding houses, and brothels leaned balconies over the street. A few men were seen on the balconies, blankets up to their chins with clay jugs and cups at their feet.

"Where is everyone?" wondered Piper.

"About their business. We were not expecting you," said Chat. "A compliment to your lightning approach."

The street narrowed as it leaned to the right. As Trefsayer's column began to round the bend, Chat threw an acrid, gray powder in the eye of Trefsayer's horse. The horse reared and nearly threw Trefsayer. Chat barely avoided the horse's flailing legs; he squinted, the cloud stinging his own eyes, and wrenched the horse's reins and bridle with all his strength, trying to immobilize the horse against the corner of a building. Chat leaned all his weight down an alleyway. The horse recoiled which served to lock it in place, its neck pressed hard on the rough-hewn logs.

"Mountain!" yelled Broadshield Chatton Holley, and more men began to move at their leader's signal.

Through watering eyes, Trefsayer fumbled with the reins, not quite grasping what had happened. Trefsayer's eyes grew large as men rushed out onto the street, spears leveled and kite shields interlocking to form a solid wall. He pulled hard at the reins of his bucking horse and tried to retreat back.

Trefsayer blurted a string of sounds to his men and attempted to draw his sword. With his right shoulder wedged against the building, his sword arm was rendered useless. He could not get off the horse either. The young man tried to draw the sword with his left hand, but it caught in the scabbard.

From amongst the buildings and back up the street from which Trefsayer's men rode, the same scene took shape, a wall of spears and shields closing in. The men seemingly sleeping on the balconies rose with short bows trained down on the trapped royal cavalry.

As Trefsayer still struggled with his sword, a spearpoint stabbed towards his face, and he smacked the muddy plank street in a slick thud.

"Sons of the Southwest, identify yourself!" called a man

from one of the balconies. "Hold your arms high. You will be untouched." He started to sing, "My eyes shine for Mira."

The four men raised their arms and instinctively began singing.

> *My eyes shine for Mira,*
> *a pretty girl is she,*
> *we'll plow the fields,*
> *tend the droves,*
> *and raise a family*

An arrow streaked down from a balcony and then another. Several of the cavalrymen tried to break the shield wall and flee back towards the gate, but they were confronted with deep ranks of spearpoints.

Caught in a tightening trap, few continued to resist. Troopers slid off their horses and begged for mercy. The four men from the Southwest under Trefsayer's command refused to partake in the slaughter but forlornly continued to sing in self-preservation.

> *My heart leaps for Mira,*
> *As fair as there can be*
> *and in caress*
> *by water's fall*
> *she declared her love for me*

A small group who survived the first attempted break-through jumped off their horses and slashed them in the hindquarters to propel the wounded beasts towards the shield wall in a vain attempt to break open an escape path. "Rally Ardalencor! Don't die on your knees!" called a soldier as he and a handful of men desperately hacked at the spears and shields.

Heward spun and jumped off the horse. He tried to aid Lisk but, as he went to help him off the skittering horse, he was greeted by a stream of blood. Heward grabbed Lisk's sword from the mud-sopped street. He crouched low, surveying the scene around him. Spearman swarmed from all sides and made quick work of Trefsayer's vanishing command. A spearman struck Piper while he fended off another attack.

Heward stayed low and hacked at the shin of a Southwesterner. Heward rose to his feet, his body surging with the desperate will to live. The old liner swept aside a lunging spearpoint and then evaded the attack of another assailant.

"What madness is this? You craven. Who are you? I'll die on my feet, you cowards!" Heward gripped the sword with both hands and spun in a circle, wondering where the challenge would fall.

"Come forward," said a stout soldier tossing aside his spear and drawing a war hammer. The soldier swung the war hammer, and Heward jumped out of the way.

"You bastards!" Heward grunted. "Log dogs! Boys, hear me!" his frantic scream trailed into a deflated gasp.

Two arrows smashed into Heward, one below the rib cage and then one in the center of the back. He fell forward. The weight of Heward's words seemed to linger. Chat lifted his eyes to the sky, wary of a reply to Heward's call.

"Get these bodies removed and burned far from here, especially this one." Chat pointed to Heward. "Spread word that Tavuros tried to infiltrate the town with captured standards, but their plan was foiled."

"Wait," said Ocklef as he and a man with a leathery face emerged from the shadowy folds of an alley. "We will interrogate the captives."

"Are there any left?" said the man in a low rasp as he examined the carnage.

"The town will understand that it was attacked by Tavuros," agreed Ocklef. "Jon Heward was killed. A Tavuro, a skin changer, murdered him and assumed his spirit. We spotted the insidious trap and protected the town. They have Padazar's men to thank for that."

"Drift," Ocklef said to the man with the leathery face. "Pick a few faces and learn them well."

CHAPTER 16

High Lord Eadolan and Duke Urric beat a frantic pace down the main road. In Middlepost, more carrier pigeons were dispatched to Darhax and Ravalas to make further preparations for the High Lord's return. The exhausted mounts and saddle-sore knights reached Darhax as night fell on the third day of travel.

The following day was given over to rest and readying the army for a feted return to Ravalas. The men were fed a thick beef and barley soup and given leave to visit renowned establishments in the shady narrows of Darhax's cobbled streets. The bone-tired horses were washed and brushed by an ever-growing throng of retainers, stable hands, and townsfolk who rallied to their High Lord. After the recent traumas, Eadolan felt a measure of relief to be back in lands most familiar to him and loyal to his family.

"The country is with you, Your Grace," Duke Urric exclaimed at the outpouring of support as he surveyed the camp laid out in the rolling fields just beyond the city.

Commander of the Lifeguards Alwyn Lyjos nodded and

said, "Indeed, my High Lord. Please excuse my momentary departure. I must go check on the preparations of my men." He mounted his new horse, a Swiftmane gray, recently arrived from the royal stables in Ravalas. As Lyjos trotted off and watched those tending to the horses, he said to himself in his elven tongue, "Will those who now wield comb and bucket fight under the banners?"

Watching Lyjos descend the hillock, Urric said, "Do you recall, Your Grace, when your father taught you to ride?"

"What? Yes," said Eadolan brusquely with a dismissive look.

"No, I mean the very first time." Urric assumed an avuncular tone. "Your mother thought you still too young to ride so your father and his closest friends, myself included, took a ride out from Ravalas. You went in a little wagon as we headed to the fields west of town."

Urric paused in the hope of regaining Eadolan's attention. "There not being a pony in the retinue put your mother at ease, but your father already arranged for one to be saddled at the Darhax stables and brought out to meet us. A shaggy little buckskin. Your father held you steady in the saddle, and I led the horse. I can still see it all clearly. In point of fact, it was not too far from where we are today that you truly first started to ride. I feel that your father is here with us."

"Where were the Boscawent banners? Why did so few heed my call?" demanded Eadolan.

"Your Grace?"

"Let me further test your recollection," said Eadolan starkly. "Do you recall the war with Velenharn?"

"Yes, of course," puffed Urric.

"Do you think we gave in too soon? Should we have fought on?"

"My dear boy, the whole of the Southwest was lost. Velenharn has ten times the people as we do. Our boys fought valiantly against long odds and made them pay. You made a difficult but very wise decision. Better to lose a few toes than the leg. Droswild struck a better bargain for us in the treaty than I thought possible."

"Later I heard Padazar had sent Latrobh across the Mountain Trout to retake the offensive. Why was I not told this?"

Urric spat at the question and whisked the spittle from his freshly shaven cheeks. "You can ask Padazar himself. Do you now find him more credible than those loyal to you? Eadolan, your distress pains my heart. Padazar's betrayal grieves me. It grieves me ever still to see you in this state. Do not believe those old lies about a southern offensive. It's pure hubris. Hubris is the escape of a defeated people. We were within a hare's breath of losing the whole Southwest. The Velens were closing in on the Avenbair and Ravalas as well."

"The enemy was nowhere near Ravalas. Crowiler and Crosstimbers checked the advance at Pelham." Eadolan looked Urric directly in the eye. "But the Velens were raiding into your prized lands in the south. The Southwest had much more fight in them than you did. Do you agree?"

Urric looked back in gaping silence.

"And your banners are late to arrive. Why are contingents of your vassals and men-at-arms just now coming up the road?

With feebly restrained emotion, Urric said, "How Padazar would rejoice to hear you ask these questions! By Indalos, I beseech you! Do not go looking for enemies amongst your dearest friends!"

Urric looked to the sky and fidgeted, trying to control the stampede of thoughts and find a prudent horse to ride. "Most of my life and uncountable sums of my family's treasure have been freely given in support of you and your family. What other noble family brings you such support? Stokes? Billengrath? Tarpley? Ajhax? The Boscawents have always supported the Arkwens. We have never wavered. Much of the cavalry with you now rides under the Boscawent bull. My vassals and armed men are traveling great distances. We have already seen many on the road these past days, and many more are close behind. Padazar will be crushed, and the Tavuros expelled from our country."

Wounded and aggrieved, Urric continued, "It makes me weep to have to state such a plain truth. Your father's last command to me was to protect you."

Eadolan's face quivered, but he composed himself. "I am sorry, Duke Urric. You and your house have delivered great support and comfort to my family. I know that you will fight to the last to defend Ardalencor."

"I am here to serve you, Your Grace."

Eadolan smiled, and Urric gave him a reassuring hug across the shoulder.

———

The following morning the High Lord and his loyal knights entered Ardalencor's capital city through the Arsenal Gate. To increase the size and sound of the army, noble formations and infantry met on the road had been turned around and forced marched back to Ravalas. Some formations of knights and retainers widely scattered during the battle had reformed as well to ride again beneath the High Lord's standard. In addition, scores of the Darhax Sentinels with their halberds and distinct black gambesons also found a place in the ranks.

Eadolan judiciously decided not to use the Processional Gate when he entered the city. This gate was closed for most of the year and reserved for triumphs, feast days, and events significant to the continuance of the royal family: births, weddings, funerals, and coronations. The current situation was no less significant, but the aura of devastating loss and retreat was not to be strung through the Processional Gate.

Prominent in the stone and brick archway of the Arsenal Gate, the city crest depicted three hares in full run across a burgundy field. The crest symbolized the founding myth of Ravalas when settlers' selection of a campsite scattered three hares across a heather field. According to the story, the hares took flight but paused after a short distance not wanting to abandon the idyllic location along the river. The settlers took this as an omen that the site indeed must be special to inspire such courage in even the most timorous of creatures.

Behan, Eadolan's younger brother and Royal Steward, and Lodestar Mathurin Mondray turned out the populace for the return of their High Lord. After the tumult of a generation ago and the recent war with Velenharn, the capital's population had swelled above sixty thousand with an influx of refugees fleeing marauders and devastated towns and hamlets. Rural resettlement and returning fields to cultivation met with mixed success as many preferred to stay within the immense walls of Ravalas. While swathes of Ardalencor had been severely depopulated, war only seemed to help increase the development of Ravalas, and the ready supply of labor propelled the city's voracious growth.

Under Behan's guidance, hovels and shanty towns gradually were demolished and replaced with properly planned suburbs. New wharves and drydocks were constructed and the Avenbair dredged to meet the needs of the expanding commercial center. To bolster the defenses of Ravalas, Behan recently commissioned surveying work for a new belt of fortifications around the enlarged city.

The clomp of iron hooves and drum beats of boot leather echoed along the thoroughfares of Ravalas. The blue-orange banners of Ardalencor hung in abundance from the brick and timber buildings. The majority of the crowds cheered and waved at the sight of the High Lord, but, once the thin parade passed, they grew somber for how few men still marched under the banner of Ardalencor.

The parade occasionally passed the smashed stores and looted homes of Southwestern transplants. A handful of men who had offered real and extrapolated critique of the Arkwen dynasty found themselves beaten, locked in wooden stocks, and glazed in overripe tomatoes and rancid cabbage. Behan and Mage Albright kept tight control of the city but permitted the mobs an occasional outlet to slake their thirst for convenient revenge and to gauge the level of support for the fratricidal struggle to come.

"Padazar and the Tavuros go where they please, but brave Ravalans," mocked an unimpressed woman to her husband, "High Lord Eadolan has returned home to show us that these shopkeepers will trouble us no more."

The path chosen followed the gradual climb up Shepherd's Hill. As the road widened on to Coronation Square, Eadolan, in his golden armor and diadem, led a force of around five thousand to ascertain the immediate safety of his throne. Duke Urric rode on the High Lord's right and was finely armored in gleaming steel plate, menacing bull heads prominent on the pauldrons. He wore a silver cape with a multitude of striding black bulls adorning its length.

At the other end of Coronation Square, on the top steps of the Starfield waited Lodestar Mathurin Mondray, Chancellor Weldon Droswild, Mage Elias Albright, and Sahalana, wife of Eadolan and High Lady of Ardalencor. Elven Lifeguards and members of the Zaravandian Order formed a relaxed but continuous ring of protection around the four. Supporting ranks of city watch held formation at the base and along the lengthy rise to the Starfield's porch. This Coronation Starfield, as it came to be known, represented the largest temporal portal to the Starry Fields of Indalos. Initiated twenty years ago, this enormous renovation and expansion project was a marvel to behold and, through its usurpation of Valmuros, created deep fissures amongst the faithful.

The national and spiritual significance of Valmuros was manifest in the history of Ardalencor and the Faith of Indalos. For centuries the city on the Mountain Trout River had been the center of the Faith of Indalos, the residence of the Lodestar, and the place of coronation for successions of High Lords, but Valmuros suffered heavily during the Disorders.

The Acclamation Starfield, the very first of its kind, and built on the site of the Four Acclamations which inspired the belief in Indalos, awed and strengthened believers by the fact that it still continued to stand. Although the ardent defenders prohibited despoiling forces from entering the Starfield, ultimately stemming the tide within a few feet of the doors of what would also be known as the Divine Keep, they were unable to prevent widespread structural damage. In the aftermath, Berislan, Eadolan's father, had convinced the Lodestar at the time to relocate his residence temporarily from Valmuros to Ravalas. To incentivize the permanence of the move, Berislan offered to fund the enlargement and remodeling of the formerly named Winter Starfield on the formerly named Clothbolt Square.

At the time, Mondray, Conservator of the Winter Starfield, outmaneuvered his rivals, including Woolfolk, in persuading the previous, and then ailing, Lodestar not only to keep his residence in Ravalas but also to move the religion's spiritual center to the capital. The move in some ways seemed to be fortuitous as the walls of Valmuros again came under siege during the war with Velenharn, but at the time the announcement sparked riots and nearly precipitated a doctrinal and physical rupture in the faith.

The change of the Lodestar's primary residence was one matter, but the ritualized abandonment of Valmuros with the relocation of the coronation rite and the transfer of the sacred icons, most notably, the original limewood carvings depicting the Four Acclamations and the Elosiquiad Chain, embittered many Southwesterners. Deprived of its ancient grandeur and privilege, the Acclamation Starfield refurbishment felt to many like the work of an old man attempting to claw back fleeting youth.

From atop the Coronation Starfield's stairs, a herald observed the pace of Eadolan's approach and with an arcanely amplified voice bellowed the names of the prominent figures waiting their High Lord's arrival.

When the herald said, "The High Lady, Sahalana," the crowd gave its loudest affirmation. A young woman in a loose-fitting amber gown and a gossamer mauve shawl waved and smiled to the adoring Ravalans. Sahalana, the Foreign Beauty as she was often called, mesmerized with black hair and porcelain skin. Her eyes bespoke a fragile elegance but also a protective strength. As she gracefully acknowledged the adoring crowd, cheers reached a higher pitch when she placed a hand on her long-sought maternal belly which sheltered the bloodline and a blossoming soul within.

Standing to the left of Sahalana, the Lodestar, the leader of the adherents of Indalos, was dressed in ceremonial white silk and iridescent blue velvet vestments trimmed and patterned in green and gold. Mondray stood serenely in cushioned gold slippers, raising his arms to encourage the faithful and habitually wiping beads of sweat from his brow. Except in the depths of winter, his thin face and loose chin radiated a pinkish hue. Standing in front of the great Starfield dome, his corporeal dome resembled a threadbare carpet. Sandy wisps, which resisted the creep of gray, lay wet and matted on his head.

"She seems to be faring better this time. Perhaps Eadolan will have an heir after all," whispered Mage Albright to Mondray.

Unsure if the comment had undertones of hope or sarcasm, the Lodestar remonstratively clutched his medallion that depicted the Starry Fields of Indalos. Sitting heavily on his chest, this symbol of station dazzled with finely encrusted blue opals, green diamonds, and yellow jasper.

"Is this the first time you are praying for the tranquility of womb or did the other times not work?" chided Albright.

The Lodestar glowered at the mage but just as easily swapped in a smile as his gaze returned to the High Lord's approach. At an opportune moment, Mondray leaned back in, his words wafting up through Albright's hedgerow of earrings.

"Careful, Elias. Lest it be thought by Eadolan and all the faithful that you and your Order wish ill upon the High Lady," Mondray said with icy severity.

Mage Elias Albright, second-in-command of the Zaravandian Order, posed tall and resplendent in a silver-gray robe and a cape of dark red. His oiled hair and bushy beard melded in competing shades of dark brown. Multiple small golden loop piercings sprouted from his ears: two on the lobe, three on the top. A wide belt rested snuggly beneath his abiding paunch of pastry and goose livers. A large oval warding eye served as the belt buckle.

Despite his penchant for indulgence, Albright had a muscled torso and framed shoulders. He powerfully held a staff fashioned purportedly of mammoth tusk and either the bones of a griffon or werewolf, depending on the telling. The staff, banded in silver, was carved with an old mystic form of Ardalen script which would be indecipherable to even the most literate Ravalan. The staff's top was shaped in the head of a wide-eyed maiden with long flowing hair spiraling the length of the staff.

When Mondray finally unlocked his stare, Albright gave a dismissive smirk. With still more on his mind, Albright bent down to his left to address the source of smoke puffs wafting towards him. "Will the bell be smoothly struck? A loud and resonant call?"

"Eight years crowned as High Lord and still held captive by the last person who speaks with him," the man said gruffly, not bothering to look at the mage, as his teeth clenched on the pipe for another long drag.

Chancellor Weldon Droswild wore a long goldenrod tunic with a pattern of multiple interlocking white circles. A linen belt of crimson and beige cinched the tunic. He sat dignified in a wheelchair crafted of imported cedar. His charcoal gray pants were hemmed at the left knee.

A half-orc servant, more man than orc in appearance, stood in blue and tan livery behind the Chancellor as he diligently studied and tracked the mood of the crowd. Droswild was an older man, but his short, curly butternut hair and beard betrayed no signs of the trauma which had befallen the rest of his body. He incessantly smoked a deep pipe to mask the lingering pain from the loss of his left leg. Despite his health issues, Droswild heeded Eadolan's request and accepted the office of Chancellor two years ago.

Droswild was much respected after having served Ardalencor well in customs administration in Floriana and then extensively in diplomatic service. Droswild, a Southwesterner by birth, ceded his place of birth, Brenvalbath, to Velenharn in the treaty which concluded the war.

"Where are you, ol' Blackbirds? On your way to meet us?"

he muttered to himself as he irritably blew acrid smoke through his nose and handed the pipe to his servant to refill.

Down at the base of the steps, the High Lord dismounted his horse, handed the bridle to a retainer, and ascended the steep stairs in a deliberate manner. Suspended from a braided velvet baldric, the Arkwen family sword scabbard shifted and knocked against Eadolan's leg. He placed a firm hand on the grip to steady the blade, the large purple amethyst in the pommel reflecting the sun's light in myriad directions. Urric and Lyjos followed the High Lord at a respectful distance as not to block the crowd's view.

"My High Lord and husband, it is good to see you well," smiled Sahalana as Eadolan rose from a courtly bow at the top of the stairs. The royal couple hugged as if seeing each other for the first time. The crowd cheered for the awaited reunion which was partially for appearances as they had met in Darhax the evening before. Eadolan smiled widely and felt strengthened, tenderly holding his beloved's hand as they acknowledged the crowd.

Twelve years prior, Eadolan's father, in deference to the long-standing Arkwen practice of arranging foreign matches for the heir apparent, arranged a marriage compact with King Pamurgen of Elotma. This betrothal of Pamurgen's third daughter to Eadolan gave Ardalencor an alliance with a strong naval power and a level of protection for the Floriana merchants as their ships plied more distant waves. This custom also preserved the superficial balance between the other prominent noble houses by not elevating one notional peer above the others through direct marriage to the High Lord. Other bonds of marriage to less eminent family members did link the Arkwens to the other major families of Ardalencor.

Sahalana had been a scandalous choice to some in Ardalencor upon learning that her maternal grandmother had been an elf. The enatic lineage found observable form in the High Lady's eyes and curvature of her lips. That no heir had been produced in over a decade of marriage was sign enough to many of divine disapproval. Despite Sahalana's exotic charm and the affection she had inspired among the people of Ravalas, Eadolan's unwillingness or inability to dissolve the marriage was also a source of much consternation.

As Eadolan finished greeting the other dignitaries in front of the Starfield, the herald, still wrapped up in the excitement of addressing the capital, looked to Lodestar Mondray for further instruction.

"Grab the speaking ring. We'll not profane our High Lord with some parlor trick cast about his regal person," said Mondray with restrained reproach.

The speaking ring, in fact two brass rings, one fused slightly inside the other, was held a few feet in front of the High Lord by two heralds to project the royal word. Eadolan cleared his throat and stepped forward.

"Sons and Daughters of Indalos. Loyal subjects of Ardalencor and your High Lord." Eadolan spoke with measured practice and then let his gaze wander across the shoulder-pressed sprawl below him in Coronation Square.

"Here we go, Lad. Strong and steady," Droswild murmured to himself in between puffs of smoke.

Mondray softly spoke the next words which drifted gently to return Eadolan to his work.

"We have again been stirred from peace by an enemy invader," proclaimed the High Lord. "This time the intruder enters our home with the help of deceitful brothers. This is a breach of duty to their sovereign, their nation, and their very souls!"

A roar of denouncements rushed up from the crowd.

"Fear not. The gate has been barred at Thavodyn. The

Archmage and our army hold the walls. We shall drive the invader from our home. We will deliver justice to those who betray their High Lord and imperil our lands. Let it not be said, and let it not be shown in deed, that the traitors desire our lands more than we resolve to keep them!"

"I declare," Eadolan pronounced with heavy anger, "Horace Padazar to be an outlaw and all his family lands and titles forfeit."

Eadolan motioned for the crowd to quiet and hear his next words. "Mustering sergeants are at all corners of Coronation and Feneric Market Squares. Every man who signs up will be given a parcel of traitor or Tavurite land at the conclusion of the war."

The crowd cheered, and the cheers of Duke Urric seemed to rise a bit higher than all the rest.

"I ask for your unwavering support. There is no safety in timidity. Brave souls and ready arms are needed. The preservation of your home is found only in swift action. Your High Lord needs you. Ardalencor needs you!"

Eadolan glanced at his wife and then towards the skyful fold of Indalos. "May you look upon me," Eadolan whispered upward to his father and mother and those ever before him. The High Lord pulled the sword and raised it skyward. The light through the amethyst flashed across Coronation Square.

Albright nodded approvingly at the sight. The sword called Dominion was presented many generations ago by Rhodwyt, a founding member of the Zaravandian Order, as a symbol to cement the alliance with the Arkwen dynasty and to acknowledge the fledging Order's primacy in arcane matters. While the pommel had been repaired and refashioned over the centuries, the blade was the original. Rhodwyt labored for nearly a year, it was said, meticulously working, shaping, and infusing each bend and fold of the metal with arcane force.

Eadolan lowered the sword and placed it horizontally in his upturned hands. "I pledge before Indalos, my ancestors, and all gathered that I will not rest, that I will not stop until all foreign invaders are driven from our lands and traitors punished for their treason. This I pledge," exclaimed Eadolan and let the sword bite into his hands. He felt the steel sting, and then blood began to flow. He pressed his hands tighter on the blade, letting globs and rivulets drip down his hands.

As Arkwen blood wetted the blade, it shimmered, and a translucent field of energy enclosed Eadolan.

The heralds nearly dropped the speaking ring so awed and unnerved by the display.

"Indalos, guard soul and soil," Eadolan said to a hushed crowd. "Ravalans! Ardalens! Are you with me?" Eadolan again raised the dripping sword above his head.

The crowd roared and began shouting.

"Eadolan!"

"Ardalencor!"

"Eadolan!"

"Ardalencor!"

CHAPTER 17

Inside the Starfield, Sahalana looked admiringly and worriedly at the depth of the cuts on Eadolan's hands.

Lyjos removed a tin disk from a pouch on his belt. "High Lord, if it would please you," the Lifeguard Commander said to his charge while motioning for him to open his palms wide. He flashed Eadolan an approving smile and carefully sprinkled coarse blue-green powder into the gashes. Lyjos clasped both of Eadolan's hands closed and placed his own hands over top. In almost a whisper Lyjos repeated a rhythmic elven incantation. Stepping back a pace, Lyjos asked Eadolan to open his hands.

The wounds closed pink and fresh as Eadolan held up his palms. "How about that?" boomed Eadolan with a broad grin. "I think that was a speech worthy of the Arkwen name."

All gathered for the council clapped and cheered.

"Well done, Your Grace! It is good to see you well. Have no doubt that the people are behind you," said Mondray.

"Your father would be most proud," added Urric.

"Splendid and befitting of a High Lord. Forgive me, but I

must return us to matters of state," said Chancellor Droswild. "Trawfarne's ambassador indicated that they would be willing to discuss terms of assistance, but he is not authorized to negotiate the terms. We would need to send a delegation."

Droswild cleared his throat. "Regarding Domariadin, as we know the Domariads are sympathetic to the fate of the Southwest and are at a loss to reconcile the current events. They have no love for the Tavuros, but I do not think they will declare in our favor. They, however, stated their commitment to keep the border closed and not permit the passage of Tavurite armies."

"Will they prevent Padazar from recruiting mercenaries in their lands?" asked Eadolan.

"Officially, yes, but I think it hard in practice to stop the movement of men in small numbers. As the Lodestar is acutely aware, the fate of Valmuros means something on the other side of the border as well." Seeing the worried look on Eadolan's face, Droswild added, "I don't see them violating our friendly relations and making common cause with Tavuron."

"And Velenharn? Our peace treaty was for seventeen years. Thirteen still remain, at least on parchment," said Behan.

"Corentin is very ill. A succession crisis is looming. Their attention is inward. As to matters within our borders, if I am the first to tell you, then I accept the target of your displeasure; Treasurer Braithwaite and some clerks left Ravalas shortly after your departure with the army. They are presumably in Delun or tucked away far from here. The treasury has been accounted for. What could fill only a few small chests has gone missing or perhaps southbound as it were."

Behan approached his brother and whispered in his ear. Based on their expressionless faces, Droswild was unsure whether Behan previously had informed Eadolan of the missing gold, but the Chancellor was not going to be accused of covering up the misdeeds of a fellow Southwesterner.

The bond of the two Arkwen brothers was readily apparent by their pale blue eyes, a gift from their mother. Behan was nearly as tall as his elder brother but of a slenderer build which was drawn into stark contrast with Eadolan presently encased in golden armor. Behan wore a slashed doublet of black with griffons in circular patterns of orange and gold silk and black breeches tucked into tall black boots with white gold fasteners adorning the sides. Behan's sandy brown hair and beard were both closely cropped. He wore a ring studded by offset star-shaped diamonds, two white and one purple, in stylized depiction of the Arkwen family crest.

Behan's wife, Avlina, daughter of Rafal Stokes, General of the Line of March, leader of the Ardalen infantry at Boruma, was not present to attend today's pageantry. Lachrymose and inconsolable by the capture and rumored betrayal of her father, Avlina opted to remain at the Royal Steward's palace with their two young daughters. Behan had an abiding loyalty to his brother and quickly acceded to his wife's request, in part, not to subject her to rumor and slander and also to limit overt reminders to the people of Ravalas that the other Arkwen brother had found a match presently more capable of securing the continuance of the family.

"Chancellor, what of the Tavurite embassy? Have you granted them safe passage to the frontier?" asked Behan trying to set aside the image of his weeping wife.

"The ambassador has requested leave. I offered him escort to Floriana. He can take the long way home. I will not vouchsafe a Tavurite retinue, no matter how trifling, to survey our disposition between here and Thavodyn."

"Careful, Weldon. Lest our envoys be treated in similar fashion," cautioned Mondray.

"Your Grace, may I suggest that you write to your sister. Pavtanarell can provide troops, and we can provide for their upkeep," offered Droswild. "I know the Pavtanari can be of dubious quality, but I think this can be easily arranged should recruiting efforts not fill the ranks."

The loss of a battle, the loss of my army, the loss of multiple provinces, the loss of loyalty of several noble houses, and my first move is to contact my sister to rescue me? Eadolan dismissed the thought, imagining the laughter across the country.

"How did my trusted advisors fail to uncover this treason?" snapped Eadolan. "Who is our ambassador to Tavuron?"

Not wishing to indulge the High Lord, Droswild said, "Drevell Swan," in a tone reflecting that all gathered knew the answer.

"Swan. Yes. Our diplomatic service seems to be staffed by Blackbirds," said Behan half-listening. "Who made that unfortunate choice?"

"Your father. And if you are referring to me as well? Your brother," said Droswild with annoyance, rapping his fingers on the wheelchair. "If you think me part of those traitorous fools, then throw my chair down the Starfield's stairs, and let the crowd tear me to shreds!"

Behan no longer could meet Droswild's eyes and spun his attention to Mage Albright. "Excellent smithing of the family sword. A great asset. Truly brilliant. Too bad you and your conjurers have not produced another iron pounder like Rhodwyt in your renowned Academy. How is that?" Behan shook his head in frustration. "With all your comet chasing and salt sniffing, you couldn't figure out what was going on in the country you are sworn to protect?"

For a while Albright stared at Behan and then lowered his eyes in apparent anguish.

"Your Order has proved to be as wayward as it is loyal to our family," chastised Behan.

Quickly recovering his usual pluck, Albright asked, "And

you, Behan, son of Berislan, Royal Steward, tell us what you heard from your network of informants?"

"We looked again over the recent messages sent by agents in Delun," Behan muttered, his eyes rapidly darting between Eadolan and Albright. "We now believe the messages to be forgeries. We think it months since genuine messages have been received. One of our couriers also was killed in a horse-riding accident near Swiftmane, or so we thought at the time."

"And the whereabouts of the other agents?" wondered Duke Urric.

"They are at the bottom of the Mountain Trout with all the other bones," Albright speculated with a mix of rebuke and grief.

"Were they turned? How much of the network is compromised?" asked Eadolan of his brother.

Behan's silence did little to mask his own worry and uncertainty.

"A common suspicion pervades all Southwesterners; they have a distrustful yet devoted disposition," said Mondray.

"Closer than toes in a sock," said Droswild. "Shared traumas have a way of binding people together."

The faint sound of an iron latch interrupted the discussion before Droswild could continue. The line of elven bodyguards near the main door rippled, beaded, and then reformed as a small group entered the Starfield. Court Chronicler Cadmus Quill traipsed a swirling path into the vast interior. His two attendants fretted as they struggled to keep a constant spacing while guessing in which direction the next foot would fall.

"High Lord Eadolan!" said Quill when he spotted the council and took a more direct line.

Briskly making his way to the High Lord, Quill motioned for one of his pages to open a wide satchel. Rolled parchments crisply peeked from the satchel's corners. When the page started to unfasten the hasp, Quill abruptly slapped away the man's hand and grasped a plain-looking glass disk clipped neatly to his own waistcoat. Quill seated the monocle and gave a surreptitious look around the Starfield's vaulted glass dome and across the vast interior.

Four pillars aligned to the compass points gave form to the interior and upheld the massive dome. Much of the marble pillars were overlaid with carved alabaster and gold leaf depicting the Acclamations, four separate occurrences of divine intercession which happened on the same day and originally retold at the lone crossroad of Valmuros when it was barely a village.

Adherents to the faith pointed to the truth and authenticity of the belief in Indalos as it did not have a central founder to serve as exclusive conduit for divine instruction. The four individuals who recounted their experiences, all separately but distinctly seeing the brilliance of a radiant starbolt close about them and hearing the name of Indalos carried in the light. These separate accounts confirmed for many the veracity of the message. Word of the Four Acclamations spread gradually, and a doctrine slowly codified in custom and practice centered on the virtues of duty, perseverance, repudiation of evil, sanctity of life, and cultivation of the land.

Forgetting his initial purpose, Quill shifted his eyes between the pillars to admire their beauty. To the north, an old man defending his flock against a pack of wolves; to the east, a young woman blessed by delivering a healthy baby after concerns about the loss of both mother and child; to the south, a man enduring through failed plantings and then raising an abundant crop with green shoots readily growing before him; and to the west, a girl taming a horse which had been possessed by an evil spirit, and the expulsion of the evil by Indalos.

Each story revealed on the stout and soaring columns

depicted greater detail than that shown on the original paneled limewood carvings. A fifth wooden carving, long and slender, sat above the four panels and was carved with the sky and Starry Fields of Indalos. Marble masonry gave expanded form to the fifth image as well. A ring at the top of the columns joined with the contour of the ceiling. Rising up from the marble ring and across the open space between the columns, a blue-gold iron frame held clear panes of glass which reached wide and high to link the faithful with their divine protector.

Quill carefully trained his eye across a stretch of empty scaffolding and risers used by the painters and artisans. Returning his gaze to the lower levels, he briefly swept his monocle across the range of finished and half-finished paintings of exemplars. Exemplars were those ordained, most often posthumously, as the best embodiments of the doctrines of Indalos.

Along the walls reaching out from the main entrance were depictions of the formative parables from the lives of the Sixteen Exemplars. More men and women had been given the distinction of exemplar, and some featured more prominently in the art of local Starfields, but all followers of Indalos were expected to know of the renown sixteen, their piety and practical virtues.

Quill swung his attention back to the Starfield entrance. It had a low ceiling, as if he had just passed through a short but wide tunnel before stepping into the airy grandeur of the Starfield's interior. The mural along the entrance's walls and ceiling commemorated the defense of Ardalencor during a time which had been called by various authors the Dark Calamity, the Orc Wars, the Disorders, the Red Moon, the Disturbances, and then triumphantly entitled as the Vanquishing. This time of desperate struggle had created a brief period of unity between most nations to counter the overwhelming threat of servitude or death. This devouring threat which pervaded many continents began as an outgrowth of magic unleashed by two warring elven states, earning all elves increased enmity and suspicion.

Quill had spent his life recording the deeds of others, most significantly those of royal blood and doers of martial feats. While Quill was neither noble nor warrior, it was through the tireless exertions of his frail body which proved to be a strong sinew to bind the present with the past. He was lost for a moment, caught up in the scenes of a not-too-distant past. He admired the brilliant artistry: defenders of the Faith of Indalos painted in heroic detail and the Arkwen family and its sprawling side branches bravely leading the nation. Tucked in between the gallant soldiers were spellcasting figures banishing the great evil, but none in the Zaravandian red or others not fitting the orthodoxy.

Satisfied with the results of his inspection, Quill removed the ocular aid. "One can never be too careful," he said while re-securing the monocle with his ink-stained and age-spotted hands. In the jostle, long wisps of hair leaked out from underneath a floppy velvet hat with wolf teeth corded into the hatband.

"We have already checked for interlopers and eavesdroppers," said Albright with ill-concealed irritation.

"Harrumph!" grumbled Quill. His cumulative decades from clerk to Court Chronicler gave him a noteworthy scholarly curvature of the spine. Despite his age, Quill was still as sharp and inquisitive as in his youth. He lifted his broad face to straighten his bearing. His eyes had a lively glow as bright as candles when he met those of the High Lord.

"Your Grace, I bring to you with utmost speed the latest dispatches and messages received at the rookery."

The satchel bag was promptly opened, and Quill unfurled

a parchment. "This is a transcription of a message sent on the wing by Gann Goodwinds." Quill's eyes seemed to dim and droop as he re-read the content of the message.

"High Lord Eadolan, Sovereign of Ardalencor and Guarantor of the Chartered Cities, we trust this message finds you and your family well in this time of troubles. We write with pressing inquiry as to the disposition of the royal army and our militiamen who fought at Boruma. We have received distressing news from Commander Jerris, now captive at the camp of Padazar. We humbly inquire as to the measures being taken to secure the preservation and release of our men."

Quill hesitated and then resumed reading. "We remain true and loyal to Your Grace and Ardalencor and further pledge to send whatever supplies may be needed for our nation's armies, but we ask understanding of our precarious situation. With deep regret, we honorably inform you that we have no additional militia to send until such time that the abiding safety of our men already under arms can be secured."

"Cowards and traitors in all corners," snapped Behan.

"Where is the original message?" demanded Albright.

Quill gave a knowing look and tapped a buttoned pocket on his waistcoat.

"Forgive me, Your Grace. I must relay a second message. This one was written with less restraint. I shall skip much of the words included as the High Lady is present."

"Get on with it," said Eadolan.

"Tavuros are advancing in the Northwest. Camhorn Thorpe has abandoned Thornhelm. He has evacuated the populace into the depths of the Great Thicket," summarized Quill. "Thorpe complains as ever in detailed, flowered vulgarity about the lack of regular troops to guard the frontier."

Eadolan sighed heavily and raised his hand to stop Quill.

"Quite like those leaf lickers to go running at the first sign of trouble," said Duke Urric.

Quill looked ready to say more, but Eadolan said, "Thank you, Chronicler Quill. Unless you have more news from other fronts, you are dismissed."

"May I..." Quill's voice trailed off when Lyjos gave him a stern look.

Once the door had latched behind Quill, Eadolan grimly remarked, "We are beset on three fronts. Rebellion in the Southwest. A large Tavurite host before Thavodyn. Another Tavurite army at Thornhelm."

"Four," said Behan gravely. "The Chartered Cities refuse to send new troops. An ill-dressed plea for sympathy to hide a naked act of capitulation."

"How they cherish their privileges and then betray the very source. They are skittish and should regain their nerve in time if stronger men can show them a way," offered Droswild. "Summon a new militia levy. They'll be greener than goose shit, but summon them all the same, My High Lord."

"What about the second Tavurite army near Thornhelm?" asked Urric.

"Camhorn will need to fend for himself for the time being," said Eadolan. "The harvest is in. New formations can be raised and drilled. If we can hold until winter, we can counterattack in spring. What I urgently need are commanders. Where are Crowiler, Bernard Tarpley, Crosstimbers, Vraim, and most of all, Stokes?" he said with diminished energy as the list extended. Recovering himself, the High Lord asked, "Is Long-cloak still at Avenbair Castle? He is a commoner but capable."

"Summon him here immediately," said Eadolan to break the silence. "The other Tarpleys and the Pickfords will need to hold the line for now on the Leteb and in the Midriver provinces. Send more infantry to reinforce the group already headed upriver to Pelham and Croydon and hold tight the ferry crossings. Secure all boats on the southern stretch of the Avenbair or have them burned."

Urric did his best to conceal being parts embarrassed and relieved that Eadolan had not appointed him head of an independent army. Despite the apparent slight, the Duke knew full well that his position of influence was secure as Eadolan would rely upon the thousands of troops that Urric could still raise and equip from his estates.

"My High Lord, you know you have my tireless support to rally and to sustain the faithful," said Mondray. "Indalos has always protected us no matter how great the challenge. The conservators will speak this message from every Starfield and square, calling men to the spear and defense of our faith."

With the great care of urgent counsel, Mondray continued, "I think you have a fine plan, but it is just that. Calbaric Longcloak is to be fashioned a general? So be it. Armies must be raised, and we must be quickly on the march. This is the third time in your young life that invading armies have despoiled our country. I am filled with grief for our clergy and faithful. I received word that the conservators of Arandis and a few loyal soldiers have barricaded themselves inside the Starfield of the Bountiful Harvest. Whatever you do, do it quickly and free our lands. Crush the Tavuros, and Padazar's followers will lose heart."

Lyjos spoke in a low voice to ensure the Lifeguards would not be able to hear. "Your Grace, if you are open to considering a Castellan for field command." He paused momentarily. "What about the Castellan at Sevengate to lead our forces operating in the Midrivers?"

"What?" said Albright in alarm, not least at the Lifeguard Commander offering advice on who would command an army.

"Your son?" coughed Urric.

Lyjos glanced over his shoulder to see if his men had heard, but their disposition remained unchanged. Lyjos had expected a reaction, but the attacks seemed to fall heavier than anything he had sustained in battle. He felt unsure of his next move, having already ventured this far. "He is a decorated officer and of noble blood," Lyjos rejoined before Urric cut him off.

"You exceed the bounds of your station. Berislan had a soft spot for you. You have used his kindness to bore holes into our country and customs."

Lyjos flashed with contempt for Duke Urric and with the impulse to defend his family. "I have dedicated much of my life to the defense of the royal family. Rylar is the most skillful officer that the country now has in the south. He can take a small force and increase its effect. Keep Padazar off balance. My sons, Kalmon and Vedulien, serve in the Lifeguards. My family is entirely pledged to Ardalencor." Lyjos continued, distress cracking his usual calm. "I offer this only as a way to protect our country. It is in your silence that my voice is heard and that you claim offense."

"How much blood has been spilled the world over due to elven perversions?" Mondray shook his head in disbelief. "We all have our place in the creation of Indalos. Know yours. Do not presume to remake our country as you see fit. Your claimed marriage to Lady Talia Berryhill is unsanctioned. There is no record in any Starfield. I am sure you have heard the Four Acclamations many times, but how many times have you said them yourself?"

Sahalana looked with pleading eyes at her husband. In the High Lord's inaction, Albright seized the opening.

"Lyjos. You are one of the bravest of the brave," Albright began. "I have waited a long time to say this but remained quiet in such assemblies." With the Archmage far away, he relished such an opportunity to shed the restraint of many years. "You have opened the question." Albright's eyes narrowed and fixated on Lyjos as he spoke his next words. "My resolute answer is that you are an oath breaker."

Albright leaned heavily on his staff and pointed his finger. "You came freely to Ardalencor on the condition and vow to defend the High Lords and their families. This you have done, even defending this land against the abysmal scourges of disgraced elves; in this matter, I make no claim against you. But you have broken your oath. You have used your position to expand greatly the holdings of an impoverished noble family. You own land, engage in enterprise, and have made your purpose far more than just the defense of the High Lord."

"I take your military counsel as well-meaning but think it unwise, and it would not be taken well by the local nobility," said Albright relaxing his grip on the staff.

Lyjos felt his nerves tingle throughout his body. He fought to control his tongue and sword hand after such excoriations. The foreign elf glanced over his shoulder again.

Lyjos' searching look prompted a reaction from his soldiers. "Commander, is something the matter?" called one of the Lifeguards.

Mage Albright gripped his staff tighter.

"No. All is as it should be," Lyjos replied flatly to his son, Kalmon.

"Stop this," pleaded Sahalana. "Shall we rip each other apart in this holy place?"

"Commander Alwyn Lyjos," said Eadolan belatedly. "You have served the Arkwen family with virtue and distinction." Eadolan moved to shelter his own guardian. "I would not have reached Thavodyn without the aid of you and your soldiers. The sacrifices of your family and of your gracious consort, Lady Talia, do not go unnoticed. Your sons have provided vigilant service beyond reproach. Your daughter, Revna, is a fine young woman. Is she currently in Ravalas?"

Lyjos appeared thankful for the reverse of roles and the measure of protection provided, but his heart fell heavy when the High Lord used consort to refer to his cherished Talia. "No. Revna is away," he responded after a moment.

"Now," said Eadolan, "as to the question of command of the Midriver army. Rylar Lyjos is indeed the merited Castellan of Sevengate. He has been most effective against the smugglers bypassing Floriana and rogue kaldoons in the marshlands. Would you agree, Commander?"

"Yes, Your Grace," said Lyjos.

"Then I think it prudent to leave him at his present station." Eadolan turned to his brother. "Royal Steward, please dispatch half of the Sevengate garrison to reinforce the town of Tarpley. Send instructions to Roderick Tarpley to assemble what local forces may be gathered."

All members of the council wore dour, fretful expressions.

"Let us pray." Mondray invited all, especially Lyjos, to join hands in a circle.

"Lodestar, there will be time enough for that later," said Eadolan. "Mage Albright. All wizards will accompany the royal army. You will ride with me as a member of the war council."

Albright pulled at his beard in hesitation. "I cannot do that, High Lord. I received strict instruction from the Archmage that I am to remain and oversee the Academy. Votark and I will remain in Ravalas. The defense of Ravalas should not be overlooked. The siege lines are forming around Thavodyn. Forgive me, if I had not mentioned this before, but I received word from Tovenward Thiepval Bracelaw."

"Wonderful. You've finally named a new Tovenward," snapped Behan as he started pacing.

"Wizards and apprentices are provisioned and ready. Wizard Artos will join your war council. I have already made arrangements. Waydun is on his way from Floriana and will lead another contingent in support of the Midrivers."

"What of the wizards at Ravenroost? Farcloud is crazy and best left to his astronomical notations, but what of the other wizards there? Send for them immediately," demanded Behan.

Albright looked pensive and preferred not to speak. "Best leave things with Farcloud undisturbed. Ravenroost is a safe perch. Unassailable."

Eadolan and Behan looked at each other, at a loss whether to arrest Albright or stew in impotent rage.

"Mage Albright, it gives me great comfort, and no doubt to all in the city, to know that you and Mastersmith Votark will remain in Ravalas," said Sahalana graciously.

"Thank you, High Lady," bubbled Albright at the unexpected support.

Sahalana placed her hand on Eadolan's shoulder to calm him but in a deft, cultivated way as to convey deference. "My High Lord and Royal Steward, as you are seeing to the protection of this city, Duke Urric, may I make a request of you as well?"

"Of course," Urric said with great flourish.

"It would give me great comfort to have your lovely wife and son here in Ravalas. Kamila's presence will be a welcome blessing to me as we await our own child."

"My High Lady, I think..." said Urric with apprehension.

"It is well past time that Fost receive a proper education, one befitting him as heir to all Boscawent lands. The teachers at royal court have no peer."

Urric let out a warbling laugh. "Perhaps we can discuss this another time. Matters of state are more pressing."

"Duke Urric, you have already acceded to my request, and I shall hold you to it," said she with a demur smile.

Shallow beads of sweat formed on his brow as he twitched like a cornered animal. "My son is not well. Any journey may worsen his condition."

"I shall not hear of a sick child as precious as your Fost suffering a moment longer. A detachment of Lifeguards will be sent to protect your family. One of the royal physicians will attend to whatever ails him."

"I offer our services as well. We can care for him very discreetly at the Academy," said Alright helpfully.

"No!" stammered Urric. "No."

CHAPTER 18

Bambenek, Dronor, and Bayard trudged on bleary-eyed. They had said little since leaving the Darienwood and coming across the still smoldering frames of Pinemeadow. Few survivors had been seen on the way to Talonglade, the next major settlement located at the edge of the Great Thicket. Those fortunate to escape could manage few words beyond that the Tavuros had razed Pinemeadow and marched the remaining population westward.

"As recent experience has taught us, best to stay within the tree line," said Bambenek. "We'll enter the Thicket and loop around to reach Talonglade. I'm sorry, Dronor, two, maybe three, more days on that leg, but after this open stretch we'll be back in cover."

A shallow grunt was Dronor's only reply.

"Maybe more made it out," said Bayard breaking the silence when they eventually reached the beginning of the woods. "Maybe we just have not seen them."

The Great Thicket lived up to its name. Beneath the high twisting canopy, a dense undergrowth of ferns, thorns, bright green moss and clumps of broad orange fungi carpeted the deadfall. Bambenek gave Bayard a skeptical look as he scanned for disturbed flora and signs of passersby.

The forest seemed to pull the travelers in as they waded into the thick underbrush and close press of trees. Bambenek led the way, making a trail and judiciously slashing corridors for Dronor.

"Well, I need a rest," said Bayard as they moved along a narrow game trail. "Can we stop here for a bit? My feet are killing me."

Dronor shot a glance which made Bayard reconsider his words. "I mean, it would be good to see what share of the plunder we got from the battle. Never really did a proper tallying of what we have. Maybe trade amongst ourselves and know what we can barter for food in Talonglade," he sputtered.

"You'll not want for food in these woods," assured Bambenek.

After a short distance, they reached the outlines of some forgotten hunter's camp. Bayard put down Dronor's shield and emptied out the contents of three saddlebags. Sergeant Farrior had overseen the distribution of the battlefield spoils, but at the time all three had been too preoccupied with more immediate concerns to give their share more than a cursory look.

Bayard started to sift and sort out the three small pyramids. Each varied in composition, but the total catch contained earrings, some with nubs of flesh still attached, Ardalen and Tavurite copper coins, flint strikers, a miniature statue of a cat, small coils of rope, a tiny mirrored glass in leather binding, a tin of horseshoe nails, a small pliers, a crimper, a set of needles, two spools of gray thread, a small knife, a ring fashioned of bone, a fist-sized cube of salt in a folded cloth, fragments of three gold teeth, an assortment of cubed and triangular dice, four small pearls, a gouged but still dazzling ruby, dried and shredded leaves wrapped in parchment, an empty pewter flask, moldy drinking skins, and a silver shoe clasp ringed with ragged shoe leather.

Bayard did not display the few personal effects of his fallen friend, except for a talisman of Indalos which he wore around his neck. The talisman and all the other items he planned to return to Arvid's parents one day, but for now he was headed in the opposite direction, into the unknown. The ravages inflicted by the Tavuros on the common folk were a new sight for the young man spiraling him between panic and resolve in his choice to follow a scout and half-orc into the forested depths.

The past several days of roiling pain and prolonged marching had dashed the thought of treasure from Dronor's mind, but now the half-orc covetously eyed the trove of redis-covered possessions. He eagerly sifted through his portion. Dronor opened the parchment and sniffed the shredded leaves. After a few more sniffs which brought a faint smile, he stuffed the whole mess inside his lower lip and kneaded the softening glob with his tongue.

Seeing Dronor in slightly better humor, Bayard seized the moment. "Say, Dronor, well, I was wondering. I'm from Amberfield, but you probably already knew that. I was wondering where you are from. You speak Ardalen well enough."

"I spent some time in Trawfarne," he slurped and spit, while contemplating his next words. "Couldn't tell you every-thing before that. It comes and goes on the dark sails of the moon, sometimes I'm on a ship, sometimes," he caught himself. "Latgalen is a good city, but I had enough. I was dock muscle, protection for whatever merchant paid the most. Once you are in Trawfarne, picking up Ardalen isn't hard. You hear it some-times in Latgalen."

Dronor stopped suddenly when Bayard looked away.

"Bayard!" the half-orc instantly recalled the young man's attention. "When you look like me, you can't afford not knowing what's being said around you."

"Heard there was work in Jevatryn with the Queen of Lace," Dronor said with a curling grin, "but I never stopped there. Royal paymasters were offering real coin when I landed in Floriana, and I joined your army mustering at Stokesbridge."

Bayard tousled his scruffy blond hair and smiled. "The Queen of Lace. She's a real beauty. I heard her daughter is as well. Dallen would always talk about bedding them both, but I don't think he'd ever been near the city. She could buy Amberfield a hundred times over."

In a cracked and bruised hand, Dronor scooped up a pearl and ruby and slid them inside his padded jack along with his cut of the coins. He benignly shifted through the other items and held up the bone ring for closer inspection. After a light investigative bite, he gave the small ring a disdainful look and flicked it towards Bayard's pile.

"Don't be so quick to part with that," offered Bayard. "You could probably trade it in the next village. Some milkmaid may fancy it for a necklace. Would you be interested in swapping it for some of these dice? Always great for passing the time."

Dronor grunted and motioned for Bayard to toss the ring back to him.

Bambenek had paid little concern to the saddlebag treasure and paced around his two companions while looking into the woods. "No sign of any livestock tracks or our people."

"If you saw Dronor coming, do you think you would run away, too?" said Bayard in partial jest.

Bambenek smiled. "If we happen to encounter any of our people, if they're simple folk, let's not bother them and just press on."

After a few more moments of arboreal study, Bambenek

said, "Alright, enough admiring of shiny objects. We best get moving. Pack up."

Dronor shouted in pain as he stood with the help of his two companions. Bambenek now fully comprehended the cumulative drain of vitality from the long journey.

"Bayard, go get some branches so we can fix that leg straight."

As Bayard obligingly headed off, Dronor fixed his slate eyes on Bambenek. "Why are you doing this?"

"Might be time for Bayard to carry your axe for this stretch. He is having a hard time with the shield, and he can help clear brambles. I'll help you sling the shield over your back."

"Hey!" Dronor pushed the shield back at Bambenek's chest. "Why are we walking through this fucking forest? Why all this trouble for me? Desert the army to help a half-orc?"

"Do you want me to leave you here in the woods?" said Bambenek with an icy snarl as he threw the shield to the ground.

Dronor took a step back at the unexpected response.

"Nothing to say? Put your shield on your back. I have my reasons."

The men were not facing each other when Bayard returned but, seeing the shield discarded on the ground, he immediately sensed the tension. "I'll carry the shield," offered Bayard as he approached with a handful of branches.

Dronor sniffed twice and jerked his head around the woods. The half-orc growled. "Smells like—"

Bambenek picked up on Dronor's concern and spun in all directions. The scout fixated on a point deep in the woods. He unsheathed his sword and moved it to his left hand and readied his curved knife to throw.

Thundering footfalls shook the ground and quivered the tree tops.

"What is that?" said Bayard as the brush started to rustle. "A bear?" he said with a perplexed look.

"A demon!"

"Bayard, give me the shield!" demanded Dronor.

Bayard stood wide-eyed as a massive bear with glowing yellow eyes propelled straight towards him.

"Bayard. Give me the damn shield!" yelled Dronor.

Festering boils covered the bear. Withered, rotting gray skin had consumed most of the healthy flesh with scant remaining patches of brown fur. As the bear charged, sallow orange claws dug deep grooves in the forest floor.

Bambenek moved to avoid the onrush. With a running step, he launched his long knife and struck the bear in the upper flank. The necrotic bear let out a low bellow but barely slowed, fixated on the squire.

Dronor pushed Bayard out of the direct line of the impending charge, and the bear lurched to a near stop as it shifted direction. The force of the shove sent Bayard careening to the ground and scampering to hide behind the oaken shield.

Dronor roared at the bear. The intensity of the shout dissuaded the bear from pursuing the spindly squire and forced it to take stock of this rival for forest supremacy. The bear raised to its haunches. Dronor heaved his double-headed axe towards the center of the bear's chest. The bear timed its riposte and swiped at the incoming axe, catching more of the haft in rotation than the blades.

"Shit!" was all Dronor could muster as the axe harmlessly thumped to the ground.

Bambenek ran forward with his heavy sword and slashed at the back of the bear's knee. The bear winced and smacked Bambenek with a sweeping blow, sending him crashing to the ground.

The bear dropped down to all fours and landed a paw on

the oaken shield. Bayard let out a blood-curdling shriek as the bear scratched at the shield. "Help me! Help me!"

The bear roared. The malignant girth of its breath rotted the shield instantly, turning it to the consistency of parchment. A foul paw pressed on Bayard's stomach.

As the bear went to bite Bayard's face, Dronor swung his sword towards its open jaw. The half-orc sheared through rows of teeth with an arcing strike. The bear started to pull away, pus and blood squirting from its gruesome mouth.

The bear choked out a dripping roar and turned towards the half-orc. Seeing what had become of the shield, Dronor dropped the sword, recoiled and tried to cover his face. The enraged bear limped and rumbled after Dronor. As the bear started its pursuit, Bayard swiped wildly with his sword and caught the bear's foot just enough to slow it an instant.

Calling forth the same magic used in the fight with the Tavurite cavalry, Bambenek tried to ensnare the bear with entangling vines, but they immediately desiccated on contact with the corroded flesh. He swore and tried to shake his foggy vision. Bambenek ran forward as Dronor frantically limped between one tree and then another that quickly were gouged and splintered by the rampaging bear.

Bambenek closed an eye to steady himself. With a broad target he plunged his sword into the bear's hip. The bear wailed. Bambenek evaded the bear's kick and worked the blade deeper. He dodged the anticipated claw attack and continued to saw at the leg. The bear attempted to twist but thudded to the ground, finally succumbing to the totality of blows.

Dronor rammed his broad knife into a shimmering yellow eye of the beast. Sinister energy started to crawl up the blade. Dronor jumped back in panic, releasing the knife.

The bear ceased to move, but all over the massive beast a dark energy tingled in the motionless carcass.

"Fire." Bambenek removed a tinderbox from a belt pouch.

"Burn everything that withered in the fight." Bambenek removed his cloak and tossed it over the bear's head. "We need to bathe the blades in the fire to purify them. Just a light pass once it's going." With the relief of laughter, Bambenek said, "This one is a bit larger than the more benign variety of Ardalen brown bear."

The front of Bayard's surcoat was on the verge of disintegration. He ripped it off and placed it to help fuel the growing fire and then hurried to gather more kindling. As the fire crawled from tinder to cloth and eventually flesh, the stinking mass reverberated with the shrill howl of an evil spirit.

Voices in the distance echoed through the woods, a string of words not recognized by Bayard, but Bambenek seemed to know how to reply.

As Bambenek and Bayard scrounged for more wood to complete the bonfire of the corrupted bear, a small group of people sprang through the bush. One of the new arrivals gently placed multiple silver-green fern boughs on top of the heap. Another man with cupped hands and with the aid of a few phrases created a flame and directed it to the existing fire.

Three of the new arrivals stood in a triangle around the bear and began chanting. The slowly growing fire immediately heightened to a full conflagration.

"Who are these people?" asked Bayard in a hushed voice.

"They are the healers," responded Bambenek softly in reverence.

"Fire is only part of it," said the group's leader, a woman with braided, golden hair, as she walked closer to Bambenek. "Evil will always seek to coalesce and return. The application of Hunbertys leaf will purge the evil to a far greater degree and forfend its return."

"Do you know where the bear's den is?" the woman inquired.

"He paid us a visit," Bambenek replied dryly.

"There are still seeps of evil magic in these woods. Remnants from the Dark Calamity. We are trying to purge them all out, but it is a slow process. Poor bear picked a bad spot for a den. Did you come across any others like this?"

"One was quite enough," exclaimed Bambenek. "We need help. We have come a long way."

The woman approached Dronor with a disconcerted look. "We must move quickly. If you can make it to Talonglade, we can see what is possible. I can make no more promise than that."

CHAPTER 19

"Heavy weights at work," mumbled Castellan Erstchester watching from atop the Duskwall Gate the gathering dust clouds converging on his fortress.

"Beg your pardon, Castellan?" apologized Constable Dunbar as he sorted pages of duty rosters. "Eight hundred and ten able bodies to defend the walls."

"And nearly as many to open the gates," remarked Erstchester gloomily. "What did the Tovenward say about the people now in the garrison?"

"Too much confusion during the night of the battle. Something could have been left in any of the buildings but would have to be sharp and clever with wards or cloaks to keep the Order from noticing it," Dunbar replied without annoyance. Despite the repetitive question, Dunbar shared his Castellan's concern. "The wizards checked all remaining with the garrison for magic somesuch or signs of spellbinding. Only Jernivan so far."

"An embarrassing reminder that we must be alert at all times." Erstchester looked over his shoulder with uncertainty towards the citadel. "The wizards have that poor boy locked in a room. I don't think Jernivan has raised swords with Padazar, but he may be our undoing from within." The Castellan kept his eyes high on the citadel as members of the Order started to gather by the signal beacon.

"We can't look through every thread and stitch, but myself and the other officers have performed random searches," offered Dunbar. "We've tried to be discreet, part of inventory checks."

"Bad for morale if we allow suspicion to take too firm a hold, but we must plan for the worst," said Erstchester dutifully. "This black rock is as stout as any, but the Archmage in his slippery wisdom built her with low walls. A fast ladder or a cat could climb these walls, but they'll have to cross bleeding ground to get here."

"On next watch, we'll start the rotations," said Dunbar trying to ease his Castellan's mind. "The troops won't have permanent positions. They won't be able to hear nightly serenades or bribes to open the gate. It'll also give us a fresh perspective on the relative strength of the fortifications. The newcomers are sprinkled in, always less than half of a defense group. Most are assigned to labor crews or as reinforcements to relieve pressure on a threatened area."

"The Archmage and Tovenward said they will have members of the Order patrol the walls every night as well," added Erstchester.

"Any word from Sawmill Falls or about Trefsayer's patrol?" asked Dunbar.

Erstchester furrowed his brow. "No, and I think Middlepost will be abandoned or surrendered."

"Excuse me, Castellan," said Cambrell Glover, Steward of Thavodyn, responsible for the maintenance of the fortress. "The carpenters are ready to install the palisades on either side of the gatehouse. We can wait. Don't want to cause you trouble with all the noise."

The Castellan stared blankly at his Steward. Thinking the Castellan displeased, Glover added, "We'll have all movable sections ready by tomorrow. Hides tacked on, too. Won't be any scrambles up a quiet ladder either."

"Very commendable," acknowledged Erstchester. His eyes seeming to gain a new flicker. "Trip lines?" he said. "Are the trip lines all set?"

"Yes, Wolfwind's troopers completed the last of them well before dawn. The Tovenward said the apprentices left a few surprises on the road as well."

***

"Brenio, that acid had some bite. Took a while, but Dahey and I were able to stop the corrosion and remove it."

"Good work." Eager to reclaim his helmet, Brenio motioned for Thiepval to follow him into the mustering yard.

Nearby a clutch of washerwomen, army camp followers who pleaded to remain in the relative safety of the garrison, sliced and ripped canvas tents into varying lengths for use as bandages.

Thiepval raised an eyebrow and pulled back the helmet, forcing Brenio to re-enter the arsenal forge. "Listen, you crazy fool." Thiepval traced his fingers over sections of the helmet. "The steel and the fibers of your padded coat are still sturdy enough, but the ethereal bonds, the wardings, have been eaten away in places."

Brenio listened intently. His patchwork of facial scars contorted disquietingly with each piece of information.

"And what remains may recede over time," continued Thiepval. "I've stabilized it." Brenio started to turn away, and

Thiepval grabbed his arm. "I can't guarantee it will hold. I would need more time and Votark's help to reset the ward."

"It will be fine." Brenio slapped him on the shoulder. "Thank you."

Thiepval eyed him steadily. "Do be careful. You are not invulnerable. Try to teach the apprentices some good habits and not take unnecessary risks. This will be a long war, and we will need you for the duration."

"Lad," said Brenio. "You worry too much, and you worry me. You are smart; and you'd be much smarter if you stopped chasing perfect."

"I'll be careful. I'll stay close." Brenio humored Thiepval. "If I fall, you can revive me. I know you would do a better job than Tomas." Brenio winked. "Give me that helmet. Let's go. You don't want to keep the Archmage waiting. You wouldn't want the apprentices seeing bad habits from their new Tovenward."

On the floor just below the citadel's signal beacon, the Archmage sat on a low iron chest and leaned forward. The door to the small room was closed. Malu pondered what she would say next as she strained to stand as tall as she could to appear at eye level with the Archmage.

"I did it to save Brenio," Malu said exasperated, choosing the simplest answer. The truth.

"Was that the only way?" The Archmage picked up the fused crystals again as if examining them for the first time. "If you are tired after such a short fight, what then will you use? This may prove to be a long siege, and an even longer war."

Malu did not reply. She heard the footsteps outside the door and the muffled voices of Falanika, Brenio, and the others as they climbed to the top of the citadel. She wondered what they must be thinking. Malu felt nervous to speak lest they conclude what was transpiring.

The Archmage waved his hand to regain her attention and raised his eyebrows. He assumed a more serious tone to maintain her attention. "These crystals are unusable. Good that you have more, but don't count on resupply from the Academy." He dropped the fused crystals back on the iron chest with a thud. "There will always be another battle. You must always be prepared for the next battle. A wizard must always take the long view. You are not a wizard yet, Apprentice Littlecheek; but you did well. Brenio was worth saving," he said with a kind smile.

Malu nodded. "Yes, Archmage."

"Now, let us join the others." The Archmage pointed to the door. "The footfalls have passed. Go ahead, and I will join you shortly."

A short while later, a long, gray-white lock of hair and then the wizened and bearded face of the Archmage appeared from the stairway that led to the highest level of the citadel. He dressed humbly in a coarse gray robe which would be worn by an aspirant to the Order. The robe was not even that of a formal member but worn by one who caught the attention of the Order and petitioned entrance. An old length of rope served as a belt.

He grinned at the assembled members. Those now present were a fraction of the Order, but many bright examples of the fruits of his long life's work, his dedication to rebuild the Order.

"Please, there is no need for this." The Archmage waved his arms, inviting the wizards, apprentices, and attendants, twenty-one in all, to spread out and move back into the open space they had left in deference to him. He studied the construction efforts in the fort's courtyard, the vigilant watch on the walls, and the flat, empty landscape beyond. No trees. No two stones stacked one upon the other.

His eyes lingered for a moment on the billowing and rolling clouds up the main road. The Archmage finally began, "Of all places, let the battle happen here. We must make the enemy plow resources into this rocky soil and waste the season. Force them to winter outside the walls or retreat. We cannot stop the movements of cavalry, but any supplies during the winter and after the spring thaws require the main road. Much of the Tavurite army has ridden east, but even still they cannot ignore our presence here." He returned his eyes to the assembled Order, but his thoughts remained on the horizon.

"Our country is pulled in many directions." The Archmage's thoughts extended beyond the rocky field. "Some of our fiercest warriors and best commanders find our High Lord to have dishonored them and despoiled tradition. Our land is ravaged by the enemy. Merchants push seaborne adventures while fields lay fallow and abandoned. Countless other cracks and rivalries swell to new life by our family quarrel." He moved his head very slowly and looked each in the eye. "We defend the mysteries. We defend our culture. They shall not pass from this land for the people and the land are one. You must see yourself in this way, as an eternal protector, a member of the Order. You must see past the sun's daily rise and fall. Do not wait for some man on a horse to save your nation."

"Many in Floriana, half the population of our largest city," the Archmage emphasized each word, "were not born in Ardalencor. In some quarters you will scarcely hear a word of Ardalen spoken. What of it really? Floriana is our lone seaport, our watery cord to the world. Why would we not expect those along far-flung shores to visit, to trade, and still to speak their mother tongues? Many an Ardalen trader earns profitable gain, and many a noble kitchen contains exotic spices and peculiarities of all manner. But we must consider matters beyond coin and cooking pot. To foreign minds, Floriana is just another outpost to brim their pocket, a dot on a map in a spidery trade network, a spot of land where they have wharf and warehouse. For me, it is my country."

"Their level of affection for our country must be assessed correctly. What bedtime stories are told and in what language? Do their children dream in Ardalen? Have they heard Ballatane's tale? And better yet, can they recite it? I am focused on the course of the future. Will we absorb the world or will the world absorb us? Foreign banners shadow our lands, our own brothers betray us, and as we defend in the west, what is occurring in the undefended east?"

The Archmage looked at the giant Ardalen flag on the pole anchored into the basalt citadel. "Does a man have true roots in this land? Will he be toppled over by the slightest breeze, or all too eager to drift along? If things are changing all about him, would he even see it? If our country continues to fall prey to foreign powers," a great pain streaked the old man's face, "or disappears from the map, would he know how to reconstruct it? Would he want to? Is Ardalencor worth saving?"

"Are you giving us up for lost?" demanded Brenio channeling the collective anguish. "I'm not!" All gathered quickly added their affirmation.

"Good," said the Archmage. "I would not have expected any other reply. I am very proud of you all. I have dedicated my life to all of you, and to Ardalencor."

"We must understand that we are in a far worse position than when the Velens crossed the border six years ago. Our country is far smaller than Velenharn, but we were unified."

Several nodded in agreement. An old attendant said, "Many fell in the last generation. Bravery and prowess not so easily replaced."

Thiepval shifted uneasily at the old attendant's remark. "We are at your command, Archmage."

The Archmage nodded. "Now what is to be done about all this? Are we to bleed the Southwest dry and destroy them? Are we to content ourselves with a Tavurite treaty where the Southwest is cleaved away? Neither of these can occur."

No one else spoke for a moment. Tired of the silence, Falanika asked impatiently, "What are you suggesting, Archmage? Mage Albright's letter said Eadolan has already declared Southwestern lands forfeit and open to settlement."

"The Southwesters are a different kind of Ardalen, too cunning, too resourceful to see them perish," the Archmage replied. "The Ardalen spirit flowering in those river valleys is like no other where our word has taken root. We must draw the Tavuros away from them and seek reunification." He paused. "Who will do this?"

"We have no spies in their camp, at least, none whose word has reached us," said Thiepval.

"Spies or not, I don't see Eadolan agreeing to this without the Blackbirds paying a heavy price," said Telfair.

"Well, he must sooner or later. If we come to the same conclusion when we are drenched further in blood, then truly we will be unable to defend our frontiers," said the Archmage. "Eadolan is gathering a new army. We must do what we can to give him time. If he defeats the Tavuros, the Southwestern soldier may abandon the cause, not wanting his farm to be turned over to another."

"I agree with Tomas," said Falanika, her voice rising with disbelief. "I don't see other nobles agreeing with leniency. Padazar killed or captured their men, fathers, sons. How can this ever be forgiven?"

"Padazar can go and some other leaders. Fat-fingered Ray. Latrobh, now, he is too valuable. We need him. Who do we have? Stokes is too predictable, unimaginative. Crowiler is just moustache and sword. Slash everything. Latrobh wins battles with shovels or boots before a single arrow is loosed."

"I don't think they made this decision lightly," barked Brenio. "I think they damn well understood their decision. Eadolan will lose the throne in a thousand other ways if he gives favorable terms to traitors. I know these people, and I fear a return is only possible if the Southwest is bled and broken."

"Giants grow wise when much harm is done," chimed Malu repeating a smallfolk adage.

Archmage shook his head. "Best to bring the Southwesterners willingly back under the tiger. If we need to topple the mountains to convince them, they will only be trapped wolves biding their time."

"So, what do you recommend, Archmage?" asked Telfair folding his arms.

"Winter provides a man with time for consideration and cooled passions. The Tavuros will seek winter quarters. Let the Tavuros and the Southwesterners huddle close against the howling chill, and we'll see how much common cause they share. If Eadolan does intend to fight again before winter, the battle will be east of Thavodyn. He must win, or the whole country will be open. But if our country is dependent upon a few noble families to hold it all together, then what kind of land do we really have? We must tie down a portion of the Tavurite army in observation, if not outright siege, of Thavodyn. If they don't engage in an active siege, we will strike at their supply lines."

"Every soldier watching the black rock is one less out for rape and ruin," concurred Brenio.

The Archmage continued, "The successful raid by the Tovenward and the raptor force made ignoring Thavodyn impossible. We must ascertain the whereabouts of Padazar and the Southwestern forces. If we must fight a small war, so be it. On the harshest winter nights, we will seek out the enemy and give them no rest."

"Towns and villages occupied by the Tavuros may rise up if we support them. The Burzina Monastery may still be holding out," said Thiepval. "I didn't see any monks in the retreat."

"I fear all those in Burzina have perished," despaired the Archmage.

"Small war or not," offered an apprentice to break the silence. "The Southwesterners know our tactics."

"Yes. Would they be willing to share with the Tavuros?" questioned another apprentice.

"I think they would only share just enough," added Thiepval.

"Who will abandon Padazar and return to the flag?" the Archmage prodded.

"Not Latrobh. For him to listen, we'd have to win crushing victories. Shift the battlefield mighty steep, almost to where he'd slip off the edge before he'd consider kneeling," said Brenio.

Thiepval was lost in his own thoughts for a moment, questioning his leader. Was the Archmage formulating his own policy? Is that why he refused Eadolan's order and remained at Thavodyn?

"Latrobh commands iron. Woolfolk compels souls," said Thiepval. "The Tavuros will maul all they touch. If the Lodestar were to offer concessions and to mend their rivalry, that may work. I think there is limited time where Woolfolk would condone the spilling of the faithful's blood. He will need to account for his own deeds before the Starry Fields, and any prior deeds will not redeem recent conduct."

The Archmage nodded at Brenio and Thiepval. "And who could establish this contact?"

"If this were known, it would cast doubts on the Order's loyalty and undermine our standing," said Thiepval.

"No one is discussing placing Padazar on the throne. We are only discussing willingness to open a channel," the Archmage clarified.

"What about releasing some of the Southwestern troopers from the jail? We could be convinced of their loyalty and return them to duty. They could break away during a patrol and join their brethren," offered an attendant.

"I can think of a few who would be up to the task," said Thiepval.

"Send me," said one of the elderly attendants. "Send me."

"You expect them to believe that after sixty years you've had a change of heart?"

"Well, they've never given me the opportunity before. We've always been on the same side as I recall," the attendant said with a pitiful chuckle. "I am an old man. I've lived a good life in service to the Order. Talking is the right course; at least, try. I dare say Padazar can't be killed quietly. Nestor and his harvesters couldn't come anywhere near Padazar. He is too well protected. Those dogs will sniff out any magic or poison that I've ever seen. Maybe that Jernivan Shield, that might be something. Undetectable to even a dragon," he said with a trace of regret, having never had the opportunity to see one of the great scaled beasts.

The attendant continued, "I can gain their trust and find the right time. I grew up not far from Shimmering Orb. As kids, we called that crystal or whatever it actually is, the Dragon's Eye." He motioned theatrically, opening his hands by his eye. "My sister and I would watch the young divers trying to reach the depths and listen to them long into the campfire nights about new ways they tried to protect their eyes in the bright depths. I can tell Padazar I have discovered how to get it out."

"Quite fortunate timing," smirked Falanika.

"Really? It's early in this war, and I'd switch sides to help my home. I'd have no reason to reveal a long-held secret until now anyway. I'll tell them that we know all about it, and the Archmage ordered it undisturbed. Something like a kaldoon trap if anyone with half a wit showed up and took a real interest in it."

"And when they ask you to retrieve it?"

"Well, I'd hope to have talked to them about other matters before then. Maybe disappear along the way, but plant a few seeds about ending this whole mess. Just to let them know the door is open."

"You'd have to divulge too much about the Order for them to listen to you. No. I forbid it." The Archmage quickly turned to Thiepval. "What of preparations for the siege?"

"The defensive preparations are nearing completion. The garrison is ready for a fight." Thiepval looked at Falanika. "What news of our convalescent? Is the shield ready for our use?"

"I will not provide any more sedatives; he requires too much," interjected Telfair. "If he is now a moon-touched kaldoon, let's be done with him or remove him to a jail cell."

"The shield is connected to him; at least, it's starting. The energy portal, Thavodyn, revitalized the shield, but it's, well, I'd say it's disoriented. When awakened, I think the shield expected to find its battle companion," Falanika mused with dramatic flair," the great, great whatever relative, but instead it found Jarvis. It's a masterful piece of work; the bloodforge still holds. We did not waste time learning about it."

"The secrets of the shield are only revealed to those of the Jernivan line. At least, that's what the stories say," Falanika pondered. "I think the two can be separated, but I wouldn't recommend trying to wield or command it now. I need to determine how to switch the bond."

"Can't suppress what is in the blood. You can only destroy it," Telfair said.

"I think it better to keep him in the citadel," countered Falanika.

"Is he our distinguished guest until we think of something better to do with him?" asked Thiepval.

"He wouldn't be the first," grumbled Brenio.

"I won't have him guarding the walls," pronounced Thiepval.

"Can we move the shield and break the link? Just let it slumber again?" asked Malu. "What harm can it do locked away?"

"The citadel should prevent the transmission of magic so that link should start to fade if Jarvis is isolated from the shield, but remember the stories," said Falanika. "The shield was known to resist dragon magic."

"We don't understand it and don't have time for research. The enemy is here," uttered Thiepval.

"Archmage," announced Falanika. "I will continue to research."

"Your duties in defense of this fortress remain," said the Archmage.

"I will perform my duty. I will find time to study this shield, Archmage."

"No more potions," said Telfair. "They are needed for fighters."

"Done," said Thiepval, again asserting his authority as Tovenward and first wizard of Thavodyn.

"Wizards." Falanika looked at Thiepval and Telfair. "Don't worry. I'll solve this mystery and tame this lion. Without your help. And the shield is mine."

CHAPTER 20

Croydon's harbor stirred with activity. A discordant rhythm of thump, thump, thump pulsed as soldiers hurriedly jumped off their ships and onto the wooden docks. A flat-bottomed barge arrived at the next pier carrying warhorses; retainers and grooms readied the horses for return to dry land as soldiers secured a plank bridge. Another barge caught the attention of Conservator Woolfolk as a small mammoth and its mother embraced trunks, awaiting their turn amongst the multitude of river transports.

Croydon, the City of Clay, as it was known for the large deposits nearby, an important crossing point on the northern shore of the Avenbair, was now under Padazar's control. Beyond the harbor, the brick-lined streets were full of soldiers and porters hauling provisions and supplies while other materials of war were craned off the ships and then carted or moved by ropes and capstans up the streets.

The straight streets of square brick buildings cast a weighty presence of their own. In contrast to the sounds of the harbor and movement of Padazar's army, the town stood silent.

The town was an architectural sight with buildings intricately tiled in angled patterns, mosaics, and embellished with cool blues, greens, or lavish rose and pink, but the city walls were short and thin, more a customs barrier to regulate access to the harbor than intended to resist a siege. The royal garrison withdrew at the first sight of Padazar's army, and the remaining prominent merchants had already opened the gates when the first cavalry patrols approached.

"Your horse is ready, Conservator. The advance guard already crossed the Avenbair."

"Thank you. I shall be along in a moment," acknowledged Woolfolk. He glanced briefly at the shuttered second and third story windows and then waved off his guards as Jannon Padazar strode up the street.

Jannon gave Woolfolk a concerned look. "I have not seen you in over a month, and now you are headed back south?"

"You have not heard? The news of what happened in Arandis is spreading. I must leave for Valmuros. A number of conservators barricaded themselves in the Acclamation Starfield. No doubt Mondray's men are behind this. I cannot let this spread."

"When will you return?"

"As soon as matters are settled. I fear I will be gone too long and miss the battle for Ravalas. Remember that winning battles is a small part in securing a nation. If this Valmuros matter is not addressed, it will lead to more strife. Mondray will advise them never to surrender. I am sure he already quilled pronouncements honoring them all as exemplars. We'll see how spirited their resolve will be, but we must avoid spell and steel."

"I am grateful for your tutelage through my entire life, Conservator. I look forward to your continued counsel when my father and then I are on the throne. I hope you will not be gone too long. We shall miss your distinguished presence. You are an example to all."

"Blood need not be shed in a Starfield." Woolfolk had not ruled out the option, but even voicing the thought pained him. Woolfolk looked again at the harbor where Jannon's troops were still disembarking. "You've done well. More men than we had expected."

"Many joined us on the march. None have seen a Tavuro in their lands. They think it more a struggle against Eadolan, or just simply a chance for coin after a weak harvest."

"A true leader draws men to the standard."

"I wanted to thank you for the amulet." Jannon tapped his breastplate to show he could not retrieve it.

"Best to keep it safe. Take care of it. There will never be another one ever like it. Did your mother give it to you in our holy river as instructed?" Woolfolk moved his hand to signify the pouring of water.

"She did. Thank you. I don't know what to say." Jannon hesitated. "What does it do?"

"Fear not the water. It is the channel of life. The land is nothing without water. Your mother needed to be the one to give you the amulet. We receive many bountiful gifts from Indalos, including that of very life itself, but that is a gift only a mother can convey."

Woolfolk let his hand rest on Jannon's shoulder. "I feel its energy. In the tumult of all that is before us, be still. Find time to focus on the amulet. Do not stray from it. This is the power of Indalos. The amulet is a gateway to the entirety of creation."

Jannon's eyes grew wide at the thought, and he looked down at his chest.

"The waves will guide you. While Kerjelaft will remain with your father as my representative, he won't be able to guide you in focusing the power of the amulet."

Woolfolk started to say more, but Jannon interrupted. "Conservator, if this be the last time I see you." Jannon nodded his head downriver towards the looming battle for the control of Ravalas and all of Ardalencor. "I heard tales. Is it true that your parents were members of the Order?"

"Yes," he said, unsurprised by the question. "They were both wizards of the Order. They chose each other and me over their vows to the Order but pledged never to reveal what they had learned. Their loyalty was never in question; they just wanted a family." Woolfolk's bright eyes narrowed. "They were barely left alone before the assassins went looking for them. We were always moving. I'm not sure how many attempts they made, but when I was three, they killed my mother. She did not go easily. My father did not avenge her, but, how could he? He could not fight the Order himself, but he eventually made a deal to leave us alone when Silverface became Archmage. My father trained me in secret, and my parents' knowledge lives in others as best I could convey it. I am his vengeance. I have learned things of my own as well." Woolfolk looked skyward. "And, unlike the Order, my blood continues; the ancestral link is unbroken. I think my great grandson has promise. I hope Indalos permits me time to begin his journey."

"Now the continuance of this truce is much in doubt." Woolfolk frowned and raised the hood of his cloak. "There's a man I want you to meet. He is waiting not far from here." Woolfolk motioned to two men by a door up the street. "He is not a student of mine, but he is quite good in his own way." Woolfolk swept his hand across his face. "It is wonderful to see you well. Greet me again in Ravalas."

"Indalos, guard soul and soil," the old man and the young man said together as Woolfolk departed.

The great hall of the Glazer's Guild bespoke its wealth: walls paneled in decorative wood, a spacious arched brick ceiling with plasters of white and gold, tapestries and paintings memorializing practical scenes of industry and leisure: potters dutifully tending kilns, counting tables hidden beneath precise rows of coins and stacks of ledgers, hunts and the ensuing feasts, a patchwork of portraits of the Guild's bygone leaders. The hall now served as Padazar's temporary headquarters.

"Father!" Jannon exclaimed as he entered the hall.

The gathered men cheered as father and son reunited. The elder Padazar's face filled with joy and, after a long embrace, he looked his son up and down in approval. "You must be famished. The food should be along shortly."

"I am well, Father. Adventure fills a belly," said Jannon repeating a common Southwestern phrase.

"The Conservator—"

"Yes, I know. I saw him as he was departing."

"He is too important to us, but if the situation in Valmuros is as he says, he is the only one who can resolve it. I pray he will return soon. Listen to him in all matters." Padazar looked towards the door as if others would be entering. "Have you heard from Teague and Marland? It has been far too long. When will they arrive?"

"They are not coming," Jannon said in a lowered voice and handed his father a small fold of letters.

"What?" snapped Padazar bitterly. The sharpness of his voice grabbed the attention of the other men in the room.

Jannon motioned for the group to converge towards the hall's high feasting table. As Jannon acknowledged the other men, he beamed at his younger brother, Asmund, who returned a happy nod.

"Friends, it is good to see you all well. As we had assumed and now confirmed, internal strife is roiling in Velenharn.

About three months ago, Teague, Marland, and others accepted secret charters to raise companies for one of the expected claimants. There are so many, I forget the name. Some dispossessed daughter, or general, or favored bastard. Our people," Jannon said, referring to Ardalens who remained in Ardalen territory ceded by treaty to Velenharn, "have already agreed to rich contracts. All sides are preparing should Corentin not survive, or even to speed his departure. Gold and silver are flowing and promises freely given. Our people don't want to jeopardize Forris and the towns. There have been promises of lesser taxation and a reduction of the Velen garrisons by more than one claimant. Many sides are eager to win Ardalen fighting men to their side and are offering a lighter rule than Corentin's oppression."

All men gathered grumbled but struggled to find words as they considered their own actions if they were in the boots of Teague and Marland.

"Their country is still Ardalencor. They haven't forgotten," Jannon remarked. "They said they will send an honor guard in support of us and defense of the homeland." Then Jannon added, "But, in truth, I think it will be so small that the Velens won't notice, and neither will we. It is all contained in the letters."

Padazar crumpled the packet of letters and dropped them on the table. "How about supplies from Forris?

"Yes, but prices are rising." Jannon quickly shifted topics. "Mother is managing communications with Domariadin and the prominent borderland nobles to confirm our eternal friendship and secure their support; or, at least to ensure they don't actively support Eadolan. Our alliance with Tavuron unnerves and may ruin—"

"Enough," interrupted Padazar. "The Duchess will make them understand."

"At least, we can expect some volunteers," Jannon waivered, "but I don't think they'd arrive in any number until spring."

Padazar clenched his fist, trying to force patience. "What news from Mathis?"

"I have not heard from Mathis, but I don't take that as bad news," said Jannon. "I am sure he and Durwood are moving fast and causing mischief."

Padazar nodded and pointed to a stack of papers. "We have missives to be distributed to town and manor that our quarrel is with Eadolan. It is his failure time and again to defend Ardalencor. He despoiled the connection of Valmuros to Indalos. He is the deserter of land and faith. For those who see truth and join our cause, their lands will be spared and rewards given."

"An excellent plan, Your Eminence. Make your intentions clear," said a primmed man in fine garments. "There are those in Ravalas with no love for Eadolan."

"Did you have any trouble leaving the capital, Treasurer?" asked Jannon.

"Not at all," said Lanning Braithwaite, the former Royal Treasurer of Ardalencor and now perhaps the most famous thief in the country. "It was all done discreetly. Never a chasing rider. The gold is safe, and we are safe." The Treasurer restrained his desire to recount his own adventure in front of truly brave and battle-hardened men.

The chime of a bell and dramatic knocks at the door signaled the arrival of food. "Your Eminence, the meal is prepared."

Wiley and Brasher, Padazar's faithful hounds, eagerly sniffed the air and expectantly waited, hoping for their own choice morsels.

A procession of servants entered with platters of herring

baked in folds of bread, dishes of roasted quail and tripe, slender wooden platters with charred winter cabbage, wide bowls of pickled dwarf onions and mushrooms, salted lizard tail soup in steaming ceramic kettles, cubes of hard cheese stacked into small towers, plates of sticky pies with plum and pear preserves thickly smeared in honey, bowls of heavy cream, and trays of small, thin glasses and decanters filled with fire rye along with larger cups of stewed fruit.

"Mind the maps," called Padazar as long runs of stitched velum were quickly rolled up as the servants engulfed the high table in food and drink. "Enjoy the feast. We are ever closer." Padazar raised a glass of fire rye, as did the others. "Our next feast will be in Ravalas!"

As the group helped themselves to the food, another man entered the hall. "Please forgive my delay, Your Eminence. The crews and soldiers are working to clear the burned and sunk craft from the piers. We have just two piers cleared and fully receiving," said Almaric Sands, proprietor of the largest transport fleet in the Southwest and now responsible for the entire flotilla. "The river is riding high so the wrecks have not been much issue for the flat bottoms."

The fair-haired Sands was a Domariad by birth. When he was a boy, his family came on pilgrimage to Valmuros. Like other Domarese pilgrims traveling along the now well-worn route, they were so inspired by the power of the place that they never left. The Domarese connection to the Faith of Indalos began when a merchant, Elosiquiad, traveling through Valmuros heard about the Four Acclamations and became the first foreign convert. Before departing for home to spread word of this new faith, he gifted a jeweled chain to sustain those spreading the nascent teachings. The chain was never sold, instead becoming a prized symbol of devotion and gratitude to Indalos.

"Almaric, thank you for seeing my son and his army safely across the river. My Admiral of the Avenbair," said Padazar amused with his impromptu bestowing of the title. "How many vessels were you able to gather?"

"The Southwest is with you, Your Eminence. One hundred forty-three ships and boats of all sizes. Swift sails are scouting downriver," Sands said in a humble, matter-of-fact manner. "We've only seen isolated ships. The river is clear. We hear from the merchants that much of Eadolan's garrison departed with confiscated ships for Pelham, or perhaps farther downriver. Pelham is still holding out as far as we know."

"Mathis should be nowhere near Pelham," offered Jannon. "He knows to strike east and not allow the Midriver nobles to send forces to defend along the Avenbair. Even if Mathis was nearby, I don't think he can take Pelham. He doesn't have the men nor the siege train. Pelham still has the earthworks from the Velenharn war, and its walls are much better than Croydon's."

"How many men does he have with him?" asked Latrobh as he inspected the fish with a knife.

"When Mathis left Delun, a little over two thousand: quickfoot raiders, mostly archers, and about three hundred light cavalry."

"Our scout ships will learn more about Pelham," said Sands. "Taking Pelham would benefit us greatly by opening up shipping on the Greenseed and its tributaries."

Latrobh's one eye glared at Sands for stating what all gathered knew. Latrobh slurped his soup. "Can you supply us and maintain the fleet without Pelham?"

"Yes, I think so, but downriver Avenbair Castle will be a problem and then farther on the great bends of the river before reaching Ravalas. It's a long stretch to have to move the fleet. Even with Pelham there could still be a pinch or two, but

IN TIMES OF WAR: A TALE OF ARDALENCOR

having Pelham would be a mighty good harbor." Sands eyed the food but felt unease as a commoner to help himself without noble permission. "Even without Pelham, we need free navigation of the Avenbair."

"To control the Avenbair is to divide the country, or unite it, depending on one's intentions," stated Padazar. "We don't have the pack animals nor the carts to supply a stationary force at Ravalas engaged in siege, especially in winter. Any supply train would be vulnerable to attack, and the animals would end up just carrying their own fodder. We must look beyond victory. The city must be fed. The grain stores may be removed or spoiled, and any lingering rebellious northern provinces may not be forthcoming with bread."

"We can start executing nobles if no grain is sent to Ravalas. After three or four, the rest will get the idea and there would be so much food the horses would be shitting pastries," declared Latrobh. "Speed. Each moment delay is another stone, another foot of trench in front of Ravalas."

"The boys need rest, Cousin," poked a wild-eyed man seated next to Latrobh. "No sense going in dog ass tired. A few days of hot food and no marching will do them good."

"You were always the slow one, Jordy," quipped Latrobh but conceded the point.

"Behan is an able steward, a real talent for planning and construction. He will be strengthening the city's defenses," said Braithwaite. "If Weldon is still serving as Chancellor, he will be a force to rally the city as well."

"We need to float the stone throwers, and they are still sometime away," said Padazar. "If we can't take Ravalas on the march, we'd just be shivering outside with a fat prick. Holley's Broadshield will guard the barges from Sawmill, but they'll be vulnerable all the way down the river until they reach us."

"Before I left Ravalas, word was that Admiral Zelihis

would be out at sea for several months, and any remaining
warships were assigned to protect the approaches to Floriana
lest lurking pirates descend upon the city. There is," emphasized Braithwaite, "no fleet to oppose us."

"None that we know of," cautioned Jannon.

"With respect, who would lead this opposing fleet? Some
Pelham fisherman?" asked Braithwaite as gently as he could.
"With his army lost, that will be Eadolan's priority, not
constructing warships. And, he's short of gold now."

"If the wizards have bolstered the garrison at Avenbair
Castle, that unassailable island will be a viper pit on the river,"
said a muscular man with a sallow face. "It will fall only
through starvation. And, if they hold the north bank, they will
put the whole river in a vice."

Sands furrowed his brow. "Yes," he fretted for the fate of
his ships.

"You are right, Kerjelaft, but, if the wizards are at Avenbair
Castle, then there would be just as many fewer in Ravalas or
with Eadolan," said Asmund pleased with his own
observation.

"Avenbair Castle is no concern to the wizards. It is part of
Eadolan's damned senseless grand plan to ring Ravalas in
protection while diverting money which could have rebuilt our
lands," seethed Padazar.

"Jordy and I'll take most of the cavalry ahead and sweep
the northern bank. We have, what, about fifteen thousand
under all arms already here? If Eadolan wants to offer battle,
then let's have him! The fleet can well avoid Avenbair Castle
by sticking close to the north bank," assured Latrobh. "Bite is
already in the air. With the growing cold, the fogs will continue
to thicken. Need to make sure we have good pilots who won't
smack into a mud bank or one another."

"The river is high so that should not be a problem," refuted

Jannon. "We have men with us who have navigated these waters."

"I have sailed this stretch of the Avenbair for half my life," said Sands.

"In winter?" asked Latrobh skeptically.

"Even in winter."

"And how about the hundred and forty-two other captains?"

"I will ensure the safety of the fleet," Sands said in a dignified tone.

"How many forts guard the bends?"

"After Avenbair Castle, none. The great bends are all flood plain, lots of creeks and inlets and winter channels."

"Very well, Admiral." Latrobh smiled wryly. "Your soup is getting cold, and this batch is quite good. It's pushing three years in the salt. Even some lungs packed in with the tails. I got a real taste for this while serving beyond the seas with the Rithgurians."

"Thank you, Lord Latrobh," Sands said with a slight bow. Addressing the group, he said, "If there is to be a battle on the river, we would require soldiers to protect the boats as well as for boarding. We have no warships and would need to fight any large clash as a land battle."

"I like the sound of that," shouted Latrobh.

"Admiral Sands!" came the cheers, and decanters of fire rye were passed around.

"What news from Corneleo?" said Jannon wincing as he set down a small glass now emptied of its fire rye.

"I received a dispatch from Lord Ray on the road to Middlepost. He is leading the bulk of his cavalry while the infantry remains at Thavodyn. Lord Swan is with him as well as your two brothers. Nabrensus is taking most of his army east with an observation force still positioned around Thavodyn."

Padazar tried to conceal his trepidation. "Swan failed to keep Nabrensus focused on besieging the fort. Tavurite cavalry are fanning out into the countryside in order to lure Eadolan out. If Eadolan marches out, the cavalry raiders will be recalled to rejoin the army."

"I doubt they will give the common folk a light touch," worried Braithwaite. "The Tavuros help us secure the throne and hand us an impoverished country..."

Padazar seemed not to hear his Treasurer. "It will take Eadolan time to assemble a new army, but, if Eadolan rides out to meet Nabrensus, then we may find the city all but empty. We must plan our approach carefully, and be first to Ravalas."

CHAPTER 21

The cart lurched forward over the rough and rooted ground, approaching a clearing in the woods. Bambenek, Bayard, and Dronor had been on this narrow, forest road for more days than Bayard cared to remember. For a stack of coin and service as porters, Bambenek and Bayard found space for Dronor in the northbound caravan.

In Talonglade, Dronor's injuries were lightly treated and covered in fresh moss and bandages. The healers found along the way refused to help, claiming their skill too little or the investiture of effort too great. Bambenek learned that the most renowned healers had been summoned north by Camhorn Thorpe. Much of the Northwest was already under occupation by the Tavuros, including the regional capital of Thornhelm. Worse still, the region was hard pressed to deal with intensified raids by mountain tribes from beyond the northern border.

Bambenek had traveled this forest road many times before, but he knew not what lay ahead. The caravan finally stopped, and the carter motioned for Bambenek and Bayard to follow him towards the center of the clearing. A man stood prominently, barking orders about the provisioning of his gathered forces.

The man abruptly turned and demanded with a raspy rumble, "Who are you? Did you bring my birds? Where are my birds?"

Bambenek and Bayard walked forward with empty hands.

The man said sternly, "No carrier pigeons. When will Eadolan return all the damn birds that I sent? And bring us the help we need!"

Bambenek and Bayard gave no reply.

"Silver ingots? We are desperately short of silver."

"Camhorn," said Bambenek cautiously as if trying to calm a rabid dog.

With a morose smile, the man put up a hand to demand silence. "Bambenek Morley," he said recalling a name from half a lifetime ago. "Still running to and fro and never at hand where you're needed. You're far from atonement, so I suppose you've traveled all this way on an official mission to bring us good tidings from the High Lord?"

"They claim to have killed a necrotic bear on the way here," said the cart driver.

"Really? Did it touch you? At least you have the damn sense not to drag the carcass here."

"We burned it," offered Bayard proudly.

"Well, that's a start of some royal support."

Camhorn Thorpe, Ealdorman of Thornhelm and de facto governor of the Northwestern Wilds, had a round face set on a thick neck with hair and eyes a deep brown. His eyebrows on passing glance resembled furry caterpillars, and his moustache seemed bequeathed from a walrus. His nose held a flattened shape after being broken and reset several times over the past decades.

"Why are you here?" pressed Camhorn. "Who is this? Your son?"

"No. This is Bayard Summers, squire and soldier." After a moment, Bambenek said nervously, "I came to ask the help of the healers to save Dronor's leg. To save his life."

"Well, how about that. Why start with a greeting or a small request?" Camhorn said shaking his head in disbelief. "Must mean a great deal to you to return all this way and after all this time," he said with a wash of rebuke and pity.

"Is Anora?" asked Bambenek in a shallow tremble.

"No," Camhorn said sharply.

Bambenek wasn't sure if that meant she was dead or just not immediately present, but he understood that Camhorn had no interest in recounting the course of over two decades.

Camhorn walked towards the caravan to inspect the newly-arrived supplies. He glanced at the pale, sweat-streaked face of a half-orc slumped in the lead cart's dirty, straw-strewn bed. "Well, look at this wart-faced tusker. That bear probably smelled the rot of his leg before you entered the forest."

Camhorn came closer. "Dronor? A half-orc with a dwarven name. How did you come by that?"

Dronor stared blankly and pushed a few incoherent syllables through his blistered lips.

With Camhorn's attention focused on Dronor, Bambenek searchingly peered across the faces of those mustering, guilt and shame bright on his own face.

"Death stalks in tightening circles," said Camhorn flatly. "This leg is near past amputation. The corruption is seeping into the blood. Trying to save this stranger is a burden too great. We are neglected by Ravalas and pressed on all sides. Thornhelm is occupied, raids from the mountains, and deep, lingering evil in the forest."

"What are you offering in return?" demanded Camhorn. "I

see you still have that sword, Morley. At least you have not parted with everything you held dear."

"You may take all we have." Bambenek opened his bag of spoils and motioned for Bayard to do the same. Bayard dumped out Dronor's share of the spoils as well.

A large ring caught the eye of Camhorn. "That bone ring. Was it always this big?"

"No," said Bayard in amazement.

Camhorn took the ring and placed it on one of Dronor's fingers. Faint waves of iridescent runes emerged and submerged as Camhorn inspected the ring. "The magic is nearly gone from this one, but it clings to its ancient energy and has chosen him. We'll see to his wounds if he has not yet slipped beyond the horizon. You two are coming with us now. I'll consider you the vanguard of the long-awaited reinforcements from Ravalas."

"Thank you," said Bambenek with deep relief as he and Bayard lightly touched Dronor on the head before the carter trundled off to another section of the camp.

Camhorn ignored Bambenek. "A Drivach warband was spotted not far from here," he said, directing his attention to Bayard, enjoying a new audience on which to pour out his frustrations. "The Tavuros' invasion lured the Drivach out of their mountain wastes in ever larger swarms. It's too costly for us to follow them across the border and into the uplands. We need to crush them on open ground. Drivach are a scourge. They are either groveling at your feet or slashing at your throat. Best kept far away."

"Who? Drivach?" wondered Bayard as they moved back towards the center of the clearing.

"Never been this side of the forests?" jeered Camhorn. "The mining guilds bring Drivach in for the heavy work, detecting gas pockets with torches at the end of sticks. Most don't last too long before they're maimed or dead. Poor, miserable bastards. But if you let them build up in any area for too long, they're a bane on our people; cruel, vile, and they'll dissolve like acid whatever we have built."

"The trees know for how long I have written to Ravalas. That busybody Quill; he is no supporter of ours. Does he still wear that hat with wolves' teeth? He would not last a week out here. Do you think he has stared down a wolf let alone run with the pack? A city like Ravalas softens and bends a man. I have asked for a permanent frontier garrison of a thousand cavalry and a chain of forts and watches to deter raiders. Smash them before our homes and flocks are threatened." Camhorn sighed. "We are alone out here, and we must do it our way."

"Prepare my armor," Camhorn shouted to no one in particular, but several retainers started moving quickly.

"Son, have you ever faced a Drivach?" Camhorn asked as he tucked a chain with a large peridot set within a wavy-rayed silver sun into his drab hempen shirt. As he tied the shirt laces about his chest, Camhorn was careful to keep a second necklace of small beads of opalized wood and fresh pine above the shirt. Blood and sweat stained his quilted shirt of coarse hemp which had an apron to mid-thigh to provide additional protection. On the apron was a coiled snake, stitched in leather, eyes peering out from the center.

Bayard just shook his head, and then his eyes grew wide as Camhorn's armor was brought forward.

"These boys you are about to face are like no other." Camhorn stood still for a moment as the heavy steel breastplate and backplate were readied. As the two light brown tinted pieces were positioned closely, the retainers quickly withdrew their hands, and the pieces of armor rushed to fuse together over the final distance.

"Secure the fastenings," Camhorn said with a look to each

shoulder and a hint of concern more than to remind the retainers of their duty.

A low ridge to protect the neck extended nearly from shoulder to shoulder of the breastplate. Seated within the ridge and wired tight sat a wide lower jaw bone filled with a dense packing of angled, razor-sharp teeth. Bayard tried to ask what creature bequeathed the jaw bone, but he just muttered breathlessly.

Camhorn continued, "The Drivach take a stimulant found up in the mountains. They don't need sleep for several days and can move with rapid speed. If they are cut, it also helps to clot the wounds even though the heart is beating like a hummingbird's wings. If you think you get the best of one and he surrenders, if you turn your back, he will cut your throat."

"Stimulant? What is it?" questioned Bayard.

"We've tried to reproduce it. We call it demon drink. I don't think we are even close to understanding how they do it, even with scraps of wisdom we've gathered over generations. The potency has evolved. There is an evil quality to it. This is not something you want to consume for long; it rips you apart from the inside."

After the torso armor was secured, greaves of the same light brown steel backed with leather were placed over Camhorn's golden yellow pants and brown boots.

Camhorn then cinched a thick hemp belt strung with pockets and pouches formed of stitched beaver tails. From a small pocket in the apron of his hemp shirt, he produced two polished iron rings with gold veins. Each had a tooth embedded in the ring which matched those in the jaw bone. For a moment, Camhorn seemed to lose all interest in those around him as he carefully slid the two rings on his left thumb and forefinger.

An approaching attendant lifted Camhorn from his thoughts. Camhorn accepted and donned a midnight blue felt cap; three eagle feathers stitched into the fold of the cap draped over his neck.

A retainer ceremonially presented Camhorn with his war hammer. Blackened, fire-hardened wood formed the shaft. The iron head was forged into that of an eagle, tipped beak protruding forward. A fan of three feathers completed the design.

As a final touch, a twisted band of Hunbertys leaf and straw was secured to Camhorn's upper left arm. A retainer also tossed two bands to Bambenek. "You'll need some more protection than elk fur," the retainer said, pointing at Bambenek's leather jerkin. "We have some thick tabards that might fit you."

Bambenek motioned for Bayard to present his left arm. "We use these to identify friend from foe. The Drivach don't have much in the way of metal working skills so they generally prefer armor and weapons taken from our dead. Hunbertys does not grow in the mountains so this is good a way as any of telling friend from foe at a distance. We vary the pattern and materials and wear them on the arm or head so the Drivach can't infiltrate the ranks."

A large man with long, wild, red hair and a massive beard sprinted towards Camhorn. The man's beard was apportioned into three sections: side braids descended from his cheeks and were shaped with alternating bands of greasy green and white plaster. The preserved head of a snarling wolverine held tight the thickly tangled central braid. The big man moved easily even with carrying a giant maul with a head of petrified wood across his shoulder.

"Cam, if you got your tin shell all strapped on, we best be on the way. Two of Hake's birds just returned. They're pretty cut up. The Drivach may be trying to reach the herds just north of the woods, or they are moving down to link up with the Tavuros."

"No, Mannix. Can't let either happen," said Camhorn shaking his head. "We move."

CHAPTER 22

"We have to catch them on the move," Bambenek declared to Bayard as they rode out of the woods. "Or bait a trap; hard to force the Drivach to fight on ground of our choosing. Really only happens if the drink wears off, and they're dragging feet to the mountain passes or moving at a crawl with stolen herds and our people in bindings."

Bambenek gave Bayard an admonishing look. "Don't get all worried, Squire, riding that pony. Be glad they gave you a mount. I told them you were a renowned horseman from the capital," he winked. "Sure, it's not a knight's horse, but don't worry. They're hardy; they can live off the tougher grasses up here. Don't need the same kind of care that your war mounts need either. They survive outside through the frost and chill."

Bayard frowned and shifted in the saddle.

"You best make friends with that horse," warned Bambenek. "They can spook easily when that Drivach fermentation pervades the air, especially when they're in the thou-

ANDREW ZIMBA

sands. That war howl will spook a man, too, just as easy as a beast."

Bambenek urged his stout horse towards the front of the pack, challenging Bayard to keep pace. Bambenek's proper place was scouting ahead. It was in his blood, but, as the grasses north of the Great Thicket climbed in height to the horses' knees and beyond, he kept to the group, uncertain of the forgotten terrain and fearful of ambush.

The veteran scout had been away for many years and was met by shuns and kind smiles which wetted his eyes alike. Bambenek had run before and told himself he would not run again. The autumn wind whipped his face, blowing him back and carrying him forward as past and present reunited.

Bambenek estimated Camhorn's assembled force some-where upwards of two thousand fighters. Many of the fighters rode two to a horse, the accompanying rider often with bow ready or carrying a bundle of javelins.

Bambenek hoped Camhorn and others noticed him near the front ranks, though he did his best not to glance too obviously in the Ealdorman's direction. Camhorn was an imposing figure in his heavy armor, the large reptilian jaw bone jutting up from his breastplate, shielding his chin. To carry the weight of man and armor, Camhorn rode a big-ribbed, thick-necked, skewbald warhorse, a breed not native to the Northwestern Wilds.

Camhorn's father had been sent as royal authority, and the position had passed in time from father to son. Warhorses and draft horses from the heartland of the country were prized commodities and denoted prominent connections back to the more settled elements of Ardalen society. The gigantic Mannix Splitwood, the Reeve of Woodstretch, a remote settlement in the depths of the Great Thicket, rode a draft horse with a golden chestnut sheen. A gift from Camhorn, this carefully-bred heavy horse, more suited to plowing clay soils or pulling carts loaded with ale barrels, took to loyal martial service for the almost four-hundred-pound Splitwood.

Camhorn's small retinue of mounted men-at-arms in plate and chain mail was the closest approximation to the heavy cavalry of a crown army. While soldiers would decorate their arms and armor, generational heraldic devices never took hold in the dense forests or rolling steppe. For the hit-and-run tactics used in the sparsely populated areas, carrying large banners never made much sense. While the Thorpe family rapidly had embraced the peculiarities of the Wilds, the knightly traditions still held a lasting sway over Camhorn as a warrior and protector of these lands.

Two flagbearers hoisted fluttering standards: the first, the banner of the Thorpe family, a broad rectangle of white and orange, halved vertically with an indented triangular pattern; featured inside the fields, a raised orange gauntlet in the white field and a downturned white gauntlet in the orange field. Orange fringe embellished the full sweep of the banner.

The second banner towered above like the sail of a mighty ship plying its way through a deadly sea. Nearly twice the size of the Thorpe family banner, the banner of Thornhelm and by extension all the lands governed by the Ealdorman, fluttered in the light of midday. With a ripple of wind, the flag took its full span: green field with a vertical yellow stripe at the hoist, short, horizontal bars of yellow at the opposite end that extended into a compact swallow's tail and, emblazoned in the center, a yellow owl, wings spread and carrying a white war axe in its talons.

"Up ahead!" came a call from down the line. Birds of prey swirled in the sky. A multitude of raptors slashed, raked, and speared with their beaks and talons.

A quick succession of low horn blasts resounded among the cavalry.

Bayard ran his fingers over the tops of the saddle-high grass as he searched the long, low horizon beneath the warring birds. "How would you ever find anyone in here?"

"Form up!" came a shout and then a long horn blast. The horses slowed, and second riders dismounted to form the battle line.

Bambenek jumped off his horse and tugged at the bulky tabard. "Bayard, you never fought these stone fuckers before and don't know the way of fighting up here. Come on," he said, motioning for Bayard to dismount. "Take the horses to the rear."

Seeing the sternness in Bambenek's jaw, Bayard felt crushed but did not argue.

As Bayard led the horses back to a gradually forming wagon corral, he attentively took in all before him. The squire's attention locked on an elderly man, all withered and white, gripping a twisted staff of vortexwood while directing those about him. Eleven individuals with skin of a deep copper and clad in foreign dress joined the old man. The outlanders wore long white robes with a multitude of folds. Bright sashes of intertwined reds, yellows, and oranges spanned their right shoulder and chest. Striped and angular patterns of black and white masked their round faces.

"Not a cloud in the sky, Eldren," called a voice. "Can't summon lightning."

"Then they can't call it either," said the old man tersely; and then with a twinkle, "Ever been in a lightning duel?" He smiled, remembering days gone by.

Eldren Spruce, the venerable power of the Deepwood and presider over the conclaves at Long Tongue Lake, a gathering place named for the lengthy orations and not its shape, mediated and settled disputes amongst the factions. It was on his word that healers from Talonglade and other hamlets headed north to join Camhorn's force. The forest folk were fiercely independent, reluctant to leave their own territory and would only rally together in the direst of circumstances. With the Tavuros also devastating the land south of the Great Thicket, answering Camhorn's request for fighters and healers was not any easy decision, but when Eldren Spruce complied, it was all but impossible for others to refuse.

Bayard stared at Eldren and the circle of strange faces painted black and white. Eldren eventually shifted his gaze to Bayard. "Young warrior, thank you for coming all this way," he said gently. "May I trouble you to return forward? I hope to see you well."

"Thank you, Grandfather," sputtered Bayard.

On his return, some fighters, those who Bayard thought passed for captains or sergeants, positioned the troops into a wide and shallow arc to attempt to extend the ranks of the Drivach and deter their attempts to envelop the Ardalen force in the inevitable onrush. Once positioned, the Ardalen fighters started to slash and trample the grass along their front.

"We're too thin," said Bayard looking around as he approached Bambenek, stunned that the men were not armed and arrayed like a proper field army. "Where is the line infantry?" He shook his head worriedly. "And just a small reserve."

Bambenek stared at the horizon as he agitatedly hacked the grass with his heavy sword. "They don't fight the same way up here. It's not all shield walls pushing and shoving. Small groups, peapods. We'll keep formation if we can, but it's usually single combat, double up if you can, and then move to the next. When you strike, make sure they are dead. Don't turn your back."

"Use your spacing and speed," Bambenek continued. "Most will have a polearm and swinging like a demon. Keep your head and you'll keep your head." Bambenek sheathed his sword after clearing about ten feet in front. "Watch out for hot steel and clubs whirling around, even from our boys. And watch for grassfires."

"No shield wall? What?" squealed Bayard. "We just wait here to be gored by some demon!"

"The Drivach are an old foe. Our casters will smash them with a gust of wind, thorn bursts or whatever sparks between the ears. Don't worry. Our folk won't let the howlers get a clean run. When our spellweavers unleash, they try to mind our boys, but it can get blocked or redirected back at us. I know you've seen some battle magic, but it's more common up here, so stick close and don't wander off."

Bayard nodded, the moment of panic subsiding.

"The Drivach are about power blows. They aren't much for feigning. They'll give you openings," the old scout said reassuringly. "But without a shield, you need to be especially mindful." Bambenek stopped suddenly, weighing his own advice and lamenting the loss of his own shield splintered in the desperate fight at Boruma.

Bambenek fumbled with a stone and sling, unsure if he told young Bayard all he would need to know to save his life.

Bayard glanced to his right and saw a small group of fighters, one with a moose antler for a shield, discussing tactics. The fighter had stretched his arms out wide, but with Bambenek trying to impart a lifetime of instruction, Bayard could not make out what the other group was saying.

"And don't put your toes beyond the others," added Bambenek. "If the Drivach retreat, don't rush after."

Bayard wondered whether Bambenek's decades-old recollections would prove accurate, but he dismissed the thought.

He tightly cinched the strap on his nasal guard helmet and said a short prayer to Indalos. The squire cradled his sword in a two-handed grip and moved through a series of flourishes to stretch his limbs. His eyes suddenly darted upward.

Blue-green streaks launched from the reserve ranks arced high over Bambenek, Bayard, and those in the front rank.

Purple-black smoky shards twisted out in retort from multiple directions well beyond bow shot.

"They're testing distance," said Bambenek coolly. "This up ahead. It's a puff show. Nothing behind it. Couple of our strikes must have landed. They'll try to smash us up close."

"Horsemen will try to funnel the Drivach towards us. Stay back. We'll have a surprise for them," called a voice down the line.

Two other men closed up to the left of Bayard. They nodded to the squire and scout, and a fighting unit was formed within the overall battlefront.

"Cullen," said a rugged man with a fire-hardened spear, javelins, and a leather-covered wicker shield. The shield hung from a baldric, a stag's head painted in herbal dyes on the face. For armor, Cullen wore a simple, felt-lined iron helmet with a ringlet aventail to protect his neck and throat and an iron disk strapped to the center of his chest.

"This is Val," Cullen said of a thin-boned archer who stepped into the gap between the spearman and Bayard. The man wore a bark brown mantle with a deep hood and held a yew bow wrapped in Hunbertys boughs and sheep intestine. He carried little gear beyond back and side quivers stuffed with arrows. The archer was clad in dirty buckskin pants and coat with a faded red homespun shirt beneath, leather bracers snug on both his forearms. His shrouded face fixed ahead on the sea of tall grass.

Bayard stared at the hood, waiting for the archer to acknowledge him. "I'm Bayard Summers of Amberfield."

A yellow eye peered out from the shadowy recess of the mantle. Bayard gasped at the sight, the same eerie glow as the forest bear. Loosening a flap of cloth from a wood button that covered his face, the man fully turned towards Bayard, his left eye a ghastly yellow, the right, the milky white of blindness.

"Indalos, protect us," exclaimed Bayard.

"Val," the archer said with a scratch and slight bow to Bayard. The skin and muscle on his face and neck were nearly scraped to the bone. What still clung to the frame looked like cured, cinder-gray meat which jerked and spasmed as he forced a thin grin.

The men nearby chuckled at Bayard's fear. Bambenek gave the hooded man a grim look, unsure if he would have known that face even before the horrid disfigurement. Bambenek thought the man could be fifteen or one hundred and fifty. He had no idea.

"Don't mind old ghost head," said an onlooking warrior.

"Val's a drop shot so give him room to mark his targets," said Cullen, still smiling at Bayard's unease.

A group of raptors broke off from the aerial skirmish and started to return to the Ardalen line. A man and three old crones in the reserve line beckoned and welcomed their return.

Two vultures raced after the returning falcons. One of the birdmaster crones conjured sinewy cages around the vultures, and they thudded to the ground in front of her feet. A human voice growled deep within the birds. "Nice to see you again, Zhokatan," she said as she stepped on the chest of each bird, ribs cracking and organs popping beneath her feet.

At the front, Bambenek's eyes grew wide as a wall of swirling darkness came forward, moans and howls emanating from within.

With intoned defiance, a rhythmic series of short grunts and long, deep exaltations strengthened the Ardalen fighting spirit.

Bursts of light and opalescent energy waves slammed into the dark wall. The conjured shadow weakened and cracked but still held together. Glimpses of snarling and reeling Drivach could be seen within. Specters and dark tendrils jutted out in a multitude of directions to confuse with feigned movements where the heaviest attacks would fall. Arrows, javelins, and stones from slings whizzed and cracked, disappearing into the shadows. As portions of the darkness ebbed, it would expand back into the voids knocked open by the Ardalens. The mass came inexorably forward.

"Now!" came a succession of calls from the officers. After an expectant moment, they grimaced and gaped in shock as whatever they had in mind did not materialize.

"They've grown stronger," murmured Bambenek with a sickening feeling.

Draped in darkness, the Drivach horde moved in a dense column and positioned itself to smash the Ardalens in echelon, one portion of the Ardalen line to be hit first and then adjacent segments in succession.

The staggered order of assault disrupted the cohesion of the Ardalen line; some fighters stiffened, spears leveled to meet the onrushing mass, and others fell back, fearful of their ability to contain the charge. As the Ardalens braced for impact, a sweep of thickened darkness punched out in a mad rush of stampeding mountain rams.

"No! Hold!" called voices, but those most pressed by the charging shapes panicked and broke. The ethereal rams dispersed. From the smoky wisps of the illusion charged dozens of Drivach, polearms crashing with ferocious hacks and rising again in wild sickle strokes, severing heads or felling Ardalens with a torrent of blows. The war-frenzied and bestial screams echoed from the Drivach, their eyes bulging and legs driving at a manic pace.

"I wish Dronor were here!" yelled Bayard over the fury of battle.

"Why aren't the spellbinders reacting? First try got foiled and now what?" Bambenek launched a stone, but it sailed high in his haste. "Get on your front feet, Bayard. Can you see them?"

"What!" shrilled Bayard in terror.

With disaster looming nearby and Drivach fast approaching their portion of the line, Val, unphased, kept up a steady rate of fire. Even within the blackness, the yellow-eyed archer seemed able to mark targets.

"Can you see their shamans?" asked Cullen.

Val gave no reply, just drew and fired.

The Drivach warriors quickened in the final rush. With the impending onslaught, stone axes came arcing out, but they largely missed their Ardalen quarries and thudded to the ground. Still partially obscured in darkness, but now at close range, Bambenek was able to pry apart the illusion and see his own clear target.

The panoply of the Drivach varied from one man to the next, an assortment of pieces sewn, stolen, bartered, or roughly forged. Some wore sturdy armor of Ardalen, Tavurite, or Pavtanari make, others donned crude imitations hammered in home forges, and still the poorer ranks wore lumpy woolen tunics stuffed with layers of knotted grass.

Twisting his body, Bambenek hurled a stone at a lightly-armored charger. He struck his intended target, albeit in the shoulder, but the force of the blow momentarily slowed the attacker's rush and tangled his long axe with the charger next to him. Val dropped a Drivach rushing towards Bambenek with a fast arrow to the throat and repositioned a few steps behind Cullen and Bayard.

War cries raised anew on both sides.

"Indalos! Ardalencor!" yelled Bayard.

Bambenek and Bayard moved in a short burst to surprise the Drivach, getting their swords in close to negate the reach of the polearms. Another Drivach swung wildly, but Bambenek ducked and using his assailant's momentum, tossed the man over his back. Bambenek dangerously turned his attention away from the Drivach horde in order to confront the threat rising behind him. With hacking two-handed sword blows he cratered the man's puddling face.

Bambenek's allies shielded him from peril. Bayard parried a reaching blow meant for Bambenek, and Cullen crunched his spearpoint into the Drivach's ribs. Val dropped another Drivach with two arrows to the chest.

"Pull back!" came a command from the right.

The Ardalen warrior with the moose antler shield raised it above his head and slammed it into the ground. The antler expanded, points up into a short wall.

"That was close!" exclaimed Bayard as he and Bambenek jumped back, nearly being left on the hostile side of the antler.

The Drivach halted, unable to hurdle or pull down the chest-high barrier. They were met with a barrage of arrows and javelins swarming at eyeball range. A small eddy formed in a swirling sea, but the reprieve was temporary. The Drivach regrouped and started to bunch at the sides of the antler and to slash at angles towards the heads of Ardalens holding the edge of the barrier. Poleaxes, spears, and shields became broken or intertwined in the struggle for the antler palisade.

A Drivach shaman who had evaded Val's attention conjured an ear-splitting howl, but the sound was quickly snuffed by a silencing arcane counterstrike on the Ardalen side.

The shaman's flint black pupils consumed his entire eyes. Cackling, he raised his tattooed hands to his mouth and chanted. An arrow punched through his wrist, but the shaman only seemed to squeal in delight. The Drivach closed ranks to shield him from further attacks.

While the Ardalen caster who won the initial skirmish with the now-wounded shaman remained ready to foil future attacks, another Ardalen spellcrafter in the depths of stilled concentration suddenly rippled in pain as his creation took shape. Blue-green, snake-like flares plunged and circled about the heads of the Drivach disorienting them and occasionally prompting swipes which wounded their fellow fighters in the close press.

Not about to see his force dissolve into transfixed contemplation of illusory eels and maiming their own brothers-in-arms, the flint-eyed shaman made a weaving sprint and propelled a searing green mist from his mouth. The vigilant Ardalen arcanist deftly froze the particles in a shroud of frost, and the miniscule particles knifed back through the ranks of Drivach. Icy shrapnel tore through two rows of compressed Drivach ranks. The shaman's face welled in a curtain of blood from hundreds of tiny rivulets, and then the body hit the threshed grass with a lifeless smack.

Enraged at the sudden loss of several men and the measure of protection afforded by the shaman, the Drivach prepared a frenzied final assault on the makeshift position. Cullen, staggered from blows to his helmet, fell to the ground. He tried to stand, but the edge of his shield was split with an axe blow. The heavy blade stuck in the shield. He struggled to lift the baldric from his neck and left arm, but there was no slack in the stretched leather.

Cullen frantically strained to hold his position, his spear moving in rapid, desperate thrusts. Bayard and others tried to rescue Cullen. The press was so thick that Val had trouble finding clear targets. In the tumult he risked an arrow through a narrow flash and ripped the ear lobe off a fellow Ardalen as the arrow hissed towards its target. Despite attempts to save Cullen, he was dragged beyond the antler, and like a log in a saw mill, awaiting Drivach iron and stone blades glimmered with anticipation.

Val's hood swung widely, and a crackly word of warning went unheard in the swirl of battle. So thick was the press that when Val grabbed Bambenek's shoulder, Bambenek barely restrained a responding sword attack.

Predatory birds from both sides slashed through the skies looking for opportune strikes on exposed heads and faces and then racing skyward to attack other birds and spot fresh targets. Bambenek spied a blackened form above him and then just as suddenly felt razors groove and scrape down to his skull. He reeled, but the bird was already out of range as he raised his arms. Bambenek's neck was soon slick with blood and pouring freely in the pulsation of battle. He backed away, narrowly avoided another attack, and vainly tried to squeeze shut the multitude of bloody furrows.

With collapse a distinct possibility, the two Ardalen casters who thus far had stabilized their frontage, although weakened by the efforts, readied a desperate attack. One of the casters, sapped, veins blue and protruding on his face, summoned the vestiges of his strength. Two heavily-armored Drivach fighters wearing Ardalen metal helmets drew the caster's attention.

Ice soon sprawled across the iron helmets. These fighters screamed, dropped their weapons, and tried to press their way back while ripping off their helmets. The other Drivach, fearful of a reoccurrence of the reversal of fortune with the green mist, panicked and were engulfed in an explosion of ice and metal which shredded flesh and fighting spirit alike. The already enervated Ardalen caster collapsed to the ground, enfeebled from the exertion. As what Drivach remained in that stretch of the line retreated, Val took opportune shots before untangling corpses and quieting still wriggling bodies before sorrowfully kneeling by the fallen Cullen.

An Ardalen runner frantically moved along the right of the line and called, "Rusk, Fowler, Snout, move your men to protect and rally on Eldren!" The line was so thin it was hard to pull forces out and contract the line in good order, but the successful defense of the moose antler wall allowed for more fighters to reinforce other areas.

"Let's go, Val! No time for that now," barked a man wielding a blood-splattered long axe. Turning to Bayard and a few others still in fighting shape, he added, "The bunch of you are coming with me." In the clamor Bayard searched for Bambenek, but at the squire's hesitation the man intoned, "Move, there is no time!"

While the right side of the Ardalen infantry line had weathered the initial onslaught, the main Drivach attack had fallen on the left of the infantry and shattered the left and center of the line. Drivach warriors poured into the breach.

With the moose antler proving an impenetrable barrier and growing causalities taken from Ardalen missile fire and magic, shouts within the Drivach ranks called for warriors to fall back and send fighters to aid the final push against the left and center. To screen their movements, red cinders and smoke started to appear in the grass.

"Fire!"

On the far right, Camhorn Thorpe deployed with the bulk of the mounted force. His cavalry had yet to engage fully, remaining at distance and peppering the Drivach horde with missile fire. The Drivach and the Ardalens had been perpetual adversaries. The Ardalens relied upon an edge in ethereal knowledge and mastery; the Drivach, on their unassailable mountain valleys. Despite the incessant warfare, large pitched battles were a rarity. The Drivach raiders who swarmed across the countryside hunted in packs between fifty and a few hundred. A set-piece battle, even of this small scale, was a new experience for many in Camhorn's ranks.

"Something dreadful has happened," grieved a blind caster who rode alongside Camhorn when the trap of restraining magic failed to materialize. "Strong forces," he agonized, straining to identify the source.

From Camhorn's vantage point, the infantry on the right seemed heavily pressed but held its ground. The riders dispatched to check on the center had not returned; also troubling, no raptors conveyed a signal from the center or left, but the skies were a battleground all their own. The only scouts to return had reported a few Drivach horsemen galloping between the main force and a distant party of cavalry and jumble of carts awaiting plunder to haul back into the mountain refuges should the Ardalen army be destroyed or put to flight.

"Ealdorman!" snapped Mannix Splitwood, the wolverine head on his beard bouncing wildly. "The boys are in a bloody scrap, Cam! I'll charge them myself. If you're worried about the damn horse, I'll leave it here," he bellowed as he pumped his giant maul in the air.

While Camhorn's immediate cavalry command presently was little more than an observation force, it served the purpose of holding ranks of Drivach fighters to protect the flank and to prevent them from engaging elsewhere.

Most of Camhorn's force rode steppe ponies and would have little effect at closer range, unable to deliver the shock of heavy cavalry even if the riders had been equipped with lances. The steppe ponies were at another disadvantage over short distances; the elixir consumed by the Drivach invigorated their movements, and in a rapid burst they could chase down a pony whose rider clumsily ventured too close to launch a javelin.

Camhorn had selected this site, committed his fighters to this unnamed tract of grass, unremarkable mile after mile. He ordered his soldiers to fight, proven and green alike, but his magical conjurers had not delivered.

Camhorn still held his cavalry. The few true warhorses that he had under his banners were incredibly difficult to replace and with the Tavuros swarming over lands once under the Ealdorman's protection, he knew he would need these forces to fight another day; yet battle raged in front of him, and his people were fighting and dying now.

"Wheels fell off the wagon, Mannix." The Ealdorman worriedly stood up in the saddle. He strained his eyes to the west. "No sign of the falcons? Maybe the damned Tavuros aren't as close?" Camhorn's eyes raced back to the Drivach formation and the ebb and flow of battle. "Can't afford this becoming all fists and teeth. We don't have the men."

"Can't spend all day reflecting on it. Better the butcher than the calf!" raged Mannix. "If you won't lead us, I'll take a hundred picked men and wade into them. I'll smash those cravens so hard their heads will be rolling up the mountains!"

Camhorn fixed the giant with an intense look and then called to his shieldbearer, "With me!"

On the far left, the second force of Ardalen cavalry, smaller in number and primarily unarmored missile cavalry, kept up a steady rate of arrow fire but with apparent little effect against a motley array of shields bolstering the Drivach flank. Even the plunging fire seemed to have scant results, and Rodney Starling looked nervously to the skies for further instruction. His role in the battle plan was to be one of pursuit, but in the tattered plan and ensuing carnage, he was unsure of the right course of action; every attempt he had mustered to close the distance prompted feigns and countercharges by the Drivach.

"What should I do?" murmured the tormented Starling.

In the middle of the Ardalen forces, the infantry on the left and center attempted to rally. Those unfortunate Ardalen fighters who were isolated and cutoff from relieving counterattacks were inevitably cut down. The more fortunate found refuge behind renewed and more effective magical barrages.

In the reprieve, these fighters formed up adjacent to the small wagon corral. Infantry outside of the wagon corral formed layered ranks, spears forward in the style of the High Lord's line infantry. With a final defensive position readied, the Ardalen magical barrage started to ebb as those with healing powers started to triage and staunch the lacerated and maimed.

As the Ardalen magical strikes lessened, the Drivach reformed and brought up fresh warriors concentrating those with shields in the front for a final attack to collapse the Ardalen center.

"Bayard, keep your feet under you," said a familiar voice as a man with a fish tattoo on the sides of his head and down his neck offered his hand to Bayard to climb into the wagon corral. Bayard marveled at the sound of Bambenek's voice, but soon the scout's presence found physical form as another hand pushed Bayard up. Bambenek quickly followed, a stone readied in his sling, his face a swirl of half-dried blood.

"I'm alright," Bambenek said. "Just be ready if the spears can't hold them."

Archers inside the elevated platform of the improvised fort snapped off arrows, but the Drivach still in the froth of bloodlust inexorably pressed forward.

Back on the right wing, Camhorn prepared a dismounted cavalry force to strike the Drivach in the flank. "Send messages again to Eldren and Starling. Sunsmoke, you have command."

About two hundred fighters formed up in a shallow column. The Thorpe and Thornhelm standards fluttered in the center with spellcrafters placed within the second and third ranks to bolster and ward the formation before the point of contact. Camhorn stood in the center of the front rank. Haldanar, the Ealdorman's shieldbearer in heavy armor and closed helm, guarded his left; Mannix took the position to Camhorn's right. Among the cluster of the Ealdorman's plate and mail-clad bodyguards, Mannix's massive frame was armored modestly in a brown gambeson, shoulders and collar embellished with wolverine fur. Snaking lightning and shooting stars brightened the sleeves and culminated in sunbursts of brass riveted to the cuffs.

"That dog hair going to be enough?" asked one of the men-at-arms studying Mannix's gambeson.

Mannix winked. He raised his giant maul, cradling the petrified wood, and pressed it to his forehead. As flesh and petrified wood separated, his face and hands took on the appearance of living rock. He tapped a stony finger on the bodyguard's pauldron with an echoing clank. "Hope you make it through in your maid's teapot. If you get into any trouble, yell my name." Mannix roughly shook the man's shoulder and declared with a wild grin, "I'll come save you, but yell loudly; I'll be making the Drivach wail."

The Drivach smashed their weapons together and raised a war cry. Their champions salivated at the opportunity to fight and slay Mannix Splitwood, Camhorn Thorpe, and other famous defenders on the Ardalen frontier. Most Drivach had only heard stories of these men and their magic arms and armor, and the chance for their own songs of martial glory seemed close at hand.

Like the collision of two weather fronts, casters on both sides tested one another. There developed an initial equilibrium in the open space between the forces. The Ardalens quickly asserted their control, sending moaning wind gusts which reached through the Drivach line; while harmless effects, the gusts signaled to the Drivach fighters the lesser skill and fatigue of their own casters and served an ill omen should strong magic soon follow.

Camhorn stepped out from the line, faced his troops, and raised his war hammer. "Forward!"

The Ardalens cheered, and Camhorn led his men at a quickened pace. As he moved, he intoned short phrases and gently rocked his head back. Camhorn clenched his fist; the gold-veined iron rings united. As the gold veins glinted, the carnivorous jaw bone on his steel breastplate sprouted to life.

Camhorn's awakened armor transformed his head into a long-necked lizard, leathery, with a loose chin. Camhorn increased his pace over the final rush. The broad lizard maw widened; a deafening roar reverberated through the angled rows of razor teeth.

Drivach shamans tried to reengage the previously successful shadowy veil but to little effect. The shamans and the front ranks of the Drivach line felt the steppe grass come to life and snake around their feet and shins. The Drivach seethed with panic, struggling to free their feet, and then hit with the true fury of a wind gust, the Ardalen column smashed home.

In the final rush Mannix surged ahead of the line. He relished feeling the slamming gust of wind tingling the tip of his nose. He timed his approach perfectly, the tail end of the gust adding more force to his attack.

"Hear me, you shit lickers! Death calls!" Mannix swung his maul like a streaking comet catching a stout Drivach with all his might. The Drivach instantly collapsed back, the petrified wood maul shattering the chin and crunching breastbone beneath rusted chain mail.

Drivach pikes and polearms extended to stop the Ardalen charge. Those leveled near Camhorn, found their heads snapped off in the lizard's maw and the chunks of wood and iron ruefully spit into the hapless ranks of Drivach. Attacks by the Drivach shamans against the rampaging lizard-man did not slow his assault. Camhorn kept his left arm tucked close to his body, sheltering the rings while his right arm and eagle-head war hammer swung furiously at all before him, denting armor and breaking bones.

Mannix exploded into the second line. Another wild swing caught several Drivach and created a wide berth which the men-at-arms were quick to exploit. Furious at how quickly Mannix dispatched their initial champion like the swift felling of a great tree, the Drivach swarmed at him. Plunging strikes from the back ranks hungered to slay the stone-skinned giant. The Ardalen men-at-arms exploited the attention garnered by Mannix and Camhorn, striking with precision stabs and thrusts in gaps in the Drivach armor. A clubbing blow struck Mannix in the lower back which buckled his legs, but he regained his feet and pressed the attack with greater determination. Seeing his friend in danger, Camhorn's lizard maw snapped at exposed faces and outstretched arms, limbs and blood sprays cresting above the fray.

As Camhorn and Mannix pried open the Drivach line like a rusted trap, the blind Sunsmoke still with the cavalry turned towards the center, a great sadness unfolding on his wizened face. He gave no heed to the unnecessary approach of a galloping rider.

"Camhorn! Camhorn!" shouted the messenger. "Where is the Ealdorman? The line has collapsed. We need help. Please!"

Around the time when Camhorn ordered his dismounted cavalry attack, the Drivach renewed their assault on the Ardalen center and the last line of defense, the wagon corral.

Penned in and engulfed in the stench of the Drivach approach, the spooked horses trashed and bucked. Horses tried to climb the cart walls, hooves rattling in the clamor to break free.

Several points of the line did not hold. The intensity and press of the onslaught fell so heavy that many Ardalens died upright, bleeding out or crushed between Drivach fury and the tethered carts. Bayard averted his gaze as pleading hands extended from the multitude.

"Help me! Please!"

Within a small pocket, still strong against the Drivach, a white bison stood, a collar of twisted wood about its neck. With a slight turn of its head, the panicked horses calmed. Floral bloom covered the bison's horns and green shoots emerged from the hooves and glided supply around its legs. Wounded and unnerved troops touched the warm, shaggy hair. The now healed and comforted did not heed the calls to break the link and return to aid their fighting companions.

"Hold the line! Fighters forward!" yelled officers with anger and dread.

The bison groaned, highly distressed at the continual transfer of vitality. Its eyes bulged and body grew colder. Frantic shouts and attempts by the old crones and those with faces painted black and white found small gain.

Brutal, concussive magic eventually freed the bison from the people it had saved. "Away!" shouted a crone, her forearms erupting in lesions and revealed bone from the effort.

Blades were scything so close that the crone was cut on the cheek by a reaching stab. "Eldren!" she screamed oblivious to her own wounds.

The bison, recently of a coat resembling fresh fallen snow, now ice gray, tongue long and languid, moved its head to open a channel in the Ardalen line. Drivach polearms and axe thrusts at the bison's face bent back towards the attackers.

The bison raised its right hoof, and a thundering aura projected across the Drivach front. The wave nearly seemed to shake the Drivach from their stimulant-induced fervor, but the assault continued, Drivach beginning to crawl over or slither under the wagon corral.

The bison wheezed, and the flowering vines shriveled. It bucked up, raising its front legs and crashed down with a massive wave of bright light which finally ended the Drivach charge. The light blinded all around, and the stunned Drivach began a lethargic retreat. In the pulse of the light, the bison was no more. The vortexwood staff, faintly smoking, lay coiled like a serpent on the charred and bloody ground.

"He died as a wildhide," choked the crone through a rush of tears, the cut on her cheek slowly fading. "I felt his spirit travel through me."

Camhorn had sent a strong cavalry detachment under Starling and Sunsmoke to make good the Drivach retreat and ensure the herds were unmolested. The ground was strewn with corpses and crawling wretches. Circles formed around the spot where Eldren had vanished. Pleas for forgiveness by the healed were drowned out in the recriminations.

"It's your fault! All of you! You killed him!"

When words of pardon were not spoken forth, accusations flowed. "We'd have never been in this bloody pit, if you all had done your work!" rose the furor of those with sword and spear.

"You are not worthy of his greatness. Get away from me!" shrieked the old crone as she sought comfort amongst the painted faces.

Words spoken in horror, terrified of this moment when Eldren Spruce's counsel and courage were no more. All shared a common, unspoken feeling of insignificance; who among them would be that powerful in their own self-sacrifice?

"Get these carts untethered," called an officer trying to restore order. "We'll take the fallen back with us to rest beneath the trees."

"Mind your rituals, but don't touch our people," a crisp voice shot back. "Lay them bare in the swaddle of the tall grass. Just so as they came."

"Some are not recognizable. Can't sort tree from sky. We all fought together. Let's bury our brothers and sisters here and consecrate the ground," called another voice.

"Oh no!" called one man as another pulled at a corpse. "Don't remove that knife!" Some Northwestern customs called for the body to be interned with all close worldly possessions; others considered the implements of war still of pertinent need to the living and less useful to the departed.

"Stop this!" called Camhorn. "This is not our way. The Drivach will enjoy us destroying ourselves." The Ealdorman looked austere but also as if a flick of a finger could knock him over as he surveyed what had transpired in the center while he had commanded from the right wing. "Observe the rituals, but not at the expense of the living. Make ready to move."

Bambenek slowly approached Camhorn. Carts began to be stacked ignobly with Ardalen dead as they spoke.

"It's my fault. Another victory like this, and the Northwest is completely lost. Eadolan is not coming." Camhorn let out a long breath. "Eldren is a great loss. I relied upon him. The branches obeyed him."

"Don't lose hope. Do you think the forest folk will let his death be in vain?"

"Permit me this weakness. I cannot share it with anyone else." Camhorn looked at Bambenek as if across time. "No royal support, but Bambenek Morley returns as if from the dead. Your head is a mess."

"Looks worse than it is. Just a few scratches."

"Let me see your teeth," asked Camhorn. "Well, it's good to see you haven't lost many more than ones I smashed out."

"That orc you brought us." Camhorn lowered his gaze and leaned in, the teeth of the jaw on the breastplate almost touching Bambenek's face. "I'll save no orc at the cost of one of our own people. We both know that. If he has survived, we'll see what can be learned and extracted in the fever swamps."

Bambenek tried to respond, but Camhorn gave him a rough shake of the shoulder and walked off to comfort the others.

The number of wounded made the return to the forest agonizingly slow. The horses needed to be calmed repeatedly and rotating groups of twenty men assigned to push and pull the carts. In addition to honoring the forest burials, spots on the carts were allocated for choice Drivach weapons and armor; anything of iron was loaded or clanged on the sides in gloomy toll to the dead. Some horses were tethered in tandem to drag a sling between them for those unable to walk. Raptors patrolled the skies without alarm. News of the battle was carried swiftly on the wing and urgent calls for relief to be provided on the return march.

"Did we win or lose today? After every battle, it's fall back, fall back," said Bayard frustrated with trying to bend his sword near enough to straight to put in its scabbard.

"This is what you wanted to do, right? An Amberfield knight in training or did you just want to polish steel and dream about battle? The battle with the Tavuros was your first?"

Bayard nodded.

"And now you've fought in four battles before the moons have passed." Bambenek glanced at the blackening sky. "We win by surviving. People are safe because of you, Bayard." Bambenek gave the young man a scrutinizing look. "You did well, Sir Bayard of Amberfield." Bambenek shot Bayard a grin. Bayard found it hard to resist returning his own.

"What bleeding demon got loose back there? I thought you said these people knew what they're doing. We just stood there waiting to be charged," Bayard said, reliving the agony. "I thought you said the Drivach are bad at magic."

"There'll be plenty of blame to go around. Hope Camhorn can keep the forest folk together, especially those from the Deepwood. It'll be hard after Eldren's death."

"Would you blame them if they decided to leave? I mean, you left Sergeant Farrior and the others."

To end the sting of his own unease, Bambenek pointed at Bayard's bent and chipped blade. "When we get back to the clearing, we'll have a blacksmith take a look at your blade. If it can't be saved, we'll get a new one for you."

Bayard studied Bambenek like a scorpion observing its prey after delivering a venomous strike. "Now that the healers are looking after Dronor, do you think we should go back to the army? We did our share here."

"You don't think this is the army?" Bambenek lifted his eyes from the hypnotic swish of the grass around his feet. "We're protecting our country, right?"

"I guess I meant when do we go home?" Tears started to well as Bayard watched family members approaching to welcome back loved ones or collapsing in grief at their absence. "It's just that my family is probably wondering where I am. Do you have people waiting for you or is this your home now?"

"The people here need you." Bambenek was silent for a long moment, observing the same scenes. "You've got to make your own way. If you decide to go, I understand, but I won't walk you back."

"I'm no child," responded Bayard contorting his face and ready to unleash his frustration, but a shout at the tree line shook Bayard from his thoughts.

"Where is the Ealdorman?" came the calls.

Two dirt-covered men with drawn faces behind black beards walked towards the returning army. They looked like they had not slept in weeks. The men carried large packs and satchels. Despite the evident fatigue, they refused all offers to share in the carrying of the burden. The men wore drab green gambesons with a radiant golden star faintly visible on the chest.

Bayard observed them closely and even weighted down with the packs and satchels he knew their demeanor and stride befit those of hardened warriors. He stared transfixed, amazed at warriors carrying such weight in porter's drudgery. "Who are they?" Bayard murmured as he stole closer behind a tree to observe their audience with Camhorn.

"Yes?" called Camhorn impatiently. "What demon is loose now? My ears are wilting," he said, not recognizing the men. "This better be about more than counting hay bales."

"We are Faolan and Cobart, monks of the Burzina Monastery. By chance has our brethren monk, Eafford, preceded our arrival?"

CHAPTER 23

"Make way for the Lady of Jevatryn! Katya Billengrath!" called two liveried heralds in quick succession as adoring crowds pressed forward to get a better view.

"The Queen of Lace," mocked Mage Albright.

"Why does Eadolan put up with this?" wondered Votark as he took in the long procession accompanying Lady Katya. "You should talk to him, Elias," the stout dwarf said distractedly, still finding flecks of iron and soot in his dull red hair. Votark kept his moustache bushy, his head and chin shaved, and his beard split into twisted tapers with multiple thin iron rings to maintain the shape. His clothes displayed a two-tone reminder of his labors after the removal of his smith's apron.

"You know the stories of Katya and Berislan. Word is she just glided over to the next in line," said Albright with a sneer. He thought Lady Katya caught his eye as he watched the procession down Temple Street. The rampart of the Academy of Alchemy and Arcane Phenomena towered forty feet above the street. The Academy, headquarters of the Zaravandian

Order, was also a massive stone redoubt anchored within the eastern quarter of Ravalas.

Lady Katya rode in an elongated chariot covered in pristine white lacquer; a deep, shimmering cobalt blue trimmed the chariot walls and wheels. The chariot wheels mirrored the spoked weaving wheel design of the Jevatryn town crest. Pulling the chariot were two white horses covered in silken blue caparisons richly brocaded with cerise and peach hibiscus.

The Queen of Lace, one of the richest people in Ardalen-cor, proprietor of the lucrative Jevatryn textile mills, owner of several towns and villages, and wielder of ever-expanding commercial influence: cornering markets in sticky wine, quietly backing new mining operations near Ironhorn, and financing distant trading expeditions at levels rivaling the great merchants of Floriana. Much of her wealth found its way back into Ardalen society through the sponsorship of veterans' hospitals and charity houses and gifts and small loans to lesser noble houses.

Lady Katya's sense of fashion long held sway at the royal court. Smiling brightly from her resplendent chariot, she wore a light green taffeta dress with dark blue and golden brocade on the long sleeves and bodice, white lace accentuating the collar and cuffs. Her deep chestnut brown hair was braided with elegant lace ribbon.

The chariot driver was a small man as not to obstruct the world's view of Lady Katya. Serving as immediate bodyguard, also with her on the chariot platform, was a foreign kaldoon who nodded and smiled as the situation required.

"Who is the spellbinder?" asked Albright trying to take his measure.

"His name is Agozeru. Recent arrival," offered Nestor Catalfo, the Order's Spymaster. Even standing in shadow and sheltered behind obscuring wards, he still wore his cloak hood up and a false long blond beard. The Archmage would not have permitted Catalfo, even with the utmost precaution, to risk the chance of being seen standing next to known members of the Order. Albright was less concerned and relished the small deviances in protocol with the Archmage away.

"Keep eyes on him," said Albright. "What happened to the last advisor?"

"He was a man of some talent," whispered Catalfo. "It took some time to arrange plausible circumstances."

Catalfo was a Milikanthai, part of a now small religious minority with scant-remaining enclaves scattered around Ardalencor. Their numbers dwindled after High Lord Varhan the Pious initiated a purge against Milikanthai ritual, then forbid the creation of burial mounds, and then sanctioned massacres of recalcitrant adherents. As immediate tensions and hostility faded over the past three centuries, the Order actively recruited from the Milikanthai as guards, servants, and stewards such that their presence in the Order's ranks swelled disproportionately to their actual numbers in Ardalen society. Milikanthai service to the Order ensured protection of the Milikanthai enclaves, which in turn reinforced their loyalty to the Order. If the Order would ever fall out of favor with the High Lord or face a widespread societal revolt against their influence, the two minority groups would find common cause.

The onlooking members of the Order watched as more units of a several-hundred-strong contingent of the Jevatryn Guard paraded into view. The Queen of Lace had a scintillating, martial fascination with dwarves, and they composed the majority of her personal guard. The dwarves marched in uniform panoply of white padded jackets overlain with chain mail. Ruffled blue silken undershirts flared out from their collars. The sun glistened across polished steel helmets, long cheek plates and nose guards masking most of the faces. Atop the helmets, a distinct cruciform ridge deterred skull-shattering head blows which were the ever-shadowing bane of a dwarf. Dwarven officers in the Jevatryn ranks had blue plumes of musk ox or horse hair affixed to the apex of their helmets.

An elongated hexagonal shield, heavy javelin, war hammer and short sword slung on the hip constituted the common kit. The one nod to individuality afforded the soldiers was the ornamentation of their shields. Within the required pallet of white and blue, a variety of fearsome images covered the shields from shark jaws, to skeleton heads, to fang-draped vipers, to snarling demons.

Teleg Drenith, the leader, or Eredurkar, of Lady Katya's personal guard, marched at the head of the column, his chalky ginger beard meticulously braided. Eredurkar, the name of a legendary dwarven warrior, a name so revered that it passed over the centuries into more common usage to denote a dwarven general or commander.

Votark scoffed as he caught sight of Drenith.

"You know him well?" asked Albright.

"We have met on occasion. Very distant connection through the old clans."

Two notable flourishes distinguished Drenith's armor from the other dwarven officers. The first, his helmet boasted a large horsehair crest of alternating blue and white. The second item, an ornamental collar, was a recent gift in recognition for a decade of loyal service. The collar, which sat expansively across the upper chest, depicted Kveruk, the patronymic deity of Drenith. Fashioned of whale bone, the piece of martial art told the sweeping story of Kveruk's formation of the world and creation of the dwarves. The usually austere and irascible Drenith wept heavy tears of surprise when he received such a gift. He wore it proudly, his chest puffed out even more than usual, as he led his men through Ravalas. Armed with just the mark of his station, the Eredurkar raised and lowered his war mattock as he barked orders.

Half-orcs, bare-chested Drivach, and other imposing, grizzled soldiers for hire marched with great swords and polearms. Svelte elves marched near the front and back of the column, carrying repeating-dart crossbows which were recently imported through the docks of Floriana. Squadrons of blue-caped light cavalry formed the end of the procession.

"Is this all for show or are they going to march beneath the royal standard?" grumbled Votark.

"She'll make sure her contributions are acknowledged. She may loan Eadolan the savages, expendable and cheap to replace," said Albright.

"She keeps around four thousand under arms and will pull in more rabble and foreign hirelings to her private army," said Catalfo.

"What do you think happened to all the Southwesterners in her service?" raised Votark. "I am sure they're trying to keep their heads down, or they left already?"

"You mean those in household service or the mills?" asked Albright.

"In her personal army. I am sure they're weighing their odds and will make up their mind depending on whether Padazar shows his black beard. Right now, they're receiving regular pay for just dancing on cobblestones."

"Loyal men or units from the Southwest are a good sign, and if lace and lacquer keep them in step, then so be it," said Albright. "Still, better to keep them marching. I'll talk to Behan. We don't need idle foreign savages in the city. And dwarves aren't much for standing watch on the walls," Albright chided Votark.

Votark lightly punched Albright in the gut. "Better short and strong than soft in the belly," laughed Votark.

"She is a slippery eel," reminded Catalfo. "Best get to Behan quickly. You may be too late. He already could have agreed to adding her troops to the city's garrison."

"He can't agree to that without my approval!" snapped Albright.

"She is a power in her own right. Best to keep her good graces," stated Catalfo.

"Go easy, Elias," added Votark. "Mind your temper."

"Are we going to have another parade when Urric's wife and son arrive?" Albright muttered. "I am sure he is enjoying this sight. And what a time for the child's tutelage to begin. We'll see whether this boy will have the talents worthy of the Boscawent name or if it skipped another generation."

"What do you know of them? Kamila is Chetwin Claypool's daughter, yes?" asked Votark glancing in Catalfo's direction.

"A lovely girl. The hem of her dress may not always be straight, but a lovely girl," said Catalfo.

"Yes, most certainly. Your Grace should have received a message written in the Archmage's own hand. A battle has been won by the Order at Lost Bugle Bridge. The Tavuros have been forced to keep more troops at Thavodyn. Our strong presence blocks—"

"A great battle indeed!" shouted Eadolan. "Your plan is working? Did it stop Padazar from moving? He took Croydon without a fight. He's fifty miles from here!"

Albright contorted his face but held his tongue.

"Did your Archmage stop Nabrensus from moving? He's past Middlepost, a few days ride from here." Eadolan glanced out a window of the council chamber as if to catch a glimpse of the Tavurite approach. "We are receiving countless reports of cavalry loose and burning the countryside. A group of blood-soaked women arrived this morning with tales to burst your heart. Have you consoled them with your Archmage's brilliant plan?" Eadolan paced and then approached Mage Albright, their faces almost touching.

Behan started to stand, wondering if he may need to defend his brother. Chancellor Droswild clenched his pipe between his teeth and looked on with peaked curiosity.

Albright took a step back, stammering between reassurance and apology. "Ride out to meet Nabrensus on ground of your choosing," he said finally. Eadolan was about to interrupt, but Albright raised his hands. "It's over fifty miles from Croydon to here. If Padazar's force is of any size, he'll need the river to supply it, especially for a siege train that could even begin to threaten Ravalas, let alone to feed and house his army over winter. The Tavuros are the immediate threat, but if Nabrensus intended to lay siege, he would not divide his force. He'd ride straight here. Nabrensus wants battle." Albright shook his head, affirming his own thoughts. "Padazar will float the river. He depends on it. With Longcloak at Avenbair Castle—"

"Longcloak is here, in Ravalas," corrected Behan. "Brother, you summoned him to take command of a field army, but with Sir Crowiler's return, the original purpose has been resolved."

"Yes, with the return of our champion, I don't need Long-cloak here." Eadolan slightly relaxed, finding a ready solution for one of his many problems. "Although I still have an expanded command for him." Eadolan stroked his cheek as if in deep thought. "Avenbair Castle is impregnable and well worth the money. Send Longcloak back on a fast ship with supplies to Pelham. He will stiffen their resolve. Tell Longcloak to hold Pelham to the last man. Confer on him noble title and tell him he will be granted lands should he fulfill his High Lord's wishes. And lastly, confirm Longcloak in independent command. He can ignore any requests or demands from Lord Tarpley for reinforcements for his Midriver army. Pelham must be held."

Behan finished writing the instructions. He rang a bell, and a courier entered to carry out the order.

"Lady Katya Billengrath is here," the courier whispered to Behan. "She's waiting down the hall in a receiving room."

As soon as the courier left, Eadolan resummoned his fury with Albright.

Albright rushed to speak. "Your Grace, the Order defends Ardalencor. Here is my advice. One. Ride to meet Nabrensus. If their army is scattered, move quickly and force a battle. Nabrensus wants a battle before winter and departing back home. Wizards Artos and Cyra and two hundred men-at-arms as well as several of our most promising apprentices will join the royal army. When we work together, we will beat Nabrensus."

"Two. Assembling a river fleet needs urgent discussion. I will offer apprentices and attendants to aid the fleet."

"Three. Much of the Order will accompany Your Grace or is already fighting the enemy. I will remain in Ravalas and direct what members remain in assisting Behan with the defense of the city. Should Padazar or Nabrensus approach," Albright's eyes shown with bright intensity, "I will die in the rumble of the walls to bar their way." Albright breathed heavily, his body tingling.

Eadolan stared at Albright for a moment and then clasped him on the shoulders. "Marvelous."

Eadolan turned to Behan. "Now, what of our river fleet?"

"I suggest we bring Rafal into this discussion. He is waiting outside. Lady Katya is also waiting."

"Summon them both."

In his late twenties and still unwed, Rafal the Younger, as he was called to distinguish from his father, entered somberly. Rafal Stokes, the only son of Duke and General of the Line of March Rafal Stokes, was heir to Stokesbridge; his name and claim to a stone bridge carried countless more weight than his own achievements. Stokesbridge, a major commercial and manufacturing center and Ardalencor's third largest city, was notably, and vitally, the only spanned point on the Avenbair. The center arch of the incredible stone bridge allowed all ship traffic to move unhindered.

Displaying little interest in knightly training, Rafal was highly educated and well prepared to inherit his father's title of Duke. Rafal exemplified the part in a luxurious cream-colored tunic, a red jacket patterned in white, cream, and horizon blue, jeweled pendant and rings of gold. His hair was razor short; a trimmed goatee and beard framed his jaw.

After exchanging pleasantries, Rafal said dutifully, "I am not a soldier, but I am compelled to join the army. A man must step forward. I ask not to replace my father as General; I am far from deserving of such a position. I ask only to serve."

"Rafal, don't be so dramatic. You are amongst family," said Eadolan. "It is welcome news to have another Stokes in my war council. We pray for the return of your father and are working to secure his release."

"Our knights were under your banner at Boruma," began Rafal. He glanced in amazement at Lady Katya entering the council chamber along with two attendants carrying small chests. Rafal continued, "More of our family's forces will be arriving soon and without a self-indulgent parade."

"Will you send enough fighting men worthy of a parade, dear Rafal? I raised the sprits of the entire city. Your jealousy is as bright as your coat!" Lady Katya raised her finger, and the two attendants opened the chests. "My High Lord, some gifts for Sahalana and the future heir." Katya pointed to the second chest. "And Royal Steward. Some toys for your precious girls and fragrance bottles for Avlina."

"Very gracious of you as always, Lady Katya," said Eadolan as her attendants took their leave.

"Quite the distant trip from Jevatryn. I trust it was uneventful. We're honored by your presence in the capital, Lady Katya. Perhaps you are looking to make a suitable match for Barbora during your stay?" prodded Chancellor Droswild trying to put a stop to her theatrics.

Behan glanced at his brother-in-law, but Rafal was expressionless.

"Yes, Barbora is of ready age. I wish to seek the High Lord's blessing, but that is not a matter for today. The defense of Ardalencor is the vital issue. Our country will stir and raise a new generation of heroes."

"Why seek the High Lord's blessing?" Droswild asked with a raised eyebrow. "Unless you are considering a foreign marriage for Barbora?"

"What a strange question, Chancellor? Do you have a foreign match in mind as you are considering alliances and securing Ardalencor's position beyond our borders?"

Droswild gave a sly grin at goading Lady Katya into saying more on the topic than she perhaps had intended.

"You shall not marry off my daughter without my agreement," she admonished but warmed just as quickly. "I would be interested in hearing your thoughts, but I must ensure Barbora's happiness. She is my only child, and she will not be used as a trinket."

"You may rest easy, Lady Katya," replied Droswild. "I have no such designs for your lovely Barbora."

"Even with your fellow Blackbirds abandoning the High

Lord for the Tavuros, you've lost none of your charm." Lady Katya shook her head. "A splendid creature you are to represent this country in the most delicate diplomatic matters." She reflexively swept her sleeves as if to physically banish the remarks of the Chancellor.

"Might we all look to our common problems and find a solution. All this bickering can wait," Behan scolded. "Rukez is weaving wonders to provision the army, however, he is anticipating that food will be in short supply come summer. We need to be importing more grain and food of all kinds now to make up the shortfall in the harvest and the likely destruction of some existing stores."

All nodded in agreement.

"If ships are to be sent to acquire more food, let's also talk about the need to maintain control of the Avenbair," said Rafal.

"We can try to get a message to Admiral Zelihis but with him protecting the long-range merchants, who knows where he is along the sea roads," said Behan. "Any message waiting for him in port will be on his return anyway."

"Yes, but if the right port is chosen to wait with a message," said Katya, "it may hasten his return."

"The Admiral is too far out. We'll need to assemble our own river fleet," added Eadolan. "Swift's Broadshield is already on its way here. I cannot leave Floriana completely defenseless. The warships at Floriana will stay to protect the coast."

"I am not sure if you all are aware, but Robard Bracken of Masthead has already foreseen the need. He is assembling a fleet, much at his own expense. I am helping to subsidize the costs of supplying the fleet and raising archers. The merchants of Stokesbridge will also provide ships," said Rafal proudly before looking at Lady Katya. "I don't know how to say this, so I will just say it plainly. Katya, I understand you have put forward no ships."

"A mishearing," she blushed. "I assure you."

Katya fixed her full attention on Eadolan. "Your Grace, I am above all else loyal to you and Ardalencor. I came here to affirm my loyalty and to pledge two thousand of my own forces, and I will provide funds for the equipping of two thousand line infantry. With the plots of land that you are offering, this should excite many a young man to march forth with shield and spear."

"Furthermore, I offer my cavalry to protect the northern plains to keep the caravan and animal drives open. You will forgive me, but my cavalry are not the mighty warhorses suited for a frontline charge, but they certainly will discourage banditry and deter Tavurite raiding parties. This should ease the mind of Duke Urric as he musters his own forces. I presume he is seeing to the army at this moment."

"Yes, Duke Urric and Sir Crowiler."

"In addition, as there is much rumor being spread," Katya winced, "let me also make another offer. I have heard about Braithwaite's thievery. If a small loan is needed, I am here to assist and understand if installments on the loan funding the expansion of the wharves need to be paused. And, if a new Treasurer is needed, I can provide someone from my coterie, temporarily, of course, as you consider the best replacement."

"No one is questioning your loyalty and generosity, Lady Katya. We have a new Treasurer but know that your graciousness to this family and to the country will always be remembered."

Satisfied that her position was secured, she turned to the welfare of others. "What of the nobles and officers from our army?" she said, looking between Eadolan and Rafal. "Any word as to their return?"

Behan shook his head vehemently at Lady Katya to smother the question and raced to fill the silence. "There will be a dinner tonight, and you are our invited guests," he said, pointing to Katya and Rafal. "If Barbora is in Ravalas as well, we would be honored by her presence. Two great houses of Ardalencor. Stokes. Billengrath. Rafal is unwed, and Barbora is ready for marriage. Seems like a perfect match to me," he said with a smile.

"Barbora is in Jevatryn. Stokes is a great and ancient family of Ardalencor," Lady Katya said with a slight nod to Rafal, "but Barbora's future husband, Royal Steward, is not a topic for discussion in open committee." She moved towards the door. "Please excuse me. Good day, Lords."

CHAPTER 24

Bayard collapsed in sleep not long after Camhorn's army returned to the forest camp. After sleeping most of the following day, as Bayard started to move about the camp and contemplate his return south, he heard a jovial voice call, "It is good to find a true believer of Indalos."

The assertion of his faith surprised Bayard; then he remembered the talisman about his neck. A talisman of Indalos that he took from Arvid, his dead friend, after the failed attempt to reach Thavodyn.

"Yes," Bayard said, relieved to find a connection to something familiar, as the two Burzina monks, Faolan and Cobart, walked over. "I've heard the stories of Martoz the Black." To most men across Ardalencor, there was a legendary aura around the Burzina Monastery which up until recently had been the last stronghold of the increasingly reclusive Arm of Indalos.

"Every story you've heard of Master Martoz and his black armor is true." Cobart smiled. "There is no one like him."

"It is our regret that we could not stand with him to the

302

end," Faolan remarked with melancholy. "We obeyed his orders to begin the monastery anew."

"Would you excuse us?" Cobart said to Bayard as Camhorn approached. "We shall speak again."

Camhorn motioned for the two monks to follow him to a quieter part of the encampment. "Forgive my temper yesterday."

Faolan raised his hand to waive off the need for an apology. "Ealdorman, have you had time to consider our request?"

"I have, and the answer remains no. I have no men to spare." Camhorn shook his head. "It's certain death. Incursions like this were abandoned years ago. The last one of any size, no one came back."

"Fifteen."

"What?" grumbled Camhorn.

"Fifteen came back," Faolan calmly responded. "Your father sent a thousand men into the mountains to free captives and burn out the Drivach. Our monastery sent brothers to help. Master Martoz answered your father's call when he was Ealdorman. One of the fifteen who returned was a monk named Bagdarin. He recounted the grim stories. Fateful to say, I took more interest than most. I have heard these stories countless times. I feel like I know the mountains."

"You don't," Camhorn said sharply and then took a more hospitable tone. "You are welcome to stay as long as you like. We need fighting men. If you want to re-found the monastery here, we can help you select some possible sites."

"Our monastery answered your father's call. Has his son forgotten?"

"I am responsible to protect thousands and guard hundreds of miles of frontier against the Drivach, and now the Tavuros; and you want to march into the mountains to look for relics and magical tomes or whatever else because you think, think, the Drivach have taken them."

"We know," Cobart stressed. "Eafford carried the most sacred relics. The oldest, they are infused with centuries of stored energy and prayer."

"The Drivach would never have been near Burzina. Why do you think the Drivach have them? Maybe the Tavuros captured Eafford?"

"We escaped one by one through tunnels and made our way through the Tavurite siege lines. We were all to take different routes and make our way to Thornhelm. It is possible something happened along the way."

"Possible!" scoffed Camhorn. "And now the Drivach have full access to their power?"

"They are shielded, well, it is complicated to explain," Cobart began.

"Best that they are recovered quickly," finished Faolan.

"I cannot make this decision alone. Venduva must be consulted." Camhorn stopped and looked at both men, now more fully recalling the return of the survivors to Thornhelm so many years ago. He grated his teeth. "You answered our call, and I will answer yours. Whether Venduva sanctions the journey or not, I'll order two men, good men, to join you. Let it be an equal undertaking," he added cynically. "You can ask for volunteers as well after Venduva has provided her counsel. If she refuses to affirm the mission, I will demand she perform the divination."

The two monks glanced at each other. "Thank you, Ealdorman," Cobart said disappointedly.

"I know this is not what you wanted," offered Camhorn. "I admire much about you monks. You still carry the more heroic age of the faith, and not what Mondray represents. What I most respect is your reverence of silence, of protecting secrets.

There are thousands in this camp, and there is much chittering already about your arrival. For the divination, I must tell Venduva the true nature of your mission. When the volunteers are sought, the mission will be a return and search of the monastery grounds to seek what survived the pillaging. You can give the adventurers, those you trust, the true destination closer to departure. The two men I am ordering to join you are trustworthy beyond doubt. I also will see that you are well-provisioned. Discreetly."

Camhorn knelt and peered between the trees and into the canopy. "In the forest camps, there is some number, we think very small, of Drivach informants, and then an untold number of craven opportunists. Silence. Or your mission will be spoiled before you reach the tall grass."

"Do you believe them?" repeated Venduva Greenbond. The most renowned seer in the Northwest grasped a large crystal hanging from her bracelet and cradled it in her thick fingers.

Camhorn still pondered the question as he stared and sniffed at some of the smoldering bowls placed about the great room of Venduva's log house. It was Venduva's home and nearby Seer's Grove which served as the rallying point for those fleeing both the Tavuros and Drivach. "Something happened with our magic. We were unprepared or complacent in thinking it would work. Maybe the Drivach learned to repel or counter."

"You think Eldren would have let that happen?"

"No, but something happened. Something he did not consider. Either they are better now or we were lazy," Camhorn said bluntly, his thoughts lingering on Eldren's death and the narrow victory that it salvaged. "That was the last battle until the snows. We'll harry the Tavuros during winter, try to push them out of Thornhelm before the thaws."

"This winter the snows will be deep," said Venduva gently fingering her long golden-white hair. "I imagine your wife will be spending another season away. How many years has it been now? If you—"

Camhorn irritably did his best to ignore her questions and offer. "Rusher's asking for men for the eastern edge. He said more Drivach are coming down, and he's worried they'll build stockades in the forest. I wonder if Eadolan stopped the payments to Bersadok, or if they just gave up trying to control the Drivach."

"So, send more men to help the Foxpaw. Rusher would not ask if he did not think it dire. Did you come here to ask my approval?" she said jokingly, knowing there was more on Camhorn's mind.

"I want your blessing for the monks' mission."

"Into mountains?" she laughed, her heavy breasts bouncing beneath her linen dress as she swayed. "Did some Drivach club knock your senses loose or are you thinking with that lizard brain?"

"I'm returning the obligation of my father and the monks' service to us."

"Ah, so there it is," she said disapprovingly. "Stubborn and oath-bound."

"I didn't come here to beg you. If you refuse, then perform the divination."

"Eldren's dead. Rusher's pleading for help. Now you want to make this an issue? Some mad march into the skyward wastes? A divination for this? This farce may cost you the commitment of many. Few will remain through winter, and those who leave may not return."

"It is my right to demand the divination. You will perform

it!" growled Camhorn. "I am honoring their commitment to my father and to us. I think our people will understand even if you do not."

"They will understand? Then tell them the true location."

Camhorn wrung his hands and pulled at his thick moustache. "They will understand helping the monks. A return to Burzina is not an easy journey. If they think this is the reason for the divination, so be it. Obligation binds our people; I am fulfilling mine. Don't worry. I'd only send two men. I will not have it said that I turned away those who helped our people."

"Who are you sending? Two so lame they can just tend a fire?" chuckled Venduva.

Camhorn returned to Venduva's comment about possible camp desertions. "If there are those who are thinking of not returning, of scattering in the wind." He stabbed the air with his finger. "Help them remember their word. If you will just stand back now and observe. If you are just a pair of puffed-up eyes, then what difference is there between you and a crippled fire watch?"

Venduva glared at Camhorn. His harsh words had the intended effect. Camhorn did not think of Venduva in this way, but he had been drained of any patience. When Camhorn Thorpe told man or woman that they were not doing enough, even in a private discussion, that was a deep wound. A wound that could be healed easily but not easily forgotten.

"I am always grateful for your guidance. Perform the divination. The moons are right. That is sign enough."

"Placement of the moons? You'll need a stronger argument than that," battled Venduva, not ready to concede after a bruising insult. "I will perform the divination, but I determine the right time."

"The moons control the waves and the moods of women.

And now the moons are aligned. What stronger force can there be?"

Venduva began to grin but forced a frown to suppress the impulse.

"Seer, I need your help. Perform the ritual tonight. What you portend may persuade the monks."

Worried of growing discontent among the factions, Camhorn walked again through the camp to offer reassurances and raise morale. As he moved from one campfire conversation to the next, he glanced at the descending sun, in great doubt whether Venduva would perform the divination.

"Are you alright, Mannix?" asked Camhorn uneasily, taking a true assessment of his friend for the first time since the return to the forest.

"Something ain't right. Getting worse, but I'm waiting." Mannix's speech slurred, and his breath was rank with drink. The giant of a man was hunched over, barely able to stand. "Others worse off than me."

"Healer!" called Camhorn.

"Cam, shut your mouth or suck a root," snapped Mannix. "I'll wait. Just bring me a big jug of barley. I'll be alright."

"Healer!" Camhorn called again.

Not long after, Venduva approached with two female votaries. Venduva now wore a vibrant turquoise dress of fine wool faintly patterned in deep blue. A thick bear stole was pulled tightly across her shoulders. She was barefoot with bracelets of vines intertwining crystals on her ankles.

The two young votaries wore loosely spun gowns of black sheep's wool and further woven with bursts of color. The faces, arms, and legs of the young women were painted similarly with varied patterns to symbolize the infinite possibilities of the future.

"The Ealdorman has demanded a divination. Mannix Splitwood, you by right of strength, are selected to perform the honor of presenting the Hunbertys." Venduva assessed his state more fully. "Have you been healed?"

"Does it look like I have? Were you able to help Rusk and Fowler?"

"Yes, the poison is purged. They'll be fine."

Mannix nodded in thanks, but Venduva did not let the gratitude linger. "Good that you are of pure form to participate in the ritual."

"What ritual?" Mannix asked through squinted eyes. He tried to straighten himself but needed the help of others.

"Your Ealdorman and protector of these lands has demanded a divination," she repeated. "Your spine is bruised like a gnarled tree, but you can walk. By right of strength, it is your role among all gathered. Or shall you ask some stripling to stand in your stead? If you cannot do it, that is omen enough."

"Mannix," said one of the men helping the giant, but Mannix pushed the man aside.

Camhorn crossed and uncrossed his arms, trying to appear calm.

"As shoots grow towards the sun, a man is drawn to duty," said Mannix loudly.

"Very well," Venduva said with a wry smile; and then she seemed far away, transfixed in the start of the divination. "Let it begin." Her eyes flickered in a multitude of color.

Camhorn patted Mannix on the shoulder and gripped his hand.

Mannix hissed into Camhorn's ear. "The day keeps getting better." The giant squeezed his friend's hand with all his might so that Camhorn had to pry his hand out before the bones popped.

Venduva gave a series of rhythmic calls. The crowd, now in the hundreds and still growing, hummed and chanted, no words, just tonal waves to bind the energy of the group. Mannix grinned, feeling the energy pulse across his skin and tingling the hairs of his beard.

The divinations were used for undertakings of high risk and danger to glean the outcome or to call off expeditions, however vital or well-founded, if the divination revealed hidden disaster. All those present at a divination were expected to participate in one manner or another, a communal experience to beseech clarity into their shared future.

The rest of the encampment continued to gather and formed a procession behind Mannix. Immediately behind Mannix followed Venduva flanked by the two votaries. As they approached Seer's Grove, the votaries stripped Mannix to the waist and gently rubbed oils and colorful powders onto his back and shoulders. Venduva took position in the center of the grove and continued to intone, her head swaying, her eyes closed and black.

Two men and two women from the crowd were selected to verify whether Mannix would be able to remove the chosen fern without aid of any kind. The votaries then motioned for Mannix and the four others to follow them deeper into the forest to the selected Hunbertys.

In the remaining light, the leaves of the Hunbertys were especially a shimmering silver. Magical resonance, fed by energy pulsing across the planet, imbued the rich shade of silver. Of all plant life in Ardalencor, Hunbertys most attuned to this energy, and the fronds gave clear outward sign.

Mannix had observed and participated in such rituals before but loudly muttered, "You sweaty bitch," when he saw the selected plant. The Hunbertys was wide and no doubt had deep roots. Mannix slapped his arms and legs to awaken his muscles and to channel the pain away from his back. The two women ceremonially cleared some of the dirt from around the base, but it was the rite and duty of the strongest man to rend the sacred plant from the soil.

Mannix circled the Hunbertys twice in showy display, but his true goal was to find the best place from which to attempt the harvesting. The fern's trunk was over a foot in diameter, and the numerous fronds, long and leafy, dazzled in translucent silver.

Having chosen his spot, Mannix dropped to one knee and grabbed where the root crown started. He leaned a shoulder, testing whether the fern's roots would easily release their clutch.

The group of four looked on pensively. They understood that this would not be easy and could stretch on into the black of night and may ultimately end in failure through exhaustion or the misfortune of insufficient roots being preserved. "There is merit in the struggle," mouthed one of the women as all four quietly hoped for Mannix's success.

In the Northwest, where capable crafters of magic were more readily found than in the rest of Ardalencor, great trials completed without the use of magic were still highly revered. In a ritual such as this, the use of magic would interfere with the portent and blur the vision of the future.

Mannix paced his breathing. The fern did not yield to his shoulder. He released the pressure and worked his fingers deeper for a better grip. Mannix pushed, driving his feet into the earth, and with a loud grunt dropped to his knees. Panting and gulping air, he pushed his hair back from his eyes and noticed the fern had moved slightly.

Gaining a surge of energy, he quickly jumped up and

strained to loosen the side further. He felt the fern's trunk move again. Veins bulged and rippled in his neck. He shouted as he lifted to free the Hunbertys, but the fern still clung to the earth. He lost his footing, reeled, and thudded to the ground like a felled tree.

Bleary-eyed and breathless, he waived off the expressionless votaries who came over to peer down at him. "Not over!" he screamed. "Camhorn Thorpe, you fucking bastard. I'm going to break your face when I'm done with this," he roared in anger and release.

Mannix stood and slapped his arms and legs with such fury that even the votaries winced at the force of the blows. He dropped again to one knee, causing the four observers to exchange worried glances. Mannix then launched himself like a charging bear at the Hunbertys, smacking it with his shoulder and lifting with his huge arms. The roots ripped and popped. The Hunbertys listed to one side.

After what seemed a perpetual wait, the crowd murmured at the sound of footsteps crunching on leaves and branches. The crowd vibrated in silent cheer as Mannix returned. Mannix, weary but triumphant, carried the Hunbertys over his shoulder, a thick tangle of exposed and dangling roots leading the way. As Mannix moved to the center, the two votaries took the bridle of an elk from a servant and led the animal to Venduva.

Bayard watched on in wonderment and used the shoulder of a bemused Bambenek to propel his jump higher, hoping to catch a better glimpse as the crowd moved and swayed.

Mannix's knees started to wobble as Venduva seemed to take her time in examining the roots and instructing him how to place the massive Hunbertys atop an oblong divining stone so that most of the roots would not touch the ground. With each passing moment, his face seemed a new shade of pale red.

Venduva calmly flicked a finger to show the angle of placement. His feet jittered but regained their hold, and his whole body cried out in relief as the trunk rested upon stone. Satisfied of the placement, Venduva raised her arms to signal a burst of whoops and cheers in recognition of Mannix.

As Mannix straightened, agony pulsed through his body, but he ground his teeth shut to maintain the required silence. Between proud strides and painful half steps, Mannix passed out of Seer's Grove, took a few more steps for good measure, and then collapsed to the ground in a howl. Healers in their multitude rushed to his aid.

Oblivious to what transpired beyond the grove, Venduva and the votaries continued the ritual. The bridle was removed from the elk. The animal remained calm despite the noise of the crowd. Venduva whispered in its ear and embraced it around the head. She kept the elk soothed and walked it around the Hunbertys.

In a blur, she drew a long blade from beneath her bear stole and swiftly sliced the animal's neck. She placed a hand on the elk's head and then quickly moved to observe the cascade of steaming blood over the maze of Hunbertys roots. Silence. The only sound in and around Seer's Grove were the two votaries softly chanting as Venduva fixated on the rivulets, the pooling, and the full course of the blood.

Bambenek could not see the ritual, but he felt the energy of the place. Eyes closed, he, like many others gathered, hoped to glimpse shards of the future.

After a while Venduva started to move within the grove.

Camhorn and the monks stood immediately outside the grove. The Ealdorman grabbed both their arms and whispered, "Don't say anything until she is finished. She is not one to argue or haggle about her divination. You may get one question if you are lucky."

The votaries attended to Venduva and wiped away any blood. Venduva's face did not betray any indication as she walked towards Camhorn and the two monks.

"Ealdorman, you have requested a divination. I have seen. I have seen in the tendrils of time and memory," she said in a raised voice as the crowd pressed closer. "White is all around. You must go in winter. Heed to leave until snow carpets the ground for two days. What is taken may never be recovered. I cannot see your path out. It is obscured in rock and snow."

As the two monks stood open-mouthed, working through each line, Venduva and the two votaries quickly departed.

As the crowd churned and repeated to one another the vague and foreboding message, Camhorn shouted to the crowd to follow him to hear more of the purpose for the divination. Camhorn led the group back to the main camp and stood on a raised platform for the crowd to get a better view. A healer amplified Camhorn's voice by spiraling the sound around the larger trees.

"We will help these monks. I know many of you know, all too well, the tale of the lost searchers. And if you know the story well enough, you know the monks stood by us, and their brothers perished alongside our people."

"Burzina Monastery is almost certainly destroyed. These monks seek to return and assess what can be salvaged. Hope that they may find survivors. I asked Venduva for a divination to help guide their journey. It will not be easy moving across the plains. If you think," Camhorn continued, "I am doing this just to uphold the word of my father, well, then you don't think I can look past the end of my own nose. Help is what we do for one another. I'll let these monks say what they want, but you need to understand that these are two of Martoz's best."

"There were better," said Faolan quietly with sincere humility.

Camhorn glanced at Faolan, not sure how many heard the monk's words. Camhorn looked at the monk but spoke in a way for the crowd to hear. "Your humility is admirable, but he would not have sent you two unless he trusted you to continue the traditions."

The Ealdorman returned his attention to the crowd. "Based on what you heard, volunteers will be permitted. I know you all are concerned for your own families and many here are not with more than what you wear on your back, but I ask that you hear them out. But before volunteers can join, I'll announce who I am assigning to the mission."

"Why are you doing this, Cam? We got enough problems," shouted a voice. Others added to the clamor. The trees echoed, and the healer stopped the reverberation. Another caster restarted the amplification to add credence to the crowd's concerns, but all the voices mixed in little more than muddy babble.

Camhorn raised his war hammer and shouted, "Enough." That restored order.

"The hammer is plenty. Don't get ol' jawbone. We'll listen," called a voice.

"I just told you why I am doing this. Hear them out. If you want no part, then you are free to make that choice. Any mission should be back before the thaws. I am assigning two men. Any who volunteer will serve under the monks, but you shall all return before the thaws."

"What do you pay?" called another voice.

"Nothing," said Faolan without inflection. "We have no money."

A spate of laughter followed.

Faolan's voice carried in such a way that all could hear. "I think we are like many of you who have fled the destruction of your own home."

His words quieted the crowd.

"We only seek those of pure intention," affirmed Cobart. "We would rather have a fewer true than a bunch of nervous feet. If there be true believers of Indalos, we call upon you to aid your faithful monks after the destruction wrought by heretics." Cobart nodded to Camhorn to signal that they were finished with their appeal and not inclined to lengthy speeches.

Camhorn nodded. "Before volunteers, the two—"

"Who is it?" blurted Rodney Starling with a worried look on his face, thinking this subordinate journey with the monks a possible punishment for him after the recriminations about the ineffectiveness of his forces through most of the battle with the Drivach.

Camhorn laughed. "It ain't you, Starling. I need your ass in the saddle all winter watching the Tavuros."

Starling seemed relieved and then frettingly considered what was the better option.

Camhorn looked like he was ready to brawl with the entire crowd as if daring someone to say another word. His eyes scanned the mass of people, feeling a sense of overwhelming responsibility for their care. "Don't despair. We shall regain our homes and drive out the enemy. This mission with the monks may give us a better sense of the enemy's strength and movements."

"The two men selected. Fishbone. And Hack. Hackett Bale."

The crowd eventually started to part from different directions as the men approached.

Fishbone reached the platform first, ignored the few steps, and leaped up. Fishbone had a wide smile as he greeted Camhorn and the monks. The sinewy man in simple hemps and leathers had long, light brown hair shaved on the sides and tied up in the back. Tattooed on both sides of his head was a fish; the two fish joined in a shared tail down his neck.

Fishbone tapped his foot and played to the crowd. "Are you sure you want this old man? He can't keep pace!" Fishbone offered Hackett a helping hand up the platform, but Hackett slapped it out of the way and nodded respectfully to the monks.

Both were young men in their prime with Hackett a few years older. Hackett had snow eyes, the narrower eyes of the mountain folk, best suited to avoiding snow blindness. In comparison to Fishbone's gauntness, Hackett had a full build and cheeks and a swarthier complexion. His head was shaved except for a thick tuft of black hair down the middle.

"These are two of the finest trackers that we have," said Camhorn. "Good in a fight, too."

"Do you know them?" asked Bayard as he and Bambenek looked on.

Bambenek shook his head. "I've been gone a long time."

Something scratched in Bambenek's mind that the mission was more than a return to the monastery. That seemed easy enough. Why all the emphasis on a scouting mission? Why didn't Camhorn just assign some men and be done with it? Was this Camhorn's grand way of welcoming the monks to try to win favor with Ravalas and the Lodestar? Was this a way to get the silver and birds and cavalry? Bambenek didn't think this forest display would make any difference. Was this Camhorn creating an elaborate show when, in fact, he just was declining the monks' request and only committing two men?

Something seemed off and not just with the arrival of the monks. Bambenek looked around for Dronor, but there was still no sign of him. Bambenek had not seen Dronor since he departed the forest for the fight with the Drivach and any question about Dronor's health or whereabouts was vaguely answered.

Bambenek emerged from the depths of thought and asked
Bayard, "What do you think?" Receiving no answer, Bambenek
turned. Bayard was gone. A dozen paces ahead, Bayard weaved
his way towards the platform.

Bayard approached deliberately with a serious edge on his
face. "I am a stranger to these lands, and yet still it is Ardalencor. I am a believer in Indalos. It is my honor to join." The
monks smiled warmly and embraced Bayard.

"Let's go, you frog snatchers," jeered Fishbone as additional
volunteers were not immediately forthcoming. "We'll be back
well before planting."

"Alright," said Fishbone as the crowd separated to reveal a
slight man shrouded in a hood. The man tipped his bow in affirmation of accepting. "That's Val," pointed Fishbone. "It's a
long story, but he's the best archer."

Bambenek had followed in Bayard's wake through the
onlookers and now stood close to the platform. Bambenek
moved quickly after the introduction of Val. As Bambenek
bounded up the steps, he said to the monks, "My name is
Bambenek. Royal army scout. It will be good to provide a
detailed report about the monastery when I return." Bambenek
eyed the monks for any reaction. Turning to the gathering, he
said, "And I will take the place to save a younger man, some fire
taster, who is considering. Stay with your family and let me
take your place."

Standing quietly, Bambenek felt the shift of a heavy weight,
lost in his own thoughts as to why he was volunteering. Was he
accepting the mission as a favor to Camhorn in order to remain
in the Northwest? Or were the words he spoke genuine and the
best way to return to the army and defend against a possible
desertion charge? He wondered where Farrior and the others
ended up and if he would cross paths with Portnay again.

CHAPTER 25

"Patience, Young Master. We will be there in due time."

"I should be riding. I'm a knight in training. I should be scouting ahead," pleaded Fost.

"All in due time."

"I don't see why he can't be riding," said his mother, Kamila. "We're all stuck in this carriage like a flock of chickens."

"Fost, your horse could stumble," worried an old woman wringing her bony hands.

"It will not!" the boy challenged.

"And it's raining. You could catch a chill," fretted the old woman.

"The Duke has given strict instructions. The roads are too dangerous. The Tavuros, and maybe even Padazar himself, are known to be lurking along the roads," said a thin and dour man. "It is far safer in here. We shall be in Ravalas soon enough," he finished cheerfully.

Kamila pulled back the curtain and slightly opened the heavy wooden shutter. A trooper riding alongside the carriage glanced at her fine features and wavy black hair before abruptly turning his eyes back to the road.

Inside the velveted interior of the carriage with Kamila and Fost Boscawent sat one of Kamila's ladies-in-waiting, although in truth the old woman was simply an assigned minder of Duke Urric's rather than a confidant of Kamila's. Also in the carriage was a man who played much the same role as observer of Kamila's whereabouts and held the official role as instructor and physician to young Fost.

Kamila was forty years younger than her husband. Duke Urric, the lone survivor of the Boscawent line, previously married and divorced three times, had never produced an heir. About ten years ago, while on a return journey to Vryvond, Urric and his retinue had stopped at the manor of Chetwin Claypool, a minor noble sworn to the Boscawent family. As the festivities of entertaining the Duke's retinue rolled into the late evening, when Chetwin and a servant went to get two more casks of mead, he heard the cries of his daughter. When Kamila was found to be pregnant not long after and as the pregnancy progressed, honor became satisfied with Kamila's marriage to Urric. Chetwin Claypool's land holdings expanded tenfold as well. To Urric's immense delight, Fost was born the following year.

A long retinue accompanied Kamila and Fost on their journey to Ravalas. Other carriages, also painted clover green and trimmed in yellow, carried more attendants and served as decoys should the column fall under attack. Careful instructions had been given to carriage drivers and the armored escorts to break into smaller groups to evade capture if circumstances warranted. The rest of the servants rode in myriad wagons skinned with canvas. More carts were packed full with luggage and other essentials as Kamila and Fost would be occupying

Bellis House, the largest of several residences owned by Duke Urric in Ravalas.

After Tavurite scouting patrols were spotted in the fields beyond Vryvond, Duke Urric grew concerned that the patrols were preparation for a direct attack and finally relented to move his family to Ravalas. To deter attacks and to protect the extended column, Duke Urric assigned twenty knights and mounted men-at-arms and nearly three hundred archers and foot soldiers. Assembling the strong guard was not without difficulty as the Boscawent forces were already stretched in garrisoning Vryvond and sundry other towns on both sides of the Avenbair, in addition to forming a significant portion of the royal army.

"Duchess Kamila, may I propose we use this time wisely. I cannot stress how displeased Eadolan and Sahalana are with this delay. There is quite a tone in the correspondence from Chronicler Quill."

"It wasn't my decision. Ask the Duke," she sniped.

"Yes, well," fumbled the man. "Nevertheless, you must do your utmost to impress them and show yourself as a dignified woman pleasing of the royal court. Please do all you can to ingratiate yourself with the royal family. Lady Lucia and I, we will be by your side to guide you. There is much intrigue at court, and you must be careful."

"A beautiful cage for two fragile birds," mocked Kamila. "No doubt you'll stay close to me and protect us in this strange and wonderful city."

The dour man ignored the insult and addressed Fost. "Young Master may well brush up on his knowledge of rhetoric and courtly procession. When you arrive, the royal tutor will start with tests of learning. You should impress him with your knowledge. It is part of being a knight. It must be done before they'll let you fight in any tournaments."

Fost watched his instructor pondering whether his assertions were genuinely to help him in his quest to become a knight. The boy wrinkled his face, trying to recall if he had heard this ever before or if this was an ill-disguised attempt to get him to pay more attention to his studies. Fost's body ached, and he had trouble thinking in the stuffy carriage. He and the instructor stared at one another briefly before Fost grew distracted.

Fost grinned as he pulled out a small knife and started to strop the blade. "A knight's weapons are what's most important."

"Put that away with all the jostling of this carriage! It will leap out of your hands," begged Lady Lucia.

Fost gripped the blade tighter and more intently stropped the blade using what light that filtered in to judge its edge.

Kamila laid a hand on her son's forearm. Fost relented, putting the knife away. "Instructor Olbram is right. You will need to be good at speeches when you win the tournaments. Think of what you would say to all the lords and ladies." At that, Fost beamed widely and seemed a world away.

"Let's open the shutters," demanded Kamila. "It's too stale in here. He needs some air." Kamila wiped aside the old woman's arm and flung open the carriage shutters.

Fost breathed in the chill and listened to the soft splash and squish of the road softened by the horses, carriages, and wagons up ahead. Riders flanking the carriage nodded their heads, and the young heir to the Boscawent fortune greeted them back.

"Where are the Lifeguards?" Fost eagerly hoped to catch a glimpse of the fabled protectors of the High Lord and royal family.

"They are to meet us farther down the road. Don't worry, Master Fost. We will let you know the moment they arrive."

Fost peered out the window and saw boots and legs

dangling from the roof of the carriage. Archers belted into seats at each of the corners provided elevated protection and early warning of approaching raiders. The seats had a system of pegs, flanges, and foot braces to allow the archers to shift their position and not topple from the carriage. In addition, heavy wood sidings protected the driver. A crossbowman sat next to the driver to provide additional protection and serve as secondary driver. Six big horses pulled the fortified carriage.

"Riders spotted!" came a faint call from up ahead.

The men-at-arms nearest the carriage called to the archers up top. Boots thudded against the carriage walls as the archers shifted to find potential targets.

"Don't worry. They're just observing us. We have too many here; they won't fool with us," called a man-at-arms assuredly.

Kamila leaned her head out as more messages were relayed up and down the line. A knight rode towards her carriage. "What's going on?"

"Duchess, the outriders have spotted the enemy some distance ahead. It's a small number. Pavan wants to keep the column moving. I don't see a need to stop or move off the road. Do you agree?"

This was the first time a question of any consequence had ever been put to Kamila. She stared blankly at the knight.

"They're scout cavalry, Tavuros, and maybe some Blackbirds. You are quite safe in the carriage," the knight said helpfully. "We will let you know if anything changes. Best keep the shutters closed for now."

The caravan continued to move albeit at a slower pace. The rumble and jostle of the wheels was punctuated periodically by the shouts of the archers and horses galloping up and down the column.

The three adults tried to convey a poised demeanor to Fost, but in truth it was more effort just to comfort themselves. After a short while the noise subsided. The caravan continued at its slower pace, but then more shouts precipitated the carriage to move at greater speed.

"The archers are shooting!" said Fost excitedly.

His excitement was quickly dashed as the carriage started to swerve and move off the road. Shouts surrounded the carriage. Horses screamed. The carriage lurched back onto the road but kept veering back and forth, increasing speed as the road dropped, following the contour of the land. Small thuds hit the carriage. "What is that?" cried Kamila clutching Fost.

The carriage wheels bounced and slammed back to the road. With one wheel cracked and split, the carriage shook and crashed to one side.

Outside the carriage men yelled and whimpered in agony. All within was still.

The nearby screams had subsided into eerie quiet. Time seemed empty. Kamila squinted at the rays of light streaking in. Her head swam with stars. She heard voices and shrank in silence, contemplating whether rescue, or captivity, or worse awaited.

A crash of light smacked Kamila as the carriage shutters were forced open. She seemed to know one man and then another man wearing a blue cape appeared who she did not recognize. Her voice returned with the torrent of a river. "Help! Fost!"

More men arrived to lift Kamila and Fost, the two survivors, from the carriage.

"Are you alright, Duchess?" asked a panicked knight. "You are safe now." His voice did little to hide his uncertainty.

Kamila's full attention was on her son. Fost was stirring and softly moaning.

The blue-caped cavalryman examined Fost. "He has a badly bruised arm and shoulder. Could be broken." The trooper scanned the crowd of worried soldiers and servants. He waved hurriedly to another man to approach. The knight instructed the retinue to step well back and ordered soldiers to form a cordon with their backs to the injured Kamila and Fost.

The summoned man knelt; his eyes weighted with dark bags of shadow. He began to examine Fost, seemingly indifferent to the injuries as he traced his hands along the sides of Fost's face. "Most peculiar."

"Can you treat him here?" asked the knight.

The man was silent for a long while, peering over Fost.

"Hey!" the knight shook him roughly.

"No," the man finally said. "I need to take them to Jevatryn."

"Jevatryn! That's the opposite way, a long way. We're much closer to Ravalas. We can call out support."

The man laughed. "Any help is two days' ride away. Tavuros will be swarming this place before then, especially if they know who was in the carriage. I am sure Padazar would love to have Fost in his custody. There is no time to waste. The way to Jevatryn is safer, and we can travel at a slower speed so as not to disturb his injuries. Once the Duchess and the boy are recovered, the Avenbair will be a much safer way to travel."

The fear-stricken knight mumbled a response.

"What will Duke Urric do when he learns of your incaution?" challenged the man. "Do you want to risk Fost's capture? Or—"

The man did not need to finish the thought. The knight was already imagining his own gruesome demise should Fost die. The knight called to a man-at-arms. "Ride to Ravalas and inform the Duke of what happened. We are taking the Duchess and Fost to Jevatryn."

CHAPTER 26

"What happened!" yelled Telfair from inside the gatehouse as he watched the raptor force return.

"Must have been expecting us! Saw us coming all the way!" yelled Brenio hobbling heavily and carrying a soldier over his shoulder. "Get over here, Tomas. Whip's stomach is all torn up."

The Thavodyn garrison sent up another cluster of light-bursts to illuminate the moonless sky. Tavurite Skytamers and horse archers galloped tauntingly beyond effective range of the torsion crossbows. Small groups of Tavurite horsemen raced forward in irregular patterns, venturing close enough to loose a few arrows and then quickly gallop off to repeat the maneuver.

"Hold" came the calls from the officers, not wanting to waste precious bolts on isolated, erratically moving targets. The artillery crews and soldiers on the wall settled for hurling insults and were met in reply with bare Tavurite asses and shouts of "Coward! Come and fight!"

These quick dashes and then hasty retreats by the Tavuros signified more than a symbolic display. While few arrows landed harrowingly close, far more importantly, each iron arrowhead was a psychological attack seeking the heart of Ardalen morale. The current balance showed that Thavodyn's perimeter of safety was ever shrinking. Not even standing at the very foot of the walls proffered complete safety.

"Troopers, fall in! Now!" yelled Wolfwind to several of his troopers; concern splashed across his face that his men would launch a suicidal retaliatory charge on the Tavuros. He worried that this skirmish would develop into something larger as other members of the garrison may follow their lead and rush out to attack.

Inside the gatehouse, Brenio tenderly laid Whip down in the gateway and helped Whip position his own hands to hold his guts in. The wiry man was pale and growing cold. Telfair waved over two soldiers. "Carry him to the infirmary." Telfair and his medical attendants looked for others who had a better chance of survival. Telfair turned to Brenio. "Are you injured?"

Brenio's coat was slick and dripping blood. "I'm fine."

Wolfwind finally succeeded in getting his last troopers to return inside the walls. The horses added to the tangle of triaged wounded. The troopers had to tread carefully into the gatehouse. With the ceiling not much higher than the heads of their riders, the press of the walls, and the scent of blood preying on the horses' disposition; troopers struggled to control their skittish animals.

From inside the fortress, Malu weaved her way through the gatehouse, stepping deftly between the wounded and avoiding horse legs. She stopped for a moment to check on Brenio, but he seemed not to notice her presence.

"The Archmage will need a full accounting of any injuries within the Order. What about your leg?" demanded Telfair.

"Tend to the others, Tomas." Brenio exhaled deeply. "I got a little cooked, but the wound's far from the heart. I've had worse." Brenio turned and sprinted back outside the fort to see if any stragglers were still fighting or crawling their way back.

Malu started to follow Brenio, but Telfair ordered that she help with the wounded.

Brenio emerged from the gatehouse and raised Serpent, wildly offering a tempting target and direct challenge to any horse archer or Skytamer who would venture closer. His eyes swept the plain for signs of life, friend or foe.

Back inside Thavodyn, Thiepval acknowledged the returning fighters as he descended the stairs from atop the walls.

"At least ten killed, Tovenward. Several badly wounded," said Master Sergeant Dudley, while helping some of his men towards the infirmary. "We think we knocked out two, maybe three, but that ring is getting tighter and tighter. They seemed to know our tricks or at least had a quick reaction."

Thiepval waited before entering the gatehouse tunnel while the remaining wounded were moved to the infirmary. He touched each of the injured men softly on the back of the head.

Back outside the walls, Brenio stood alone, his challenge unaccepted. To his left, a rippling of bent light caught his eye. "Rufus," he exhaled with relief, the invisibility subsiding around the long-haired apprentice.

"I'm the last," called Rufus fighting his rage.

Motioning for Rufus to get back into the fort, Brenio shielded him from any precise arrows guided by a Skytamer.

"Last in. Close the bars."

The portcullis was lowered. Brenio put his arm around Rufus and motioned for all except Telfair and Thiepval to return to the walls.

"Is Dahey dead?" said Telfair as he cleaned and gathered up the last of his medical tools. "Is he here?" The wizard frantically started to search the length of the gatehouse, as if he had been unaware of a member of the Order in his immediate proximity. Finding the gatehouse empty, he asked in disbelief, "Did you not carry back his body?"

Rufus just lowered his eyes.

"How about his gear?" asked Thiepval churning inside and trying to appear calm. Rufus and Dahey were like younger brothers to him.

"There's nothing left," Brenio said softly.

"No," Telfair gasped. After a stunned moment, he retreated further into the fort. "I must look after the others."

"I will tell the Archmage and send a testament of Dahey's life for the annals," offered Thiepval avoiding his own thoughts for now about the heavy cost of the raid.

"I know it is a wizard's place, but I'd like to write it," appealed Rufus. "Or at least give some ideas."

"No time for that now. The pigeon wouldn't be able to take off if you wrote the tale. The bird would be like a toad flopping back to the Academy," joked Brenio. "Let's all agree now. The last one of us to go writes something nice and long-winded about the others. Truthful, but ink in the full glow so people will tell our tales just like Rhodwyt and Mulvanoc."

The humor did not seem to ease the collective pain. Brenio added, "They'll be time enough to get fish drunk and remember Dahey properly and all who fell today." Returning to immediate dangers, he said, "Tovenward, we saw clearly that the Tavuros are preparing. They are coming sure as the dawn breaks. Expect the throwers to open up. We fired one and got a good scorch on another. They will be launching stones and looking to close the lines even tighter."

As the sunlight stretched over Thavodyn's black stones and the surrounding field, the soldiers atop one of the bastions were at a loss for words. Eventually one called out, "Tovenward! Where is the Tovenward?"

Thiepval stood in the mustering yard, conferring with Falanika and other members of the Order. As the frantic calls reached him, he ran quickly towards the bastion.

The faint sound of large ceramic balls shattering and splinters bouncing and crashing against the rocky ground met his ears as he reached the top.

The soldiers pointed at the far distance.

"Ceramic shot. They are testing ranges," said Thiepval without concern. "Still too far away."

A soldier shook his head grimly. "We know, Tovenward. We did not call you because of the clay shot."

Thiepval furrowed his brow and looked, squinting further into the distance. Winding lines of individuals advanced, hands bound and seemingly connected together. "Our people," said an alarmed Thiepval.

"They're screening movements as the siege engines are brought forward," said a soldier.

"Thank you, Sergeant. Please send for the Castellan."

Thiepval walked farther down the rampart to speak to Falanika. "It will begin in a few days. They will move up the stone throwers, concentrate on a section of wall, and then use our people as living screens to shield the scaling parties."

"When's the last time you slept?" asked Falanika.

"About four days ago," said Thiepval intensely but cracked a smile. "Is it that obvious?"

"You hide it well from others, but we've known each other for a long time."

"How about you? How are things with the shield?"

"With Jarvis?" replied Falanika. "It will take time. Not the best circumstances now, may need to wait until things quiet in winter. I just need to spend some time with him. Observe what magic remains in him. Is the shield permanently bonded to an ancestor, or can the bond switch to him? I'll stop it before that takes place. He is still groggy, but it will not be long before he realizes he is a prisoner. That will make the work harder," she smiled. "As the sounds of the stone throwers get closer, I'm sure he will try to crawl through the keyhole and join the fight."

Thiepval seemed not to be listening. Falanika offered, "You've done very well in readying the defenses. We can try to destroy the throwers again. Take a longer route and strike from behind."

Thiepval nodded but didn't seem keen about the idea given the casualties from the recent raid.

"What can be done to keep our people out of the way?" Falanika pointed to the lines of human shields in the distance.

"Out of the way? Hundreds? Thousands of them?" asked Thiepval incredulously.

"Maybe they're bluffing? You think a waiting massacre like this would sit well with Padazar?"

"Maybe it's his idea?" said Thiepval.

"How do you want to handle this, Tovenward?"

Thiepval looked towards the citadel. From high atop the citadel, the Archmage looked at the same unfolding scene. He signaled Thiepval that he was dispatching a message to Ravalas.

The Archmage called to an attendant. "Get a bird out. Inform Eadolan that the siege has begun. The captives are being used as human shields," the Archmage said icily, wondering how any understanding could come about to restore the country.

"And where is the Castellan?" the Archmage called after the attendant. The attendant dropped to the lower level and hurriedly dispatched a messenger bird back to Ravalas. The attendant then went to the Castellan's chambers. As he descended the stairs, he heard footfalls coming up and towards the Castellan's door.

The attendant and the soldier nodded at their common duty and knocked on the door. When several attempts produced no answer, they pushed open the door.

"Castellan! Castellan! Grammel!"

The Castellan's face was down on his desk, blood thickly pooled and languidly dribbling onto the floor.

CHAPTER 27

E adolan read the small piece of paper again. He folded the letter into a tight square and clenched it in his fist.

"Calm, Your Grace," whispered Lyjos seeing the distress spread across the High Lord's face. "The envoys will be returning soon. Listen to all voices, but trust your judgment."

Eadolan fought the urge to pace and impatiently stood under the awning of his grand pavilion. The others assembled for the war council did less to conceal their own dread and discomfort, pacing and muttering to themselves. Even Wizard Artos Calaspon's pet otter fidgeted and dropped the fish head it was nibbling. The otter stood on its hind legs, contorting its body to see the commotion outside the lofted tent.

"What of the return of our nobles and soldiers?" called the High Lord, not able to wait a moment longer as the envoys dismounted their horses.

The envoys hurried their pace. "We shall recount it all, Your Grace," said Lockard Newman cheerfully in a showy bow. The boots of the three envoys quickly pounded up the short rise of the pavilion's stairs so as not to say more in the open area. The members of the war council retreated deeper within the pavilion.

"Forgive me, My High Lord, as I must relate what was conveyed to me," Lockard said in a more somber tone, now out of earshot of a multitude of retainers and servants.

"Go on," demanded Duke Urric.

"The Tavuros would not discuss ransom of the prisoners. They would barely discuss the topic of our men, their condition, their whereabouts. The terms they proposed are unacceptable to even recount."

Rafal the Younger sighed, faint glimmers of his father's restoration swallowed in darkness.

"There is, however," Lockard continued, "a proposal for a champion's duel. Corneleo Ray has challenged Sir Crowiler. As we returned from the parlay, Ray took to riding across the field between the armies, doing tricks and well, being Ray. He may still be there now. He has, he has..." stammered the experienced diplomat in a rare lapse of verbal prowess.

"What?" asked Eadolan.

"He has your sword. Sir Crowiler's, I mean. The one bestowed by Your Grace after the great victory at Pelham."

"Ray! That bloated piglet. I'll gut him in a few strokes," shouted Crowiler, his eyes wild.

"Did you surrender it to him?" gasped Duke Urric, more from shock than disparagement.

Crowiler leveled his eyes at the Duke. "No. I tried to bury the blade. We were trapped. None of your cavalry came to our relief. I would not command my men to be butchered."

"Cyp and the Lanterns fought nearly to the last man." Crowiler stared at the alternating blue and orange sheets of canvas forming the pavilion's ceiling. The spray of color looked like the broadshield banners, one pressed against the next. "Shine the light; lead the way," he murmured, tracing his mind

over each of the words, the saying of the Lanterns, the First
Broadshield of Ardalencor, and his decision to take a different
path. "I concealed myself in hopes of fighting another day and
avenging the betrayal." He bit his lip and snarled at the
thought.

"Did you see him, Lockard? Cyprien. Is he well?" Crowiler
asked through a quaver of rising hope.

Lockard gave a regretful shake of the head.

Crowiler turned quickly to Eadolan. "Your Grace, allow
me this honor," begged the Tigerclaw.

"Sir Crowiler, he is trying to provoke you," said Lockard.

"He already has! So, what do you recommend?"

Lockard paused, unsure of a better course of action. "To
give no reply to the insults and direct challenge would be far
worse for the spirits of our men. I only suggest that a counter-
proposal be given after due consideration. If fat Ray prancing
his horse is to cause us to abandon all sense," he stopped,
restraining himself, and turned his eyes to Eadolan.

"What conditions did they offer?" asked Crowiler.

"Blades or blunt weapons. No magical meddling. Four to a
side as attendants and observers. To the death or until one man
yields," Lockard said uneasily, weighing his words with great
care.

"What else, Lockard?" Crowiler demanded. "Ray got
under your skin, too."

"Ray says he will spare your neck and trim your moustache
instead. He boasted of the thickness of his own moustache and
general virility. He shouted this as we rode back to our lines. I
presume he is under some misapprehension about the current
length of your facial hair."

"What do we get when Crowiler kills Ray?" asked Quartermaster Rukez.

"If Sir Crowiler were to slay or force Ray to yield, Sir

Cyprien Crosstimbers would be released as well as one hundred men who served at Pelham in honor of their defense of the southern part of the country. And, if Sir Crowiler is not slain on the site of the duel, he must enter Tavurite captivity in Gersai."

"Why has Ray challenged me?" wondered Crowiler. "He can't possibly win."

"It's a trap," grimaced Duke Urric. "They're up to something."

"Are there any men? Anyone of heart left in this country? Or are they all dead or turned traitor? I can beat Ray!" Crowiler circled like a caged animal. "I see no downside to this. I'll cut his head off. If they betray the customs of the champion's duel, then they will be proven to be completely without honor."

"A little late for that, don't you think?" chaffed Rafal.

Crowiler looked into the eyes of the assembled men as if compelling them to agree. "Ray tried to kill our High Lord." Finally, Crowiler looked only at Eadolan. "And now Ray mocks us and waves your champion's sword. Your Grace, I revere the honor you placed in me as Linmarch. I hold this position temporarily, in the hopes that General Stokes rejoins us in time. There are other able men, other broadshields, who can assume the role. Please, Your Grace," he pleaded. "Give me the wizard to watch my back and mind the rules."

Eadolan pounded his fist on a table, scattering curls of parchment and figurines depicting opposing forces. "We must respond and quickly," ordered Eadolan. "Put an end to this mockery. I'll burn down everything they own. There won't be a Padazar or a Ray alive when this is finished. Those exiled Jernivans and those chopped and rotted at the gates, the bards will say, they were treated lightly."

Remembering the repeated commands of the Archmage, Wizard Artos said, "I think one member of the Order is sufficient for such a brief encounter. Apprentice Dalton is well versed in battlefield medicine and can readily spot any Tavurite trickery."

"See, Your Grace, the wizard doesn't think it much risk after all."

Artos paused, deep furrows in his brow accenting his otherwise bald and rounded face. Artos was a highly competent practitioner of the arcane but not one accustomed to speaking on behalf of the Order. He had barely ever been in the High Lord's presence and never without the Archmage or Mage Albright. "On second thought, both Apprentice Dalton and I will accompany Sir Crowiler."

"I would like to see Ray again." Artos felt for the amulet on his chest, a large disk of quartz embedded with a series of copper circles within circles and a warding eye in the middle. "Your Grace, I regret I was not able to remove Ray from his saddle at Boruma. Should this duel devolve, I will not fail again," he remarked dispassionately.

Satisfied, Crowiler noted, "Then we have our four. My shieldbearer, two from the Order, and one of my retainers to mind the horses."

"I am unfamiliar with the intricacies of duels," said Artos pointing to his otter with sincere trepidation. "Would bringing Sailor imperil the terms of the arrangement? Five, instead of four, I mean."

"It would not," sneered Lockard dismissing the wizard's literal meticulousness. "I don't think an otter would draw a second glance."

"Sir Crowiler, go get Tigerclaw back. It cost a damn fortune to make, and you look like just another village tough without it," grinned Eadolan. "Make it quick. There is no need for Ray to breathe a moment longer."

"You got trousers on under that robe?" asked Crowiler.

"What? Yes."

"Don't look so serious, like you were just pulled out of a burial shrine. You're making me nervous with all this silence. Show some anger, some fire. Keep an eye out for deceptions or illusions or whatever else, but don't look like you're squeezing your asshole to plug the dam."

"Fire? Do you know how to bring it forth?" Artos extended his empty hand, palm up. The wizard waited for an instant and just got a smirk in return from Crowiler. The taciturn wizard added, "In silent stillness, much is possible. Everything really."

Artos was most comfortable in the depths of the Academy's library or tinkering with new concoctions and spells in the open fields near what the Order called the Hayloft. He was not a frontline fighter in temperament, rather excelling in long-range attacks and wardings.

The cloth of Artos' robe began as dark gray at the hood and shoulders and softened to a bright white at the sleeves and lower hem. Shapes of stylized smoke and flames in bright teal adorned the elongated sleeves. His faded black boots betrayed his passion for alchemical labors, splotches stripped of color or eaten through by drops of acid or other astringents.

"I heard you and the Order were up all night. Several came back through the pickets just before dawn." Crowiler mulled and mused, "How many smiling necks did you leave the Tavuros?"

"None. We were surveying."

"Surveying! The demons drag you under!" snapped Crowiler. "Hope you'll help us this damn time. I don't need you droopy-eyed and slow coming up the road like your kind were at Boruma."

"We don't require much sleep. A terrible use of time." Artos smiled politely and tried to dampen Crowiler's erupting ire, but not before Sailor hissed in disapproval.

Sailor rode in a specially-constructed basket attached to the back of the wizard's saddle; the inquisitive otter alternated between peering out of its carriage and climbing up its friend's shoulder for a better view.

"What's the otter's part in all of this? Chew off the cuff of Ray's boot?"

Artos dismissed the questions. "Best focus on what you know, Sir Crowiler."

In keeping with the ritual and pageantry of a champion's duel, Crowiler rode in the first line, his horse maintaining the customary minimum of half a body length in front. Crowiler insisted on being the flagbearer, but, in the stillness of the day, the Ardalen battle standard with its snarling white sabertooth tiger lapped weakly against the flag pole. His own family banner, the leaping ibex, a reminder of the family's highland beginnings, was left in camp.

To Crowiler's right rode Pollard, his shieldbearer. Long serving as a member of Crowiler's private retinue, at the outset of the war, Pollard had been tasked with maintaining order across Crowiler's landholdings. In the wake of the disaster at Boruma and Crowiler's unexpected reappearance at Ravalas, Crowiler summoned Pollard to lead reinforcements assembled from the Herring family's armed retainers and peasant levies.

Prompted by dual motivations, Apprentice Dalton rode in a second line of sorts: first, deference to the champion, and most pertinently for Dalton, to display deference to a wizard of the Order; second, with all attention likely to be fixed on Crowiler, Dalton's partial concealment obscured any view of his sweeps and scans of the ground they were traversing.

Following Ray's showy exploits in the saddle, Dalton was

troubled over the number of surprises which could await them on the field. The apprentice dressed in a simple gray robe with a dark red fringe on the hood, the only sign of ornamentation. He carried no visible weapons but deftly cradled a small crystal ball beneath a long sleeve. Dalton rhythmically swept his arm across the field, eyes pulsating and ticking from one location to the next.

As the fifth member of the champion's assembly, Demps, the groom, trotted behind and led a spare horse gently on a trailing bridle. He glanced back over the mile by which they came. He kicked his horse in startled wonder at the sight, such a sight that it took him a moment to regain control.

"The army," Demps stammered quietly. "The High Lord. They are mounted and watching." The groom turned his attention forward, smiling and wondering whether he should tell Crowiler but judged it best not to disturb his lord, seeing him locked in conversation with Pollard.

"My Lord, remember the ring and pennant relay in Swiftmane this summer?" asked Pollard. "Ray twisted his knee when changing horses and did not dance in the closing celebrations. Try the knee."

"Do you think I could not beat him otherwise?"

Pollard, much used to these boasts and verbal sallies, quickly replied, "I know you want to stalk him, see him squirm. This will add another shade of panic to his eyes."

The sun towered over the wide plain, pushing to its height and the arranged moment for the champion's duel. "Almost highpoint," observed Crowiler gazing skyward. "Well, look at that!"

Across the field coming into greater view, Corneleo Ray rode a white charger resplendent in a caparison checkered with bright crimson and white. The horse wore a head covering of supple white leather with painted red and blue rowels with a blue-feathered plume. The horse's mane was thickly braided and lacquered upright in stocks painted in blue, white, and red. Oversized brass disks twinkled on the bridle.

Ray wore a long, padded jack to below the knees and vertically divided in blue and red. For a second layer of armor, Ray wore a chain mail hauberk with added plating to cover the elbows. As a third layer, Ray had donned a polished steel breastplate and backpiece to prevent an alacritous stab to the heart. The breastplate included articulated lames at the belly to provide for greater movement. Brass riveting and brass depictions of the Starry Fields of Indalos gleamed from the breastplate beneath the highpoint sun.

In his hand Ray carried his helmet, a solid piece with a t-shape forged out for the eyes, nose, and mouth and then small holes punched on each side to provide some measure of hearing. Adding flourish to the simple design, a snorting horse head was etched in the front and etched wings swooped back from the horse head down the length of the sloping neck guard.

Ray rode at the front of his group of five arranged in a shallow chevron formation. Tavurite horse archers, bows stored in saddle quivers, rode at the formation's edges, and closest to Ray rode two men-at-arms dressed in the Ardalen style.

The men clad in the Ardalen style served as flag and shield bearers. Two banners hung limp in the languid air. The first, on a slightly shorter staff, was the Ray family banner: a white field, fringed in red with a red, four-pointed rowel and then four red horseshoes at the cardinal directions radiating from the rowel. The rowel and horseshoes were outlined in deep blue.

The second was the Padazar black falcon banner and the ubiquitous symbol of the Peregrine Lands. Four equal quadrants divided the field: light blue in the upper left and lower right and red in the lower left and upper right. A black falcon with elevated and displayed wings dominated each quadrant.

"No disturbances, Wizard," Dalton whispered.

"I concur, Apprentice," acknowledged Artos and then quietly remarked to Crowiler, "No invisible figures either. They seem to respect the terms."

The respective parties stopped about twenty paces apart. Carrying the Ardalen standard, Crowiler waved off Pollard and Artos and walked alone to the center. Fighting to suppress a grin, Ray dismounted, gripped an ornate sword and scabbard attached to his belt, and walked alone to meet his rival.

Crowiler wore a long, faded, golden brown, padded coat with interlocking diamond and teardrop shapes stitched in cream-colored thread. Stains of sausage grease, dried mead, and faint traces of aged blood further patterned the gambeson sleeves and high collar. For added protection, he wore chest armor with a leather backing and fortified with thin, horizontal metal plates securely bound with small metal rings. The armor was cut inward and rounded at the armpits so as not to restrict Crowiler's sudden strikes and slashes. He wore light bracers on his forearms and steel-splinted greaves which extended over the tops of his boots to deter blows to the lower leg.

A horizon away from Crowiler's jeweled trophy now in the possession of his enemy, his current sword was simply designed and yet skillfully forged by a master smith from Ironhorn. The sword's handle was indistinguishable from hundreds of other swords in an arsenal's racks with its round pommel and faintly upswept crossguard. The scabbard, nearly as unembellished, featured the protruding head of an ibex in carved black wood between the hangers of the sword belt.

"Sir Crowiler, where's your moustache?" called Ray with a sly curl of the lip, trying not to let curiosity get the better of him.

Crowiler gave no reply, eyeing his opponent who stood an arm's length away.

"I hope you are well. I knew you would come. Your personal honor demanded it. I most admire that about you." Ray glanced around in a conspiratorial fashion. "Sir Crowiler, how do we strike a deal here? How much of Urric's land would you like? Cyprien is willing to make a deal. Stokes already has."

The Tigerclaw, Crowiler's sword, hung temptingly, a quick lunge and easily within his reach. The hilt, lavishly inlayed with orange topaz and imported, opaque, deep blue stones which the Ardalens called ocean stone, dazzled in the sun. The sword was a gift of Eadolan in recognition for Crowiler's service and in replacement for his sword that was fractured in the defense of Pelham. Beyond the hilt, an upturned guard stylized as two tiger claws sat above a scabbard ornamented in white lacquer and sun-bleached bone. The scabbard was dirtied, scuffed, and some of the inlays chipped away, but the design was still visible: a snarling sabertooth tiger's head emerging from a swirling fog.

"Bring General Stokes here now. Let him make the pronouncement," said Crowiler. "I want to hear him order his soldiers to stand down."

Crowiler reflexively reached for his now-shorn moustache and shook his head. "The boys of the Peregrine Lands, the great protectors of the nation, have welcomed the invader. Turned their back on their country. How many thousands have already been sent to the Tavurite slave markets? How many towns and Starfields looted? How much of our land did you sign away to them?"

Bitterness turned to sorrow for Crowiler. "Whatever grievances Padazar has against Eadolan, let that be his matter. Petition the High Lord. You have bled our lands and turned brother against brother. Some of the boys who defended the Southwest were butchered at your hand!"

"I butchered no one," admonished Ray in a hushed howl. "I

would not slaughter fighting men!" Ray gained a measure of composure. "Eadolan is not fit to lead. You value strength, speed, decisiveness, and yet you cling to this child."

Crowiler mulled the idea for a moment, inviting a growing brightness in Ray's eyes. "I see the Tavuros sent you an escort. What an ending for a proud people who fought one invader and then welcomed the next."

"Do you see a Tavurite standard? I don't."

Crowiler eyed Ray's four retainers. "You can't win this. I know your knee is still bothering you. You favor it even still." Ardalencor's fastest blade slowly extended his hand with the Ardalen battle standard. "Why don't you return to this flag and ride back to camp with us?"

Ray blinked but did not move. "Don't look past this opportunity to free Cyprien and make good your losses from the prior war. I heard you had to sell—"

"Enough." Crowiler walked away and motioned to Pollard for his shield.

"Crowiler!"

Crowiler abruptly spun around, leveling the spiked flagstaff as if expecting an imminent attack.

"You're fast but predictable. I've been watching you for a long time."

Crowiler's eyes narrowed.

Ray savored his next words. "I'd suggest you scribble a farewell note to your wife, if you could write. Pity. Maybe that wizard can bring her some comfort."

Crowiler walked back to his retinue and planted the flagpole deep into ground.

All retainers on both sides dismounted as required by Ardalen custom to signify acceptance of the combat and that its commencement was close at hand.

While the Tavurite archers stood watch alongside their

horses, Ray conferred with his two Ardalen retainers. They both pulled round shields from their arms. Ray lifted each shield in turn. One displayed a single black falcon, and the other depicted a pile of decapitated orc heads. Ray opted for the shield with the spread-wing peregrine, a three-prong lightning bolt clutched in its talons.

Ray unfastened his sword belt and turned slightly, hoping to catch Crowiler's eye.

One of Ray's retainers pulled another sword and belt from a saddle sling and helped his champion secure the new weapon.

"Steady," said Pollard trying to re-capture Crowiler's attention as he gently lifted the aventail and helmet over his lord's head and smoothed out the chain mail over Crowiler's neck and cheeks.

"Hurry up," snapped Crowiler.

Crowiler unsheathed his sword and accepted a round shield, two white tigers encircling a blue field with an orange rim. "Wizard, are there any dust pinchers with Ray?"

"No," said Artos lifting Sailor up on his shoulder.

Crowiler nudged his shield towards Artos and Dalton. "Then you watch those archers. If they make a move for the bows, you finish them. Do you hear me?" Crowiler's eyes were inflamed. "Don't watch me." The Tigerclaw stretched his arms and strode to command the center of the field.

Ray took a measured pace, pausing to hop twice. "Knee feels good."

Crowiler made a rushing lunge, and Ray peeled off well wide to avoid the movement.

Ray's retainers grabbed their horses by the reins to create more space as Ray worked to keep distance between himself and Crowiler. Ray circled rapidly, moving in and out and making half-hearted slashes. Crowiler's rushes and strikes were avoided by Ray with rapid retreats and lateral movements.

Artos and Dalton were disciplined enough to resist the temptation of watching the Tigerclaw in single combat. Each independently contemplated whether he could fix a spell and disable a swift bowman or stand fast against an onrushing horse. It had been a long time since either had practiced such circumstances. Neither had ever experienced when blinks were the thin veil between victory and death. Dalton's brow started to bead, and he hoped Artos would not notice.

Sailor stood on Artos' shoulder. The otter dug its claws into the wizard's bald head.

"What is it?"

The otter gestured forward, and Artos saw it. In the distance, the Tavurite army had begun to move.

Artos extended his hand and began to intone deeply, his hand twisting, gripping, and molding an unseen force.

The Tavuros started yelling at one another and lifting their bows.

"Crow!" shouted Pollard as he rushed forward. "Trouble!"

Crowiler raised his shield and made a rush at a nearby horse archer. The Tavuro reacted quickly and jumped on his horse, peeling away towards safety. Crowiler looked back at Ray who was running to his own horse. To screen him, one of Ray's Ardalen retainers dropped the peregrine flag and ran forward with sword and the shield painted in homage to the annihilation of the orcs.

Crowiler sidestepped and positioned his shield to redirect the oncoming blow and moved his sword arm with cat-like speed to strike the knee of the Southwesterner. As the man buckled, Crowiler stood tall and plunged his sword overtop the man's shield, the sword burrowing into the man's eye.

As Crowiler wrenched his sword free from the crumpled

man, a Tavurite arrow struck Crowiler in the back of the leg. The horse archer, to whom Crowiler had earlier given chase, fired more arrows. The next arrow sailed just wide, and a close follower Crowiler deflected with his shield.

"Go, Demps! As quick as you can," yelled Pollard motioning for the groom to summon help.

Back on the other end of the unfolding skirmish, the second Tavurite archer unleashed two arrows towards Artos. Sailor scurried down and took refuge behind Artos' feet. The wizard stood his ground and released the conjured fire. Engulfed in the flames, the arrows were immolated and wobbled harmlessly to the ground. The flames, while dispatching the immediate danger, did not reach the archer. Unaccustomed to close quarters combat or the rhythm for quick casting, Artos' focused connection with the ethereal could not match the speed of an archer's bow.

Seeing the flood of fire, Artos' immediate nemesis mounted his horse and loosed more arrows in rapid succession.

Artos ignored the archer. Ray, now remounted, was charging at a wounded Crowiler. With hand extended, Artos targeted Ray. The wizard's hand jerked slightly as an arrow hit his body. Two more arrows bit in quick succession. The momentum of the arrows slowed greatly as they passed through a dense pocket of air shrouding the wizard, but the arrows still had enough force to prick and jab his flesh.

Flame leapt forth from Artos' hand. It passed higher than intended, but the flame's lower wreath caught Ray on the side of the helmet. The sudden rush of fire spooked Ray's horse and caused it to wield erratically. Ray desperately clawed at his helmet while struggling to remain atop his horse.

Dalton, with hands cupped around his mouth, directed conjured bursts of discordant shrills at the Tavuros' mounts. The horses writhed and recoiled from the reverberating sounds denying their riders a stable platform from which to launch more arrows.

The remaining Southwesterner with Ray's family flag rode after his lord, attempting to steady him and aid his retreat.

Pollard reached Crowiler and lifted underneath his armpit to stabilize him as they retreated to the horses.

Artos removed one of the arrows and grimaced at the sound of Sailor's inquisitive sniffing. "Wet with wax. Poison. Three entries. Apprentice, to me," he called to Dalton.

The Tavuros circled their mounts, and Dalton found it difficult to keep the sounds vectored at the horses. The master horsemen began to soothe their animals as no physical threat accompanied the ominous sounds. The Tavuros, seeing the conjurers' focus diverted and Crowiler and Pollard in no position to attack them, unleased a volley of arrows at the two warriors. Most of the arrows missed or were unable to penetrate the men's armor, including a shot skittering off Crowiler's aventail. One arrow did hit, thumping into Pollard's elbow.

The Tavuros now followed a different tact. Very mindful of the two members of the Order, including evading another flame strike from Artos to deter their direct approach, the Tavuros fired several arrows at the anxious remaining horses of Crowiler's retinue. Two of the horses were struck, and their squealing put all to flight back to the royal camp.

"Down," called Crowiler as he and Pollard tried to contort their bodies behind his shield.

"Crow, been an honor. A better man would be hard to find."

"Damned if we are dying like this," rebuked Crowiler.

Finding the range, Artos propelled a wild torrent of fire bursts at the two Tavuros, finally maddening their horses into flight.

"Knights!" called Artos as he and Dalton rushed over.

"They think we'll run, but we won't make it back," he remarked fatalistically. "We need to hold tight until our soldiers arrive."

"Wizard, I will assist you," proposed Dalton noting the rising blisters on Artos' hands. Artos breathed deeply and listened to the growing rumble of the ground.

Crowiler scanned the horizon, but it was hard to focus. He squinted to push away an encroaching blurriness. Ray was a diminishing form, and Crowiler lost sight of him as thousands of Tavurite light cavalry swarmed forward. The Tigerclaw frantically looked behind him. He thought the royal army had begun to move, but the Tavuros easily would reach their position first.

"Sir Crowiler, you and Pollard have been poisoned. It will be entering your blood," said Dalton calmly as he could.

"Well, maybe you're right after all," Crowiler uttered to Pollard, foam starting to pool around the edges of his mouth.

"You must remain alert. Please drink this," Dalton said, offering Crowiler a small vial before deciding to pour it directly down Crowiler's throat. "Depending on the strength of the poison, it may take some time for the elixir to have a countereffect, if indeed I selected the correct antitoxin."

"We need to get out of here!" screamed Pollard preparing to stand.

Dalton tried to grab Pollard and force him down.

"We are going to be crushed by a thousand hooves! Indalos, protect me!"

Dalton rose to tackle Pollard. In the struggle the vial of antitoxin intended for Pollard fell to the ground. Sailor deftly grabbed the vial and scurried back more or less unscathed. Dalton tried to reach for Sailor, but Pollard was flailing wildly to break free. Dalton struggled to find another vial in his belt pouch and also invoke a spell to subdue Pollard. For his inattention, Dalton was kicked in the face, his nose splattered by an iron boot heel. Breathless and frantic, Pollard ran.

"Let him go," said Artos without inflection.

"We're not dying on our knees." Crowiler sighed and patted the ground, searching for his sword. "Stand. Take as many with us."

"Keep your legs inside," commanded Artos as he lightly charred a circle to denote the boundary. "Are you ready, Apprentice?" the wizard said, emphasizing Dalton's title.

"Yes, Wizard," exhaled Dalton with the pop of resetting his nose.

"We're staying?" yelled Crowiler.

"Quiet!" commanded Dalton.

Sweat beaded across Artos' reddened pate. He raised his inflamed and bubbling palms upwards and began to trace arcane arcs like a potter molding clay. Dalton, crystal ball again in hand, followed the movements, adding strength and form to the growing dome which gradually took on a green brushstroke pattern of the surrounding plain.

Crowiler started to reach for the forming dome, and Sailor bit him on the fingers. "Ouch, you river rat. I'll skin you when this is over." Crowiler shook his head. "Can they see us in here?"

CHAPTER 28

In the Ardalen camp, although no order was given, the royal army had begun to move. Keenly watching the site of the champion's duel and with the unexpected arcane fire, High Lord Eadolan instinctively moved his horse at a gallop. The Lifeguards, the Hearthguards, and then all the cavalry raced to keep pace. While Eadolan had ordered all knights and mounted fighters to make ready in show of support for Crowiler upon his departure for single combat, and doubly wary of deception by the Tavuros or the Ardalen traitors, orders were never contemplated for a general attack. Many of the senior officers, like Duke Urric and other nobles, had stayed with the High Lord to await the result of the champion's duel, rather than remaining with their formations.

No plan of battle, no precise sense of what lay ahead, but a spirit had captured the royal army and swept all forward. The loyal knighthood of Ardalencor surged across the field. Noble standards of bulls, bear paws, ship prows, woodpeckers, white roses, pheasants, crossed axes, dolphins, stags, red boars, castle towers, and dozens of other flags and pennants lifted in vibrant rush against the sky. The largest of all the symbols, the royal banner of Ardalencor, the crowned white sabertooth tiger, served as orientation point for the movements of the army, but the movements were far from orderly.

On a fleet gray mare, a woman dressed more like courtly lady than combatant weaved between the warhorses. Her copper red hair streamed wildly underneath a circular cap fringed with bear fur. In rhythm with the movement of her horse, a warding eye pendant bounced from a silver and bone choker about her neck. Her arcane wand was held snug in offset loops on her belt.

"Blackcliff, you have command." Cyra whistled as she mounted her horse. With Artos currently unable to issue orders and as the only other wizard present, Cyra had been in nominal command. Jereon Blackcliff, Overseer of Companions or Headman of the Zaravandian Order's elite men-at-arms, had the good sense to send some mounted fighters and apprentices chasing after Cyra to provide Eadolan, and Cyra herself, a measure of the Order's protection. During the champion's duel, the Order had drawn up farther away from Eadolan so Cyra had far to travel and scant time to reach him.

The broadshields, who were present in the High Lord's pavilion and also witnessed Eadolan's sudden departure, deemed it more prudent to return to their units. They hurried to direct an orderly advance of the line infantry as well as footmen of private noble retinues, the archers and slingers, and those mercenary companies which were best not left to linger in the camp.

In the widening void between the advancing cavalry and the gathering infantry, the Order's remaining contingent of about two hundred men-at-arms and handful of arcanists trundled forward in their carts.

"A beautiful sight to behold." One of the Order's men-at-arms frowned with a sense of awe and dread. "They'll burn out the horses before they even reach the enemy. I hope the boys did their work, or we'll be fixing a fort soon," he said to a companion, twirling his finger to simulate the circling of the wagons.

Pulled by two horses, each cart carried three or four men-at-arms. Apprentices and attendants were sprinkled throughout the caravan. Large wooden shields hung on the outside of the carts. Unlike the teardrop shields of the line infantry, these shields were rectangular, weighted at the bottom and with an extendable support beam and spike to fix into the ground. These shields could be deployed as a freestanding wall to shelter crossbowmen and billmen and other Order members in their preparation of arcane components. Large lengths of rope and chain also were stored in the carts to bind the carts and shields together should the situation warrant.

In the very vanguard of the army rode High Lord Eadolan. Leading from the front, he yelled, "No mercy!"

The Ardalen knights were in a furor, unsure if Crowiler, their great champion, still lived. Calls of "No honor, no mercy!" reverberated through the cavalry.

In the pell-mell charge, keeping cohesion of the ranks became a growing concern as some knights began to take a more rational assessment of the advance.

"We must dress the ranks, Your Grace!" shouted Lyjos. "Form up."

Eadolan barely acknowledged the shouts from his elven protector.

"No honor, no mercy!" came the cries again, drowning out Lyjos. Consumed by the long-awaited moment to put an end to the retreats, to change the slide of fortune, to ride out and to meet the enemy on the battlefield, Eadolan and his army again had fallen victim to ruse and deceit.

Tavurite horse archers were approaching the site of the champion's duel. The Ardalen army, still far off, appeared to be moving piecemeal with a large mass of knights in the lead.

"How long can this pocket hold up? Can they ride over us?" worried Crowiler as if floating under the churning seas in a fragile bubble.

"Do not disturb him." Dalton leaned in with bared teeth and violently motioned for Crowiler to cover his mouth. Dalton lowered his voice. "I must help Wizard Artos. Speak again, and we are dead."

A group of Tavurite horsemen paused to inspect the site of the champion's duel. One rider galloped forward to claim the abandoned Ardalen battle standard and Padazar's flag and pumped them into the air with a celebratory whoop. The horse archers inspected the fallen Southwesterner and sniffed the air seasoned with the lingering smell of char.

The Tavuros exchanged puzzled looks at the disappearance of tracks near a tiny nub of elevated terrain, but then footprints reappeared, and a few hundred feet beyond stumbled a man back towards the Ardalen camp. Finding the site otherwise deserted, they pressed on. More waves of horse archers quickly trotted by.

Crowiler tried to assess the total strength of the enemy, but the Tavurite army seemed an impenetrable mass, a rippling tide, surging forward to the rhythm of hoofbeats. "Horse archers screening the whole field. Beyond that, still the cataphracts," he whispered to himself.

Suddenly, the earth groaned with a deep pain.

"What's that sound? By Indalos!" exclaimed Crowiler elated and panicked at the same time. He covered his mouth and rocked back and forth in excitement.

Within the mass of advancing Tavurite cavalry, an eruption of energy split the ground. Although a fair distance away, the fountain spout of clods of dirt, flotsam of helmets, lances, armor, and legs and limbs seemed close at hand to Crowiler.

"A simple matter of surveying," voiced Dalton, unable to restrain his own excitement.

The Tavurite army seemed to freeze and skittered to a halt like a young fawn on thin ice, hearing cracking all around. All stared wide-eyed, nervous even to speak above a whisper. One of the nearest horsemen anxiously pointed at the concealed position of Artos, Crowiler, and Dalton.

Crowiler gripped his sword. Dalton shook his head and lightly put his hand over the flat of the blade.

A massive cheer went up in the royal army. The Ardalen cavalry collectively reined up to gawk and marvel at the plume of wreckage.

Lyjos, himself gape-mouthed at the distant sight, called to Eadolan. He struggled to be heard through the cheers. "Your Grace! We'll spend the horses. Stop and reform. Allow the Hearthguards to move up. They need strength to deliver the charge."

"We must press the attack. Press the attack," shouted Eadolan, although he saw even his horse grateful for the breather. "A brief rest. A count of thirty and no more."

When the royal camp had been set near the waypoint of Bride's Arch, the muster rolls, such as they were, counted just over seven thousand mounted fighters under the Ardalen banners. Most of this number was now present or hurriedly racing to form up around Eadolan. The foot soldiers were still too far off to allow for effective coordination.

Eadolan's cavalry varied from the elite flower of the nobility to little more than stable boys given hauberk and sword and pressed into emergency service and also included all manner of long-serving noble retainers, glory-starved squires, provincial men-at-arms, and experienced freebooters.

Ellard Ajhax moved amongst the Hearthguards and feverishly waved. "Lances to the front. Kite shields to the front." Both were in short supply and still being brought up by squires and retainers.

Messengers crisscrossed the field, delivering instructions to arrange the order of attack.

Lyjos felt the closeness of the grave. Something tingled in his blood. He and his elven Lifeguards had protected the royal family against assassination attempts, shielded them from tumultuous crowds, and defended the Arkwen men on the field of battle. Now Lyjos was being called upon to lead a charge into swarms of Tavurite horse archers and behind that cataphracts, some of the heaviest cavalry formations on the continent.

"Sir Ellard, the position of honor is yours. My Lifeguards will assist you with a torrent of bolts, pierce their armor at close range. Keep moving. Never stop. We will have one chance to drive the Tavuros from the field. We are now committed and must slay Nabrensus." Lyjos grabbed Ellard by the hand and leaned in close. "Tell your cousin not to make it easy for the Tavuros. Please tell him not to ride in the front rank."

Lyjos returned to his men to inform them that the Hearthguards would take the lead ranks and then added in the elven dialect used by the Lifeguards, "We must protect the life of the High Lord even though he is not concerned with it himself. If he has a death wish, we must not let it come to pass."

While Ellard and Lyjos were seeing to the cavalry's order of battle, Eadolan called, "Where are my wizards?" The High

Lord's bloodlust ebbed for the moment, imagining Nabrensus protected by cataphracts and his own adept spellweavers.

"Lady Vraim!" Eadolan said with unrestrained relief as Cyra approached. "It's good to see you again."

The renegade daughter of Clayd Vraim reined up her speedy mare, letting the reference to her renounced family origins pass. "Thank you for waiting, Eadolan," she said to her childhood playmate from distant years. "I feared you'd become a pin cushion, rushing off into a hail of arrows."

"You were rushing off again without the protection of the Order." She trailed off now, considering that her actions were not any different; she being the only wizard immediately present and not a mage for miles and miles.

"We have our own surprises! That blast ripped them apart! Devastatingly brilliant. That will give the Tavuros something to think about!" He smiled widely with childish delight. "Keep the kaldoons away and try to keep up. We must not give them time to recover."

"Your Grace, the Tavuros are not advancing on our right. The explosion seems to have halted their movement," called the royal standard bearer as he approached.

"Indeed," acknowledged Eadolan, his desire to renew the charge gathering strength. "What of Crowiler and Artos?" he asked in a more serious tone.

"Hard to say. I'm picking up some residual magic where the duel took place." Cyra paused, uncertain, and pushed back her copper locks. "It could just be remnants of the shockwave from the explosion."

Eadolan squinted, weighing Cyra's words. He turned his charger in a small circle to face his warriors now in proper battle order. "If this battle is lost, the entire nation would be open to ravage and rapine. We will be victorious! Ardalencor will not perish this day." His horse rose on its hind legs. "And Crowiler. Crowiler lives. Let's go save him!"

The High Lord looked into the eyes of his cousin, Ellard Ajhax, and into those of the closest knights. "Hearthguards! Will you fight by my side?"

The Hearthguards cheered.

"Knights of Ardalencor! Will you trample the enemy and carry the day?"

Another cheer.

"Lifeguards!"

The elves held their heavy crossbows in their left hands and thumped their right fists over their hearts, clinking their scale mail. "To defend," they intoned in unison.

"Are we going to set off something like that?" asked Eadolan pensively of Cyra, nodding his head towards the site of the explosion.

Cyra shook her head. "We only placed one. It takes time to craft and hide it." She wheeled her horse, and with wand raised her voice eased into the cadence of a lady-in-waiting. "Step boldly, brave knights!"

Eadolan unsheathed Dominion, its amethyst crystal pommel gleaming in the sunlight. "No mercy! A great reward to the man who kills Nabrensus!"

His warriors roared their approval.

The Tavuros had started to withdraw away from the slight rise where a horseman claimed he heard a voice.

To Crowiler, the Tavuros seemed to be in great disorder, at least on their left wing.

"Skytamers!" was the constant call as men and women in blue coats were those few on horseback still moving about.

Skytamers were one of the steep pinnacles, an elite class, in favurite society. The Skytamers served multiple functions: the priestly class, sought-out practitioners of medicine, and battle casters. While no two Skytamers dressed exactly alike, the distinguished symbol of station was the knee-length hide coat dyed a vibrant blue, usually elk or sheepskin, but presently tiger hides were more fashionable. Sewn into the bright blue skins were asymmetric patches and pockets of reds, yellows, and pokeberry purple. Small disks of mirrored glass, elongated crystals, chicken feet, coins, porcupine quills, tin jewelry, braids of horse hair, and a myriad of other ornamentations stylized each distinctive coat.

Simple, squared-off black felt hats with a short brim contrasted with the multi-colored coats. Skytamers with griffon feathers, real or purported, encircling the band of the black hats, occupied the positions of highest status. The curled toe of their boots, a simple reminder that the focus should always be skyward, completed the ritualized look.

Two Skytamers advanced under escort of more horse archers. Both were treated with reverence by the other Tavuros, even though neither had griffon feathers in their hats. The Skytamers told the horse archers to stop escorting them.

Alone the Skytamers continued forward and began to intone. The hands of the Skytamers were covered in a chalky substance which they sprinkled liberally on their horses' necks. Seeking similar traces of the magic which caused the explosion, they started to twirl knotted cords with seated copper pots which soon were spinning over their heads.

"One-eyed magic!" called a Skytamer pointing at the small protuberance in the land. He signaled any still curious horse archers to get farther away.

The other Skytamer, more inquisitive, jumped off her horse and put her head to the ground.

The Tavuros were quietly shouting at her to return, but one did not become or remain a prominent Skytamer by always acting cautiously.

The more courageous Skytamer started to crawl towards the spot. As she deftly moved low to the ground, she grabbed a few blades of grass and chewed. She approached the small rise slowly as if it were a wild beast and again grabbed a blade of grass, sniffed, and warily chewed twice. Her face contorted with deliberation.

Crowiler thought the woman was looking right at him. He raised his sword, the point barely a foot away from the Skytamer's bosom but still hidden within Artos' spell.

The Skytamer sniffed again. "Otter?" She mumbled and then took a few steps back in disgust. "Arrows. Tie some cloth around them. Hurry. We've wasted too much time already," she shouted at nearby horsemen. Soon an improvised cordon of arrows served to signal approaching units to bypass the feature.

"An illusion. A trick." She waved her arms to signal safe passage.

A Tavurite officer approached the Skytamers to seek their guidance.

"Ride!" yelled the woman. The officer frantically ordered all horsemen forward, knowing well that the twin impact of the devasting explosion and the delay to search for more nefarious magic had led the Tavurite army to be separated. The right wing and center moved forward unsupported by the left.

"Where is Nabrensus?" called Eadolan trying to peer around ranks of Hearthguards and Lifeguards in front of him.

"We'll seek him out. We'll find their kaldoons, and we'll

find Nabrensus," declared Cyra, her hand moving in a flash of signals to members of the Order.

"Flying iron!" came the call as horse archers reached bow range and peppered the charging Ardalens with arrows. The air whistled and hissed as a steel rain poured into the knights in the vanguard. Aggressive iron rang off protective steel and occasionally found soft horse flesh.

Lifeguards stood in their saddles to snap off bolts over the Hearthguards, but their crossbows' rate of fire was a fraction of the Tavurite bows which also had the benefit of plunging fire. As the Lifeguards spanned their crossbows with goat's foot levers for another salvo, Lyjos signaled to conserve their fire for closer killing.

The Tavuros kept up a steady rate of fire and then gradually fanned along the flanks of the massed Ardalen cavalry, creating an enfilading crossfire.

"Indalos! Guard soul and soil." Men looked at one another as the fervor started to diminish in direct proportion to arrow wounds and brotherly cries.

With more Tavurite horse archers occupying flanking positions, the front of the Tavurite cavalry gave way to a thin line of Skytamers summoning power drawn from their belief in the limitless skies. Billowing waves of smoke and stench began to descend and blanket the lead ranks of Ardalen knights.

"Wizards! Do something!" demanded Eadolan. Dominion, the Arkwen family sword forged long ago by the finest smith in the Order's history and attuned to the duress of royal blood, awoke to protect its charge. Radiating from the amethyst pommel, a shielding aura enveloped Eadolan and his steed.

The most heavily armored knights were having the worst of it as the smoke crept into the narrow openings of the armor and sunk into the spaces inside the panoply. Gagging and gasping, they futilely tugged at layers of linen and iron, many desperately abandoning shield or lance, or both.

The slim number of the Order's casters present struggled to break the choking weight of the cloud. The cloud pressed thick and heavy and spilled forth like a bolt of cloth with so many Skytamers focused on its conjuring. Unable to dissipate the cloud, the Order scarcely managed to channel a pocket of fresh flowing air underneath, giving reprieve to the front of the column and staving off disaster.

Desperate pleas came from all sides. Arrows swarmed along the flanks compressing the Ardalen cavalry further, most outside riders sought to veer inward, which only encouraged the Tavuros to venture closer and tighten the net. In maddened anger, small groups of Ardalen cavalry would peel off the main body to attack their tormenters. Units of Tavurite horse archers would appear to panic at the sudden onrush of Ardalen horsemen, feign retreat, and then massacre the isolated Ardalens who gave chase.

With the Skytamers fixated on maintaining the cloud and suffocating all beneath, Cyra spurred her horse forward. She leveled her wand as if in farcical impersonation of a lancer. Her hat flew off, and her copper hair streamed in the rush.

Her wand pulsed a myriad of colors, and the orb swelled with crackling energy. "Please," she whispered to herself as she raised the wand in full martial and arcane pageantry. She dropped the reins from her right hand and extended her arm, tracing over the ground.

The Skytamers appeared unphased or even unaware of Cyra's display, still ever focused on the smothering cloud.

Slowly a Skytamer and then another looked over their shoulders. A faint tremor began to echo with a low rumble. The Skytamers started to wave wildly and scatter. Impacting the Tavurite approach, units or individual riders darted in random directions, unsure whether to advance, stop, retreat, or veer to one side or another.

The Ardalens could not hear what the Tavuros were yelling, but from the frantic movements it was clear.

"Dread naught, gallant knights! Dread naught!" exclaimed Cyra in an expanded voice.

The Ardalen flag, sooted by the cloud and ripped by arrows, still fluttered full and proud in the firm grip of the standard bearer.

The cloud parted in patches and vaporized which led to hoarse cheers and bursts of joyful rasps at the deliverance.

Those Skytamers who remained in the ever-narrowing space between their own heavy cavalry and the advancing Ardalens, now sensed the ruse and tried themselves to manipulate the ground and cleave a trench in front of the first rank of the Hearthguards. The trench started to appear and did drop a few riders in a concussive tangle, but other horses leapt the sharp cut, and successive ranks avoided the danger. Not having the desired effect, the Skytamers abandoned the plan and as nimbly as the wind slipped back through the ranks of their own reformed cavalry.

"Storm approaching!" called one of the Hearthguards. Within the Tavurite army, if the horse archers' deluge of arrows and Skytamers' magic could not put an enemy to ruin or flight, for the close work, the shock troops were the cataphracts, well-trained men in full armor atop their nearly as heavily armored mounts. The weight of man and beast channeled into the iron tip of a lance could readily smash any remaining vestige of resistance in an enemy formation.

At Boruma, it was the Ardalen right wing under Duke Urric's command that offered little resistance before falling back against overwhelming numbers. Leaving prolonged pursuit of Duke Urric's scattered command to the horse archers, the cataphracts then turned to shatter many Ardalen infantry formations which chose to stand and fight rather than immediately surrender. For the Hearthguards, they had fought against the traitor Ray and his cavalry, but soon enough the Hearthguards would test their martial skill with the cataphracts.

Within the cataphracts, this wall of living steel, a devoted group occupied the position of honor in the vanguard. Picked solely from sons of noble families, and only those who already displayed unparalleled talent and ferocity, they formed the elite of the elite within the Tavurite cavalry. Beneath the pulsing sun, their fluted midnight blue armor shimmered like rippling water. If they were constructs or conjured forms, and not flesh and blood men, it was difficult to distinguish the difference. The only visible parts of the rider were through tiny slats in the helmet to maintain the senses. A fine film covered the eye slats which muted the sun's glare as well as hostile magical extremes of blinding radiance or deep darkness.

In contrast to the uniformity of the steel-tempered midnight blue armor, jagged silver accents on the cheeks and forehead distinguished the helmet. The bright red fingers on the gauntlets were the other notable contrast and homage to their bloody work. Among the Storm's multitude of weapons: spiked maces, swords, and lassos, each rider reputedly carried a lance with a magically-infused tip which could disrupt magical wardings and pierce and crumple armor on impact. To the Hearthguards, all the Storm's lances appeared to ripple and crackle with energy.

The ominous Tavurite war flag, a blood-red field with a knot and fan of horse hair, lacquered dark blue and still slick with the blood of a young foal, flew high above the formation. This flag of war, distinct from the Tavurite royal standard, was always carried in the position of honor.

IN TIMES OF WAR: A TALE OF ARDALENCOR

As the final prelude to the cavalry battle, some Skytamers in the rear ranks of the vanguard cradled caltrops in their palms which then leapt from their hands and over the heads of the lead elements of the Ardalen cavalry. Using the Ardalen royal standard as an aiming point, the caltrops fragmented and did great harm.

The Tavuros raised an echoing war cry which seemed to bounce skyward and reverberated in its intensity. Any final commands from the Ardalens would have been useless and unheard as both sides braced for impact.

Lyjos had watched the caltrops and moved closer to shield the High Lord. A caltrop fragment deflected off the protecting aura from Dominion and passed inside Lyjos' helmet. The iron shrapnel sliced open his cheek and pinned a flap of flesh inside the steel check guard.

Lyjos' mind pulsed. The pain was raw, but as he tasted blood, he delighted that his sight was still intact. He had endured far worse injuries over his many decades of soldiering across the world. Now a far worse pain tore at him, piercing from his ear to his heart.

As his awareness returned to the battlefield, Lyjos looked to the High Lord, still unscathed, and then took account of his men. Several had horses sliced and lamed by the shrapnel. His men looked at him in fright, but despite the gash and blood trickling down his ornate armor, he signaled that he was alright. He tried to pull out the piece of iron but ended up tearing his cheek further and abandoned the effort.

Lyjos looked for his sons, Kalmon and Vedulien, but within the tens and hundreds of Lifeguards and knights around him, it was impossible to know their whereabouts. He could not dwell in haunting possibility. Lyjos commanded his men to stand again in the saddle and fire at will. "Pour it on!"

Many of the crossbow bolts from the Lifeguards would hit

the fluted cataphract armor, but the bolts struggled to bite and penetrate as anticipated. Shots which struck the scale armor of the horses had more success. A precise bolt smashed a horse in between the eyes, buckling its legs.

"Their wards are too powerful. We can't disrupt them," called an apprentice to Cyra in a voice filled with the terror of hurdling into a devouring chasm.

"Ardalencor!" roared the Hearthguards, and they spurred their tired mounts in a final burst.

Often what happened in the final approach before impact, casters of magic, so as not to disorder their own troops, tried to create a dead space where wards prevailed, and the moment of impact was left to iron and wood and will.

Cyra blinked with heavy foreboding, but her eyes sparkled. She yelled to the apprentices, "Focus on the strongest lance and amplify the energy!"

"What?"

"Do it! Now!"

Although not able to see between the ranks of cavalry, Cyra raised her wand to locate the lance with the strongest magical force. The apprentices quickly followed her lead.

The two armies, the Hearthguards and the Storm, charged, moments from collision.

One Tavuro's lance tip sparked and glowed white hot before he realized what was happening. The energy crackled and leapt from one lance tip to another. The surge of magical energy roasted Tavurite horse flesh beneath the heated scale armor and found pathways through eye sockets, bursting horse heads in horrid explosions.

More alert riders seeing the pulsing energy wave dropped their lances, but still the energy wave reached several lances on the ground, shearing through horse legs as it traveled. A Skytamer in panicked madness jumped from his horse and levitated above the field. Screaming as he rose above the cataphracts, he channeled his life force to unleash one final spell. Four bolts from the vigilant Lifeguards dropped the Skytamer back to the ground in an unceremonious thud.

Over a dozen horses and riders were killed outright and more taken out of the fight by Cyra's quick thinking, but the effect was far greater. Fear again erupted in the army of Tavuron.

The two sides smashed into one another. For members of the Storm unphased by Cyra's magic, their couched lances smashed into the Hearthguards, punching holes into armor, flesh, and bone.

Ardalen lances also struck their targets. Shouts and screams punctuated the growing clang and clash of steel. A number of Storm and other cataphracts who had survived initial clashes with the Hearthguards swung swords or spiked maces trying to cut a path to Eadolan and the flag of Ardalencor. Hearthguards, Lifeguards, and other knights barred the way and fought with their own ferocity, giving as good as they received. The Ardalen flag in places was little more than tatters and shreds, but the crowned sabertooth tiger could still be made out and still fluttered in the breeze.

Brought forward on an ethereal wind, a Skytamer appeared in the Ardalen ranks, launching a sudden attack and then drifting back as abruptly as he arrived. On a subsequent attempt, two Skytamers appeared before Eadolan. Lyjos, like most elves, could see the manifestation of magic faster than a typical human and positioned his sword well to await the Skytamer's arrival. The other Skytamer tried to attack Eadolan but was thwarted by Dominion's ward. Still hovering before the High Lord, the Skytamer, in stunned disbelief at his own futility, was unable to retreat in time when Eadolan turned in the saddle and cleaved the Skytamer beneath the ribs.

"Where is Nabrensus?" yelled Eadolan scanning across the innumerable Tavurite flags and standards. "There!" Eadolan guessed, finally spying the Tavurite royal standard, a crowned silver stallion with lightning bolts forming part of the flowing mane against a field of midnight blue.

Within the mass of Ardalen cavalry, from his position farther to the right, Duke Urric had observed the billowing cloud over High Lord Eadolan's position and choked down the peach pit of fright in his throat. The Ardalen army was again hard pressed, but for Urric the sting of defeat, personal humiliation, and the scorn heaped upon him as commander of the right wing at Boruma had created resolve and determination within him.

Duke Urric was not on the far right of the Ardalen formation as he had been at Boruma but was now in a center-right position. The cavalry around him moved less from his own orders, but from the general impulse which captured the entire army. While lacking knowledge of where most of his vassal cavalry were, immediately surrounding the Duke rode his own knightly retinues, a smattering of provincial cavalry, and a small contingent of Pavtanari warriors. These knights of Pavtanarell were sent by Eadolan's sister in support of her brother and her native land.

To Urric it appeared the Ardalens were riding into another trap, but the right wing was less threatened compared to the intensity of fighting in the center. The Tavurite cataphracts which should have been confronting the Ardalen right wing were shaken by the great explosion and still seemed less than willing to move forward at rapid speed. Horse archers formed most of the forces opposing Duke Urric and the Ardalen right wing, which also contained contingents of horse archers. While the Tavuros had superior light cavalry to the Ardalens, the Ardalen horse archers were holding their own this day and preventing encircling movements on the right.

Duke Urric contemplated what orders he should give. He glanced to the center and saw the Ardalen royal standard disappear into the tumult, briefly reappear, and then sink again. "Indalos! We shall not let Ardalencor perish. Halt! Halt!" Urric called, signaling his knights and the cavalry around him to stop.

Still following the cavalry, the infantry moved at a quickened step. From their position, at first there was uncertainty at the muffled rumble from the explosion, but the resulting cheer by the Ardalen cavalry made the foot soldiers' panoply feel lighter and seemed to give them wings. They still had far to travel, and their test was yet to come. Lacking any orders, the broadshields decided to divide the foot soldiers and send their men to the wings of the army to prevent encirclement.

"The fight is in the center," exclaimed Urric to a small cluster of nobles and officers as arrows flew just above them. "We must cut a path before those cataphracts hit us," he said, pointing farther along the right wing. "One charge. Break the center, and put all those shit-licking bastards to flight. Move quickly and follow my banner."

The heaviest cavalry under Urric's command had been reformed into two wedge formations. The first stood beneath the black bull of Boscawent and the second led by Pavtanari knights under their national flag, a radiant sunburst over a mountain top. Some provincial cavalry and other formations were added to the back ranks to bolster the attack.

These adjustments were made rapidly, but the Tavuros still kept up a harassing rate of fire. Duke Urric gave the command, and units of provincial cavalry galloped towards the Tavurite horse archers. The Tavuros fled, turning back in the saddle to fire. In this real or feigned retreat, the Tavurite horse archers had uncovered the flank of their cataphracts and Skytamers engaged in the center.

Duke Urric led the heavy cavalry in the direction of the retreating horse archers and then signaled to charge the Tavurite center. The charge crashed into the stationary cataphracts. After the snapping of lances, the Pavtanari knights pulled slender three-foot swords. The thin, four-sided blade was razor sharp and well-suited to finding armpits, eyes, and other soft spots in the Tavurite armor.

Surrounded on two sides, the cataphracts fell or tried to retreat which caused other units in the center to give way. Exhausted Skytamers conjured mists to obscure the retreat from the enraged Ardalens.

On the Ardalen left an encircling attack by Southwestern cavalry units was made half-heartedly. At the approach of broadshields and the gleaming halberds of Darhax Sentinels, the Southwesterners withdrew.

On the Ardalen right, to preserve their honor and hopefully prevent a full pursuit of the retreating center, the delayed cataphracts made attacks on the approaching broadshields, hoping to repeat their success at Boruma and perhaps salvage some measure of victory. After a few charges were stubbornly repulsed, the cataphracts withdrew. Seeing the cataphracts attacking the infantry on the right, Blackcliff moved the Order to support. The Order launched fire bursts at the withdrawing cataphracts to deter any further approach. Thin arrow volleys from fleeing Tavurite horse archers sailed errantly, pushed away by up or down drafts conjured by members of the Order.

IN TIMES OF WAR: A TALE OF ARDALENCOR

"Bathed in blood and washed in glory!" called one passing Hearthguard to another.

"The field is yours, High Lord! A fighting spirit has been restored amongst the men," said Duke Urric. He reveled in the euphoria of bloodlust as he rode towards Eadolan. "What a celebration there shall be in Ravalas!"

Eadolan's eyes swept the field of carnage around him. Despite holding the field, he saw more Ardalen dead than Tavuros. He had won a victory, and he would not trade that, neither would the men, but how many such victories could he afford? "I am not returning to Ravalas. I am keeping the army in the field. I must keep Nabrensus on his heels. If we are aggressive and pursue him, he'll have to keep the horse archers with him which will spare the countryside."

Eadolan breathed deeply and motioned for a courier to scribe. "Duke, please return to the capital. Tell Behan of our victory. I charge you to oversee the gathering of more troops from the eastern provinces to replace our losses and to create a third field army. Secure more financial support from the towns on the lower Avenbair. They must open their coffers wider, knowing that victory is possible, and unless they support us, there will be no army to defend them should the Tavuros make it to their doorstep. The new soldiers must be drilled and ready to fight in the spring."

"Yes, Your Grace," said Urric. He watched Eadolan for a time as the High Lord congratulated the men and checked on the wounded. Urric saw Eadolan kneel next to a pale-faced Ellard as Cyra delicately tended to the Hearthguard Commander's shoulder mangled to a fleshy pulp by a Storm lance.

Duke Urric did not immediately depart for Ravalas. He wanted to remain on the field. He savored the acknowledgement of the men, stopping to greet and thank many. Urric sat tall in the saddle and led and received cheers as he went. He moved through the infantry on the right wing, hoping for redemption and removal of the scorn he felt after Boruma.

Urric approached a group of wounded soldiers convalescing and attending to one another. "The country is saved by your bravery. You have done well."

A man looked up and, seeing it was the Duke of Vryvond, stood to attention on behalf of his comrades.

"My compliments, Sergeant. I will send for my personal physician," said Urric seeing the man's face.

"Thank you, Duke," said the sergeant looking around and not seeing any physician in sight. "There are men here who need more attention than me."

"Send for my physician," Duke Urric called to a retainer.

The apparently genuine offer surprised the sergeant. He grimaced as he tenderly removed his helmet, the nasal guard bent back over his broken nose. A swelling purple bruise the size of a mushroom sprouted beneath his eye. "One big bloody slug," he said, motioning towards the center of the battlefield.

"Boys got their spirit back," gleamed Urric.

"We never lost it." The soldier spat a thick stream of blood. "Duke," he said with more formality.

"Indeed," said Urric good-naturedly. "What's your name, Sergeant?"

"Kellin Farrior. Armstead's Roamers. Twelfth Banner Company." Farrior's voice trailed off. "Or what remains of it."

"Yes, well, is there anything else that I can do for you, Sergeant Farrior?"

"Most kind of you, Duke Urric," Farrior said in astonishment and gave the unexpected question a long thought. "Yes, a simple request really," he said finally. "I was wondering if a friend of mine is currently in the army. I mean, is he here now? I think he serves under your banner. Sir Dallen Portnay of Amberfield. Could one of your couriers help me find him?"

CHAPTER 29

"I will double the invocations to Indalos," affirmed Lodestar Mondray repeating his words to a larger crowd as he wheeled Chancellor Droswild into the hallway. A line of courtiers and servants waited with brass candleholders, the protracted council having plunged into the depth of night. "Indalos has guided Eadolan to victory and saved our city. We must now entreat the abiding protection of Sahalana and her precious ward."

"Prayers have their place, Lodestar," cautioned Droswild. "Still trenches to be dug and earthworks to be raised before the ground freezes. Few men to defend the works. Tell the conservators to keep the prayers during the breaks. Indalos calls men to the spade as well."

"Not to worry, Chancellor, I am overseeing the fortifications personally. They are well underway," said Behan as he closed the council chamber's door. Behan paused briefly to reflect on the saying carved in the door mantle. *Reasoned words and virtuous deeds.*

"Weldon, your brooding grows more distressing in the

373

pallor of the moons. Do spend some more time in the sun. It will do wonders," said the Lodestar charmingly.

"I think it a truly splendid idea, Lodestar. The High Lady and her tender ward are always in my prayers," said Katya Billengrath placing a reassuring hand on his shoulder.

"Thank you, Lady Katya. You are an inspiration to us all."

Droswild grabbed a candleholder and waved the servant off so he and the Lodestar could speak in private. The Chancellor used the candle to relight his pipe as the Lodestar gradually quickened his pace to move ahead of the other dignitaries.

"She has never progressed this far. I am hopeful," remarked the Lodestar in an unconvincing tone.

Droswild unclenched his pipe and peered around. With others approaching, the Lodestar asked, "I am anxious to know more of the returning embassy from Trawfarne. Several conservators sailed from Floriana on one of their ships, the *Westwind*, I think it was. The ship has been missing since late summer and presumed lost. Did the mission inquire into their whereabouts?"

Still lingering by the council chamber's door, Duke Urric asked Lady Katya, "Might I have a word with you?"

"Oh, it is late, but yes, of course. Nary tarry time nor tallow," she said demurely. Wishing good night to the remaining dignitaries and dismissing her waiting attendants, she held a candleholder in her left hand and coiled her right arm about Urric's arm. Duke Urric and Lady Katya walked down the hallway in the opposite direction from the others. Lady Katya's flowing gown of muted orange swished softly on the tiled floor.

The pair descended two flights of narrow stairs. In the light and shadow of the stairwell, Urric removed his arm and upbraided, "Where are my son and wife?" His voice echoed faintly between the stones.

Lady Katya placed a finger to her lips. "Patience. As I said in council, they are safe."

Urric gave her an annoyed look. "You seem to know your way about the royal residence," he chortled at the memory of walking in on Eadolan's father and Katya in a reclined position. Urric had always wondered whether these encounters predated the death of her husband.

Lady Katya paused to listen for any sounds by a door and then slowly opened it. She quickly went about the small room, lighting a series of candle sconces. In the revealed space, Duke Urric fully took in the room's theme: a memorial to the High Lady Floriana, the only woman to wield power formally in the Arkwen dynasty's history.

Urric looked smugly at the painting of Floriana with her arm outstretched, endowing the foundation of the eponymous city, superseding a small fishing settlement. Other paintings depicted the expansion of the city: dredging marshes, driving pylons in the silty river, and mapping out the city's districts with a mindful Floriana overseeing it all. A floor-to-ceiling portrait of Floriana and large paintings of family gatherings set in idyllic forests covered much of the other walls.

A long couch anchored the center of the room. Two ornate wooden chairs faced one another in front of the fireplace.

Katya bolted the door with a small slide near the top. It was a light bolt but would deter a servant making rounds to ensure fireplaces were properly banked for the evening.

From a clutch of golden lace, Katya produced a sphere, smaller than a miniature plum, with a concave top. She licked her finger and gently moved it around the lip of the sphere. After two passes the glass sphere hummed and turned a dim blue. She walked the perimeter of the room and stopped several times to admire the paintings. "I've always liked this room."

Urric took a tuning fork from a thin compartment in a decorative dagger holder. He flicked the tines which vibrated benignly. With no threats detected, he discarded any restraint. "Where are my son and wife!"

"They are under my care. Safe in Jevatryn. It was not safe to bring them directly to Ravalas. The prudent decision was to head in the opposite direction and avoid the Tavuros. They seem to be riding free across your northern lands," she jabbed but took no joy in the devastation of the country.

Urric started to pace the room.

"Forgive me. I see you discomforted. Can I send for some water or fresh fruit?" she said with feminine sincerity.

Urric saw the door's closed bolt and moved to put himself between Katya and the door.

"My physicians examined your son."

"Tell me more of the injuries," fretted Urric.

"Just a bruise on the shoulder." Katya studied Urric for a long time. "It must be quite a sorrow to be an old bull. To be the last. Your wives, four is it now? And no heir?" She paused. "But now you have Fost, a sickly boy. Sorrowful face. In examining him, my physicians, they are quite good, very good, they discovered something most peculiar."

Urric rushed towards Katya, but she quickly moved behind the couch.

"Oh, your troubles will grow if you take another step." She kept her voice just below a shout. She softened. "Only a few know. It can stay that way."

Urric retreated a step. "What is your aim, you conniving viper? Eadolan will have no time for this intrigue. Your lies and slurs. Padazar. You serve Padazar." His eyes widened. "Treason. A betrayal of your High Lord." He started to glance around the room as if hidden figures would emerge and kill him.

"Is Silverface helping you? Was this his idea?" Katya

considered that permutation seemingly for the first time. "Why would the Order need you?" She stopped as if in deep thought to feign consideration of the possibilities but wanted Urric to confirm her suspicions. "If not Silverface, then a kaldoon's black magic. I am sure the Order would want to pay an inquiring visit."

"You wicked bitch."

She raised her hand for him to stop. "Urric. I need your help."

"Enough of this, Woman. Sensible men are rid of you." He moved towards the door. "I am sure your husband found great comfort in his early grave."

The veins in Katya's neck strained. Pleased his words had struck such a raw nerve, Urric forgot about the door's bolt and stared at her. Katya needed a long moment to regain herself.

She finally raised her head. "I know Fost is not your son."

Urric said nothing.

"I think you've always known, but over the years it became clearer that he looks nothing like you, nor much his mother. You are altering his face. A ghastly process for a growing boy."

Slick tears pooled in Urric's eyes.

"What is to be the fate of your lands? Picked apart? What would your forefathers say to see it all drift away?"

"He is my son!" shouted Urric with clenched fists. "All he knows is because of me."

"I am told he is quite a rider. He spends his time outside Jevatryn, riding near the Avenbair. Much talent. In that way, he is your son." Katya rubbed her arms, suddenly feeling a chill coming on. "I did not bring you here to quarrel with you. We share a common interest in lineages."

"The Billengrath name ends when Barbora marries," said Urric.

"You men are overly concerned with names. It seems a simple bargaining chip."

"You hold Fost and Kamila in Jevatryn as hostages. A word to Eadolan will fix this, or I'll storm the city myself."

"I'll parade them through every town on the way here. Let the crowds get a good, long look. Fat Albright and a gaggle of apprentices may even want to meet Fost on the way to start his education, but the road is dangerous. Maybe travel to your southern estates is better. Avoid Ravalas all together."

"What do you want?"

"Elf and human make for a tenuous physiology. The union can endanger the realm for generations to come. The elf mark is a slumbering pox to introduce into the royal blood. It can make for barren wombs and spoiled seed."

"I am told you performed admirably on the field of battle, Urric. I think you have brought us a momentary reprieve, but our long-term stability still needs attention." Katya took a few steps closer and lowered her voice. "I only want to strengthen and stabilize the land. I need you to propose the idea to Eadolan to end his marriage and consider a native born. Barbora, perhaps?" she said with a slight smile.

Urric backpedaled and almost smacked into the door. Sahalana departing and Eadolan marrying again was not a new idea, one with the weight of frequent whispers, but never one put to him so directly. He laughed. "And if I refuse? Your threats will have no compulsion over me!"

"You can refuse, but I still know your secret. You will have my unwavering support. Should there be any claims against the integrity of your lands and titles, I will swear up and down that I believe and know by the radiant day of Indalos that Fost is your trueborn son and heir. In return, I require all your cultivated lands and rents along the Avitsa watershed between Wild Rose and Jevatryn and a third interest in your glassworks at Coldbridge. Also, my scholars have done extensive study and think the Jernivan Shield is somewhere in your arsenals or treasure holds. Do you have it?"

"What guarantees do I have from you?" Urric blurted in stunned retort. "I, I need some payment from you."

"You're in no position to ask for anything, but this can all turn out well."

"If Eadolan produces no heir, what of it? Behan already has two girls, and surely a male heir will follow in time. The Arkwen name is secure. I see wasting no more time with this." Urric fumbled at the door. "I'll speak with Behan now."

"I shall deny everything. Remember you're the one in front of a line of gossiping servants that said you wanted to talk to me. Do you want to provoke a crisis? Who has done more to feed, fund, and cloth this army? If you are successful, Fost will keep all his titles and privileges and maintain Boscawent prominence at the royal court. I'll even support your claims to Padazar's confiscated lands. That would make up twenty-fold for what I've asked for in return."

She continued, "If you provoke this, Silverface and his clutch will investigate. At best you'll have to pay a big bribe, and they may end up confiscating much of your lands anyway. Think of what Eadolan could do to restore a depleted treasury by auctioning off your lands? Other than Chetwin Claypool, who truly will fight for Fost?"

"You heard in council, as did I, that Sahalana is not well, but if a child is born, then I shall only require the Avitsa lands and rents and the portion of the Coldbridge revenues. It's a modest request. In your sprawling lands you will hardly notice the difference. I'm sure you will have plenty of occasions to find the right time to discuss with Eadolan." She motioned the Duke aside and unbolted the door. "Good night, Urric."

CHAPTER 30

"Stand before me, Coward. Receive what seasons have held from you. Why did you come back?"

"My home is under attack. I had failed before and I—"

"Yes, you did, but I doubt that's the reason. You ran and now return with that thing."

"When I saw the baby was twisted, an orc, I knew again the eternal shame of being late. Anora never told me. I felt such sorrow in caring the, it, to the woods, of what it represented and the pain it brought to her. A pain she carried alone."

"And made worse by you leaving!" The woman's broad face boiled with anger. "She survived the pregnancy but seemed to lose all heart, all hope when you never returned. She was strong, and you were not. You caused her death!" the woman screamed. "And now you mock me and her by carting that thing up here."

The old woman, Anora's mother, tightly gripped Bambenek's face.

"I accept your judgment. Do as you wish. I am not here for forgiveness. I am going into the mountains."

The woman's fingers pressed into Bambenek's face. He let out a shallow groan as his cheeks started to wither. The anguish of his cold breath escaped through his mouth and cracks in his face, his desiccated skin drifting like flakes of ash in the air.

Bambenek gasped again and stared into the woman's eyes.

"Better you had stayed away, stayed dead. Now you return with an orc to be saved and running off again. What a fool you are!"

"I felt compelled." Bambenek tried to speak, air and sound leaking in all directions. "There is a greater purpose. I thought I could save him."

"And Anora! Your betrayal."

"I wish I could change it all. Took wrong path. Late." Bambenek's face quivered.

The woman loosened her fingers.

Bambenek inhaled deeply. "I feel guided by forces beyond pity. It would have been easier for me to stay away, but we were guided here. I have taken no other wife and forever carried Anora's memory, but I cannot remove the disgrace. I did not come back to torment. I accept your judgment." Bambenek lowered to both knees, staring up at the woman.

The woman glared deeply into his eyes. She released her grip. Bambenek's skin started to return to its prior state, save for an ashy mark on his cheek. "Let that serve as a perpetual mark."

Bambenek touched his face in disbelief.

"I am so very sorry." Bambenek began to sob as the woman walked away.

"Who are you?" said Dronor, still quilted in fog.

"Your leg is now healed," smiled a woman, her pinched features barely moving in her small face. "When you are ready, do you want to learn the secrets of that ring?"

"I want to learn my own secrets," he said but could not feel his lips moving.

"Not sure they would be helpful to you. Best to forget what is already buried."

The bone ring rested on the pointer finger of the half-orc's big right hand. The tiny woman moving like a hunched rat, and barely tall enough to reach, gently grasped the bottom of Dronor's wrist. She gave a little tug to get Dronor to hold out his hand, the smooth blanched bone ring now illuminated with pale blue markings and emitting a faint light.

"This is the edge of the woods. Beyond are the fever swamps."

Dronor looked up to the towering trees. Thin light drizzled through a gray rain.

"Make your choice," the woman said.

Dronor felt her hand release, and, when he looked down, she was gone. He spun around and found no sign of her. The half-orc sniffed and found nothing. He reached for his sword and found just a tunic of coarse sackcloth.

As Dronor considered the situation, he grunted and kneaded his lip with his stumpy tusks. His left leg seemed healed; it carried his weight. He studied the leg and found no trace of a scar, but the muscles had atrophied. He fought to grasp how much time had passed. The air was much colder now.

Dronor sniffed again and looked in all directions. No path seemed particularly favorable, and he had no idea where he was. He remembered the voice of Bambenek, the scout who had saved his life, and wisps of other voices since being pulled from a cart, but these fragments gave him no bearing on the present.

"Alone," Dronor said in a dwarven tongue. This he noted was the first word passing between his lips, which caused the hair on his neck to tingle. Sweat beaded on his forehead, and he wondered if his leg truly had healed.

After testing his legs for several moments, he took a few tenuous steps in one direction, passing between trees cautiously, bracing against the trunks, uncertain of what may lay ahead. The ground became damper and squished beneath his bare feet. He found a drier patch and stayed to that track.

The gray sky grew wider, the trees starting to spread apart as ferns and grass tufts took their place with stream-fed ponds and smaller pools of stagnant water dotting the marshy landscape.

A rustling in the tall grass stopped Dronor. He raised his hands and snarled a warning. With a roaring grunt, a massive boar appeared between the grass. Dronor decided the grunt was more a welcoming call than a threat. The half-orc relaxed slightly, his muscles uncoiling.

The boar abruptly charged. The speed of the sudden rush stunned Dronor, the huge boar barreling towards him. Dronor hesitated, looking to the water on either side and whether that offered any safety. His legs felt heavy, empty, and he tried to move. The boar lunged forward, maw open and teeth bared.

Dronor recoiled and extended his right hand to blunt the charge of the boar. As the boar's force collided with the ring, an explosion of light and memory flashed across Dronor: childhood toil under dwarven whips, fighting in streets, the deck of a ship, wounds and triumphs of recent battles, a looming crag mountain, and the slick delirium of fevers.

Dronor was again quilted in fog, all black and silent before him.

CHAPTER 31

"Another message has just arrived from Mage Albright," said the Archmage as he entered Thiepval's quarters. "Preparations continue in Ravalas. There are also new reports coming in of the Southwesterners marching at will through large swathes south of the Avenbair, although no reports of concern from the Hayloft. No word if the river fleet has clashed with the traitors."

"The Tavuros have us under half siege," said Thiepval, finally looking up from several open spell books and ledgers. "Very cautious, hiding behind a living shield of our men. I want to hit them back, hit them back hard, in revenge for Dahey's death, Erstchester's death, and the mockery of parading our captive men. I want to send a large raptor force but not led by Brenio. Falanika—"

"You will lead it," the Archmage interjected.

Thiepval leapt from his chair. "I am now the Castellan of Thavodyn!"

"And you are the Tovenward of the Order."

"Who will be?" Thiepval started but did not need to finish his question.

"You will retain the title of Castellan," said the Archmage assuagingly before adding, "until such time that Eadolan names a new Castellan or confirms you. I will see to Thavodyn's security while you are away."

Thiepval struggled to remain calm, eventually saying in a flat voice, "Do you hold me responsible for what happened to Erstchester?"

"It was most unfortunate to have the most secure area of the fortress violated in such a manner."

"I disagreed with Erstchester allowing any of the recent arrivals into the citadel, even to perform menial tasks," protested Thiepval, his voice rising. "At least the three were discovered when trying to escape the walls." Even now Thiepval struggled with comprehending their brazenness, even the cleverness of the infiltrators. "Scum. Filth. And a washer woman."

"Audacity comes in all forms. Are they the only three?"

"They used no magic. Other than trying to read the thoughts of everyone in the fortress, I don't think we could have discovered their intention."

"Commitment is itself a powerful magic."

Thiepval, ever sleepless, was in no mood for the Archmage's quips. "The garrison is in a state of serious unrest. Dunbar and Glover fear it will only get worse. Too many unknown faces and suspicion. There is talk amongst the soldiers of wanting to expel anyone that at least two garrison members won't personally vouch for."

Thiepval blinked his blood-shot eyes and smiled. "This is madness. Anyone expelled would just be captured by the Tavuros out on the road. And we aren't likely to get reinforcements anytime soon. Spies and assassins are nothing new in an army. I'd like the apprentices and assistants most skilled in reading thoughts to begin covertly assessing the newcomers."

"Do you think the three were unaided by anyone in the garrison?"

Thiepval shook his head. "I don't know, but Wolfwind won't stop asking for the release of the Southwesterners in the jail. He's right that they did not kill the Castellan. Wolfwind thinks it would raise morale to release them. Show we dealt with the problem and we're not fearing of shadows. In any case, I think it better that I stay. I know the men better, and I can keep this from growing further and weakening their resolve."

"You don't think I can handle it?" questioned the Archmage.

Thiepval suppressed a smirk. "I know the men better. I would not want morale to be any worse. When's the last time you have talked to anyone who wasn't a noble or member of the Order?"

The Archmage glanced out the window but appeared unmoved by the comment.

"I have served with these men for years. We've trained alongside one another and endured the same hardships. And, if you are about to say that Tomas Telfair will remain and that is same enough. No," Thiepval shook his finger at the Archmage, "no, it is not. He is respected, but he is not a battle commander. A physician is not viewed the same."

The Archmage nodded, acknowledging the point, but Thiepval barely noticed, still churning through his own thoughts.

"If we kill Padazar, is the rebellion over?" Thiepval considered, running through the permutations. "Is Catalfo working on this?"

The Archmage had a strained look on his face. "Nestor.

He," the Archmage said, judging his words, "has been focused on other areas. It would—"

"So, he doesn't even have agents close to Padazar." Thiepval intuitively knew this to be correct. "Is this because of Woolfolk? Who is he? Stop these games. Is he an expelled member of the Order? Enough of keeping us in ignorance. We must know! Or are your secrets and lies going to get us killed?"

CHAPTER 32

"We're about in the slop shit of it now!" howled Elgar Anchorsmith, the muscled arms of the dwarf steady on the tiller and bare feet tapping against the sand-strewn deck. His bare, massive chest and bulging belly sported a large tattoo blending an anchor and an octopus. Despite the quickening approaching of winter, Anchorsmith dressed only in drab, checkered wool pants. Even in the chill, sweat beaded across his stubbly bald head. "I missed this!" He stroked his goatee while watching low profiles of charred and smoldering skiffs drift by.

Captain Robard Bracken glanced at his helmsman. The two were inseparable sailing mates over the past three decades. They both smiled, recalling wild fights against pirates from their youth. It had been nearly as long since the two had served together in Ardalencor's navy, but they sailed once again in defense of their country.

"We fared well, but there's ships alight and bunched on the left side," worried Bracken as he surveyed the two fleets about to engage across the breadth of the Avenbair.

Bracken pulled on the broad brim of his galaswack skin hat. Teeth sewn into the brim gave it a decorative and serrated edge. A falcon's foot jutted out from the band and three tall feathers were tucked in the side for good measure. Sprouting from inside his galaswack rain slicker, he wore a bright orange scarf high on his neck, determined to be a visible symbol to his crew and the other captains. Bracken started to call to his lookout, but the man was already calling back.

"Captain, three. Four ships alight. One badly listing." The lookout was gripping the ropes and leaning his body back and forth to get the best view. "Crews are—"

"Fire boats! More coming!" came a call from multiple sailors as more red-orange auras came alive.

"Take care of yourself," said Bracken to Anchorsmith. "Keep an eye on the river and one for any missile fire."

Anchorsmith only nodded as another sailor warned of even more fire skiffs.

Bracken stood high on the castle of his cog, the *Harrier*, a river and coastal trading craft, and now the flagship of a motley array of vessels under his command. The *Harrier* had high sides, a stout transport built to resist boarding by pirates while on runs beyond Floriana to the ports of Trawfarne or Pavtanarell. To defend the *Harrier*, Bracken had brought on additional men, mostly archers, to augment his experienced crew who knew how to defend their floating fortress.

An experienced shipbuilder and modest merchant captain, Bracken had never led more than a handful of ships. Many of the other captains, especially those in the service of larger commercial ventures or the great noble houses, were reluctant to subordinate themselves to him and put their ships at risk for this voyage.

Bracken was chosen to lead as he was first to step forward and propose the idea of a river fleet when the small Ardalen navy would not be put to this use. While others prevaricated, Rafal the Younger was steadfast in backing Bracken as lead captain, and ever more so when the river fleet gathered commitments and coveting command became more opportune.

"Courage, more than wind, moves men," Bracken had told the other captains in part to scold and to inspire, before they set sail on the Avenbair to confront the Southwesterners. The saying was from Bracken's father and one often repeated when he was a boy and had long been painted on the stern of the *Harrier*.

"Let's see what kind of fleet we have," Bracken said to himself, deeply concerned about the left squadron and the nerves of the squadron leader. Political considerations had determined the other senior officers in order to ensure the arrival of ships.

Bracken would have preferred to launch raids up the Avenbair, up and down the tributaries, even to Delun itself to disrupt the Southwesterners and deprive them of any sense of safety. Instead, battle was to be given a short sail from Ravalas to entice the merchants to deliver on their promises and incentivize them to defend their wharves in the capital and establishments farther downriver.

Bracken had arranged for long red banners to be raised to avoid misidentification once the Southwestern fleet had been sighted, and he saw several ships flying these banners now in distress. Small boats lowered as more desperate men jumped into the water to try to get away from the burning ships. He assumed that one of the small boats carried an urgent request to him to send ships to reinforce the left.

This assembly of ships had never sailed together, much less in war. The left wing could still put up a fight. Bracken wanted to see whether the left squadron would continue to battle on or strike their colors before he considered shuffling ships across the river. He reasoned that such dramatic movements would only cause more confusion. The flow of the river was also against his fleet. Sailing against the current and moving across the course of more fire skiffs was not to his liking. Bracken reminded himself that he needed to maintain a blocking fleet to protect Ravalas, not necessarily win a decisive victory. "We need to stay afloat and keep the flag flying."

"When are those wizards going to appear? The Order said it was going to be along the bank or on one of these little islands. I haven't seen or heard a thing," grumbled Anchorsmith straining to stand a bit taller. The dwarf scanned the northern bank and multitude of islets in the great bends of the Avenbair.

"Padazar has cavalry roaming the north bank. Most of our troopers are supposedly with Eadolan." Bracken decided not to give his overflowing disappointment more voice. "Can't fix the clouds, nor the currents." He folded his arms and evaluated his options.

"Fire! We have them in the flames, Admiral," a young aide called with delight, nearly wondering aloud if combat was really all this easy.

"We hit a few, but they were ready," said Jannon to the teen, admonishingly but not too strongly.

"We spread them out too thin, except on the right. Should have concentrated them. Stop sending the fire skiffs!" shouted Admiral Sands in disgust as more were lit and sent in an unco-ordinated fashion. After screaming at several crew members to ensure the order was relayed across the fleet, Sands turned back to Jannon. "We should attack on the right. Force them into the deep mud or surrender." Blood coursed through Sands' reddened face. "Let's see how much fight is in Eadolan's fleet.

Who is willing to risk it all? We're not going to win control of the Avenbair with just fire boats."

"These are tall ships. They've handled pirates before." Jannon tried to assess the best option and sourly wanted the fire skiffs to have made things easier.

Sands' flagship, the *Slippery Sprite*, like most of the larger Southwestern crafts, was a flatbottom barge with open decks for cargo save for a small mast and pilot house. If not hauled back up the river, the larger barges could move under oar power. In preparation for battle, palisades were added to the sides of the barges, including overhead protection to shelter the oarsmen and platforms for men assembling to climb and board opposing ships.

"Pirates want easy prey. Oh, they may fight, but plundering is not within divine sanction. By the strength of Indalos, we fight for our country and our future. Those captains ahead will see a different sort of man scale their walls and take their ships." Sands' eyes focused. "I think it's Molunby's ships alight and smoking on the right. I wager that oat groper won't wait around for us to pay him a visit."

"Do you know who is in command of Eadolan's fleet?" asked Jannon.

"We hear it is Robard Bracken. He is an earnest man, a fine shipwright. Pity he is not on our side."

Jannon nodded. "We'll ready the men. Kerjelaft prepared some surprises as well." He studied the river, imagining the final approaches and collision of ships. "I think we should release all fire ships now. They can screen our movement. No sense in saving them and best to give them time to burn before we get too close."

Sands concurred and turned to his aide. "Signal release of all fire skiffs. Tell them to mind their flames and the currents. Get them burning hot when at close approach," he said without any hesitancy at reversing his earlier order. Sands then called to his boatswain, "Ready the oars."

The deck of the *Slippery Sprite* was crowded with fighting men. The oarsmen slid out their oars, licking and then dipping into the water. Having space for the full movement of the oars proved problematic with the number of fighting men aboard. The fighting men were pressed together, shoulder touching shoulder. Many soldiers decided to fight unarmored, more fearful of the Avenbair's pull than their enemies' weapons; even so, each soldier looked above the short palisade, imagining the high sides of the ships and a deluge of rocks, arrows, and whatever else would descend upon them.

As soldiers helped Jannon secure his breastplate, he looked across the river. "See there!" Jannon pointed. "The falcons. Those have to be Freprew's falcons circling there. Latrobh and Freprew are keeping pace with us. If Eadolan's fleet breaks for the north bank, they'll be rounded up."

"Signal to all ships on the right and center," called Sands. "Large vessels and troop transports to converge towards the right and prepare to board. If captains surrender, accept their word and avoid unnecessarily spilling of the faithful's blood. Tell Captain Hamern to keep his squadron near the north bank to coordinate with Latrobh and the cavalry, and it'll serve to hold part of our adversary's fleet in place."

"Boatswain," called Jannon. "Can your crew get up enough speed to ram?

The boatswain shook his head in disbelief. "The *Sprite* ain't built for that. Lot of extra weight on board, too. We use the oars when empty and headed back upriver. No telling what would happen."

"Swimmers!" ordered Bracken, and soon after small row boats fanned out from the center of the fleet. These boats with just two or three men with axes and small drills rowed to intercept and sink the fire skiffs. In the cloudy gloom above the river, the flaming shapes cast a more ominous presence on the rippling water.

Bracken figured these skiffs did not contain any arcane accelerants to increase the potency of the fire. He had not seen any used in the previous skiffs and hoped the Southwesterners did not possess any of these materials. If they did, Bracken now grimly assessed, better for this to be discovered well before a skiff drifted too close to a ship, but the thought of sending men out to be engulfed in magical flame twisted his stomach. He ran his hand over his beard to douse these imagined flames.

"We'll get these fire boats cleared and give us some angles of attack," remarked Bracken as he calmly strode the deck. "We'll be coming to bang sides soon enough. Those aren't warships up ahead. These men are no pirates. Most of them have never fought on water."

The knob nails of his boots scratched across the sand-strewn deck. Bracken looked at each member of his long-time crew and the recently mustered archers. "Ravalas is the heart of our country, and the Avenbair is the life vein. We will not be dislodged from this place. We will bar the way. These men were our brothers, but in betrayal they are no more. We must remind them of their forgotten loyalty." He pointed at the baskets full of rocks and boxes with small ceramic pots placed at points along the length of the ship. Bracken strode to the prow and stood near two small catapults. "As hard as it may be to meet them in anger, remember they welcomed a foreign invader. There is one fate for traitors."

"Yes, Captain" came a half-hearted cheer, solemn but committed to the work ahead.

"Captain!" called the lookout. "The traitors are turning ships towards the left."

Bracken spun and saw several of the Southwestern ships in the center lines preparing to move towards Molunby's ships. Bracken wondered how many would turn and what kind of hole this would leave in the center. "Norwell, get these catapults ready to open up at longer range."

An eager crew of Swimmers quickly had rowed out against the current and approached an oncoming fire skiff. The trio, two teenagers and a weather-whipped dockhand, used oars to try to steady their approach in front of the fiery craft, but the skiff had weight and did not yield its course. They hurriedly pushed off, bumped, and moved to the side, the wall of heat intense and roiling past their faces.

When this trio and other men of the coast formed their own free company, they selected the name of the First Ardalens, this phrase having been memorialized in the chronicle of a seafaring visitor on arrival at the shores of Ardalencor. The captains of the river fleet found the name too presumptuous and opted for Swimmers in recognition of the group's unique talents, excellent swimming and diving skills in coastal currents as well as in the Avenbair.

The three exchanged frightened glances. The skiff was more of a challenge than reckoned when the Swimmers gladly accepted the mission. The trio splashed furiously with the oars and bare hands trying to douse part of the flame and gain a hold on the boat. The skiff was well in blaze but, depending on the contents of the boat, it could still burn a long while and cause problems for the larger ships.

One teen singed his hand when hastily trying to grab the skiff's side and recoiled in pain. The other teen leaned out of the boat with a hand axe and tried to hack at the skiff's water line but the movement of both boats rendered his attempts futile. The old dockhand in a broad straw hat tried to balance keeping the boat close and avoiding the flames jumping as cinders showered from the skiff.

"Is it raining?" said one of the teens seeing a ripple in the water nearby.

"That's an arrow!" shouted the dockhand. "Let's try to douse the prow and then use that hand drill. Wet your shirt and wrap it," he said to the teen with a charred hand. "Let's try to get back in front of this thing, drench the front, and then bore a hole at the waterline. That should give us some cover from these arrows, too. Those ships will be closing!"

The trio rowed and struggled to race ahead of the fire skiff. The dockhand shouted to Swimmers nearby, asking how they were dealing with their own fiery creatures.

Suddenly beneath the cloud-covered sky, bursts of bright radiance shone near the north bank of the river. Pulses of color, white and yellow, popped and winked over the position of the Southwesterner's left squadron. Soon after, seeking stabs of swirling magical tracers raced towards the Southwestern ships.

A broad-hull longship had its sail ripped and charred as the tracers found range. The next sound was an iron thud hitting the side of the longship. The crew's shouting stopped, and in eerie silence, they wondered if the hull had been punctured. Sighing in collective relief and resuming their shouts, they were unsure whether to retreat or to engage, but most of the crew strained to take cover against the low walls of the ship. A few arrows and bolts zipped wildly in defiance back towards the shore.

The next shot from a torsion crossbow landed in the center of the ship, engulfing the mast and crew members in purple-orange flames. The fire was greasy slick and spreading. Several men were immolated. Any survivors jumped overboard.

Two more bolts were shot from the shore and hit the stern

of a nearby barge. Crews furiously attempted to put out the fire, but water only seemed to propel the oily flames across more of the ship. Seeing the rapidly losing effort, the crew abandoned ship. Men desperately pulled at armor or sword belts in the spasm to flee.

———————

"That'll get those bastards' attention!" Apprentice Dalibor whispered loudly, still admiring his work through the frame of the torsion crossbow. "Let's load another bolt."

"Not bad, three out of four," said Apprentice Rains chidingly. "I think I could have done better." Even concealed on a small islet surrounded in thick reeds, they kept their voices low to avoid revealing their position.

Dalibor shook his head. "Part of the ground was too soft for the first one. Couldn't handle the kick. Now we got a good base."

An attendant conjured a cordon of illusory flame which appeared to emerge and retreat from various points on the marshy shore to deter any ships considering a landing. "See you that falcon?" called the attendant. "Is that one of ours?

Rains said, "You worry too much. No ship is going to come close after that, and the cavalry aren't going to swim through this mess, even if they could find us in the marsh."

"Could just be a falcon that doesn't like all the commotion on the river," offered another apprentice who was tasked with observing the shoreline for signs of approaching cavalry.

Dalibor fired another crossbow bolt which splashed in between two ships which were attempting to get greater distance from the shore.

"Let's save these bolts. Took me and Gavin months to make them, and I almost lost my fingers a few times. If the ships are leaving, we've done our work. Let's cast some more tracers to keep them moving."

"One more," pleaded Dalibor. "I can hit the next one." Rains relented, and Dalibor took aim. The next bolt punched through a barge's palisade, the shaft and imbedded tube cracking under the impact, releasing a rush of arcane fire and horrid screams.

———

"Admiral, the left wing is withdrawing!" called the young aide.

"Those damn wizards must have slipped through the cavalry," despaired Sands. "If we wait, maybe Latrobh can flush them out!"

Jannon studied the river, saying nothing.

"We can still beat them on the right. With the center moving, we have the numbers and can break them. Still salvage this day," Sands pleaded with Jannon.

Jannon looked across the river again and towards the southern bank, envisioning the carnage of boarding and taking the high-walled ships.

"Please, my Lord. Give us a crack," Sands begged. "We're all here. Let's have at them."

"No," said Jannon disappointedly. "There will be another day. Signal the withdrawal."

CHAPTER 33

"Why are we doing this?" asked Fishbone tired of the repeated discussion of the smallest of logistical details.

"Why? We've already discussed it many times," said Faolan. Growing impatient, the monk pointed at Val seated against the wall, knees up and face down over his arms. "Can he hear us? Has he been sleeping all this time?"

"He's out and may sleep until we leave tomorrow night, but he'll be able to stand each watch for days on end if you'd like. His eyes can see what most of us can't. He sleeps when he needs. You'll learn to appreciate Val. So." Fishbone folded his arms. "Tell me again."

"Your Ealdorman ordered," started Faolan.

"I know what he ordered." Fishbone overly stressed each of the sounds. "But tell me again. Make me feel good about this. Excite me." He lifted his cup. "These relics are so vital to recover, but they couldn't save your monastery? How powerful can they be? Will Martoz the Black reappear to rip the top off a mountain and show us where they are?"

The monks seemed lost for words; had their sword belts not been left by the door, steel may have been swung across the large central fire. Their eyes conveyed as much.

Around the fire sat Camhorn, Mannix, Sunsmoke, the members of the expedition, and an older Drivach woman.

"Let me ask you this," called Hackett hoping to shift the attention away from Fishbone. "A lot of our people, hundreds, thousands, over the years, have been taken by the Drivach. At times I think even Indalos does not know what happened to them. A lot of people, including my sister." Budding tears loosened by drink cupped his eyes. "If we find our people, if I find my sister. We are getting them out. Forget your books."

The monks had recovered a measure of their composure, but Cobart's glance seemed to still blaze through Fishbone. "True that we could not stop the entire Tavurite army," he emphasized, "but they lay thick before our walls! More trouble will befall us all, the entire country, if these sacred objects are not recovered or if their power is released. If we can get your families out after retrieving the relics, then, yes, of course."

"We are not on a death march. We intend to live and re-found the monastery," added Cobart. "Ealdorman, I appeal to you."

Camhorn raised his hand. "They didn't say they won't go. They asked that you make them believe. They're just a bit scared and can't seem to grasp your steadfast resolve, holding on, clinging to the very end."

Fishbone and Hackett looked angered and ashamed at Camhorn's statement about them being afraid.

Camhorn continued, "Boys, it's time not to fear the shadow of the mountain, myself included. We can't just sit down here and wait to be attacked. This is also a scouting mission. Not even the traders and smugglers go into the mountains in winter so the Drivach won't be expecting you. You boys know how to cover tracks in the snow, and the monks tell me they can, too."

"Let me go with you," said the old Drivach woman. "Please."

"Golobi, you have given us invaluable information. For that we are forever grateful," said Cobart. "But you would slow us down."

"If you think me too slow, I would only go one way." Looking at Camhorn and Mannix, she said, "I'm eternally thankful for the shelter I received when I fled my own people. And yet, I would like to look upon the closeness of the sun and the valleys once more."

Mannix put his arm around Golobi to comfort her.

Sunsmoke's opaque eyes pointed towards the fire. "I can help you see your memory."

"It's already clear. I could never forget. I want to see it again with my own eyes." Golobi looked again at the monks. "You should take me with you. You won't be able to hide in snowdrifts the entire way. You will need someone who can talk to the mountain folk. Hackett and Fish speak some, but in one valley there can be three different ways to say the same word, and how it's said matters. Each tribe has pass phrases and are very suspicious, even of one another." She sighed trying to convey the importance of her warning. "Hackett can pass for a mountain man at a glance, but what if you get into a situation where a sword can't get you out?" She took a long breath and then gave the monks a hopeful look. "They won't expect an old woman of secretive work."

The monks seemed to reconsider but did not commit. Cobart said with more than a hint of regret, "I don't see how you'd keep pace. We intend to move very fast."

"You're not going to walk the whole way?" protested Golobi. "You'll need a good story in case you're spotted before the mountains. Bring a cart and go as peddlers making one last run before the snows. I'll ride in the cart," she winked.

Cobart shook his head. "And if the horses go lame? Or the cart can't go up anything near a sheer face? So, we need to travel along what passes for a road up there under observation of who knows how many eyes, and what if you start to fall behind the pace? As you said, we leave you in the snow to starve to death? Or you crawl to a village, and desperate for food, you tell them our plan?"

Golobi's eyes blinked wide at the monk's intensity.

"No. We left sisters behind once already."

There was a sound at the door. Venduva briefly entered the circular log house, and Camhorn nodded in acknowledgement.

After appearing to pick through the plates and pots of food, Bambenek said, "I need to piss," as he headed for the door. Bambenek knew what would be happening soon, and he decided it best to take his leave.

Outside the log house, Bambenek's footfalls melted and spotted the snow-sprinkled ground. The snow fell intermittently, now falling slow and thick. It was dark. Few outside fires were being tended, and the trees cast long shadows. Since he arrived seemingly long ago, the camp had transformed from tents and lean-tos into a maze of huts packed thickly with earth to keep out the growing cold.

A looming shadow approached directly ahead of Bambenek. As he followed the top of the shadow towards its source, he heard a familiar grunt.

Bambenek's head snapped up in disbelief. "Dronor!"

A small, hunched woman walked with Dronor. Bambenek heard the patter of her slow shuffling feet and watched the long strides of Dronor.

"I feel like I've nearly died many times since we met, but here I am. Still standing, and on two good legs. I have you to thank, Bam," Dronor said, gripping Bambenek in a massive hug. "No one else would have saved me." Warding his own emotions, the half-orc abruptly pushed Bambenek away. "We need to stop meeting in forests."

"At least you've had a bath since then. And they washed your clothes."

"New pants, too. I'm ready for a lord's ball."

Bambenek bowed deeply at the small woman. "Thank you for saving his life."

"He is a tough one. His will is very strong. Very fierce. You all came a long way, but it was necessary, I think." The woman gave her best pinched grin before disappearing into the night.

"When do you leave for the mountains?" questioned Dronor.

"What? Who told you that?" Bambenek frantically looked around to see if anyone may have heard.

"I saw it. Blurs. Flashes. I am coming with."

"Are you alright?" Bambenek asked incredulously. "Why?"

"I feel drawn. Like I must go. I don't think I could describe it."

"Are you strong enough?"

Dronor nodded. "It's cold here. You got any food?"

As they walked back to the log house, Bambenek signaled for Dronor to stop. They stood concealed in the shadow of a tree. Departing the building were Bayard, Fishbone, Hackett, and the two monks, now joined by Venduva and four other women. Venduva stopped for a moment as Fishbone and Hackett went their separate directions through the camp. One of the women departed by herself in a different direction. Venduva led the remaining women, Bayard, and the monks in the opposite direction from where Bambenek and Dronor stood.

"What's that about?" asked Dronor.

Bambenek just shook his head, not wanting to explain the custom to one who would never be involved. Bambenek waited a moment longer in case there was any more movement, but he was certain Val would not be participating either. The mere appearance of Val or Dronor would make all but the most venturous of women recoil at even the thought.

Half-orcs, given their unnatural origins, were thought to be sterile and that any coupling would not produce offspring. This growing realization eased the perception of surviving half-orcs. In the aftermath of the Disorders, within Arda-lencor and far beyond, of the faint sliver of half-orcs who were permitted more than a breath, most were used as soldiers, servants, spectacles, or little more than beasts of burden. Sired by creatures called orcs, men corrupted and transformed by elven magic, half-orc offspring who were given a semblance of care and attention were found, if prop-erly guided, to have an innate sense of magic bound within them. The question was, once unleashed, in which form would it manifest?

As Bambenek and then Dronor ducked in through the log house's low door, Camhorn stared transfixed as if seeing a forgotten memory. He struggled to reconcile how one so close to death stood before him. Camhorn's mind rushed to grasp how much energy went into saving this creature and perhaps at the expense of his own fighters.

Sunsmoke spoke into Camhorn's mind. "This one is more than a brute."

"Dronor, is it?" Camhorn stood in greeting. "Good to see you well from that cart from so long ago. Bambenek is a stub-born man in his own miserable way but has some redeeming qualities despite his best efforts."

Mannix stood as well and sized up Dronor. Golobi peered up at them, wondering who exactly was taller. "There is room for many trees in the forest," she chuckled as the two seemed to relax.

Dronor hungrily eyed the steaming kettle suspended over the fire. Mannix filled and handed the half-orc a bowl of hunter's stew. Dronor tilted the gourd bowl back in one slurp and gulp. Mannix roared in laughter and quickly filled another bowl.

"Pipe? Chew root?" asked Mannix as Dronor finished a second bowl.

Bambenek grabbed a flagon and took a long drink. He sat down next to Dronor, his friend whose life he vowed to save. He had made a promise and traveled as far as the Northwestern Wilds to keep it. He had atoned and redeemed himself for a deep and haunting wound, at least, in part, such that the weight felt lighter.

Dronor set down the bowl licking his teeth and tusks, considering his next course. Mannix again gave him an assessing look. "How many heads can you lop off in one swing?"

Sunsmoke smirked at the question. "Let me ask you, Dronor. What do you know of that ring? What has it revealed?"

Venduva led the monks, Bayard, and the three women to a sparsely-settled part of the camp. When they arrived at a series of conical tents with flickering fires, she studied their faces and then paired each man and woman. Another woman met the group with a platter of earthen tea cups. As each pair linked arms and drank the tea, Venduva proclaimed, "Life proceeds and vanquishes death. The bond of man and woman releases all creation."

Finally grasping the situation as Venduva escorted each

couple to a tent, Bayard's eyes were wide, and he found it impossible not to grin. He had been with a woman a time or two, but they had been long, winding pursuits and never so arranged or immediate.

Bayard thought he had seen the young woman once before, tending goats at the edge of camp. He didn't think she had been accompanied by anyone, at least at the time. No man. No children. Bayard reasoned it best not to ask. He looked again at her face and her blue eyes. She would smile but kept her focus ahead as they followed Venduva. Bayard thought her a few years older than he, but perhaps not. Maybe she been hardened by tragedy, but she still had the brightness and grace of a young woman.

The night before battles or dangerous expeditions, the older women would pair unattached or widowed men with a woman from the community. Given the number of raids, kidnappings, and general hard living in the borderlands, children tended to be raised communally. Family units vanished and reformed with the sharp ease of necessity. This arranged coupling aided in sustaining the population and in strengthening the spirits of the men undertaking these endeavors. The chance for longevity and the enduring hope through desperate situations to return and possibly meet their children kept men alive. Depending on the circumstances, however, for a returning man, confirming lineage of a child could prove dubious.

Men with wives or sweethearts were expected to partake with their beloved in the communal duty as well. Fishbone and Hackett readily obeyed when Venduva gave them leave to escape the protracted fireside council.

Venduva hugged Bayard and the young woman and then motioned towards the tent. The pair crawled in. The floor was deer skins and blankets across a fresh matting of boughs. Small baskets containing food and drink had been placed inside.

"What's your name?" said Bayard as he peered around. He relaxed seeing that no one else was in sight as he closed the tent flap.

"Mara," she said, pushing back the hood of her woolen shawl and running her fingers through her long brown hair. She wore a simple hempen dress and buckskin boots.

"Bayard. Pleasure to meet you," he uttered, barely believing the circumstances.

Mara picked through the baskets. She tore off two small chucks of bread and handed one to Bayard. "Are you a knight from the south?"

"Yes," Bayard lied but felt the assertion to be true.

Mara looked at him searchingly, not sure whether to believe him. She opened a small corked bottle, sniffed, and took a sip. She closely studied the features of his face. "Well, even if not, you fought the mountain demons. Thank you. You came to help when no other knights did. To me, you are a knight." She traced her hands over his shoulders. He placed his hand gently on her waist as she undid the lacings and lifted his shirt. "A knight's story is worth knowing and telling," she whispered.

Outside the snow fell lightly, lingering and dancing in the air. Mara and Bayard were warmly intwined within furs and blankets beneath the tree tops and pale stars.

CHAPTER 34

"We should wait for Behan. I thought he'd be here by now," complained Mage Albright as he glanced between the roaring fire and trays and plates of picked-over food. "I don't want to have to repeat all of this."

"I'm sure he is still entertaining his guests. With Eadolan away, his work is doubled," reminded Chancellor Droswild. "Keep the merchants ingratiated, reassure the foreign dignitaries, such as they remain, sniff the bright flowers of Ardalen nobility, and have a dance or two with the ladies. I am sure he has not forgotten us. He'll be along when he is able."

"Not like, Behan," considered Albright. "Not even a messenger. It's well past deep night."

"Forget it," Droswild said with a grin. "A mage has more important matters of contemplation. You were saying that sweeps of the city found a cache?"

"A small cache. Magic detection orbs along with lead tubes. They were discovered underneath the floor of a shop near the Smelting Gate. Very crude items, maybe they'd work once against as equally dirty magic. The tubes had real nasty stuff in them."

"Items infiltrated into the city?"

"Could be. But either the magic was so old that it degraded or was initially of such low quality. The soup in the tubes could be slag from some other work. The orbs could just be a profiteering kaldoon selling baubles to panicked nobles."

"Shop owner had no idea they were there?"

"Of course not. Said he bought the place two months ago. Building had been abandoned before then." Albright scratched his beard again as he weighed the circumstances. "We've been sweeping the city regularly and varying the patterns; sometimes we'd show up—"

"Enough, especially on a holiday. A toast. Let's have another toast!" proclaimed Lodestar Mondray. "Two great victories. Land and water." He cheered and haphazardly clinked glasses in a jubilant effort to refill them. "I feel the tides are turning. The Chartered Cities should not despair. I have dispatched more conservators to preach duty and steadfast faith in Indalos. Come spring the Tavuros will be on the run over the border, and Padazar crushed under heel!" Glasses clinked, emptied, and the Lodestar quickly filled them again.

"What is the latest from Valmuros and Arandis?" asked Chancellor Droswild with sincere concern. "I received some questions from the Domarese ambassador earlier this evening." Seeing Mondray's blank expression, Droswild prompted, "The Starfields."

"Oh, how you find gloom," bellowed Mondray. "Must you even ruin a celebratory toast! Ravalas is safe. Ardalencor, the tiger, stalks the enemy now." He looked away in disgust from Droswild and watched the cold fog clinging to the windows. "And with the favor of Indalos, the High Lady Sahalana should birth an heir any day now. A pity that Eadolan cannot be here with the Tavuros still moving about, licking their wounds, but they'll not try us again."

Mondray looked up from a long slurp of fruited mead as Court Chronicler Cadmus Quill entered the council chamber. Quill hung up his cloak, muttering, "Dreadfully cold."

"I hope our conservators are safe," offered Droswild. "Please let me know, Lodestar, and you too, Cadmus, when you receive word from, or about, them."

"Of course, Weldon," said Quill displeased with the lack of use of his courtly title.

Albright took a break from drowning his boredom and fixated on Quill's fine cloak of blue and bright gold thickly fringed with fur. "Is that rabbit?" he asked in false admiration.

"Red wolf, you greasy dust sniffer," spat Quill. "I hope you left some goose livers for the rest of us. May I dare to have one?" Quill and Albright grinned at one another.

"Weldon," said Quill, "I'm sure you've heard of the disgrace down in the Midrivers, the mockery the children of your wayward brothers are making of the Tarpleys and Pickfords?"

Droswild's expression was a mix of worry and amusement.

Quill added, "I have the competing letters. Ink scratching roosters who spend more time clawing at parchment than at Padazar's boy. Bernard Tarpley's arrival did little to solve things. Even he and Roderick are at odds. I have those letters as well."

"Speak clearly," admonished Albright. "I need to be returning to the Academy."

"Seems that Mathis Padazar is riding circles around our forces and then vanishing. The Tarpleys and Pickfords were arguing about who is in command, issuing orders, counter-manding orders, and then they ended up leaving a bridge unguarded. It's all char as well as the lookout tower on the far bank."

Quill continued, "Later in a brief flash of brilliance, Tarpley and Pickford seemed to have Mathis and his cavalry trapped in a river pocket and a fast current. They argued until sunfall about how and who should lead the attack, and in the night the boy's cavalry swam across the river, just wet for their trouble. They call them grass benders. That's the only sign they can find of them other than what they destroy."

Albright frowned in disgust. "Waydun had kept me informed as well and requested more support for the Midrivers. After these embarrassments, the Tarpleys and Pickfords will learn to work together, or they all should be removed from any semblance of command."

Quill gulped down a goose liver, and his eyes twinkled. Highly protective of his position at royal court, Quill relished being the first to know, to control, and to bequeath information as it suited him. He motioned for the three men to gather more closely around him. "I could not find you all together at Behan's festivities. You all will have great interest in this matter."

Quill looked at each man to ensure he had their full attention. "Sir Gavril Haldanar."

Albright, Droswild, and Mondray shook their heads.

"Yes, that was my response as well," said Quill. "He is Camhorn Thorpe's shieldbearer and trusted man, it seems."

"A good trait in a shieldbearer," said Albright motioning for Quill to quicken the pace.

"He was sent to deliver a message to Eadolan, who not being here, was directed to Behan, and Behan referred him to me. Thorpe can't escape dealing with me," Quill squeaked with delight.

"Do you have the message with you?" asked Albright.

"A verbal message only," said Quill. "Very secret."

"Is this Haldanar still in Ravalas?" said Droswild quickly. "I must know more of what is happening up north and if Bersadok is making any effort to restrain the Drivach."

"The message was relayed to me, and I will tell you," said Quill irritably, the stage seemingly being dismantled beneath him.

As Quill struggled to gather himself, the council chamber door flew open. Behan entered with the broadest of smiles.

Mondray grasped the meaning and said with great relief. "An heir!"

"A boy!" said Behan. "Healthy."

"Why was I not informed Sahalana was in labor?" demanded Albright.

"Should we let the city know? Ring the tower bells?" exclaimed Quill excitedly, seeing a larger role for him to play. "Wonderful news and on such an occasion as the Feast of the Great Hearth. The flame of the Arkwen family sparks anew and burns ever brighter."

"Now? Absolutely not. The whole city is asleep or delirious with drink," said Behan while ignoring Albright's question.

At the slight, Albright slipped through the open door.

"A joyous occasion, Behan. It is a wonderous blessing from Indalos. I think it best, for now, to keep the birth as quiet as possible. We must uphold the law of Indalos and customary twice passing of the two moons before a proclamation. The spirits of the people are already sustained by the two great victories." Mondray added with deep satisfaction, "A boy."

———

Fog and frost drifted along the wharves. A woman wrapped in a thick felt cloak and holding a small candle waited timidly in the mist. Her heart in her throat, she carefully peeked around and with slow and silent steps approached the harbor. The faint glow of candlelight revealed the festive ribbons of pale blue, white, and red braided in her hair. She tried to steady her breath, but the wait seemed unending.

"You made it," whispered the woman with great relief. She started to look around, counting the men moving in winter cloaks, light gambesons and soft-soled shoes to muffle their footfalls on the docks. "So few," she sighed, doubt swelling and permeating her limbs.

"Watch your tongue," said a tall man approaching her, a mix of reprimand and plea not to sow doubt among the men. "More will be up soon. Where are the guards?"

"They're taken care of." She gestured with a drinking motion. "Gatehouse and adjoining sections of the walls. The girls gave them big cups, but you should not linger."

"What time do they change watch? Have they been varying the times?"

"With the feast, they won't change until after first light."

"If you see women wearing these ribbons just above the elbow," she said pointing to her hair, "they are supporters." She paused. "Do you know where you're going?"

"Yes."

"I mean, do you know more than one way to get there?"

"What?" Latrobh put his hand up for his men to stop.

"There are barricades," the woman chirped. "Carts. Stones. Wood."

"Slow. Say it again."

"Some of the streets are blocked to move people in a certain direction, especially near the gates. They're changed periodically without notice."

"Are they manned?"

"I don't know. I don't think so," stammered the woman. "I couldn't get a message out. The gates are closely watched now."

"You must come with us."

"I can't!" protested the woman. As she scanned the docks, more men emerged through the fog. Several men with dogs quickly moved forward, the dogs sniffing as they made their way.

"You must. It will be alright. You will be remembered along with the great heroes of Ardalencor." Latrobh grabbed the woman by the arm and led back towards the open Harbor Gate.

EPILOGUE

Moonlight faintly pushed through the thick clouds. A man, old beyond his years, sat in front of a large barn door, softly playing a long flute, his cloak's hood up against the chill. The man had accepted watch to let the others sleep off their revelry. A long scar from temple to cheek partially sealed the man's left eye, but he strained hard into the darkness. He kept up his playing but stretched the space between each note. Listening between the sounds, he straightened his back.

A shadow, near black on black, then converging into a svelte form, burst forth in front of him.

The man spun off the chair, avoiding an incoming kick. The assailant hesitated for a moment, shocked by the man's reaction.

The assailant then moved quickly with kicks and punches, wisps of light and flame visible along the knuckles and contours of the fists.

The man narrowly dodged or deflected the strikes with the wooden flute. One punch reached close enough to singe his beard. "A woman!" called the man seeing the eyes of the assailant in the fleeting light.

He swung the flute like a club to create space and fall back. The woman easily sidestepped his attack and pressed forward. In the flash of reprieve, the man extended his hand and stopped the woman in midair with a spell.

No weapons were visible. Her clothes were muted browns, yellows, and reds, no factional patterns that he recognized. The woman wore dark leather bracers over her forearms, but he could not make out any markings. With the woman immobilized, the man inspected his cracked flute and tossed it to the snow-speckled ground.

Her eyes continued to resist despite their inability to move.

"How did you find this place? Who are you?" he said angrily, jerking the hood and yanking down her face covering.

The man stared at the face of a young woman, a short, asymmetric mop of flaxen hair, partially shaved on one side, and the slightly elongated tops of her ears. He gave her a disbelieving look, astonished by whom was before him.

He peered into her eyes, grabbed her harshly by the elbow out of rebuke and scorn, and in the same instant the woman vanished. The man hastily checked his still smoking and curled beard. "Run, girl, and never stop. Would you want your mother to know you're sneaking around?" He smiled in anticipation of a reply.

None came.

"How you worry your mother? You might as well tell me everything. I already know a great deal," he said not entirely all in bluff.

He sensed she was still close. "Your silence is commendable, Revna."

The young woman reappeared in front of him with a

readied strike, which moved faster than anticipated. It took him great effort to avoid the blow and not to ignite his cloak.

"You've come all this way to beat up an old man, is that it?"

The comment stopped her.

He looked at her gravely and stretched his arms to shake off the sting of her attack. "You are far too angry for the leisurely life you've led. So, this must be what's happening in the elf colonies near Jevatryn. Did you learn this in the fire temples, or did your father teach you? I didn't know outsiders could gain entrance to the fire temples," said he with unveiled provocation.

"I'm an elf!" she shouted back.

"Yes, and what elf is that? No elf counts all elves as kin, so what kind of elf are you?"

She just glared furiously.

"Remember it was scheming elves that almost plunged the world into total darkness!" he said, tracing the line of his scar. "Do you claim your Ardalen blood just as strongly?" He did not wait for a reply. "How you dishonor your mother? Does she not exist? All her love and nurture that birthed your impetuous self?"

"You're a Milikanthai?" she said, noting the blood red collar of a white tunic worn by some Milikanthai in remembrance of the massacres. "How can you support Ardalencor? You were the hunted."

"Bitter tears linger heavy if you stoop to carry them. There are far fewer of us now, but in time, our sacred mounds and cities are reclaimed. War between brothers is a ghastly thing, and that was long ago."

"I speak Ardalen. It's who I am. Why would I throw that away? And become what? Someone else? In Velenharn, the common folk are forbidden to hunt anything larger than a rabbit. I am sure this is not a concern for you eating at the high table as you have, Lady Lyjos, or is it Lady Berryhill?" He smirked. "Have you ever thought about what essence must flow through Ardalen bones? In your own lifetime, how do you think we were able to resist Velenharn, a much smaller nation as we are?"

Revna contorted her face, confused by the mere notion of the questions, let alone contemplating an answer.

"You have some talent," he said without understatement, struggling to understand how she found the Hayloft and made it past the innumerable wards. He thought best not to acknowledge the great feat she had already accomplished. "But then I've seen some great fighters in my time, true warriors," he added, not wanting to linger on his own worries.

"What do you want?" Revna challenged, starting to look around for signs of others stirring.

"I should ask you the same thing, but that can wait for another day. You can run away, but you will be found, and if you won't answer for this, then your father and mother will have to explain themselves when the Archmage is informed."

"Let me go, and I will not come back. You have my word," she said somewhere between plea and demand.

"I'm afraid I cannot. The Archmage and the High Lord must know of this."

She seemed to be contemplating another attack, but the man put his hand up. "I have been a fighter all my life, and now my patience is all burned up. Who did you tell that you were coming here? If you were to disappear now, who'd know where to look?"

Fear washed across Revna's eyes and compelled her to turn her gaze.

"I heard one of your brothers fell while protecting Eadolan. Your brother died defending Ardalencor. I am sorry. I know this sorrow. All," he emphasized, "of my brothers died in the defense of Ardalencor."

Revna returned her gaze now with softened eyes.

"Have you heard of the siege of Forris?" He shook his head, trying to dismiss his own thoughts. He pointed his finger at her. "So, while you are figuring out whatever you are, people are tearing apart the soil that birthed you and on which you took your first steps."

The man's eyes started to tear, the memories of his brothers rushed forward; his brothers pleading with him to leave the keep and carry the word of their fate, and he, tearfully pleading to stay to fight and to die by their side. "Ardalencor is at war. Why don't you help save our country?"

GLOSSARY OF SELECTED CHARACTERS

The list is arranged by character's last name when possible. The last name was chosen to provide a common format recognizing many characters are referred to primarily by first name, title, or by a sobriquet. Characters for whom no last name is provided are listed by first name or sobriquet.

Descriptions are written based on events prior to the outbreak of hostilities between Ardalencor and Tavuron and the betrayal of Padazar's faction as to avoid revealing the course of events described in the chapters.

Aaron ... Squire of Dallen Portnay.
Agozeru ... Advisor to Lady Katya Billengrath.
Ellard Ajhax ... Commander of the Hearthguards. Cousin of High Lord Eadolan.
Elias Albright ... Mage of the Zaravandian Order.
Elgar Anchorsmith ... Navigator from Masthead.
Avlina Arkwen ... Wife of Behan Arkwen. Daughter of Duke Rafal Stokes.

Behan Arkwen ... Royal Steward of Ardalencor. Brother of High Lord Eadolan.

Eadolan Arkwen ... High Lord of Ardalencor. Husband of Sahalana Arkwen.

Sahalana Arkwen ... High Lady of Ardalencor. Wife of Eadolan Arkwen.

Arvid ... Squire to Dallen Portnay.

Simon Audley ... Chartered Cities militiaman.

Hackett Bale ... Renowned tracker and fighter from the Northwestern Wilds.

Tryk Bearward ... Line infantryman in Fryll's Broadshield.

Talia Berryhill ... Lady of Bear Burrow and consort of Alwyn Lyjos. Mother of Kalmon, Revna, Rylar, and Vedulien.

Barbora Billengrath ... Daughter of Lady Katya Billengrath.

Katya Billengrath ... Lady of Jevatryn. Colloquially known as the Queen of Lace.

Jereon Blackcliff ... Overseer of Companions of the Zaravandian Order's elite men-at-arms.

Fost Boscawent ... Heir to the Boscawent family fortune.

Kamila Boscawent ... Wife of Duke Urric Boscawent.

Urric Boscawent ... Duke of Vryvond. Advisor to High Lord Eadolan.

Thiepval Bracelaw ... Wizard of the Zaravandian Order.

Robard Bracken ... Shipbuilder and merchant from Masthead.

Lanning Braithwaite ... Treasurer of Ardalencor.

Gerdeon Bune ... Commanding officer of Third Broadshield: The Roosters.

Artos Calaspon ... Wizard of the Zaravandian Order.

Nestor Catalfo ... Spymaster of the Zaravandian Order.

Chetwin Claypool ... Nobleman. Father of Kamila Boscawent.

Cobart ... Monk of the Burzina Monastery and the Arm of Indalos.

Corentin ... Ruler of Velenharn.

Humphrey Cotterill ... Prominent merchant in the Chartered Cities. Major of the Chartered Cities militia.

Cyprien Crosstimbers ... Commanding officer of First Broadshield: The Lanterns.

Dahey ... Apprentice of the Zaravandian Order.

Dalibor... Apprentice of the Zaravandian Order.

Dalton ... Apprentice of the Zaravandian Order.

Teleg Drenith ... Commander of Lady Katya Billengrath's personal guard.

Dronor ... Mercenary.

Weldon Droswild ... Chancellor of Ardalencor.

Barrett Drummond ... Commanding officer of Fourth Broadshield: The Long Tusks.

Emerik Dudley ... Master Sergeant and member of the Thavodyn garrison.

Harrik Dunbar ... Constable of Thavodyn.

Grammel Erstchester ... Castellan of Thavodyn.

Faolan ... Monk of the Burzina Monastery and the Arm of Indalos.

Corwen Farcloud ... Mage of the Zaravandian Order. Secluded at Ravenroost.

Kellin Farrior ... Sergeant in Eighth Broadshield: Armstead's Roamers.

Fishbone ... Sobriquet of a renowned tracker and fighter from the Northwestern Wilds.

Jordy Freprew ... Southwestern warrior. Cousin of Balian Latrobh.

Raymond Fryll ... Commanding officer of Fifth Broadshield: Handsome Lads.

Cambrell Glover ... Steward of Thavodyn.

Gann Goodwinds ... Elected leader of the Chartered Cities. Mayor of Everhall.

Venduva Greenbond ... Prominent seer from the Northwestern Wilds.

Gavril Haldanar ... Shieldbearer of Camhorn Thorpe.

Crowiler Herring ... Commanding officer of Sixth Broadshield: Sheep Dogs. Colloquially known as the Tigerclaw.

Jon Heward ... Logger from along the Falling River. Former soldier.

Hodger Hill ... Chartered Cities militiaman.

Chatton Holley ... Commanding officer of Eleventh Broadshield: The Hot Coals.

Falanika Hood ... Wizard of the Zaravandian Order.

Evret Hufyn ... Knight in service to Dallen Portnay.

Jarvis Jernivan ... Impoverished descendant of the once-prominent Jernivan noble family.

Maneol Jerris ... Prominent merchant in the Chartered Cities. Commander of the Chartered Cities militia.

Kerjelaft ... Disciple of Donald Woolfolk.

Balian Latrobh ... Southwestern warrior and renowned tactician. Patriarch of the Latrobh family.

Malu Littlecheek ... Apprentice of the Zaravandian Order.

Calbaric Longcloak ... Castellan of Avenbair Castle.

Alwyn Lyjos ... Commander of the Lifeguards. Consort of Talia Berryhill. Father of Kalmon, Revna, Rylar, and Vedulien.

Kalmon Lyjos ... Member of the Lifeguards. Son of Alwyn Lyjos and Talia Berryhill.

Revna Lyjos ... Daughter of Alwyn Lyjos and Talia Berryhill.

Rylar Lyjos ... Castellan of Sevengate. Son of Alwyn Lyjos and Talia Berryhill.

Vedulien Lyjos ... Member of the Lifeguards. Son of Alwyn Lyjos and Talia Berryhill.

Martoz ... Head Monk of the Burzina Monastery and the Arm of Indalos. Colloquially known as Martoz the Black.

Mathurin Mondray ... Lodestar of the Faith of Indalos.

Bambenek Morley ... Scout and soldier.

Myron ... Aide to Humphrey Cotterill.

Nabrensus ... King of Tavuron.

Lockard Newman ... Royal envoy.

Ocklef ... Agent of the Padazar family.

Amos Padazar ... Fourth son of Horace and Fiona Padazar.

Asmund Padazar ... Fifth son of Horace and Fiona Padazar.

Ethan Padazar ... Third son of Horace and Fiona Padazar.

Horace Padazar ... Duke of Delun. Husband of Fiona Padazar.

Horace *the Younger* Padazar ... Toddler and youngest son of Horace and Fiona Padazar.

Fiona Padazar ... Duchess of Delun. Wife of Horace Padazar.

Jannon Padazar ... Eldest son of Horace and Fiona Padazar. Husband of Polina Padazar.

Mathis Padazar ... Second son of Horace and Fiona Padazar.

Polina Padazar ... Wife of Jannon Padazar.

Brenio Pazdan ... Wizard in the Zaravandian Order.

Dobbins Pelt ... Mayor of Sawmill Falls. Owner of Pelt & Sons foundry.

Dallen Portnay ... Knight and heir to Amberfield.

Cadmus Quill ... Chronicler of the royal court. Responsible for the royal communications rookery in Ravalas.

Quinby ... Aide to Humphrey Cotterill.

Rains ... Apprentice of the Zaravandian Order.

Corneleo Ray ... Cavalry commander. Purveyor of the annual equestrian tournaments and festivities at Swiftmane Races.

Rufus ... Apprentice of the Zaravandian Order.

Jakob Rukez ... Quartermaster of the Ardalen army.

Almaric Sands ... Southwestern merchant.

Mannix Splitwood ... Reeve of Woodstretch.

Eldren Spruce ... Venerable healer of the Deepwood.

Rallis Stadrys ... Archmage of the Zaravandian Order. Colloquially known as Silverface.

Rodney Starling ... Cavalry commander from the North-western Wilds.

Rafal Stokes ... Duke of Stokesbridge. General of the Line of March, or Linmarch, of the Ardalen army.

Rafal *the Younger* Stokes ... Son of Rafal Stokes.

Bayard Summers ... Squire of Dallen Portnay.

Sunsmoke ... Advisor to Camhorn Thorpe.

Drevell Swan ... Ardalencor's ambassador to Tavuron.

Talvert ... Squire of Dallen Portnay.

Mardin Tanner ... Archer in the Chartered Cities militia.

Bernard Tarpley ... Nobleman. Patriarch of the Tarpley family.

Roderick Tarpley ... Nobleman. Brother of Bernard Tarpley.

Tomas Telfair ... Wizard of the Zaravandian Order.

Camhorn Thorpe ... Ealdorman of Thornhelm and military commander of the Northwestern Wilds.

Val ... Revenant archer.

Votark ... Master Blacksmith of the Zaravandian Order.

Clayd Vraim ... Nobleman. Father of Cyra Vraim.

Cyra Vraim ... Wizard of the Zaravandian Order. Estranged daughter of Clayd Vraim.

Waydun ... Wizard of the Zaravandian Order.

Arnost Wolfwind ... Master of Horse at Thavodyn.

Donald Woolfolk ... Conservator of Flowering Hill Starfield in Delun. Advisor to Horace Padazar.

K'jir Zelihis ... Admiral of the Ardalen navy.

Made in USA - North Chelmsford, MA
1321227_9781737703105
07.08.2022 1630